RABBITS

Terry Miles is an award-winning filmmaker and the creator of the Public Radio Alliance and the network's series of hit podcasts: *Tanis*, *Rabbits*, *Faerie* and *The Last Movie*. He splits his time between the dark emerald gloom of the Pacific Northwest and sunny Los Angeles.

terrymiles.com
publicradioalliance.com
rabbitspodcast.com
 @tkmiles
@tkmiles

RABBITS

A Novel

TERRY MILES

MACMILLAN

First published 2021 by Del Rey
an imprint of Random House
a division of Penguin Random House LLC, New York

This edition first published 2021 by Macmillan
an imprint of Pan Macmillan
The Smithson, 6 Briset Street, London EC1M 5NR
EU representative: Macmillan Publishers Ireland Limited,
Mallard Lodge, Lansdowne Village, Dublin 4
Associated companies throughout the world
www.panmacmillan.com

ISBN 978-1-5290-1694-9

1 3 5 7 9 8 6 4 2

A CIP catalogue record for this book is available from the British Library.

Printed and bound by CPI Group (UK) Ltd, Croydon, CR0 4YY

Visit **www.panmacmillan.com** to read more about all our books
and to buy them. You will also find features, author interviews and
news of any author events, and you can sign up for e-newsletters
so that you're always first to hear about our new releases.

For Luna

All your life you live so close to truth, it becomes a permanent blur in the corner of your eye, and when something nudges it into out-line it is like being ambushed by a grotesque. A man standing in his saddle in the half-lit half-alive dawn banged on the shutters and called two names. He was just a hat and a cloak levitating in the grey plume of his own breath, but when he called we came. That much is certain—we came.

—Tom Stoppard, *Rosencrantz & Guildenstern Are Dead*

RABBITS

I FIRST CAME ACROSS THE GAME IN 1983. My game theory professor took me to visit the site of the original Laundromat in Seattle. The Laundromat is no longer there, of course, but if you ask the manager of the restaurant that currently occupies the space, she might take you into the office in the back and let you see part of the original room. And, if you order a big meal and tip the waitstaff well, she might even remove the large modernist painting that hangs above the fireplace and show you the graphic of the rabbit on the wall.

Some true stories are easier to accept if you can convince yourself that at least part of them are fictional. This is one of those stories.

—SHALINI ADAMS-PRESCOTT, 2021

1

THE SCENE IN THE
MAGICIAN'S ARCADE

"WHAT DO YOU KNOW about the game?"

The smiles vanished from the assembled collection of conspiracy hounds and deep Web curiosity seekers, their private conversations stopped mid-sentence, their phones quickly stashed into a variety of backpacks and pockets, each of them doing their best to look cool and disaffected while unconsciously leaning forward, ears straining, eyes bright with anxious anticipation.

This was, after all, why they were here.

This was what they came for, what they always came for. This was the thing they spoke about in inelegant lengthy rambles in their first Tor Browser Web forum experience, the thing they'd first stumbled upon in a private subreddit, or a deep-Web blog run by a lunatic specializing in underground conspiracies both unusual and rare.

This was the thing that itched your skull, that gnawed at the part of your brain that desperately wanted to believe in something more. This was the thing that made you venture out in the middle of the night in the pouring rain to visit a pizza joint–slash–video arcade that probably would have been condemned decades ago had anybody cared enough to inspect it.

You came because this mysterious "something" felt different. This was that one inexplicable experience in your life: the UFO you and your cousin saw from that canoe on the lake that summer, the apparition you'd seen standing at the foot of your bed when you woke in the middle of the night on your eighth birthday. This was the electric shiver up your spine just after your older brother locked you in the basement and turned out the light. This was the wild hare up your ass, as my grandfather used to say.

"I know that it's supposed to be some kind of recruitment test—NSA, CIA maybe," said a young woman in her early twenties. She'd been here last week. She didn't ask any questions during that presentation, but after, in the parking lot, she'd stopped me and asked about fractals, and if I thought they might be related to sacred geometry (I did), or the elaborate conspiracy work of John Lilly (I did not).

She didn't ask me anything about the thing directly.

It was always like this.

Questions about the game were most often received as whispers online, or delivered in a crowd of like-minded conspiracy nuts, in safe spaces like comic shops or the arcade. Out in the real world, talking about it made you feel exposed, like you were standing too close to something dangerous, leaning out just a bit too far on the platform while listening to the rumble of the approaching train.

The game was the train.

"Thousands of people have died while playing," said a thin red-headed man in his early thirties. "They sweep these things under the fucking rug, like they never happened."

"There are a number of theories," I said, like I'd said a thousand times before, "and yes, some people do believe that there have been deaths related to the game."

"Why do you call it 'the game,' and not by its proper name?" The woman who'd spoken was in a wheelchair. I'd seen her here a few times. She was dressed like a librarian from the fifties, glasses hanging around her neck on a beaded chain. Her name was Sally Berkman. She ran the most popular Dungeons & Dragons game in town. Original Advanced D&D.

"Phones and all other electronics in the box," I said, ignoring Sally's question. They loved it when I played it up, made everything feel more dangerous, more underground.

Everyone stepped forward and placed their phones, laptops, and whatever other electronics they had with them into a large cedar chest on the floor.

The chest was old. The Magician had brought it back from a trip he'd taken to Europe a few years ago. There was a graphic stamped onto the lid, some kind of ceremonial image of a hare being hunted. It was an intricately detailed and terrifying scene. There were a bunch of hunters and their dogs in the background bearing down on their prey in the foreground, but the thing that drew all your attention was the expression on the hare's face. There was something dark and knowing about the way it stared out from the bottom of the image—eyes wild and wide, mouth partly open. For some reason, the hare's expression always left me feeling more frightened for the hunters than the hunted. The chest looked like it had been manufactured sometime in the 1920s or 1930s. I always used it when I did these things; its strange patina brought an authentic old-timey-conspiracy atmosphere to the ceremony.

Once the last phone was inside, I kicked the lid shut with a dramatic bang and pulled out an ancient reel-to-reel tape recorder.

I had a digital copy of the recording, of course. In fact, I'd made the reel-to-reel recording I was about to play from an MP3. But there's just something romantic about analog tape. Like the cedar chest, the old tape recorder was for show, and these people had come here, to this old arcade in Seattle's University District, for a show.

They'd come from their parents' basements, their messy studio apartments, high-rise tower penthouses, and midcentury post-and-beam homes in the woods. They'd come to hear about the game. They'd come to hear *The Prescott Competition Manifesto,* or *PCM*.

Just as I was about to press play, I heard a voice from somewhere near the back of the room. "Is it true that you know Alan Scarpio?"

"Yeah, I know Scarpio. I mean, I met him once while I was playing the ninth iteration," I said, trying to find the person who'd asked the question in the crowd.

There weren't that many people here, maybe forty or fifty, but the arcade was small and the bodies were three or four deep in some places.

"Most people believe Scarpio won the sixth iteration of the game," I said.

"Yeah, we know that. Tell us something we don't know."

I still couldn't find the person speaking. It was a man's voice, but it was hard to tell exactly where it was coming from over the drone of the videogames and pinball machines.

"Alan Scarpio is a gazillionaire playboy who hangs out with Johnny Depp," said a young man leaning against an old Donkey Kong Jr. cabinet. "He can't be a player."

"Maybe he played, but there's no evidence he won the game," said a woman in a *Titanica* T-shirt. " 'Californiac' is the name listed in The Circle, not Alan Scarpio."

"So then how do you explain his overnight wealth?" Sally Berkman replied—a familiar challenge when it came to Scarpio. "He has to be Californiac. It just makes sense. He was born in San Francisco."

"Oh, well, if he was born in San Francisco, he must be the guy." Donkey Kong Man was clearly looking to stir up some shit.

"San Francisco is in California," Sally Berkman replied. "Californiac."

"Wow, are you serious?" Donkey Kong Man said, shaking his head.

"How about I just play what you've come all this way to hear?" I said.

If I let them go on about Alan Scarpio and whether or not he was actually Californiac, the winner of the sixth iteration of the game, we'd be here all night. Again.

I nodded in the direction of a blond curly-haired woman standing near the front door, and she turned out the lights.

Her name was Chloe. She was a good friend of mine. She worked for the Magician.

The arcade was the Magician's place.

It was an old speakeasy that had been converted into the arcade–slash–pizza joint back in the 1980s. The pizza oven had died more than a decade ago, so now it was just an arcade. Nobody understood how the Magician had been able to keep the place running through the rise of home-based and eventually handheld computer entertainment, but keep it running he did.

Walking into the arcade was like walking into another age.

The brick walls and exposed pipes in the ceiling clashed with the bright video screens and sharp 8-bit sounds of the arcade games, resulting in a strange yet perfectly comfortable blend of anachronisms.

Chloe called it eighties industrial.

The Magician was out of town on some kind of research trip, but he never came down for these things anyway.

He'd started letting a few of us use the place for meetings after the eighth iteration of the game. The Magician's arcade became a kind of de facto clubhouse, an informal gathering place for those of us who remained obsessed with the game long after most everyone else had checked out.

I pressed play on the reel-to-reel recording, and the voice of Dr. Abigail Prescott filled the room.

. . . The level of secrecy surrounding the game is concerning, as are the number of candidates . . . STATIC . . . it's chaos from the trailhead to the first marker, no algorithm can track its logic . . . CRACKLE . . . I've heard the underlying condition of the game described, metaphorically, as a kind of fluid, like the cytoplasm or protoplasm of a cell . . . STATIC . . . It had been dormant for a very long time when the first clue showed up in 1959. It was something in The Washington Post, *a letter to the editor, and the lyrics of a song by the* Everly Brothers *that, when combined, provided the first indication that the game had returned. A student at Oxford put everything together and brought her professor into the thought matrix at Cambridge . . . CRACKLE . . . the name Rabbits was first used in reference to a graphic containing a rabbit on the wall of a laundromat in Seattle. Rabbits wasn't the name of that specific iteration of the game, just like it's not the name of this one . . . as far as any of us can tell, the games themselves—at least the games in this modern variation—don't actually have names. They're*

numbered by the community of players . . . STATIC . . . should be warned, we have reason to believe that the reports of both physical and mental jeopardy have been, in fact, underreported, and . . . STATIC.

The following was allegedly written on the wall in that laundromat in Seattle in 1959, under the hand-scrawled title MANIFESTO, and above a hand-stamped graphic of a rabbit:

You play, you never tell.
Find the doors, portals, points, and wells.
The Wardens watch and guard us well.
You play and pray you never tell.

There it was. Rabbits. The reason they were here, looking for some new information, a clue, anything that might lead to evidence about the next numbered iteration: Eleven, or XI.

Had it started?

Was it about to start?

Had the tenth version really ended?

Had anybody seen The Circle?

I let the echo of Dr. Abigail Prescott's words hang there dramatically for a moment, and then I continued with the Q&A section of my presentation.

"Any questions?"

"What can you tell us about Prescott?" A man wearing a Canadian tuxedo—dark denim shirt and light blue jeans—asked in a booming voice. He was playing a game manufactured by Williams Electronics in the 1980s, Robotron: 2084.

He was a friend of mine named Baron Corduroy: a plant I'd brought along to prompt certain aspects of my presentation.

"Yes, well, we know that Dr. Abigail Prescott allegedly worked under both Stanford's Robert Wilson—a professor whose main area of interest is game theory as it relates to economics—and quantum physicist Ronald E. Meyers, but nobody has been able to dig up anything else of any real value on her. Some believe Abigail Prescott is a pseudonym, but nobody knows for sure."

"A pseudonym for who?" asked Dungeon Master Sally.

"No idea," I replied, which was true. Abigail Prescott was a cipher. It was almost impossible to find anything about her online or anywhere else—and believe me, I've tried.

"Where did you get that recording?" It was that voice again, coming from somewhere in the back. I still couldn't locate the speaker.

"Well, as most of you know, *The Prescott Competition Manifesto* is extremely rare. The moment it's posted to a crowd-sharing site, it's removed faster than the big movie studios pull down their copyrighted works. It's not much, but this clip is currently our best source of information available on the game."

Another pause for dramatic effect.

"This particular clip was given to me by a friend of mine who almost won Eight." This last bit was a lie. I'd bought the recording on the darknet for twenty-six dollars' worth of Bitcoin.

A hush fell over the room.

They loved it when I mentioned anything related to the numbered iterations of the game, or the winners of those particular iterations, The Circle. And, of course, Hazel, the most infamous Rabbits player of all time.

Hazel wasn't the only famous participant. There were the two well-known Canadian players, Nightshade and Sadie Palomino; ControlG, the winner of the tenth—and most recent—iteration of the game; the Brazilian anarchist who went by the number 6878; and, of course, Murmur, the deadliest of them all, allegedly sacrificing their spouse to gain an edge during Nine. But all of those players, as accomplished as they were, existed a tier below Hazel.

Hazel was my closer. I always saved a brief mention of Hazel for the end.

"Come on, tell us something we don't know." My friend Baron again.

This time he didn't even turn around as he asked the question. I made a note to have a word with him about his commitment to earning his cut of the profits.

"Well, rumor has it there's another force at work, operating behind the scenes of the game—something powerful, mysterious, and, occasionally, deadly. Something out there watching from somewhere else, staring into our world from an infinite darkness, waiting for the players to make a mistake." I paused again for effect, and then continued, my voice a bit lower than before. "This warning was discovered written on the back of a Dewey decimal card in an old set of drawers in a thrift store in Ireland."

I cleared my throat a little, then recited:

"Remember the game, or your world it dies.
"Remember to follow the patterns and signs.
"We wait in the shadows a-twisting your fate,
"While you crawl and you stumble blind into the gate.
"It's all predetermined, no losses no gains,
"So play, little human, keep playing the game."

"Wow, that's dramatic." The unseen man again.

I looked around and caught part of a green military-style jacket moving through the crowd.

"So, that's the game," I continued. "Rabbits."

I looked around the room again slowly. "With unclear prizes for participation and sinister-sounding punishments for those who betray the secrecy and spirit of the game, it's hard to believe anybody still actually plays." I took a deep practiced breath before I continued. "Any other questions?"

"My friend says she has proof the game has started up again, the eleventh version." This was somebody new, a woman wearing a red bandana, sitting on the floor and leaning against a Dragon's Lair cabinet.

"With all due respect to your friend, experts agree the game has been dormant since the tenth iteration ended. We're in a down cycle. Nobody knows if—or when—the game will start up again."

"What about Hazel?" Baron Corduroy again, right on time.

"I'm afraid that's all the time I have tonight."

Moans from the crowd.

"But, if you'd like more information, there's a brand-new downloadable PDF on my website."

Normally at least half the crowd sticks around for an informal Q&A, which is when I'd finally share some of the stories I'd heard about Hazel or a number of other infamous Rabbits players, but there was a midnight screening of *Donnie Darko* at The Grand Illusion Cinema in about twenty minutes.

The Venn diagram of people interested in Rabbits and in Richard Kelly's sci-fi thriller from 2001 is essentially just a circle.

I said goodbye to each of the participants in turn as they collected their electronics and hurried out into the rain to catch their movie.

After the last of them had exited the arcade, I opened a small green lockbox and counted the donations. Two hundred and two dollars. Not bad. I left the Magician his cut and slid the lockbox under the counter.

"Well, that was all kinds of bullshit." It was the voice from earlier, the man in the green military-style jacket. Beneath his jacket he wore a thin black hoodie, which hid his face. He was playing Robotron: 2084, the game Baron had been playing throughout my presentation.

At some point while people were leaving, he and Baron must have switched places.

"Where's Baron?" I asked.

"Who?"

"The guy who was playing this game earlier."

"I think he went to see *Donnie Darko*."

Of course he did. Baron couldn't be bothered to pay attention while I talked about Rabbits, but he'd be more than happy to pay seven dollars to see a movie he's seen at least eighty times.

"Not bad," the man said, nodding toward the screen.

I moved closer and saw the score. It wasn't bad at all. It was much higher than Baron could have managed, and Baron was the best Robotron player any of us had ever seen.

"I used to play these things all the time." At this point, the man in the green jacket turned around and slipped off his hoodie.

I recognized him immediately.

There are two things worth noting here. Number one, the man playing Robotron in the Magician's arcade—the man who'd asked me if I knew Alan Scarpio—was the famous reclusive billionaire philanthropist and alleged winner of the sixth iteration of Rabbits: Alan fucking Scarpio. The second thing worth noting is that although I'd mentioned earlier that I knew Alan Scarpio, I'd never met him before in my life.

"I need your help," he said.

"What for?" I replied.

"Something is wrong with Rabbits, and I need you to help me fix it."

And with that, Alan Scarpio went right back to playing his game.

2

SO WHAT? IT'S A FUCKING WOODPECKER

IN CASE YOU'RE WONDERING, my name is K. That's it. Just K. One letter.

Two things I'll tell you: First, K is short for something. And second, I'll never tell you what that something is. You'll just have to find a way to cope with that disappointment.

I grew up in the Pacific Northwest: A place that, at the time, I considered the wettest and loneliest corner of the Earth. A place that, many years later, I would romanticize as a kind of dark green gloomy world of ancient secrets and hidden lives, and a place that I now see as a kind of perfectly disturbing amalgamation of all of those things.

I'm old enough to remember cabinet videogames in arcades, but young enough to have trouble recalling a time without the Internet.

As a child, my parents believed I had what's called an eidetic memory: a remarkable ability to retain images, words, and patterns in extensive detail. Back then they used the term "photographic memory," which is inaccurate. Photographic memory doesn't exist, and even if it does, I didn't have it. I was just able to remember certain things, picture them clearly, and recall them later. I couldn't remember everything, just stuff connected to patterns I found interesting. It wasn't a math trick. Although I may have been able to drop a box of toothpicks on the floor and tell you how many there were, you weren't getting the square root of anything from me.

Because I was the kid who could remember weird shit, I was occasionally able to distract a couple of the angry bullies in my class long enough to make them forget to kick my ass, but that only worked about fifty percent of the time—a percentage that quickly plummeted to zero when I reached high school and the ability to focus on details and pick out complex connections became less of an occasional act of self-preservation and more of an obsession.

It was this obsession with finding patterns and cracking codes (that may or may not have actually been codes at all) that resulted in me being labeled "slightly neurodiverse"—a diagnosis that landed me on a number of different medications and a handful of different therapists' couches. It was also this obsession that eventually led me into the world of Rabbits.

When asked to pinpoint the precise moment they'd heard about the game, people often can't remember. Maybe they'd seen something on some obscure online bulletin board, or read a snippet of a conversation about hidden "kill screens" in arcade games from the 1980s. Or perhaps it was a friend of a friend talking about a kid who'd died while playing a strange Atari 2600 game that nobody can remember actually existing.

I remember exactly where I was standing when I first heard the name Rabbits.

It was at a party in Lakewood, Washington.

Growing up in Olympia, Washington, just about an hour south of Seattle, I'd heard the stories about Polybius: the video arcade game that allegedly killed some kids in Oregon. But *this* mysterious game was different, more enigmatic, and perhaps even more sinister. Like Polybius, this game had whispers surrounding it that included men in gray suits and potential mind-altering consequences for participation. But unlike Polybius, nobody was actually talking about this game—at least not until I attended that party.

Bill and Madeline Connors were close family friends who hosted a Fourth of July celebration every year. They had two daughters, Annie and Emily—one and three years older than me respectively.

The Connors sisters had the best taste in music, and they always wore the coolest clothes—a lot of belts, and a lot of hats. At this particular party, they were both wearing tall, striped Dr. Seuss-looking hats that they'd bought at what they assured me was the hippest store on Melrose Avenue in Los Angeles. I took their word for it. At the time, I'd never been farther south than Oakland, to attend sailing camp.

While our parents were in the backyard playing a drunken game of lawn darts, I entered the house to get a Coke (something I was never allowed to drink at home) and overheard Annie and Emily talking.

They were huddled in front of the family computer staring at something on the screen.

"Did you figure out how to load EverQuest, or what?" Annie asked.

"I have something better," Emily replied, bringing up a screen I recognized. I had a pretty clear view from where I was hiding, just inside the kitchen doorway. They were looking at a Usenet news-group.

Annie leaned in to get a better look. "What's alt dot binaries dot games?"

"Gaming group," Emily replied, striking a few keys with expert precision.

"What's binaries?"

"Be quiet."

"Zelda pictures?"

"Not quite."

"Another dancing baby?"

"Just listen." Emily gently placed her hand over her sister's mouth and pressed the space bar.

A video file started to play. It appeared to be a clip from an old wildlife documentary. The voice on the screen was talking about something called the imperial woodpecker.

"So what? It's a fucking woodpecker. Let's go back outside. Luke Milligan is here," Annie said, tugging at her sister's sleeve.

"Luke Milligan's an asshole. He tried to put his hand up Nina's shirt in chem."

"Really?" Annie was clearly disappointed.

"Besides, it's not just any woodpecker," Emily said.

"What do you mean?"

"I mean, look at them all. There must be at least fifty woodpeckers in those last three scenes."

"Yeah, so what? They're big?"

"Yeah, they're big, but that's not it. This documentary was made in 1989, and the last reported sighting of an imperial woodpecker was in 1956."

"Whoa." Annie leaned in closer to the screen. "What does it mean?"

"It's Rabbits," Emily said, and shut down the computer.

"Rabbits?" Annie's eyes were huge. She was fascinated.

So was I.

There was something about the way Emily had said the word "Rabbits" that felt like a secret—like something adults knew that children couldn't possibly understand.

Emily looked around to make sure nobody was listening. The angle of the kitchen doorway kept me out of her line of sight. She lowered her voice. "It's a secret game."

Annie stared at the image of a woodpecker frozen on the screen. "What does it mean?"

"It means I'm going to be playing," Emily said, matter-of-fact.

"How do you play?"

"It's kind of complicated."

"Like how?"

"Like we're supposed to find things."

"What things?"

"Things like patterns, discrepancies. Things that don't make sense."

"Patterns?" Annie said. She was doing her best to follow the conversation, but she clearly had no idea what the hell her sister was talking about.

Emily took a deep breath and collected her thoughts before continuing. "Okay, so, there's a nature documentary released by a company that no longer exists, if it actually ever did."

I stood there in the kitchen, completely enthralled, as Emily got into some pretty wild theories about that documentary.

The gist of it was pretty simple. There was a name listed in the end credits that didn't have an accompanying occupation like makeup artist, boom op, best boy, or key grip.

One name was just hanging there, all alone on the screen—an "orphan name," I think Emily called it. She told Annie she'd overheard a discussion about this and had brought it to the others on her gaming forum. They performed some numerology and math involving the letters of that person's name, and eventually found something called The Night Station.

"What's The Night Station?" Annie asked.

"That's what we're going to find out. Come on."

I ducked out of the house and into the backyard just in time to miss being spotted by the two girls.

Emily told her parents that she and Annie were going to the store, and asked, half-heartedly, "Does anybody need anything?"

A few voices yelled out requests—cigarettes, ginger ale, chips and dip. Annie wrote everything down as Emily grabbed the keys to her mother's truck.

Mrs. Connors's voice rose above the others. "Take K with you."

"Mom, there's no room," Emily complained.

"It's a big truck, Em. Don't be difficult."

Emily exhaled and walked past me without making eye contact. "Come on, kid."

"What makes you think I wanna go?" I said.

Annie grabbed my hand and pulled me out of the house.

I definitely wanted to go—not only because Annie was the first girl I'd ever kissed, but also because of what Emily had been talking about in the kitchen. The idea of a mysterious secret game called Rabbits.

This felt different. This was something big, something grown-up.

Holding Annie's hand as she pulled me out to the old blue-and-white Chevy truck with the giant knobby tires took me right back to the moment she had kissed me.

Annie Connors was unconventionally pretty. Her eyes were just a bit too far apart, and her hair was extremely wavy and chaotic, but I found her beautiful, with a brash, powerful confidence that was both exciting and incredibly frightening.

A few weeks after my thirteenth birthday, our families were together celebrating Thanksgiving. Annie and I had been sent downstairs to dig up a game called Trivial Pursuit. On our way to the storage room where we kept our old games, Annie suddenly yanked me over to the furnace next to my makeshift bedroom in our otherwise entirely unfinished basement, matter-of-factly pressed her body against mine, took my face in her hands, and kissed me.

She tasted like grape gummy worms. It was incredible.

"Well?" she'd asked, after the kiss.

I couldn't speak, but I'm pretty sure my eyes answered with a resounding "holy shit, wow."

"Get in." Emily was already inside the truck picking out a cassette for the drive.

I crawled up into the cab, making sure I didn't sit too close to Emily. Annie Connors was beautiful and mysterious enough; Emily was a whole other world.

"Hurry up, it's almost time." Emily had the big truck moving before Annie had shut the door.

I didn't know much about cars, but the truck was at least a decade old. The ashtray beneath the stereo was overflowing with a blend of white-and-orange cigarette butts. On the floor, an old salt-and-vinegar-chip bag sat next to an empty bottle of Sprite, a few salty shards of greenish-white chips visible against the foil inside.

"The store's open twenty-four hours," I said, realizing as I was saying it that Emily knew that.

Everybody knew that.

Emily didn't answer. She just popped a cassette into the stereo with a mechanical whir and click, and a series of tiny blue and pink lights from the stereo lit up the cab of the truck. Then Tori Amos began singing "Crucify," and Emily guided the huge truck down the long, winding driveway and out onto the street.

———

We passed the store without stopping. Emily didn't even slow down.

I remained silent. I didn't want to open my mouth and risk saying something that might affect what was happening. This was an adventure—my first "wild hare up your ass" adventure—and there was no way I was going to risk saying anything to fuck it up.

Emily pulled a pack of cigarettes from beneath the visor and took her hands off the wheel to light one up. Without a word from her sister, Annie reached across my lap and grabbed the steering wheel.

Emily and Annie were in perfect sync.

Annie steered for her sister, staring ahead at the road, keeping the truck between the lines with the focus of a brain surgeon or air traffic controller, as if driving between those lines was the only thing keeping the world spinning.

We drove for another seven minutes or so before Emily took the wheel and turned onto an old logging road. A minute later, she pulled over onto the unpaved shoulder.

"There's nothing up here but the Peterman house," I said, "but there might be some kids at the gravel pits."

If I showed up at the gravel pits with Emily and Annie Connors, I'd be a hero tomorrow at school.

Emily shushed me as she turned on the cabin light and pulled a small journal from her purse.

"You sure this is the road?" Annie asked. "K's right; it's just the Petermans' up there."

Emily stared down at the journal in her lap.

The pages were completely covered in tiny words, numbers, and sketches. It looked familiar to me—not the content, but the style. It was similar to the things my friends and I would scribble onto graph paper while playing Dungeons & Dragons.

Emily circled some numbers she'd written above what appeared to be a collection of names and symbols. She thought about something for a moment, then she added the numbers together, leaned back, and exhaled.

"A hundred and seven point three," she announced. I was silent. Watching Emily Connors do math was one of the most beautiful things I'd ever seen in my life.

She put the journal away and turned to me, her expression grave. "You can't tell anybody about what's going to happen tonight."

"I won't," I said.

"I'm serious." She grabbed my wrist, hard. "You have to promise."

"I won't tell anybody." But Emily's eyes indicated that she needed more. "I won't, I promise. I swear." I held up my pinkie. Emily ignored my pinkie and stared into my eyes for what felt like forever. Then, seemingly satisfied with whatever she'd found there, she double-checked the information in her journal and slid it back into her purse.

Annie popped out the Tori Amos cassette. "What's the number again?"

"One-oh-seven point three," Emily answered.

"Got it." Annie slowly tuned the dial to that number. There was nothing but static. "Are you sure this is it?"

"I hope so." Emily adjusted the volume on the radio, then turned to the two of us and smiled.

It was beautiful and unnerving.

In my experience, Emily Connors wasn't the kind of girl who smiled.

"Time?" Emily asked Annie, suddenly all business.

"Six minutes after ten," Annie replied.

Emily touched my arm and said, "Whatever you do, don't freak out, okay?"

I did my best to look cool as Emily put the truck into drive and guided us back out onto the old logging road.

We'd been listening to the static from the radio for about a minute or so when Emily nodded to her sister, then pressed the lever that turned off the truck's headlights.

Black.

We were driving at the same speed, but now I couldn't see a thing.

We were completely blind.

Static from the radio filled the cab.

"Emily, I don't think—"

"Sshhh." Emily grabbed my arm again, hard enough that she actually left four bruises, one from each finger. "Listen."

I shut up and listened.

"Did you hear a voice?" Emily asked.

Annie shrugged. Clearly, she hadn't heard anything. Emily looked at me and I just shook my head.

I was trying, but I found it hard to focus due to the constant static and the situation. Sitting in a truck with Emily and Annie Connors, speeding along an old logging road in complete and total darkness, wasn't standard operating procedure for me.

"What was that?" Emily turned up the radio. "Please tell me you heard that."

"I think so," I lied.

I still hadn't heard anything except for a steady stream of noise. My head was aching. The static from the radio tickled my ears and a thick fuzzy hum began vibrating, moving upward from somewhere deep inside my chest. My mouth was suddenly extremely dry.

I'd always attributed that sick feeling to the fact that we were speeding down that country road completely blind, but when I think back to that time now, I'm not sure that was it. Something felt . . . off in that moment. Different, somehow.

"Maybe we should turn on the lights?" Annie sounded scared.

"We're fine," Emily said.

When she'd switched off the headlights, the road was straight as far as the eye could see, but we'd been driving for quite a while since then. I crossed my fingers and hoped that we weren't about to hit a curve.

"I don't know, Em . . ." Annie said.

"Sshhh," Emily said to her sister. "It says we have to drive in the dark."

An almost imperceptible amount of moonlight occasionally revealed a bit of the road or the trees. I chose to believe Emily was using that light to keep us safely on the road.

"There." Emily leaned forward. "Did you hear that?"

I did hear something, almost imperceptible at first, but it was there.

A woman's voice.

Just as I was about to ask Emily if she'd heard the same thing, a loud buzzing filled the inside of the truck. Emily yanked the lever, the headlights flooded the road ahead of us, Annie screamed, and the world exploded in a brilliant flash of light and glass.

When Emily had turned the headlights back on, they'd cut like two tiny nuclear blasts through the darkness, illuminating a giant bull elk in the middle of the road.

The accident was over before my mind had time to process what was happening.

Emily and I were thrown clear through the windshield, but Annie remained inside the truck.

We were told later that, due to the position of her neck at the time of the accident, Annie had died instantly, and that there was no way she could have suffered.

I had a dislocated shoulder, a serious concussion, and a bunch of cuts and bruises, but I was lucky. Emily's right leg had been badly injured. She spent almost a year in the hospital, and longer than that in physical therapy.

The last time I saw Emily Connors was a few years after the accident.

My parents and I were driving down to San Francisco to visit some family friends. On our way out of Washington, we pulled over so I could use a gas station restroom. I was walking back to the car when I saw her.

She was sitting in the back seat of the car next to ours. I smiled and waved, but Emily just kept staring straight ahead, looking right through me as if I didn't exist. I was about to knock on the window to get her attention, but there was something about the way she was staring. I had the very distinct feeling she was someplace else, some-place far away, and that a knock on the window wouldn't be able to reach her. Before I had a chance to change my mind and knock, the car she was sitting in pulled away and exited onto the freeway.

That night I had a dream about Emily and Annie Connors.

I dreamt that we were back on the road that led up to the Petermans' house, but this time it wasn't a bull elk standing in the middle of the road. This time, it was a tall twisted gray figure.

As we moved closer I could see that the gray figure was actually made up of much smaller things, broken swirling shapes that wiggled and blurred together to form the shape that was standing in the middle of the road.

I wanted to scream but I was frozen, unable to move or speak.

At that point, just like it had happened in the truck, the static from the radio filled every part of my mind, my head began to ache, and my mouth dried up. The gray thing in the middle of the road slowly started to turn.

I tried to close my eyes, but I couldn't.

Emily was still driving, looking ahead as if the road were clear, and Annie had her head down, trying to hear the message Emily had been convinced was hidden somewhere in the static.

At this point, everything slowed down.

The buzz and static from the radio became deafening, and I felt the strange hum complete some kind of horrible circuit in my mind and body.

The truck continued speeding forward, and just as we were about to slam into the gray figure, I finally saw its face—or, at least, the place where a face should have been.

There was nothing but dark empty space.

This is when I heard the woman's voice—the same sound I'd heard cut through the radio static that night in the truck.

In a voice like dry, sharp crackling fire, she said the words—the exact same words I'd heard her say on that road back in 1999.

She said, "The door is open."

NOTES ON THE GAME: MISSIVE BY HAZEL
(AUTHENTICATED BY BLOCKCHAIN)

Gaming disorder is defined by the World Health Organization as "a pattern of gaming behavior characterized by impaired control . . . to the extent that gaming takes precedence over other interests and daily activities, and continuation or escalation of gaming despite the occurrence of negative consequences."

Negative consequences are real.

Don't forget to hydrate, and remember to tell somebody where you're going when you leave the house to follow a strange clue that nobody else believes is a clue.

Be careful out there.

—HAZEL 8

3

IF YOU LISTEN CAREFULLY, YOU CAN TOTALLY HEAR THE RHUBARB

THERE WERE THREE HUNDRED AND NINETY-FIVE white tiles on the floor and four hundred black. It took me twenty-one steps to get to the booth.

Two professional sports teams of some kind were playing celebrity dodgeball on the small television that hung above the milkshake machine. There was a neon green Dodge Challenger visible outside on the street.

Dodge.

Alan Scarpio smiled and waved his fork in the air. "Can you believe this place?"

"Yeah, it's pretty great."

"I got you coffee," he said, nodding to an off-white ceramic cup sitting on the table in front of me.

"Thanks." I slid into the worn vinyl booth.

It was an old diner from the 1950s, located directly across the street from the Magician's arcade. It was exactly the kind of place you might hear referred to as a joint or a greasy spoon. There were tiny jukeboxes on the tables in each of the booths. I think a few of them actually still worked.

I couldn't believe I was sitting across from Alan Scarpio—one of the richest men in the world—watching him devour a piece of rhubarb pie.

Dodgeball.

Was that woman in the back of the diner wearing an L.A. Dodgers baseball cap? Groups of tiles on the wall—four, fifteen, seven, five—numbers corresponding to the letters in the word "Dodge."

I was nervous.

As a kid, whenever I felt anxious, I found myself unable to stop picking out patterns—often to the point that I became incapable of focusing my attention on anything else. As these bouts of anxiety became more intense and frequent, I was forced to develop certain coping mechanisms in order to deal with the stress. The majority of these involved repeating familiar patterns from memory. The most effective involved tennis.

I've always loved tennis. I can recall entire matches with remarkable clarity. I'm able to do the same thing with baseball games and horror movie dialogue, but when it came to my homemade brand of pattern-recall therapy, tennis was always the most effective. One of my favorite matches was the 2001 U.S. Open quarterfinals match between Pete Sampras and Andre Agassi. On my legs, I would tap once for each player—Sampras on my left knee, Agassi on my right. I visualized every single shot, every serve and point, and eventually whatever was making me anxious would lose its potency and I'd be able to relax.

This technique had been extremely helpful after the accident with Annie and Emily Connors, and later when my parents were killed in a ferry accident while on vacation in Greece.

In the years following my parents' death, I would go on to develop a number of deep-breathing and relaxation techniques that were effective in combating my anxiety. Those exercises, along with medical advances in anti-anxiety medication, eventually allowed me to stop tapping out tennis matches on my legs entirely.

I was almost two full sets into that U.S. Open match before I realized what I'd been doing. I yanked my hands away from my knees and took a sip of coffee.

It had been at least ten years since I'd tapped out a tennis match.

Fuck. Why was I so anxious?

Scarpio was reportedly fifty-six years old, but looked at least a decade younger. He was about five foot ten and thin, with scruffy brown hair, cool blue eyes, and a wide mischievous smile. He wore dark blue jeans, faded brown desert boots, and a white Oxford button-up shirt. He was Caucasian, with a barely perceptible accent—most likely English, or maybe Welsh.

"Did you know rhubarb grows so fast you can actually hear it?"

"Really?" I said. I had no idea.

"It's true. I have a recording on my phone if you're interested."

"Oh . . . cool."

"I'm just fucking with you." He went back to eating his pie. "I mean, it's true. Rhubarb does grow fast, and I do have a recording of it on my phone, but what the fuck do you care? You wanna know why we're here, why I showed up at the arcade, and, more importantly, why I asked you for help." He smiled. "Am I right?"

"You're right—although the rhubarb thing is interesting."

Alan Scarpio nodded. "You're lying, but that's okay." He was using his fork to hunt down every crumb on his plate. "Are you sure I can't get you anything? This pie is fucking fantastic."

"I'm good, thanks." I took a sip of the warmish coffee.

"Well, I'm stuffed," he said as he leaned back in his chair and exhaled, every bit of pie now off the plate and inside the enigmatic billionaire.

I sat there in silence for as long as I could stand it.

"So," I said, finally, "why *did* you show up at the arcade?"

"You're surprised."

"Very."

"I get it. I'm a face you've seen on television or online. I saw Gary Busey once in a bar. He looked so familiar. As I walked by I smiled at him like the two of us were old friends."

"He's the crazy conspiracy guy?"

"I suppose maybe he is, but he was in *Point Break*. Classic. Two meatball subs!" Scarpio held up two fingers and yelled loud enough for the entire diner to hear. "Get me two, Utah!"

"I don't remember that scene," I said as the server approached our table and glared at Scarpio as if he were a small child who had just spilled a milkshake on the floor.

"Is everything all right?" She looked tired. The whites of her wide grayish-green eyes were spidered with tiny red lines, and her voice carried the earned rasp of somebody who'd poured an infinite amount of coffee into the cups of an infinite number of assholes. It had to be close to the end of her shift. She desperately wanted every-thing to be all right.

"Everything is perfect. I'm sorry for the outburst. We don't actu-ally want meatball subs. I promise it won't happen again." Scarpio smiled.

"Thanks," she said. "I don't have the energy to throw anybody else out tonight." She smiled, added a tired wink, then topped up my coffee.

"Thanks."

"You're welcome," she said, clearly happy we weren't going to ruin her night.

She didn't appear to recognize Alan Scarpio. Maybe she'd look him up tomorrow when she came in for her shift and discovered she'd been given a three-hundred-dollar tip on a seven-dollar check.

Scarpio waited for her to leave, then pulled out his phone and set it on the table. "What do you know about Rabbits?"

I glanced down at his phone. I thought maybe he was recording our conversation for some reason, but I couldn't see any voice re-corder app, just the date, time, and a cute dog as wallpaper—some kind of spaniel with a light blue bandana around its neck.

"Well, I mean, I know what most people interested in the game know," I said, trying to work out the best way to answer.

"Which is what?"

I had no idea what Scarpio was fishing for here. If he was Califor-niac, the alleged winner of the sixth iteration of the game, he knew a lot more than I did. And if he wasn't Californiac, well, he was still a billionaire, and if he wanted to learn about Rabbits, all he had to do was hire an expert. I mean, don't get me wrong, I know quite a bit. Among my friends and the handful of Rabbits aficionados I know, I am considered something of an authority on the game. But Alan Scarpio could afford the best—or, at the very least, somebody a fuckload better than a perpetually underemployed gamer who'd spent the last few minutes frantically tapping out a decades-old tennis match.

"You're not worried about the warnings surrounding the game? 'You play, you never tell?'" Scarpio asked, repeating a section of the *Prescott Competition Manifesto* that I'd played earlier in the arcade.

"Of course not," I said, although, like anyone seriously interested in the game, I'd heard rumors about all kinds of dangerous things surrounding Rabbits, including the mysterious Wardens—potentially deadly figures whose job it was to protect and maintain the integrity of the game at all costs.

"Now onward goes," Scarpio said.

"I'm sorry?" I asked.

"Those are the first three words of the tenth canto of Dante's *Inferno*. 'Now onward goes.'"

"Right," I said. "'Now onward goes along a narrow path, between the torments and the city wall. I follow my master,' or something like that."

"Very good," Scarpio said.

"Thanks," I said. "I spent half a semester studying Dante's *Inferno*. What . . . I mean, why—?"

"Sorry, I've been trying to remember that line all day."

"Why not just look it up online?"

"Where's the fun in that?" Alan Scarpio smiled and took a sip of coffee, and that's when I heard the strange creaking and cracking sounds. For a second I thought I saw the lights of the diner flicker in concert with the odd noises, but I couldn't be sure.

Did talking about Rabbits somehow summon the game's Wardens into existence? Was Scarpio's Dante quote some kind of strange evocation?

"What is that sound?" I asked.

"The rhubarb," he said, and pointed to his phone. "It's so creepy. Throw a bit of reverb on it and it's a fucking horror movie soundtrack."

I nodded. It was definitely creepy.

Scarpio stared at me for a moment, as if he was waiting for something, then he finally smiled.

"Something's wrong with the game," he said.

"What do you mean 'wrong'?"

"I'm not sure exactly, but if we don't fix it before the next iteration begins, we're all well and truly fucked."

At this point, Scarpio's phone buzzed. He looked down at the small screen. "Excuse me for one second." He picked up his phone.

"What is it?" he asked.

I watched as most of the color slowly drained from his face.

"Are you sure? Okay, I'll be right there," he said and hung up.

"I gotta run," he said, clearly flustered by the call he'd just received. "Late meeting. Do you mind walking me to my car?"

"No. I mean—"

"I'd like to keep talking for a bit as we walk, if that's okay with you."

If Alan Scarpio wanted to keep talking, I'd be walking until my legs gave out.

"Um, sure," I said.

As we stepped outside, I pulled my collar up against the light rain. Scarpio didn't seem fazed by the weather at all. He started walking up the street. I hurried to keep up.

"I'm going to tell you everything I know about what's happening, I promise," he said. "I just need to get a few things straight first, if you don't mind."

"Of course," I said.

"Great. So let's start with my earlier question. What do you know about Rabbits?"

In the brief period of time it took us to walk the few blocks from the diner to Scarpio's car, I told him everything I knew about the game: how it was a hidden and secret thing, a deep underground obsession, and how, if you weren't looking for it, you'd most likely never heard of it. That it was reputedly ancient and possibly connected to the Knights Templar, the Illuminati, and the Thule Society. I detailed everything I'd heard about the alleged prizes: NSA or CIA recruitment, billions of dollars, or immortality, and about the list of winners known as The Circle that appeared all over the world, seemingly at random, before and after each new iteration of the game. I went on to tell him all I could remember about the mysterious Hazel, the most famous Rabbits player of all time, who'd supposedly checked out right after they'd won the eighth iteration. I ended with something about how most people who studied the game believed that Alan Scarpio was Californiac, the winner of Six, and that winning the sixth iteration of the game had resulted in his becoming extremely rich overnight.

I looked at Scarpio's face carefully while I was delivering that last bit of information, but his expression betrayed nothing.

"Anything else?" he asked.

"Most people interested in Rabbits believe the game is currently between iterations, and are waiting for the eleventh version to begin."

"That's it?" he asked.

"That's all I can think of right now," I said as the two of us finally reached Scarpio's black Tesla sedan.

"Can we continue this tomorrow? A late breakfast at the diner?"

"Of course," I said.

"Great." Scarpio pulled a small black leather case from his pocket, took out a business card, and handed it to me. It had been printed on some kind of thick off-white material, linen or bamboo maybe. On the card was nothing but a phone number.

"Let's meet back at that diner at eleven tomorrow morning to continue our discussion," he said. "Give me a call if you have a conflict and we'll set something else up, but this is important, and I'd really appreciate it if you could make it."

He got into the car, started it up, and rolled down the driver's-side window.

"I'll be there," I said, working extremely hard to stop myself from grinning like an idiot.

"I'll see you tomorrow," he said, and then he guided the shiny black sedan away from the curb, down the street, and out into the night.

I stood there for a long time after his taillights had faded into the distance, doing my best to digest what had just happened.

I was initially surprised that Alan Scarpio didn't have a driver, but after thinking back on our conversation, it kind of made sense. For a billionaire, Scarpio was definitely what you'd call "down to earth"—except for the part where he'd allegedly won a fortune playing a potentially deadly secret underground game that most people had never heard of.

NOTES ON THE GAME: MISSIVE BY HAZEL
(AUTHENTICATED BY BLOCKCHAIN)

Stop me if you've heard this one before. A man walks into a dead letter office and asks the person in charge of the facility if they'd be willing to keep their eyes open for one very particular stamp. It was pressed into service in 1932, and on the front of the stamp is what appears to be an arctic hare. The stamp comes from the country of Thirland. Now, if you know anything at all about geography, you're aware that Thirland doesn't exist.

It remains, however, a beautiful stamp. I've seen it.

There's something about the stamp that makes you feel strange—like you know you've seen it before, like you've been aware of its existence your entire life.

Picking out what's important from the static they use to confuse us is a key aspect of achieving success in the game of life. This game isn't so different.

Just because you're convinced there's a dangerous secret process running beneath a secret world doesn't mean there *isn't* a dangerous secret process running beneath a secret world.

—HAZEL 8

4

THE PASSENGER DISCREPANCY

My parents died when I was seventeen. I can't say that it happened suddenly, because I have no idea how long they were trapped inside that capsized ferry before they eventually succumbed to the freezing cold water.

My mother was an only child, and my father's brother—an uncle I'd never met—declined familial custody. All of my grandparents were dead by that point, which left me almost completely alone as far as family goes.

I'd already graduated high school and was waiting to start college in the fall. I had no desire to sample the hospitality of the foster care system, so, rather than take my chances with social services, I fought to become emancipated by court order.

It was easy. I represented myself. They don't recommend it, but what do they know? Trust me, there's no way you would have said no either if you'd seen me up there, just seventeen years old, arguing my case in legalese like the main character in a coming-of-age comedy from the early nineties.

I received a modest amount of money from my parents' passing, which I eventually invested in the stock market.

I did a shit ton of research and practiced using mock stocks in a simulated investment environment for a full year before I did any real investing. My ability to pick out deeply embedded patterns and causal fluctuations resulted in my turning seventy thousand fake dollars into almost four hundred thousand fake dollars. The following year, I invested my money for real. Then I sold my parents' house and purchased a modest apartment in Capitol Hill.

I was a young adult living in a hip neighborhood in Seattle—in a home I'd purchased with my own money—coasting through college with a GPA much higher than I deserved.

I should have taken things more seriously, put more work into my studies, but what did I do instead?

I played games.

And after graduation, while everybody I knew was taking global surf trips, pretzeling themselves into enlightenment at an ashram in India, downing ridiculous amounts of cheap beer with the other American tourists in Prague, or going on any number of other adventures, I was doing something else.

I was playing games.

I'd played games when my parents had been alive, of course, but after they died, I spent every minute outside of work and school devoted to nothing else. Focusing my attention on games resulted in my becoming a little bit more social, and it had another added benefit; it helped me avoid thinking about what had happened to my parents.

At first the games were effective, and I was able to use them to not only calm my racing mind, but learn how to better interact with others. But, similar to a longtime drug user, the games I'd been playing began to lose their efficacy and I needed more.

So I started playing longer and sleeping less.

From role-playing games to first-person shooters, online to dice on a table, I played them all. I became so obsessed that I was lucky if I managed to get two or three hours of sleep a night.

It was during this period that I joined an active online community of role-playing gamers, discovered alcohol in a big way, and narrowly avoided doing a long stint in a psychiatric facility.

The court referred to it as a trespassing incident, but it was full-on breaking and entering. By the time I was finally arrested in the basement of the Harvard Exit Theatre, I hadn't eaten or slept for three days.

The arresting officer claimed I'd told her I was there waiting for someone—that I'd been following important signs, and needed to be in that theater at a very specific time in order to meet somebody I referred to as The Passenger.

Full disclosure, there were a couple of things that had happened during this period that may have added to my confused state of mind. My psychiatrist had recently changed my medication, and our family dog had passed away from complications during a routine dental surgery. My dog was older, but she'd been completely healthy at the time of her accidental death. I was crushed. She was a little brown Chihuahua named Ruby, and she was the last living connection I had to my parents.

Ruby had been there for me when I came home from the press conference where they'd announced that the rescue operation—which had eventually turned into a recovery operation—was now strictly a salvage operation.

When my parents were finally pronounced dead, having Ruby there needing to be fed and walked helped me make it through the seemingly endless days.

When she died, I was well and truly alone.

One night, shortly after Ruby died, I was playing a brand-new massively multiplayer online role-playing game (MMORPG) called Underlight, when another game popped into my mind. It was something my parents had played with me when I was a kid, something called Connections.

Connections was all about trying to find patterns and relationships between a number of seemingly disparate and unrelated images.

My parents had introduced me to Connections on a weekend evening, sometime in the late summer. We were getting ready to go to the drive-in, and it had started raining really hard. I was angry, because for the first time I'd managed to persuade my parents to let me pick an R-rated movie. I'd chosen Peter Jackson's *The Frighteners,* and they'd reluctantly agreed.

I called the drive-in theater, but they told me all of the movies had been canceled because of the weather. My mother decided this wasn't an unfortunate event but rather an opportunity for a family game night.

She made popcorn and the three of us played Monopoly. It was a far cry from *The Frighteners,* but I enjoyed playing games with my parents, and I loved the way my mother made popcorn. She called it a delivery system for butter.

Later, after we'd all made banana splits (a delivery system for hot fudge), my father brought out a worn rectangular black box with the word "Connections" written in burnt orange across the front in a modern font. I'd been through the closet where our family kept our games a million times. I'd never seen that box before.

I remember my mother wasn't impressed when she saw it. I heard her whisper to my father that he was forcing things, that I wasn't ready, that this game might exacerbate something she referred to as my "condition." He told her that was exactly why it was important.

Inside the box were a variety of photographic images in a series of color-coded envelopes. The pictures had been printed on some kind of thick card stock. Each card had some words or numbers printed on the back of it.

I wasn't allowed to see the backs of the image cards, only the pictures themselves.

After a minute or two spent arranging the images and envelopes, my father lifted up one of the cards and asked me to look at the image carefully.

It was a picture of a tiger in a lush green jungle setting.

After a moment, he put that card away and held up another one. This one was a photograph of a woman sitting at a Formica table in a 1950s-style kitchen. She was doing some kind of accounting work.

My mother asked me if I could see anything in the second picture that was similar to something in the first. I told her that the patterns of the tiger's markings matched some of the patterns on the wallpaper.

Then my father brought out a third photograph.

Taken in what appeared to be some kind of honky-tonk bar, the photograph featured a bottle of beer sitting on top of an old Wurlitzer jukebox.

My father asked me if there was anything in the third photograph that matched the second. I told him that the time on the clock in the second picture matched the numbers of the song on the jukebox in the other.

This continued a few more times, until I could no longer come up with anything to connect the images.

That's when the game ended.

We played Connections a few more times over the next couple of months. It was fun spending time with my parents, but staring at cards and trying to find some kind of link between them really wasn't much of a game. After a while, I found myself getting bored. I'd started dreading the sight of the black box with the orange letters.

But the last time we played Connections was different.

My parents had taken me out for pancakes. This time there were no cards.

This time we were looking for connections in real life.

My father asked me to look for things that could be related somehow, for any kind of link between two or more things in the restaurant.

I hadn't noticed anything that stood out until after we'd eaten and were just about to leave. I pointed out a girl wearing a T-shirt with a horse on the front. It was very similar to a painting of a horse hanging above the door to the kitchen.

We followed the girl and her family as they went outside and got into their car.

As we were standing outside the restaurant, a bus pulled up and stopped. There was an ad on the side of the bus for a group of artists at the Frye Art Museum. The ad featured a horse. And just like the girl's T-shirt and the painting above the kitchen door, the horse was rearing up on its back legs. My mother grabbed my hand and we ran for the bus.

We didn't make it. My parents had a brief conversation, then we got into the car and drove to the Frye Art Museum.

We entered the museum and my parents took me straight to the painting of the rearing horse that had been featured on the side of the bus. There was something in the title and catalog number of the painting that led my parents to drive us to a park. I can't remember exactly which park, but I remember seeing a bust of a man's head attached to a small fountain, and some kind of outdoor performance stage.

While my parents were excitedly working out something related to the numbers they'd found connected to that painting, I wandered off.

They found me a minute or so later, screaming my lungs out.

I'd stumbled onto a large concrete chessboard.

It was protected from the elements by a large metal roof and surrounded by four stone benches. I remember stepping up onto the board and playing an imaginary game of chess. I'd recently learned how to play and had become fascinated with the way the pieces moved. I was still too young to be any good, but I loved the rules and the seemingly endless possibilities.

I imagined the pieces—bishop, pawn, rook, and the rest—clashing in my head as I performed each allotted movement in turn. The giant board became a mental battleground as I strode across the squares, my purposeful footsteps representing the movements of black and white in their fight for supremacy. While I was taking one of white's pawns with one of black's knights, however, something happened. A deep panic overwhelmed me, and dark blurring shapes slowly started seeping into my eyes from the edges of the world. I felt like my peripheral vision had betrayed me somehow. I was suddenly frozen in place. I couldn't move.

This is the first time I remember experiencing this feeling—a feeling that would overwhelm me again a few years later, in that truck with Annie and Emily Connors, a sensation that I would eventually begin referring to as "the gray feeling."

The gray feeling usually began with a low thrumming vibration deep in the pit of my stomach and an itchy tingling right behind my eyes. It would soon take over my upper body with a rush of what felt like fluttering moths in my lungs, then my limbs would turn heavy and weak and, finally, my mouth would be filled with a thick fuzzy tingling. This was all accompanied by an inescapable, low, hollow, metallic humming in my head.

This is what happened to me while I was standing on that giant chessboard in the park. This . . . and more.

I had the sudden feeling that I was somewhere else.

And, wherever I was, I wasn't alone.

Something was there with me—something cold. I remember being terrified to look up into the sky, because I knew that I'd be able to see whatever it was. And I understood that if I could see it, it would be able to see me.

Then I felt it coming, speeding toward me from somewhere way up in the dark clouds.

That's when I lost control of my bladder and screamed.

My parents came running and took me home immediately.

In bed later that night, I wondered if I'd imagined the whole thing. I'd been rereading The Lord of the Rings for the third time, and something about that thing I'd felt coming out of the darkness reminded me of the Eye of Sauron seeing Frodo when he'd put on the ring. I remembered feeling completely naked and exposed, like I was waiting there for something terrifying to arrive from another world.

I didn't think about Connections again until years later, while I was playing Underlight.

It wasn't anything about Underlight specifically that made me think of Connections; it was just something in that moment. Maybe it was the smell of microwave popcorn coming from the unit next door, or the way the rain was hitting my window, but something triggered the memory and brought me right back to that table with my parents, right back to the game called Connections.

At first it was a happy memory, but as I sat there reliving it, some-thing slowly began to change. I started thinking about the gray feeling and the dark thing I'd felt coming for me in that city park. This led to me picturing my mom and dad trapped beneath that capsized ferry, kicking and screaming for help, and eventually to my envisioning both of their faces, floating in the freezing water, staring up into nothing, forever alone in the dark.

My usual relaxation techniques didn't work and I was unable to get the image of my dying parents' faces out of my mind. So I left Underlight running, stood up, grabbed my leather jacket from the back of a nearby chair, and hurried out of my building into the rain.

I would be arrested three days later.

During those three days I did nothing but play my own version of Connections.

I started with the final image my parents had shown me on the last day we'd played the game together.

It was a color photograph of an old woman feeding a bunch of pigeons. One of the pigeons was different from the others— browner, with a reddish breast. I looked it up. It was a passenger pigeon, just standing there among the regular pigeons.

But the last passenger pigeon had died in 1914, and modern-day Kodachrome color photography had not come into being until 1935.

It was an impossible photograph.

The first word that popped into my mind was "discrepancy." Based on the woman's clothing and the cars behind her on the street, the photograph had been taken sometime in the 1960s. An extinct bird, in a photograph taken almost fifty years *after* that bird had become extinct, was definitely a discrepancy.

It reminded me of another extinct bird—the imperial woodpecker Emily Connors had been so excited about.

It reminded me of Rabbits.

The passenger pigeon and an address hidden in coded text on the park bench in that impossible photograph led me to a video store. Hanging in the window was an Italian movie poster advertising a classic 1975 film by Michelangelo Antonioni. In Italian, the film was called *Professione: reporter,* but in English it was known as *The Passenger.*

In the end credits of that movie was a clue that led me to a specific page in an out-of-print edition of a French mystery novel. This in turn led me to a bus stop where I got on a bus and rode it until I discovered a wall covered in graffiti.

There, hidden in the content of that graffiti, I found a message. Or perhaps I imagined I'd found a message. Either way, that message led me on a journey through the city, chasing clue after clue, until I eventually found myself arrested for trespassing in the basement of the Harvard Exit Theatre, waiting for somebody or something that I referred to as The Passenger.

By then, I was a mess. Nothing made any sense.

I actually remember feeling a sense of relief when they finally arrested me.

I was screened and assessed, then given the option of attending a mental health court or going through a normal criminal proceeding—mental health courts, like drug courts, were created to divert defendants with mental illnesses from the overcrowded and overworked criminal justice system.

I opted for the former, and they let me go once I'd agreed to attend weekly counseling sessions.

A few days after my arrest, I was back at home, and a month after that, I started my junior year of college.

I never played the game called Connections again—not only because of what had happened to me in that theater waiting for The Passenger, but because I was about to find something better.

I was about to rediscover the game called Rabbits.

5

BARON CORDUROY

I WAS STARTLED AWAKE by a series of aggressive buzzing sounds.

Somebody was downstairs hammering on my apartment's call button.

I live on the top floor of a four-story older brick building in Capitol Hill. On the plus side, there are crown moldings, hardwood floors, and leaded glass windows. Some of the negatives include an oil heating system that barely works and a shower plagued by bursts of scalding hot water that occur whenever someone flushes the toilet in the apartment directly below mine—the building's superintendent claims he's been trying to figure out how to fix it for years, but I'm not sure I believe him.

"Circle K, what the fuck is happening?" Baron brushed past me and headed straight for the kitchen.

"Have you slept?" I asked. "You look like you've been up all night."

"Spent the night working on a hookup app for a couple of grad students," he said as he scoured my pantry for something to eat.

Baron didn't actually look that bad, but his eyes had the wild faraway look of a coder, that thick wired glaze that working all night staring at a screen and listening to crazy loud music can produce.

Baron Corduroy was tall and thin, with angular cheekbones he once referred to as his "shoulders of the face." His eyes had a perpetual sleepy look, which belied a fierce intelligence and sharp wit.

He came from the world of high finance, but these days made a living as a freelancer in tech. He spent most of his time working on mobile apps for startups and college kids, but Baron could pretty much code anything. I think he actually did some contract work for the NSA at some point. Before he changed careers and went freelance, Baron worked as a broker at a large firm in downtown Seattle.

One of the keys to Rabbits is an ability to recognize complex patterns, connections, and coincidences. If you were really good at that type of thing, you had a lot of solid employment options, but like I'd discovered while still in high school, none of those options was as immediately exciting and financially rewarding as the stock market.

By the time I'd met him, Baron was starting to burn out, getting tired of the West Edge grind. Microdosing LSD and pounding Adderall had kept him sharp for a while, but when the drugs no longer worked, he needed to find something else.

That's when he discovered the game.

The mysterious history and deep Web conspiracy links got him started, but the intense pattern-recognition work and puzzle-solving—along with the camaraderie of like-minded weirdos—kept him in.

Way in.

I met Baron for the first time at the Magician's arcade when I was a senior in college.

Like a lot of us, Baron Corduroy had come to the arcade in search of the Magician. He came to speak with him about a game called Xevious—a vertically scrolling shooter videogame released by Namco in 1983.

He'd come to see Xevious because Baron believed something strange was going on with one particular cabinet version of the game he'd played in a 7-Eleven in Oregon, and he wanted to check out another cabinet in order to use it as a point of comparison. At that time, the closest functioning Xevious machine was located at the Magician's arcade in Seattle.

Five teenagers, on four different dates, had complained of headaches and dizziness before passing out while playing the Xevious machine in that 7-Eleven. Baron was on the trail, trying to solve that mystery.

He'd interviewed the teenagers who'd passed out, and they all told him the same thing. Just before they lost consciousness, they saw something—a shadow thing that spilled across the screen and beckoned to them with a thin outstretched hand. They'd all described removing their hands from the controls, hearing a high-pitched ringing combined with an impossibly low rumble, and then waking up on the ground, staring up into somebody's concerned face.

The symptoms sounded eerily familiar to me, if not the cause.

The owner of the game in Oregon claimed that his machine had been functioning perfectly fine and if the Magician's Xevious machine was different, well, then, the Magician had somehow messed with it himself.

I know the Magician fairly well now, and if he's capable of messing with the code of a videogame from 1983, then I'm Hazel—and, spoiler alert, I'm definitely not Hazel.

Baron didn't find any difference between the Magician's Xevious machine and that machine in Oregon, but while he was playing it, he did find something.

He found a kindred spirit.

He found me.

Baron poured the last of my Count Chocula cereal over a small scoop of freezer-burned vanilla frozen yogurt that I'd had in my fridge for at least a year.

"Do you have any chocolate chips?" he asked.

"I met Alan Scarpio last night," I said, doing my best to keep my voice level and unaffected.

"Yeah, right," Baron said as he picked up a spoon and started eating.

After a moment, he set his spoon down slowly and stopped chewing. He knew me well enough to understand when I was most likely joking, and when I might have actually just met Alan fucking Scarpio.

"Are you being serious right now?"

"He was at the arcade. He finished your game of Robotron."

"Alan *Scarpio* was at the Magician's place?"

"Yeah."

"Last night?"

"Yep."

"He was the guy in the hoodie who took over my game?"

"Sure was."

"Fuck. And you met him?"

"Yeah. We had pie."

Baron just stared, his mouth hanging open.

"Well, Scarpio had pie. I had coffee."

I eventually managed to talk Baron into leaving my place, but only after I'd told him everything that had happened the night before and promised to call him the second I finished my morning meeting with Scarpio.

6

SABATINI VS. GRAF

THE RAIN IN SEATTLE is different.

I've experienced the weather in London, New York, Hong Kong, and a handful of other places around the world, but nothing sticks to you like the rain in the Pacific Northwest. This deep emerald gloom is eternal, cellular. It's part of the landscape—and, before you know it, it becomes a permanent part of you as well.

It was raining as I walked down the street toward the diner.

I was wearing a faded blue hoodie, jeans, and light gray Converse All Stars.

I've lived in Seattle most of my adult life and, although I've found myself under an umbrella from time to time, I'm not sure I've actually ever owned one.

Thirty days of rain in a month isn't all that unusual here. You get used to it. I can't imagine seasonal affective disorder is something that happens to Seattleites; when you live here, that's just life. And, frankly, I wouldn't have it any other way.

I love the rain; you can hide in it.

I got to the diner half an hour early and drank cup after cup of spiritless coffee as I waited. Part of me was convinced that I'd imagined last night, but the business card Scarpio had given me was sitting on the stained Formica table, right next to my diner-standard off-white ceramic coffee mug.

It had happened. It was real.

I'd always imagined I was connected to the world of Rabbits somehow, but it was an ephemeral feeling, fleeting, always just out of reach. And yet something felt different this time—something that might finally justify the hours spent online searching for clues to a game that at times over the years I wasn't sure actually existed, saving up for road trips to decidedly nonglamorous locations like Winnipeg, Canada, following leads that turned out to be nothing, and temporarily working two jobs in order to afford a special edition of a weird roadside atlas rumored to contain information about the game.

It was all coalescing now. It felt like Rabbits was finally coming to life.

But Scarpio was late. It had been almost an hour.

I drank more coffee and stared at the number on Scarpio's card for another fifteen minutes before I finally decided to call.

A woman's voice answered after the first ring.

"Hello?"

"Um, hi. I'm looking for . . . Mr. Scarpio. I think we were supposed to have a meeting this morning."

"You *think* you were *supposed* to have a meeting?"

"He told me to meet him here for breakfast."

"How did you get this number?"

"Mr. Scarpio gave it to me last night."

There was a long pause.

"Where are you?"

"I'm at the diner."

"What fucking diner?"

I gave her the address.

"Stay put." She hung up.

I had no idea if she was going to get him to call, show up, or maybe reschedule. I was hungry, but I didn't want to be halfway through a plate of runny eggs when Alan Scarpio showed up, so I didn't order anything.

"What's your name?" the woman asked, as she slid gracefully into the booth.

She was about thirty-five, Asian, subtle highlights through shiny black wavy hair. Everything she was wearing looked expensive. I wouldn't have been surprised if she was an FBI agent or a salesperson at Tiffany & Co. She smiled slightly, and I could tell immediately that her smile didn't mean what most of us mean when we smile.

The diner wasn't packed, but more than half a dozen booths were full of people. How the hell did this woman know I was the person who'd called about Scarpio?

"My name is K," I replied.

"K. Is that short for something?"

"Yes."

After realizing she wasn't getting anything more, she leaned forward and crossed her hands on the table. "Where is he?"

"Scarpio?"

"Who the fuck else?"

"I don't know."

I wasn't sure when, but at some point during the conversation or interrogation, I'd begun tapping my fingers on the table: the third and final set from the 1991 Wimbledon final between Steffi Graf and Gabriela Sabatini. It was a classic, cementing Graf's legacy at Wimbledon. Graf was serving on my left, Sabatini on my right. Steffi was down one game in the second set. Princess Diana was in the crowd. It was a beautiful day.

There was something about the way this woman looked at me, like she could see straight through my eyes and into my mind. My pulse was racing. I did my best to concentrate on taking slow, deep breaths.

"You met him here last night?"

"Yes. Well, we met at the arcade, then came over here for pie."

She nodded, processing this information.

"Is Mr. Scarpio going to be joining us?" I asked.

"What happened after you had pie?"

"I didn't have pie. Mr. Scarpio had pie."

She just stared, waiting for me to answer her question.

Salesperson at Tiffany's was definitely off the table. This woman was something else entirely. I continued to tap out the points of the Wimbledon match. Steffi Graf was serving at five-all in the third set.

"Mr. Scarpio met me at the arcade across the street. We came over here for a while, and then I walked him to his car."

She considered this for a second or two. "Did he play any games?"

"What do you mean?"

"At the arcade. Did he play any of the games?"

"Um . . . yeah. I mean, I know he played Robotron."

"Robotron: 2084?"

"Yes."

She pulled out a worn old orange Moleskine notebook and a black roller-tip pen and wrote something down.

"I'm sorry, who are you?" I asked.

She looked at me like I imagined an overworked clandestine government agent might look just as they were about to switch interrogation tactics from asking questions to beating the shit out of their subject with a phone book. "I work with Mr. Scarpio."

"That's it?"

"What else?" she asked, ignoring my question.

"I'm sorry?"

"What else happened?"

It felt like the temperature in the room suddenly dropped by ten degrees, and the lights dimmed, just a little.

I considered telling her about the call Scarpio had received just before he'd abruptly ended our time together in the diner, but there was something about this woman that felt incredibly dangerous. I suddenly wanted this interview to be over.

I shook my head. "That's it."

It was at this point that something strange happened.

Steffi Graf lost the 1991 Wimbledon final.

This was impossible.

I'd run that particular match over in my mind hundreds of times. I see every point as it happens, very clearly, without exception. Steffi Graf wins. She won. It's a fact of history.

This had never happened to me before. Every match I'd ever re-created mentally had played out exactly as it happened in real life. I was never a single point off. I was shaken. My hands began to tremble.

"Are you okay?" the woman asked.

"I'm fine," I lied, and did my best to compose myself. "Do you think Mr. Scarpio is coming?"

"I don't think so, but if he does, please tell him to call home immediately." And with that, she stood up and walked out of the diner.

I watched her cross the street and enter the arcade.

I'd walk over later to see if the mysterious woman said or did anything interesting, but I had to do something first. I went back over that tennis match in my mind, at high speed.

Steffi Graf won, just like she was supposed to.

I relaxed a little bit and ordered some food.

I was starving.

"Hey, you're the meatball sub guy's friend."

I took the last bite of my three-cheese omelet and looked up into the familiar wide grayish-green eyes of the server who had shown a great deal of patience dealing with Scarpio yelling lines from the film *Point Break,* and who had seen that patience rewarded with an enormous tip.

"Guilty," I said.

"I have something for you," she said, then walked away from the booth toward the back of the restaurant.

I had no idea what she was talking about.

She returned about a minute later and handed me Alan Scarpio's phone. "You left this last night," she said, then hurried off to help another patron.

Either Scarpio accidentally left his phone in the booth after he'd played me the rhubarb sounds, or it had somehow slipped out of his pocket.

I stared at the cute dog photo for a moment, then realized his home screen wasn't locked. If I wanted to, I could access Alan Scarpio's phone with one simple swipe.

A few minutes later I called the server over and explained that the phone belonged to my friend, and I would do my best to let him know it was here. She told me she'd put it in the back office for safekeeping.

Once again I called the number that Alan Scarpio had given me, but this time there was no answer, and no voicemail option.

I waited until I saw the mystery woman leave the arcade, and then ran across the street to ask Chloe if the woman had mentioned anything about Alan Scarpio.

Chloe and I had almost gotten together once—or at least, that's the way I choose to remember it.

It was a week or two after we'd met. Both of us were single at the time.

A mutual friend had an art opening, and Chloe and I were there, along with a handful of other people we knew from the arcade.

I had no idea how she felt about me, but I'd been attracted to Chloe from the moment we met. She was smart and funny, and into a lot of the same terminally uncool shit I was. And even though she might come across as somebody who doesn't give a fuck, I could tell that she did. She gave all the fucks. She was deeply engaged and cared about a lot of things, you just needed to take the time to get to know her.

Chloe referred to herself as a "recovering musician." She'd lived a completely different life from the ages of sixteen to nineteen as the singer and principal songwriter in a semipopular indie rock band.

Like Pavement with "Cut Your Hair" or Radiohead with "Creep," Chloe's band, Peagles, had a hit single that overshadowed a critically acclaimed full-length album. That song was called "MPDG (Manic Pixie Dreamgirl)."

Chloe smashes the absolute shit out of a ukulele in the video. It's really cool.

Although Peagles released only one album and an EP before they broke up, "MPDG" was a big hit, and that song's ubiquity in movies and television shows meant that, unless she really wanted to, Chloe didn't need to work for the next couple of decades.

After the gallery show, a couple of our friends suggested we head back to my place for a drink. My apartment was not only large and roommate-free, it was also right around the corner, and I always had booze.

There were six of us there, but I spent most of the night talking to Chloe and her friend Amanda. It was a great conversation. We talked about games, movies, comics, television, and whatever else popped into our heads. By the time I finally glanced over at the clock, it was one in the morning, and everybody else had gone home.

I walked Chloe and Amanda to the door, and on the way there Chloe and I shared a brief look. She smiled just a little as she pulled her hair behind her ear, and I felt a wave of electricity move through me. I suddenly couldn't figure out breathing.

Was I on an inhale or an exhale?

I eventually remembered how to work my lungs, the three of us hugged goodbye, and I shut the door.

As I made my way back to the living room, I thought about the best way to ask Chloe out. Was dinner too prosaic? Definitely. Was there maybe a cool band playing The Crocodile this weekend? I would check first thing in the morning.

Then I heard a knock on my door.

I was absolutely positive that when I opened the door, Chloe would be standing there. She'd tell me she came back to suggest a late-night walk or something similar, that she'd been having a great time and that she didn't want it to stop.

But it wasn't Chloe at the door. It was Amanda.

She said she'd forgotten her glasses and suggested we have one more drink. She wanted to talk about Neil Gaiman's Sandman series.

We ended up staying together for five years.

———

Chloe was balanced precariously on a stool behind the front counter when I arrived. She wore a faded NPR T-shirt, ripped jeans, and standard-issue Apple AirPods, which she pulled out of a tangle of crimped blond hair when I walked in.

She smiled and held up her middle finger.

"Super unprofessional," I said. "This is a place of business."

She shrugged.

I asked about the mystery woman from the diner. Chloe told me that the woman didn't ask any questions, just played one game of Robotron and left.

"Why the interest in random business lady?" Chloe asked, suspicious.

I told her about what had happened with Scarpio.

"Alan Scarpio?"

"Yeah."

"Asked you to help him fix the game?"

"Yeah."

"Rabbits?"

"Yes."

Chloe stared for a moment, then shifted her weight to her back foot and crossed her arms. "That didn't happen."

I smiled.

"For real?"

"I swear. It really happened."

"Holy shit!" Chloe said, and her gum almost fell out of her mouth. "That woman did ask if I'd seen Alan Scarpio in here. I thought she was fucking with me."

"It really happened, but Scarpio missed our meeting earlier today and I haven't been able to get back in touch."

"Tell me everything," she said.

So I did.

Chloe made me describe what had happened with Scarpio down to the most minute detail—twice. As I found myself repeating what had happened, it made less and less sense. Alan Scarpio, billionaire philanthropist and possible winner of the sixth iteration of Rabbits, had told me something was wrong with the game and that he needed my help to fix it.

Chloe asked me if I was sure it was actually Scarpio and not some kind of look-alike or something.

I nodded, but, in that moment, I didn't actually feel all that sure about anything.

7

JEFF GOLDBLUM DOES NOT BELONG IN THIS WORLD

THREE DAYS AFTER Alan Scarpio stood me up at the diner, I called the number on the business card he'd given me for the last time.

Out of service.

Baron had taken on another complicated coding project and Chloe was busy at the arcade, so I spent most of my time cleaning up a couple of online trading accounts I'd been neglecting and taking care of a few things around the house.

Meeting Scarpio had begun to feel like some kind of weird fever dream—a brief glimpse into an alternate reality where I was important enough to be sent on quests and billionaires sat down with me for pie.

Since the number Scarpio had given me was out of service, and he was legendarily reclusive, I had no way of getting in touch with him.

If he really did need my help fixing Rabbits, he'd have to find me.

I did my best to dive back into my life, and tried not to think about Rabbits, Scarpio, or anything connected to our strange conversation in the diner.

Two days later, Alan Scarpio was reported missing.

One of the public relations companies he owned held a press conference. They said that he'd been missing for what they referred to as a "significant, but as yet unknown period of time." They were asking for help. If anybody had any information on Alan Scarpio's whereabouts, they were to please call the number.

"Holyfuckingshit!" Baron Corduroy's voice burst out of my phone's tiny speakers. He could clearly barely contain his excitement. "Alan Scarpio went missing right after he told us something was wrong with the game."

"Yeah. It's pretty nuts," I said.

Of course, Alan Scarpio hadn't told *us* something was wrong with the game, he told *me,* but I didn't have the heart to correct Baron. I couldn't remember the last time I'd heard him this excited.

"I hope he's okay," I said.

"Wait, do you think his disappearance might be connected to his visiting you?"

"I don't know."

"Fuck, K. Is this Rabbits?"

I ignored his question. I was still processing the news of Scarpio's disappearance. It couldn't be a coincidence, could it?

"What the hell are we supposed to do now? All we have is a cryptic visit from a billionaire and some mystery woman who cornered you at the diner," Baron said.

But that wasn't all we had.

"I'll call you later," I said, and hung up.

The diner was half full, and the staff were settled into the calm just before the lunch rush. The woman with the grayish-green eyes who'd served us the other day was working.

She recognized me with a smile and waved me over to a booth.

"Welcome back," she said as she filled my cup with coffee.

I told her that my friend was busy and had asked me to pick up his phone.

She brought it over the next time she refilled my coffee. She obviously had no idea that the person I'd been sitting with was a missing billionaire. I guess she didn't watch the news.

As soon as she handed me Scarpio's phone, I threw down a five-dollar bill and rushed out of the diner. I was worried she'd suddenly figure out whose phone it was and change her mind.

There wasn't much on Scarpio's phone. No photographs, aside from the picture of the dog that functioned as his wallpaper, and no records of any calls—including the call I'd watched him receive that had clearly disturbed him and sent him rushing out of the diner to attend what he'd referred to as a late meeting. Those factors, along with the lack of a connected email account and an empty contact list, made one thing absolutely clear: This was definitely not the missing billionaire's primary means of communicating with the world.

"Rhubarb pie?" the Magician asked, staring at Scarpio's phone as if it were the Ark of the Covenant.

"That's what he ate," I said.

"And coffee?"

"Yep, and coffee."

"Any special kind of coffee?"

I shook my head. "Just regular diner stuff."

The Magician nodded and went back to work, his wiry black hair hanging low over cool green eyes, long fingers bending and flexing as he connected Scarpio's phone to a laptop running an operating system I'd never seen before. He was wearing a light brown suede jacket over a vintage pink-and-yellow Teenage Fanclub T-shirt. He looked a bit thinner than the last time I'd seen him, and, although it had only been a month or so, he looked years older.

Chloe said he'd been in northern Russia for a while, but she didn't know where he'd gone after that; the Magician was always traveling somewhere last-minute for wildly disparate amounts of time and then just strolling back into the arcade as if he'd never left. None of us had any idea what he did for money, fun, or anything else.

"You met Scarpio here in the arcade before he had pie in the diner?" the Magician asked.

"Yeah," I said. "Right downstairs."

The Magician hit a few keys and waited for something to boot up on his laptop.

"What did he want?"

"He asked me to help him."

"He asked *you* to help *him*?" The Magician's choice of emphasis would have been insulting, if it wasn't so completely warranted by the situation. Me helping Alan Scarpio fix Rabbits? It wasn't just surprising, it was completely insane.

"And you're sure *this* was the phone in Scarpio's possession?"

"Positive," I said. "I mean, I'm pretty sure. It looks the same."

"Tell me everything you can remember," the Magician instructed.

I went through all of it: how Scarpio had told me something was wrong with the game, that he needed my help for some reason, and if we didn't fix Rabbits before the next iteration of the game began, we'd all be well and truly fucked. Then I described the pie, the mystery woman, the rhubarb recording, and, finally, the waitress who'd eventually handed me Alan Scarpio's phone.

"Scarpio was playing Robotron the night you met him?"

"That's right."

"And he received a call that clearly worried him somehow, but there's no record of that call on this phone?"

I nodded.

The Magician appeared to consider that information carefully.

It was at this point that an old yellow analog phone on the desk rang once and then stopped, the loud clipped ring echoing through the room for a few long seconds.

The Magician looked over at the phone. "I have to take that."

"It stopped," I said.

"I'll be in touch," the Magician said firmly, then carefully unhooked Scarpio's phone from his computer, handed it back to me, and led me out of his office.

I could hear him muttering something to himself as he closed and locked the door behind me.

Chloe was sitting outside on the stairs when I stepped out of the office.

"I thought the Magician never plays the game," I said as Chloe and I walked downstairs and into the arcade proper.

"He used to play, but not anymore," Chloe said, slipping a quarter into a Mappy cabinet. "He just advises those who do. You know this, K."

"I know. It just feels like he's really into it this time."

"Well, you did just bring him Alan Scarpio's phone."

"Fair point."

I watched Chloe expertly guide her tiny pixelated mouse avatar around the screen.

"What are you gonna do now?" She asked.

"I'm going home."

"Enjoy the cosmic thrill ride that is your life, K," Chloe said as she cleared another screen on her game.

I covered her eyes for a second, but she somehow still managed to keep her onscreen character alive.

"I'm unstoppable." She laughed.

"Yeah, yeah," I said. "See you later."

I woke up at two in the morning to the sound of buzzing.

I normally have my phone set to silent like a rational human being who needs sleep, but Alan Scarpio was suddenly orbiting my life, and there was no way I was going to risk missing anything important because of something as mundane as a good night's sleep.

I picked up the phone in the middle of the second vibration.

"Hello?"

"Hey, K."

"Chloe?"

"Sorry for calling so late."

"No worries. I was up," I lied.

"In the dark?"

"What do you mean?"

"I mean you don't have any lights on."

I sat up in bed. "Where are you?"

"Out front."

"What are you doing?"

"I can come back tomorrow or meet you at the arcade, if it's easier. It's just that I was on my way home when it came to me."

"When what came to you?"

"It'll be way cooler if I show you."

"Okay. Give me five minutes."

I hung up, brushed my teeth, then pulled on a pair of light gray jersey pants. I tried on three shirts before I decided on the *Red Dwarf* T-shirt I'd received in the mail that morning. *Red Dwarf* was Chloe's favorite television show of all time. I loved *Red Dwarf* as well—but to be honest, there's a one hundred percent chance that I'd bought that shirt specifically because I knew Chloe would dig it.

"Alan Scarpio doesn't have a dog," she said as she rushed into my living room. "He's allergic."

She didn't even glance at my shirt.

"What?" I asked.

Chloe picked up Scarpio's phone from the coffee table. "His phone's wallpaper features a dog."

"So?"

"That has to be a clue."

"Does it?"

"You have Alan Scarpio's phone, K. He asked you to help him fix Rabbits. This is un-fucking-precedented territory."

"Yeah," I said. "You might be right."

"There has to be something on here," she said, swiping through the application screens on the phone.

Chloe was experiencing the rush that accompanied the game.

I could see it in the way her eyes were just a little wider and brighter than normal, her movements faster and less precise. We'd all felt it—the sense that the next iteration was about to begin, and that we might be about to discover a way in.

"You want something to drink? Wine or tea?" I asked.

Chloe bit her lip and made a clicking sound with her tongue. She did this when she was thinking.

"Why don't we do tea," she said, finally. "If there is something on the phone, we might miss it if we're on our fourth glass of Malbec."

"Sounds good," I said, and stepped into the kitchen to boil some water.

———

My living room was filled with the pop culture anchors of my life—thousands of books that looked like they'd been shelved by blindfolded maniacs, vintage videogame consoles precariously piled beneath the television on a fading Ikea stand that had some funny name I can't remember, and countless shelves filled with a variety of toys, candles, board games, records, and antique nautical navigation equipment.

It was an eclectic collection of slightly useful but mostly ornamental detritus.

I handed Chloe a mug of decaffeinated Earl Grey tea, and the two of us sat on my worn-out couch with its red wine stain shaped exactly like Japan and took yet another look at Alan Scarpio's phone.

We looked into the picture of the dog—the breed (a Cavalier King Charles spaniel cross of some kind), the background of the photograph (the dog was sitting on grass in front of what appeared to be rhododendrons), and the dog's bandana (a shade of blue called cerulean). What did any of it mean? Did it have to mean anything?

We went through another pot of tea and our conversation eventually veered away from the game to other topics—like love (Chloe had just broken up with her boyfriend, a drummer named Griff whom she and I always referred to as the Muppet), life (my hardwood floors had water stains and needed to be repaired or replaced), and family (I didn't have any left; Chloe still had all of hers, but mostly wished she didn't).

Chloe's mother had recently been incarcerated for assaulting a convenience store clerk somewhere in Florida. Even though Chloe's family situation was a consistently fucked-up shit-tower of sadness and neglect, and she still got stressed out about her mom—a lot—Chloe was remarkably cool and well-adjusted. Or maybe she'd become so adept at playing cool and well-adjusted that it was impossible to tell the difference anymore. Either way, it was impressive.

I took a look at the clock. It was just after three in the morning.

"It's probably time for bed?"

Chloe yawned and nodded.

"You can crash here," I said. "The guest bedroom is all yours."

"You sure?"

"Of course, yeah. You know where the towels and everything are."

"Sure do," she said.

"Great."

I handed Chloe a pair of thin blue sweatpants and a Tanis podcast T-shirt, in case she wanted something clean to sleep in.

After she thanked me for the shirt, the two of us stood there in the hallway for a moment. Chloe toyed with the string of her tea bag, which I'd wrapped around the handle of her mug. An unreadable smirk crossed her face as she shifted her weight to her back foot.

I muttered a hasty good night, slipped into my bedroom, and shut the door.

When I got into bed, I pulled out my phone and took another look at the screen capture I'd taken of Scarpio's home screen.

I mindlessly zoomed in and out on the image as I thought about Chloe across the hall in the guest bedroom.

Was she thinking about me? And if so, what was she thinking? No way she was thinking about me. There were a million things she could be thinking about.

But what about that smirk? Was that some kind of challenge? Did it mean I should have kissed her? No. That would just complicate things, wouldn't it?

Totally.

So? What the hell is wrong with a little complication?

I zoomed in on the dog's face. *And why wouldn't Chloe be thinking about me?* I moved over to examine the details of the building in the deep background. *We're both single now, right?* I turned my attention back to the dog. *There is absolutely no reason to feel weird about being attracted to a smart and beautiful woman.* I zoomed in on the grass. *Okay, settle down. No point in obsessing like this.* The dog's bandana. *But Chloe is perfect. Okay, now you just sound sad.*

As I continued to zoom around the photograph, obsessing about what Chloe might be thinking, I eventually noticed something.

A glimmer, just beneath the bandana.

There was a bit of metal on the collar. A tag, maybe.

I zoomed in further.

At this extremely low resolution, the words on the collar were far too small to read except for one: the dog's name. Rabarber.

I jumped out of bed and threw on some pants.

"What the fuck is Rabarber?" Chloe asked, rubbing her eyes as she sat up in my spare bed. She'd already fallen asleep.

"Rhubarb," I said. "In Danish."

"Kind of a weird name for a dog," she said, suddenly much more alert.

"Right?"

Chloe sprang into action. "We should look into the history of rhubarb. Maybe there's something there?" She pulled out her phone and started to do precisely that.

"I already did a search, checked numerology, and put the word 'rhubarb' through a prelim puzzle matrix."

"Find anything?"

"Yes, but not on the Internet."

"Where?"

"On the phone."

"What do you mean?" she asked.

"In the diner, Alan Scarpio played me a recording he told me was rhubarb growing."

"And the dog's name is Rhubarb?"

"So it would appear."

"Holy fuckballs."

"I found the rhubarb file in his music library. It was the only thing there. No artist or album title."

"I need to hear that shit, right now," Chloe said.

As I hooked Scarpio's phone up to my Bluetooth speaker, Chloe stretched her arms way up to the ceiling in what appeared to be some kind of half yoga pose. "I like your shirt," she said.

"Thanks."

"Have I seen it before?"

"I'm not sure. Maybe?" I lied.

I double-clicked the audio file, and the familiar eerie creaking and crackling of the growing rhubarb filled my spare bedroom.

Chloe and I listened to the whole thing twice, paying close attention for any hidden bits of audio, but there didn't appear to be anything there—no Morse code buried behind the sounds of the rhubarb, no apparent extra-aural frequency manipulation.

Nothing.

It was only after transferring the file to my laptop for further analysis that we noticed something.

The file was huge.

It was a WAV file, not an MP3, so of course a larger file size would make sense, but not this much larger. No way. This thing was too big for any kind of audio file.

Something not known by many civilians—that is to say, people who don't spend almost every waking moment of their lives thinking about games, puzzles, patterns, and codes—is that it's possible to hide other types of data files within audio files. It doesn't work with a compressed format like MP3, but you can, however, do it with a WAV file.

Chloe and I booted up my old Linux machine and loaded a program that would be able to decode anything hidden within that audio file.

I hit a couple of keys, and in less than a second we had it.

Sitting on the left-hand side of the screen was a file entitled TabithaHenry.avi.

I double-clicked it, and a video began to play.

It opened on an empty chair sitting behind a desk on a small stage in an enormous old train station. There was text across the bottom of the screen that read:

Jeff Goldblum does not belong in this world.

8

ROWING ALL THE BOATS

THE CAMERA PULLS BACK to reveal twenty or so people standing in an orderly line in the train station. A young woman waits nervously near the back. She's in her early to middle twenties, about five feet four inches tall, with deep hazel eyes and wild curly brown hair. She's wearing a light blue denim jacket, ripped black jeans, and faded green cowboy boots. Pinned just above the pocket on the top left of her jacket is a three-inch happy-face pin featuring a small smear of blood—an image connected to the popular comic book *Watchmen*.

On the stage, there's a low leather chair tucked behind a small desk. Atop the desk are five bottles of what appear to be Fuji water, featuring a well-known film company's logo in place of the water company's usual design, and a microphone on a small black metal stand.

A colorful poster for what looks like some kind of action-adventure movie sits behind the desk on a flimsy aluminum easel.

After about ten or fifteen seconds, a studio executive walks up to the microphone and explains to the people in line—participants in some kind of contest who'd won a chance to meet the cast of Steven Spielberg's latest film via a viral-marketing campaign for a video-game property loosely connected to the film—that they would be meeting the actors from the movie one at a time over the next hour or so.

As soon as the executive finishes addressing the people in line, the first member of the cast takes the stage to a smattering of applause. It's Jeff Goldblum. He's followed by a publicity assistant from the movie studio—a six-foot-tall, thirtysomething blond woman in a tight navy blue suit.

Jeff Goldblum is a movie star, no doubt, but these people were clearly saving most of their excitement for the male and female leads of the film: that dark-haired scruffy-looking guy from the superhero movie with the plane crash, and the blondish woman from that TV show where she played an alien learning how to fall in love with a human.

After a polite wave and smile, Mr. Goldblum takes a seat behind the desk and the event begins in earnest.

One after another, people step up and onto the stage, and the tall blond publicity assistant takes their pictures with the actor.

This continues for about five minutes or so before it's the curly-brown-haired woman's turn.

After a quick hello to Jeff Goldblum, she hands her phone to the publicity assistant. Then, like he's done dozens of times already, the famous actor smiles a wide, genuine smile, puts his arm around his temporary charge, and prepares for the photograph.

But instead of smiling for the camera, the woman with the curly brown hair whispers something into Mr. Goldblum's ear, and then—with practiced precision—deftly removes a razor blade from her mouth and attempts to sever his carotid artery.

This shocking attempt on Jeff Goldblum's life is foiled by the publicity assistant, who is standing close enough to intervene, and—in a remarkable act of bravery—forces herself between the actor and his assailant.

Mr. Goldblum is unharmed, but the publicity assistant doesn't make out quite as well.

While wrestling with the famous actor's attacker, the assistant is wounded—a deep gash from her elbow all the way to her wrist. A rush of blood fountains from her arm, covering Mr. Goldblum and flooding the white linoleum floor of the stage.

It isn't until the publicity assistant looks down and notices the blood on the floor that she realizes she's been cut.

At that point, she passes out and the stage erupts in a wild flurry of blood and chaos.

The two members of the security team standing closest to the action rush forward to help, but they're unable to get their hands on Mr. Goldblum's would-be assassin due to the slippery smears of deep red blood now covering the stage.

With the security guards slipping and flailing in the blood, the woman with the curly brown hair continues to slide around the stage like a rabid deer on a frozen lake, screaming her strange message repeatedly into the astonished faces of the audience:

"Jeff Goldblum does not belong in this world."

Chloe pushed the space bar on my laptop and the video stopped playing.

"Well, that was certainly fucked," Baron Corduroy said as he sat down next to Chloe on the couch. He'd come over to my place right after we called him and described what we'd discovered on Scarpio's phone.

I leaned back and exhaled.

We'd watched it at least six times before Baron arrived.

"Fuck," Chloe said, as if another usage of that particular word was required to release some kind of pressure that had been building up.

She hit the space bar and we started watching again.

I found it hard to keep my eyes on the screen.

I've never been all that freaked out by blood or violence in movies or videogames, but there was something about the raw, visceral nature of this clip that really affected me.

Something about the video just felt . . . wrong.

I turned away from the screen, pulled out my phone, and started looking for other versions of that video online, or any corroborating evidence of this attack on Jeff Goldblum.

There was nothing.

I was able to track down various television interviews with audience members taken after the promotional event depicted in that video, but everything seemed perfectly normal, no mention of a brutal attack on the famous actor.

As far as the world was concerned, the event went off without a hitch.

"It was obviously some kind of publicity stunt," Baron said, then pulled out a vaping apparatus in the shape of an old-school Sherlock Holmes–style pipe and took a hit. "Fuck, I love Jeff Goldblum," he said, somehow managing to get the words out while his lungs were full of the highest THC-content vapor available to mankind.

"Yeah," Chloe replied. "He's cool."

I loved Jeff Goldblum too, but at the moment I was more concerned with the woman with the curly brown hair, and even more concerned with why Alan Scarpio had a hidden file on his phone of her attacking the well-known actor.

"If it was a publicity stunt," I said, "there would most likely have been some publicity."

"That's a fucking good point," Baron said, pointing at me with his vape pipe.

"You think it's some kind of deepfake?" Chloe leaned in, looking closer at the screen, as if this might magnify some previously unidentified element of the footage.

"It definitely has to be fake," I said.

Chloe nodded.

"I mean, it looks pretty real to me," I added, "but we would have heard about this, right?"

"Fuck, yes," Chloe said. "For sure."

The video file was called TabithaHenry.avi, so the first thing we did was look up the name Tabitha Henry.

"Find anything?" Baron asked.

"Just one picture on an old Facebook page," Chloe said, holding up her phone, "and it's definitely her."

It was clear that Tabitha Henry was the woman with the curly brown hair from the video. In the photograph, she was pictured smiling on a boat somewhere.

"This girl doesn't have much of an online presence," Chloe continued, "although she does follow Jeff Goldblum."

"We need more," I said.

"Darknet?" Baron suggested.

"Oh, sure," I said. "We just fire up the old Tor Browser and type in 'Jeff Goldblum murder video'?"

"Attempted murder," Chloe said.

"You're not helping," I replied as I opened up a browser and performed a Torch for "Jeff Goldblum attempted murder video."

There was nothing.

After a few hours of fruitless research, Baron had an idea. He pulled out a phone I'd never seen him use before and left the room.

A few minutes later, he came back, and before we could ask him what the hell he was doing, a text alert sent him rushing over to my laptop.

He quickly loaded a program, typed in a bunch of numbers and letters, and then waited. A couple seconds later, he opened a Tor Browser of his own and entered a .onion URL. Once the site had loaded, he leaned back in his chair and motioned us over.

I was fairly tech savvy, but whatever Baron had been doing on my laptop appeared to involve some kind of root-level modification that was way outside my experience or ability to understand.

"What the fuck did you just do to my computer?"

"I was just following instructions," Baron said. "Look." He pointed to the screen.

"What is it?" Chloe rolled her chair over to where I had recently joined Baron at my desk.

"Tabitha Henry," I said.

And there she was.

Her face occupied the center of the screen. It was a candid shot, probably taken from another old social media account. She was smiling in what appeared to be a Thai restaurant. There was some additional information surrounding that image, including links to Tabitha's now-defunct Instagram and Twitter accounts, college transcripts, high school yearbook photos, library book withdrawal info, at least one bank statement, and her recent employment records.

"None of this social shit is live anymore," Chloe said. "She must have deleted it."

Baron shrugged and took another hit off his pipe. "Deleting wouldn't do it. Probably hired a fucking cleaner."

"Where did you get this?" I asked.

"A couple of guys I used to work with at Lehman Brothers owed me a favor."

"You got this from broker bros?" Chloe asked.

"They got into some pretty fucked-up shit over there," Baron replied.

"I'll bet," I said, staring at the screen.

The stock market was a sophisticated system that I'd enjoyed exploring for a while, but the behind-the-scenes workings of the deeply crooked world of corporate high finance were a web of fuckery that made advanced game theory look like eighth-grade math.

"Do you have any Bitcoin?" Baron asked as he took another hit of weed.

"A little."

"I'm going to need to borrow it."

"Okay. How much?"

"All of it."

It took us a while to comb through the information. There was a whole bunch of useless material—dozens of photographs, expired links, and archived social posts—but not one mention of any kind of attack on the famous Hollywood actor.

There were some photographs that had clearly been taken on the day of that event—including three pictures of Tabitha Henry and Jeff Goldblum, the two of them standing on the familiar stage with the movie's poster in the background. In all three pictures, they were smiling; clearly no attempted murder, and not one drop of blood.

"It looks like that attack never happened," I said.

Baron nodded. "I told you it was fake."

"I don't know," Chloe said. "That video is pretty fucking legit. Are you sure these photos aren't the fakes?"

"Nah, these are real," Baron said. "The metadata's on point, and there are a bunch of other attempted-murder-free photos of the same event online." He took another huge rip from his pipe and leaned in to stare at Tabitha's face on the screen.

"What is your deal?" he asked, as he slowly zoomed in on the image.

But of course, Tabitha Henry's pixelated face couldn't answer any questions about her deal, or anything else.

Baron went home to do some work, and Chloe and I spent the next several hours making calls. Somehow Chloe managed to convince a representative from the movie studio that we hadn't made up this insane story just to mess with her. The studio rep assured us that nobody who worked for their publicity department had ever been harmed in a manner consistent with what we'd described. When we asked her if she was sure, she told us that she was one hundred percent positive.

That attack never happened.

According to the information Baron's finance guys sent over, Tabitha Henry was born in Queens, New York, graduated from UCLA with a degree in communications, then moved back to New York to work in digital advertising for a while before eventually returning to Los Angeles to start an immersive interactive theater company.

Tabitha's company was called Rowing All the Boats. They ran a few popular escape rooms in Los Angeles. Their events always received rave reviews, and by the end of their first month of operation, they had a two-month-long waiting list. A few months after that, they were purchased by a company specializing in cutting-edge online-gaming technology called Chronicler Enterprises.

I called the number listed on the Rowing All the Boats website and left a message asking Tabitha Henry to return my call.

She called back a few hours later.

After some awkward small talk, I finally explained why I'd gotten in touch with her, how some friends and I had discovered a really weird movie clip, and that Tabitha herself was the star.

She gave me her email address and I sent her the file. A few minutes later she called us back, this time on video.

Tabitha's hair was a bit shorter, her face a little bit fuller, but otherwise, she looked pretty much the same as she had in that clip with Jeff Goldblum.

"How the fuck did you do that? How did you copy my face and body?"

"We didn't. We found it on somebody's phone," Chloe said.

"Whose phone?"

Chloe and I looked at each other.

"Well?" Tabitha was losing patience.

"A man named Alan Scarpio."

"The billionaire?"

"Yes," I said. "Do you know him?"

"No. He's gone missing, right?"

"That's right," Chloe said.

"What's a missing billionaire doing with a fake video of me on his phone?"

"We don't know," I said. "That's why we're calling."

It looked like Tabitha wasn't sure who she should be mad at, or how mad she should be.

"What in the actual fuck?" she said. We could hear her playing the video clip again while she was speaking with us. "It's so realistic. It's creeping me out."

"You're sure you don't remember anything like this happening?" I asked.

"Are you serious?" Tabitha's eyes were huge. "You think I could forget something like this?"

She held her phone up to a desktop computer and showed us the section of the video where the publicity assistant's arm was slashed. "Look at all of that blood. Would there really be that much blood?"

"I understand this must be . . . strange for you," I said.

"Ya think?"

"I can send you all the information we have, if you like."

"Yeah. I'll need all your information."

"If you have any questions, please get in touch."

"Thanks. I'm sure I'll have questions. I mean, you do know this isn't me in this video, right?" She stared at the two of us. "Right?"

"Right," I said. "Of course."

"This is so weird." Tabitha started watching the video again. "Wait, did Devon put you up to this?"

"I'm sorry, but we don't know any Devon."

"Right—except that's exactly what somebody who knows Devon would say."

I looked at Chloe. She shrugged.

Tabitha Henry, for the moment at least, appeared to be a dead end.

9

EVERYTHING THAT ISN'T RABBITS

"THIS IS FASCINATING." The Magician pressed the space bar on his laptop and the video stopped playing.

We'd rushed over to the arcade shortly after we'd spoken with Tabitha. The Magician had watched the video three times in a row.

"Is it Rabbits?" I asked, doing my best to keep the excitement out of my voice.

"The hallmarks are definitely there," he said, "but it's hard to say. I'm going to have to think about this."

Then he kicked us out of his office and shut the door.

Is it Rabbits?

I'd asked the Magician the exact same question a number of times in the past.

The first time was the day we met.

I was a senior in college then, completely obsessed with games and gaming, and barely interested in the subjects that actually affected my grade-point average. Thankfully, I'd retained enough of my childhood ability to recall things in detail that I was able to memorize names and dates well enough to keep my academic scholarship. And as long as I remained on scholarship I wouldn't have to get a job, which meant more time to play games.

Of course it was a game that eventually led me to the Magician.

"What is it?" I asked.

"It's called Wizard's Quest Four; it works on this Apple II clone."

Andrew Goshaluk pulled a floppy disk from an old Rolodex-style case and slipped it into a cream-colored drive from another age.

"How old is that computer?"

"Fucking ancient, mate."

Andrew Goshaluk was slightly overweight, about five foot nine, with straw-colored feathered hair and gold-framed serial killer glasses. We'd met when we were seniors in high school and ended up at the University of Washington together. He was studying computer science and I was working on a degree in English literature with a minor in game theory.

Andrew had come over from London with his father after his mother and sister were killed in a train accident. Although a mutual interest in games had brought us together, my own parents' subsequent death and the fact that we'd both recently experienced such significant family tragedies made us inseparable in college.

Back in high school, Andrew and I were what you'd call hardcore gamers. We played everything from The Legend of Zelda and Final Fantasy to Risk, chess, and the strategy board game Go, but roleplaying games were by far our favorites. Dungeons & Dragons and Traveller were our top two.

By the time we hit college, not all that much had changed. Outside of the occasional unavoidable party or concert, we did almost nothing but play games.

It had been ages since I'd heard Emily Connors use the term "Rabbits" in relation to a secret game that somehow involved extinct woodpeckers and orphaned movie credits, since I'd heard that strange voice cutting through the radio static on something Emily called The Night Station—a voice that I would continue to hear in my dreams, always repeating the same thing over and over, the unmistakable phrase I'd heard that night, on that dark winding country road—a phrase I'd later learn was deeply connected to the mysterious game unofficially known as Rabbits. *The Door Is Open.*

Shortly after playing Wizard's Quest Four on that old Apple computer with Andrew Goshaluk in one of our computer science labs, I encountered that phrase for the second time.

"Check it out." Andrew pressed the return key, and Wizard's Quest Four booted up.

There was a small box in the center of the screen that included some really primitive graphics—at that moment it was a purple wizard who looked like he was dropping some seeds—but the majority of the game was plain text.

As Andrew tapped the arrows on his keyboard and guided the characters through the first stage of their dungeon adventure, 8-bit classical music blared from the computer's tiny speaker: a short song playing on a loop that sounded slightly medieval.

"What are you doing?" I asked, not sure I actually wanted to know the answer. Andrew had a habit of falling into some pretty deep research spirals when it came to computer games.

"What do you think? I'm playing a game."

"A dungeon crawl from the seventies?"

"Come on, K, look at this thing."

"What about it?"

"This is a runtime library system, my friend. Total early eighties–style."

"Okay, then. Let me ask you this."

Andrew leaned back in his chair and waited for me to ask my follow-up question.

"Who gives a shit?"

Andrew smiled. "You're funny."

"I'm serious. Why are you playing this garbage game?" I was actually a little pissed off. We were in the middle of a really great Drakengard campaign, and we'd almost reached the final battle.

"Ah, now that's the real question, isn't it?"

"Sure," I said, hoping he might get to the point. "But I thought you were going to look into that game Beverly and Travis were playing?"

"I am." Andrew smiled as he pressed the return key. "We are," he continued.

The screen changed, and we were now looking at two boxes side by side, one filled with text, the other with the graphic of an extremely long-armed dungeon monster.

"Please tell me what the fuck is going on. I have a French test in an hour." I was getting impatient. French was killing me. It was easy enough for me to memorize the verbs and phrases, but there was just something about the pronunciation and the way everything fit together that wasn't coming easily.

Andrew stood up and stretched. "I can't feel sorry for you; I'm taking astrophysics this semester."

"They call French a Romance language."

"That sounds familiar."

"It's murdering my soul."

"I've heard that can happen. Check it out." He navigated to another screen on the computer and motioned for me to take his chair.

I sat down and leaned forward to examine the screen. "What the hell does this mean?"

"What do you think it means?"

"It's fake."

"It's not."

"Bullshit."

"Oh yes, *mon copain*. This shit is real."

"What makes you say that?"

"I checked it out."

"For real?"

"For real real."

I took another look. "There's no way."

The monster on the screen, one of the myriad creatures you might encounter while playing Wizard's Quest Four, looked very familiar. As a kid, I'd seen its name and the trademark spiky hair thousands of times.

Staring back at me from that screen, in a computer game from 1983, was the main character from a videogame that wouldn't exist until almost a decade later.

The monster on the screen was Sonic the Hedgehog.

———

The reason Andrew was playing Wizard's Quest Four was because he'd been looking into another game, something our friends Beverly and Travis were playing that their friends at MIT had discovered: a game that existed in the real world, a game that the government was allegedly using to recruit secret agents.

It actually sounded plausible at the time.

Cold War films and literature from the 1980s—like the proto-hacker movie *WarGames* and the military science fiction novel *Ender's Game* by Orson Scott Card—posited a world where video-games intersected with the real world, where these games might actually train future soldiers or operatives to deal with potentially dangerous real-world scenarios like global-scale war or national security–threatening espionage.

The possibility that a game like this actually existed—a game that took place using the real world as its playing field—was intoxicating. This was everything I loved about role-playing games like Dungeons & Dragons, amplified by a thousand.

I very badly wanted it to be real.

I had no idea how it was possible, but Andrew appeared to be implying that this Sonic the Hedgehog anomaly was part of that mysterious game.

If it was fake, it was nothing but evidence of a forger with a weirdly specific set of interests and skills. But if it was real, Andrew had uncovered an interesting anachronism: Sonic the Hedgehog was there, on that screen, as part of a game that had been released almost a decade before the character would be created by the brilliant game-design team over at Sega.

We immediately sprang into action and tried to figure out what was happening.

Was it possible that this was just a crazy coincidence? We asked everybody we knew with any kind of experience in game design or videogame history, but nobody had an answer.

We called Sega, but they had no idea what we were talking about and no interest in learning more. Everyone with a more than cursory understanding of the computer gaming industry thought what we were showing them was fake. Anyone outside of that industry didn't care.

But I cared.

This thing felt strange—but strangely familiar. Something about it made me feel the way I'd felt the night of the accident with the Connors sisters, the night I first heard the word "Rabbits" connected to another mysterious game.

Andrew had gone just about as far as his curiosity would allow. He loved the idea of uncovering something cool, but actually taking the time to figure out what it might mean? That was way too much effort. He quickly moved on to solving another puzzle—some kind of marketing game related to Reebok—and I was left to dig into this weird Sonic anachronism on my own.

Andrew was out, but I was just getting started.

"What does it mean?" I asked the rail-thin brunette with the cat-eye glasses whose legs were currently draped over the back of a worn black leather sofa in a messy one-bedroom apartment. This was Beverly. She was lying on her back reading the photocopied instruction manual for Wizard's Quest Four that I'd downloaded online and printed out.

"I'm not sure," Beverly replied, and turned her head toward a good-looking young Black man wearing a Baltimore Orioles baseball cap and a T-shirt featuring the graphic of an old radio, with text below it that read: TURN UP THE EAGLES, THE NEIGHBORS ARE LISTENING. "What do you think, Travis?"

"It could be the game," Travis said. He was carefully analyzing something on his computer screen.

"What game?" I asked. "The secret CIA thing?"

"It's more than that, K," Beverly said as she hopped off the sofa and made her way over to where Travis was working at his desk. "It's something else, something much bigger." She grabbed a chair and sat down next to Travis.

"What do you mean, 'bigger'?" I said, but they completely ignored me, whispering to each other as they examined the image of Sonic the Hedgehog and the accompanying text on Travis's monitor.

After a minute or so, Travis stood up, took a photograph of the pixelated image, then turned to me and smiled. "We're going to see the Magician."

Half an hour later, I walked into the Magician's arcade for the first time.

The Magician took a couple of minutes to examine the image, then turned his attention to the photocopied instruction manual.

When he'd apparently seen enough, he stood up from behind his desk, walked across the room, and shut the door to his office.

When he sat back down, he carefully rested his elbows on his desk and slowly put his fingers together in a kind of steeple. "How much do you know about the game?"

Travis and Beverly burst into their favorite theories—how you had to follow any and all patterns you were able to find in real life to see where they led; how nobody was completely sure if it was real or not; how the CIA was probably using it to recruit agents (or maybe it was the NSA); and how some people were players and others were just observers.

The Magician just sat there, listening, until Travis and Beverly stopped talking.

"Anything else?" the Magician asked.

"It's supposed to be incredibly dangerous. And"—Travis lowered his voice—"some people have died while playing it."

Travis's words brought me right back to the night of the accident, right back into that truck with Annie and Emily Connors. I felt my face flush with emotion as I tried to ignore the images skip-framing through my mind like an action movie.

I looked over and saw the Magician looking back at me, his face expressionless.

"Like Travis said, nobody knows if it's real," Beverly said. "I mean, at least, not for sure."

"Well," said the Magician, turning his attention away from me and back to Beverly and Travis, "the players certainly know."

He let that possibility hang there in the air for a moment.

Could a game like this really exist? Were there actually players? What if this was the same thing Emily Connors had been talking about way back when?

Something in the Magician's eyes reminded me of the look on Emily's face the night of the accident.

"Is it Rabbits?" I asked.

The Magician turned to face me. He appeared surprised.

"Where did you hear that name?" The look of surprise on his face had changed into something else—a kind of half smile that I found very difficult to gauge.

"I don't remember," I lied.

I wasn't ready to share that information with a conspiracy-obsessed stranger I'd just met in an arcade.

The Magician took a moment to process this information, then nodded to Travis and Beverly. "What do you two know about Rabbits?"

"What's Rabbits?" Travis asked.

"Nothing," Beverly said, staring at me with a new kind of respect. "Wait, is that the name of the game? Rabbits?"

The Magician turned back to me. When it became clear that I wasn't going to offer anything else, he continued. "The game doesn't have a name—at least, not officially—but Rabbits has become a kind of . . . an unofficial moniker. Something to separate it from . . . everything else."

"What do you mean by 'everything else'?" I asked.

"Everything that isn't Rabbits."

My curiosity about the game began the night of the accident with Annie and Emily Connors, but if I had to go back and pinpoint the exact moment my complete and total obsession started, it was right there, in the Magician's office. Hearing the name Rabbits once again connected to a mysterious game felt like some kind of validation—as if that name and all of the strangeness I'd felt the last time I'd heard it wasn't just something I'd imagined.

Ever since that night in the truck with Annie and Emily Connors, I'd been convinced that Rabbits was something I'd either made up or misremembered, but in that moment, sitting there in the Magician's office, I felt a shift in my mind and I allowed myself to imagine something I'd never seriously considered.

Rabbits might actually be real.

"It's clearly fake, some kind of bootleg copy or something," Travis said.

"Sonic isn't listed as a monster in the manual," Beverly added, holding up the copy of the instruction booklet I'd printed out.

The Magician again examined the photograph Travis had taken, then sat back and sank into his chair. "I'll need to see everything you have on this."

"Sure," I said. "I can bring it by sometime in the next few days."

"What's wrong with right now?" the Magician asked.

"Oh," I replied. "I wasn't expecting to—"

"If that's okay?" he continued.

I'm not sure why, but I had the feeling this was an important moment. Was the Magician actually in a hurry to examine my copy of the game, or was he simply testing me in order to find out how interested I was in Rabbits? Was I serious or was I just a tourist?

Andrew's interest in the game had faded when the investigation became too difficult, and Beverly and Travis would soon follow suit, but I was just getting started. I was definitely no tourist.

"I'll be back in half an hour," I said.

I made it back to the arcade in under twenty minutes.

I was really fucking interested.

I couldn't wait to find out what the Magician was going to tell me about the game, but when I returned, out of breath from pedaling as fast as I could, he simply snatched the floppy disk from my hand and closed the door to his office.

I was about to knock—to ask him to give me a timeline or at least tell me something about what he had planned—when I heard a voice behind me.

"He'll let you know if he finds anything."

I turned around and met Chloe for the first time.

She was a few weeks shy of her twenty-first birthday, her hair platinum blond, shaggy-short, and choppy. She was wearing a ripped light gray suit jacket over a white T-shirt featuring a graphic of a pink cassette tape. The flashing lights of the arcade sparkled in her eyes as she half smiled and offered a cool, disinterested "Hey."

"Hi," I said. "I'm K."

"Chloe," she said, and shook my hand like she'd just survived a job interview.

"Do you work here?" I asked.

"Sometimes," she said as she led me back downstairs to the arcade proper. "What's your game?"

"Robotron," I said.

"There's a Robotron machine in the back. We're just waiting on a new monitor." She slipped a quarter into a pinball machine called Centaur.

"Awesome," I said.

As I stood there watching Chloe prepare to play pinball, I felt like I needed to say something interesting, to let her know I was a kindred spirit.

"Did you know that Harry Williams created the tilt mechanism for pinball machines?" I said, and immediately regretted it.

Who could possibly give a shit?

"I did not know that," she replied as she pulled back the plunger and launched her first ball onto the playing surface.

I watched her use her hips against the table to adjust the angle of the ball as it moved. She was good.

"So, how long have you worked in the arcade?"

"How long have you been interested in Rabbits?" she asked, ignoring my question. Chloe had a way of constantly reminding you she was going to cut through the bullshit, and that she'd appreciate if you did the same.

"I don't know that I *am* interested. I'm just looking into things."

"Really?" She was still playing her first ball. "Good luck with that," she said as she saved the ball with a deft shake of the table, hit a difficult target, and started the game's multi-ball feature.

It took three days for the Magician to get back in touch.

I went over to the arcade and found him playing a game called Space Ace.

Released in 1984, Space Ace was a follow-up of sorts to the much more successful Dragon's Lair. Both games featured high-quality LaserDisc animation, and both were designed by legendary animator Don Bluth. Because those games relied on memorizing patterns, it didn't take me more than a few days (and about twenty-five dollars in quarters) to figure out how to finish both of them.

Space Ace was the science fiction counterpart to the fantasy setting of Dragon's Lair. Space Ace was fine, but I much preferred Dragon's Lair. The character of Dirk the Daring was a lot more fun. He didn't take himself too seriously.

"It's a very interesting anomaly," the Magician said, handing me the floppy disk I'd dropped off the last time I was there, "but I wasn't able to find anything to connect it to the game."

"Okay, thanks," I said, disappointed.

I'd felt certain he was going to uncover something mysterious— maybe not proof this Sonic thing was connected to a strange and dangerous secret game running beneath the surface of our world, but I was pretty sure he'd find something.

I was about to leave when I looked over and saw Chloe watching me from the stairway the led up to the Magician's office, and I suddenly caught the feeling that I was standing at the precipice of a whole new world. I could turn around, walk out of the arcade, and return to my regular life, already in progress, or I could do something else.

I went back over to the Magician and tapped him on the back of his shoulder.

"What can you tell me about Rabbits?" I asked.

He stopped playing the game for a moment and turned to face me.

His expression was unreadable, but I thought I detected a hint of menace beneath the surface, and I wondered—for just a moment—if I'd made a terrible mistake.

I was about to turn around and leave when he asked me a question.

"What is it that you would like to know?"

"Everything," I blurted. Hint of menace or not, I just couldn't help myself.

His expression softened and then he laughed as his onscreen character caught a blue baby that had just fallen from the sky.

I lowered my voice and leaned forward a little.

"Is Rabbits real?" I asked.

The Magician smiled, leaned forward a little himself and whispered. "Just wait."

I stared at the action on the screen as the Magician continued his game.

"What are we waiting for?" I asked.

"The Circle," he said.

"What's The Circle?"

"It's a list of the winners of the game, a kind of Rabbits hall of fame."

"So people really can win the game?"

"Absolutely," he said.

"And that list of winners is here, in this Space Ace machine?"

"One particular list, yes."

The Magician continued to guide his onscreen character flawlessly through a series of complex moves, eventually defeating the evil Commander Borf and winning the game.

"What do you mean?"

"Well, The Circle is a mystery. Nobody knows who updates it, or where to find it. It can show up anywhere in the world at any time, but it most commonly appears when the current iteration of the game ends."

"It just appears?"

"Yes," he said as we watched the end credits of the game scrolling up the screen.

"And that's what happened to this Space Ace machine?"

"Wait," he said, and we watched as the last of the credits faded away, leaving behind an animated inky blue-black background filled with glowing space clouds and twinkly little stars.

A few seconds later, a list of names and numbers appeared.

"This," he said, pointing at the screen, "is The Circle, circa the seventh iteration of the game."

It looked just like the regular list of high scores on any video-game, except there were Roman numerals instead of regular numbers. Those Roman numerals, seven in total, were followed by seven names.

I leaned in and took a closer look at the screen.

I: Mickie Mouth
II: The Condor
III: Alison Cat
IV: Radio Knife
V: Carbon Thing
VI: Californiac
VII: Nova Trail

As I stood there staring at that Space Ace machine, I started thinking about how difficult it would be to add something like this to the game. Unlike other titles from this period, Space Ace was played using a closed LaserDisc system. All of the information was contained on that large silver disk. There was no real programming involved.

"How did they do it?" I asked.

"What do you mean?" the Magician asked.

"How could somebody create a brand-new LaserDisc for a video-game from 1984?"

"You'll have to ask Chloe. She knows a lot more about the technical side of it all."

We stood there for a moment as the game rebooted and the Space Ace intro started playing on the small screen. I wanted to slip a quarter into the machine immediately; I hadn't played that game for ages.

"This list of players just appeared on that Space Ace machine out of nowhere?" I asked.

"One day, the end credits were exactly the same as any other version of the game. The next day, there was this."

"Why this particular machine at that particular time?"

"There are many who claim that the game follows the players, that it knows exactly where they are and what they're doing."

"That's kind of hard to believe," I said.

"It's good to be skeptical, K, but you're entering a new world. There are some things that are going to appear, well—"

"Totally unbelievable?" I interrupted.

He laughed. "I was going to say a bit hard to believe, but yeah, maybe totally unbelievable is closer to the truth."

"You really believe the game might be somehow tracking the people playing it?"

"I didn't say *I* believe that; I said *some people* believe that's the case."

"Either way, all of this sounds—"

"Totally unbelievable?" He smiled.

"Okay, so how do you know The Circle is actually part of the game and not just a prank or something?"

"Because I know."

"What does that mean?"

He stared at me for a moment, and then he spoke slowly, in a tone that sounded almost reverent. "I was playing the game."

I wanted to ask so much more, but in that moment, all I managed to blurt out was: "Is all of this really . . . real?"

"Oh, it's real." The Magician turned and walked away from the game. "Follow me."

He led me upstairs to his office where he pulled out a laptop covered in band stickers from the nineties: Urge Overkill, Nirvana, Pavement, and at least a dozen more I didn't recognize.

He flipped open his computer and booted it up. When his password screen popped up, he just pressed enter.

"You don't use a password?" I asked.

"Never. Passwords are easy to hack. All you're doing is giving the world free information about yourself."

"Not if you use random numbers and letters," I said.

"Nothing's random, K." He navigated to a folder filled with images and showed them to me, one by one.

Each image featured a list of names and Roman numerals. One was a picture of a take-out menu from a pizza place, one a Billboard Hot 100 chart from the sixties, another was a list of box scores from a baseball game in 1979. The earliest image was a photograph taken of a wall in a laundromat in Seattle, featuring the stenciled graphic of a rabbit.

"These are all different versions of The Circle?" I asked, staring at each strange image in turn.

"Yeah, these particular versions were all found in North America, all validated. I've assembled them in chronological order. I have other collections from Europe and Asia."

The first image was the Laundromat, followed by a picture of what appeared to be a modernist painting featuring the name Mickie Mouth, the winner of One, then a few more featuring the winners of Two, Four, and Five, ending with the Space Ace version from the Magician's arcade and the final image: a screen capture from a GeoCities website for a pet food company named Tiny Morsels.

That website had been hacked and a message splashed across it in a spray-paint font. The message was a question that read:

"R U PLAYING?"
—HAZEL

"Who is Hazel?" I asked.

"Hazel won the eighth iteration of the game then allegedly abdicated their place in The Circle and disappeared."

I stood there staring at the image on the screen as the Magician continued: "Hazel is, or was, the best Rabbits player who ever lived."

Back down in the arcade proper, I took a closer look at the Space Ace machine. Once again, I had the urge to put a quarter in and play.

"So, this version of The Circle is from the seventh iteration?"

"Yes, it's an important artifact. Seven was one of the most highly competitive cycles of the game."

"So, what's going on now? The eighth version is already over?" I asked.

"Yes."

"When does the next cycle start?"

"When players begin discovering something we refer to as The Phrase."

"A phrase? What phrase?"

"There's a phrase that always precedes the beginning of the game, something that starts appearing just before the next iteration is about to begin."

"What's the phrase?"

"The Door Is Open."

I felt like I'd uncovered something in the arcane mythological puzzle that was Rabbits—an access point to a world as far away from our own mundane existence as Narnia or Middle-earth. It was a world of mystery that I desperately wanted to access.

The Door Is Open.

Those were the words I'd heard coming from the radio the night of the accident with Annie and Emily Connors.

Did my hearing those words coming from the radio back then mean that a new iteration of the game had begun? And if so, was it version six? Seven?

From this point forward, Rabbits became more than an obsession. It was the first thing I thought of when I woke up in the morning, and the last thing I considered before I fell asleep at night.

Rabbits was everything.

NOTES ON THE GAME:
MISSIVE BY HAZEL
(AUTHENTICATED BY BLOCKCHAIN)

It's commonly accepted by those interested in Rabbits lore that The Phrase and The Circle can appear anywhere in the world at any time. Before and after each iteration of the game, players from all over the globe flood underground Rabbits chat rooms with pictures and reports about finding the phrase "The Door Is Open" or what they believe is an official representation of The Circle.

There have been rumors of The Circle showing up spray-painted on the side of a building in Red Square, replacing the track listing on side two of a Wilco vinyl record in 2002, and more than one player reported seeing The Phrase listed in the end credits of an independent Canadian film that screened at the Toronto International Film Festival in 2010—although, so far, no video or screen capture evidence has surfaced to support these alleged appearances.

No organization has ever officially addressed how or why The Phrase or The Circle appears, which isn't all that surprising, considering the fact that no organization has ever officially acknowledged the existence of the game itself.

—HAZEL 8

10

WORGAMES

A FEW DAYS AFTER we'd brought Alan Scarpio's phone over to the arcade, Chloe called to tell me that the Magician wanted to take another look.

When I got there, Chloe and Baron were waiting. The Magician stuck a Back in Fifteen Minutes sign on the window, locked the door, and led us up to his office.

"You said Scarpio received a call while you were sitting with him in the diner?" The Magician motioned with his fingers, and once again, I handed over Scarpio's phone.

"Yeah," I said, "but we checked, there's nothing on the phone. No call log, no records of anything."

"Right," the Magician said, "but call logs are stored in a few places, both on the device and in the cloud."

"We checked the cloud," Baron said. "There's nothing there."

"Did you find something?" Chloe asked as the three of us watched the Magician plug Scarpio's phone into the same laptop he'd hooked it up to before.

"The last time you were here, I checked if this phone's data had been updated with the call he'd received while you were in the diner, but the cloud connection had been completely wiped."

"Exactly," Baron said. "There's nothing there."

"So what are you doing now?" I asked.

"Rooting the phone."

"That's definitely going to void the warranty," Chloe joked.

"Apparently, this particular phone backs up call and messaging information in a database file, and that file is accessible only by rooting the phone and using a file manager application."

"Shit," Baron said. "That's a great idea."

Rooting a phone—or, more accurately, hacking it to gain root access—isn't uncommon among people who want less "restrictive" experiences with their mobile devices. Chloe was right, however; rooting would immediately void the warranty.

It took the Magician two minutes to locate the database, and another two minutes to crack it open. Eventually, he spun the laptop around and showed us the contents of the file he'd discovered. There was one entry: the call Scarpio had received while he'd been sitting with me in the diner. That entry contained three pieces of information: the time of the call, its length, and the incoming number.

"Well?" Baron asked.

"Well what?" Chloe replied.

"We're calling the number, right?"

The three of them turned to look at me.

"K?" the Magician asked.

I nodded and dialed.

Somebody picked up on the second ring.

"Hello, and thank you for calling WorGames Seattle. How may I direct your call?"

I hung up.

The call that had clearly upset Alan Scarpio shortly before he disappeared had come from WorGames.

WorGames was the brainchild of a man named Hawk Worricker. The following is an excerpt from an article written by Yumiko Takada for *Wired* magazine in 2016:

> Not much is known about Hawk Worricker's early life, although it's generally accepted that he grew up in Washington State and moved to Southern California with his family sometime after high school.
>
> A decade later, while at Stanford, Worricker created a computer programming language similar to COBOL that he called LEMON.

Rather than sell LEMON to one of his many suitors, however, Worricker decided to give it away for free, and as a result, it's still in use today in some smaller countries' telecommunication devices.

In 1983, after a brief stint at Apple, Worricker, then forty-nine, founded his flagship company, WorGames. Less than a year later, after WorGames' first titles—Warz and Tankz—had shipped, the company was profitable, and investors were clamoring to buy in. Worricker turned everyone down.

He took an enormous risk by circumventing existing distributors and selling directly to buyers, but his gamble paid off. Big time. By preserving ownership, he was able to both maximize his profits and maintain complete creative control over his games.

Despite his success, Worricker remained notoriously reclusive. He disappeared completely from the public eye not long after forming WorGames.

The following is a brief timeline of some key events in Worricker's professional life:

1988: WorGames challenges Nintendo with Worricker's platform game masterpiece, Dragonize Wide Open.

1990: The sequel to Dragonize Wide Open becomes the second-biggest—selling sequel in gaming history.

1993: Worricker tells his board of directors that he's going to recharge his creative batteries by traveling the world and digging into the popular games and ancient traditions of other cultures.

1999: WorGames releases Alienation Nation, their biggest game to date. Rumors swirl around Worricker's potential return to the United States, but WorGames refuses to confirm or deny these reports.

2001: WorGames purchases the first building of what will eventually become the company's flagship campus in the Wedgwood neighborhood of Seattle, not far from the University of Washington. With his company now responsible for over a thousand employees, Worricker remains completely absent from public life.

2010: Hawk Worricker reportedly passes away peacefully in his home in Seattle at the age of seventy-six. If there is a funeral or memorial ceremony of any kind, those details are kept private by Worricker's estate.

Although he was an extremely well-known figure in the world of videogames and technology, almost every single thing we know about Hawk Worricker comes to us secondhand. Very little is known about his private life. He avoided all public contact with the outside world since around 1983, and only a few photographs of Worricker are known to exist, almost all of them from his high school or college days.

In the late nineties, as a publicity stunt, a well-known technology magazine offered two hundred thousand dollars for a verified photograph of Worricker.

Many tried, but nobody was able to claim the reward.

Although Hawk Worricker himself is no longer at the helm, over the years, WorGames' continued commitment to innovation has transformed it into one of the most commercially successful and critically acclaimed videogame companies in history.

"So Alan Scarpio spoke with somebody at WorGames before he disappeared? How does that help us?" Baron asked.

"It's a start," the Magician growled as he scratched his chin with his thumb.

"No matter where the call came from," I said, "the expression on Scarpio's face when he picked up was . . . well, whatever the call was about, it was clearly something serious."

The Magician nodded. "He gets a call that clearly affects his demeanor, then he disappears. These things we know."

"Scarpio told K that whatever's wrong with the game needs to be fixed before the next iteration starts up," Chloe said. "What if it's too late?"

"The game remains between iterations."

"Are you sure?" I asked.

The Magician nodded. "I'm sure."

"So, what do we do now?" Chloe asked.

"I'll see if I can find out more about the current state of things surrounding the game," the Magician said, "and you keep looking into everything connected to Scarpio and his phone."

As the Magician was speaking, I thought I saw something through the window behind him—a gray pulsing form, swirling around in the clouds.

I shook my head and looked down at the floor. Not now.

"I have a friend who works at WorGames," Baron said. "I could ask her if she knows anything about Scarpio or whatever."

"That's good," the Magician said. "Anybody else with friends over there?"

"No," Chloe said.

"K?" the Magician asked.

I shook my head again, then looked over at the wall behind Chloe. The strange shadows had changed direction and were now swirling toward her. I took a step closer, trying to position myself between Chloe and the creeping darkness moving across the wall. She looked at me and shook her head, confused. "What?"

"Nothing," I whispered. The shadows were suddenly gone.

"I might know a couple of people at WorGames," the Magician said. "I'll make some calls." He stood up and handed back Scarpio's phone.

Baron said he needed to go home, and Chloe was working until five. I told everyone I was going back to my place to see if I could dig up anything new on Tabitha Henry and the Jeff Goldblum attack video, but I really just wanted to sleep.

I was suddenly exhausted.

A green Dodge minivan sped through a busy intersection, windows down, music blasting. I recognized the song. I think it was Band of Horses, something from an album I used to listen to all the time, but I couldn't pull the name.

A tall dark-haired woman with a miniature greyhound smiled at me as she stepped off the curb and started walking across the street, her little dog's legs a furious blur as it hurried to keep pace.

I smiled at the dog and stepped off the curb a second later.

I could hear the Band of Horses song fading as the minivan moved away. The way the music echoed high among the skyscrapers in the distance reminded me of a soundtrack from the edge of a dream.

Suddenly, I felt a hand grab the collar of my jacket and yank me back. A split second later, a white Volvo station wagon sped through the amber light.

That car had come so close to hitting me that whoever was driving didn't have time to honk.

I looked across the street.

The light hadn't changed, and the woman with the greyhound hadn't actually stepped off the curb.

She was the one who'd pulled me back onto the sidewalk and away from the oncoming station wagon.

"Thank you," I said—and although my "thank you" was definitely genuine, it felt and sounded distant in my head, as if I were speaking through some kind of reverse megaphone from someplace far away. My voice was also clearly missing the requisite "holy shit I almost died" sense of urgency.

"Are you okay?" she asked.

Her dog looked up at me, maybe wondering the same thing.

"I was thinking about something else," I said, which wasn't true. I couldn't actually remember thinking about anything at all.

"You stepped in front of that car," she said.

Did she think I just tried to kill myself?

I shook my head and forced a smile. "I was just distracted."

"Maybe you should call someone?" she said, still slightly concerned, but clearly ready to move on with her day.

Saving my life—or, at the very least, saving me from a significant number of broken bones—would be an interesting story she'd repeat a few times throughout the day, probably adding a little extra drama each time she told it, but I could tell she was looking forward to the experience being over, especially if it turned out I actually was suicidal and was gearing up to try again.

"I'm good, thank you. Thanks so much," I said, waving her away with a smile.

Thanks so much. I sounded like an asshole.

When the woman and her dog were safely across the street, I took a closer look at my surroundings.

Where the hell was I?

The world in front of my eyes appeared foreign, like a word I'd momentarily forgotten how to spell. I looked up at the closest street sign. I was standing on Nineteenth Avenue, directly across the street from a restaurant called The Kingfish Cafe.

Okay, this was looking familiar.

I loved The Kingfish. I often went there for lunch, but I had no idea what I was doing there at that moment.

Then the world slowly began slipping back into focus.

The last thing I remembered was standing in the Magician's office with Chloe talking about WorGames.

I looked at the time on my phone. It was five thirty.

Somehow, I'd lost more than six hours.

I slipped into The Kingfish Cafe's bathroom, splashed water on my face, and took inventory: Everything was where it should be, no scrapes or bruises. Whatever I'd done during the past six hours hadn't involved bodily harm.

Losing time was obviously disconcerting, but the accompanying feeling of helplessness was worse. What had happened during that time? Had I done something that I was never going to remember?

Then something else hit me that was even more disturbing. The Kingfish Cafe had closed permanently in 2015.

"What's up?" Chloe said, stepping past me and into the living room.

"Nothing much," I said.

I watched as she moved around my place to see if something in her expression might reveal whether I'd contacted her during the past six hours.

"Why are you staring at me like that?"

"Like what?" I said, shutting the door to my apartment and following her into the kitchen.

"Like a weirdo," she said as she grabbed a soda from my fridge and cracked it open.

"I don't know. Let's go with lack of sleep," I said, doing my best to sound nonchalant.

She tilted her head a little. "Are you sure you're okay?"

"Yeah, I said I'm fine," I snapped.

"Okay, okay," she said. "Settle TFD."

I would have loved to have settled the fuck down, but I'd just lost six hours.

Chloe pulled out her laptop and opened a browser window. "Check it out."

"What is it?"

Chloe pointed at her screen. "You were right. Tabitha Henry is connected to WorGames."

"She is?"

"Yeah, through Chronicler Enterprises."

"What is Chronicler Enterprises? Why does that sound familiar?"

"Um . . . because they own Tabitha Henry's escape room company? Baron's finance bros dug that shit up, remember?"

"Right, I remember, but why do we care what WorGames has to do with Tabitha Henry?" I asked.

"Are you serious?"

"What?" I asked.

She pulled up a bunch of legal documents and a list of shell corporations.

"K, you asked me to look into a possible Chronicler Enterprises/ WorGames connection hours ago."

"I did?"

Chloe crossed her arms and glared.

I forced a laugh, trying to sound casual. "What?"

"Are you going to tell me what the fuck is going on?"

I shook my head. "I'm just feeling a bit tired."

"K . . ."

"Fine. I can't remember the past six hours."

"Oh, all right, Memento," she said and shook her head as she looked something up on her laptop. "If you don't wanna tell me what's wrong, I'm not gonna push."

I almost laughed. Since when the fuck was Chloe not going to push?

"I'm serious," I said.

Chloe looked up from her computer. Something in my eyes must have let her know I wasn't kidding, because her tone changed immediately. "Fuck, for real?"

"Yeah, for real."

"You don't remember calling me earlier?"

"Nope."

"Not at all?"

"Nothing . . . and there's more."

"What?"

"Before I came here, I used the bathroom at The Kingfish Cafe."

"What?"

"Yeah. Sounds impossible, I know."

Chloe screwed up her face. "It doesn't sound impossible. Just disgusting."

"It doesn't strike you as odd that I just used the bathroom of a restaurant that permanently closed six years ago?"

"It strikes me as odd that you, of all people, would use a public bathroom when you're like five minutes from your apartment."

"When did The Kingfish reopen?"

"What do you mean? The Kingfish isn't closed."

"It closed in 2015."

"Umm . . . no, it didn't. We ate there a week ago. Red velvet cake. Remember?"

I shook my head. No.

"K? What's going on?"

I definitely didn't remember eating red velvet cake or anything else, because The Kingfish Cafe *had* permanently closed. There were articles about it in *The Stranger* and *The Seattle Times*. It was big news at the time for locals—especially for people like me who lived in Capitol Hill.

Chloe came over and sat down beside me on the couch.

"It's happening again, isn't it?" she asked.

"It's not like that," I snapped.

"Hey, I'm sorry, but if you remember, the last time something like this happened, you almost died."

I looked across at the television, where our reflections stared back at us from the black screen.

Chloe had her hands on her knees, her back straight and stiff, and she was staring at me, worried.

Looking at my own reflection, I could see why she was concerned. My eyes were wild and my arms were crossed tight, way too high up on my chest.

"I'm fine," I said as I uncrossed my arms and did my best to look relaxed.

The incident she was referring to happened a few years ago. It was one of the worst days of my life—right up there with my parents' death and the accident with Annie and Emily Connors.

It was the day I discovered the building with the missing floor.

In 2016, we'd begun hearing rumors that the ninth iteration of the game had finally started, and I immediately became so obsessed with playing that I ignored every other aspect of my life and almost stopped sleeping entirely.

During this period, I experienced severe mental lapses, panic attacks, and inexplicable losses of time. I attributed all of this to months of relentless sleep deprivation, so I made an appointment to see a therapist with experience treating acute insomnia.

I arrived a bit before my appointment and killed time in the lobby drinking tea and listening to a podcast that featured a group of stand-up comedians drinking red wine and talking about the first season of *Friday Night Lights*.

When it was finally time for my appointment, I walked upstairs to the fifth floor and spent an hour sharing my most intimate thoughts and feelings with a complete stranger. I told her about the loss of my parents and how I'd been arrested in that theater basement after following a series of (what I believed at the time were) connected patterns and signs. We finished up with a discussion about the gray feeling I'd experienced as a child, and the accompanying acute sense of deep pressure that filled up the air, as if there was something dark hiding in the margins of the world, waiting to devour me.

She nodded in all the right places, and I felt a little better after speaking with her, but I wasn't optimistic. I was pretty sure they didn't have a section about "gray shadow things in the margins of the world" in the *DSM-5*.

After my appointment, I went home exhausted and even though it was the middle of the day, I crawled into my bed and fell asleep.

The next week, I returned to the therapist's office ready to do it all over again, but something was wrong.

I couldn't really explain what it was as I stared up at the building from across the street, but something just felt off. I walked up the stairs to the same office I'd visited last week, and then it hit me.

There was no fifth floor.

I hurried back downstairs to the lobby and examined the building's directory. My therapist's name wasn't there. A quick online search revealed that her office was located in a different building about a block away.

As I was walking over to the other building, a tingling feeling in the pit of my stomach forced me to stop. My breathing became shallow and forced as a familiar anxious emptiness began to fill me. I couldn't go any farther.

I turned and looked back at the building I'd just left.

The fifth floor was back.

I started running, determined to make it up to my therapist's office this time, but something else had changed. The street was darker now, the traffic sounds muted. It was as if somebody had placed a dark filter in front of my eyes and a thick gauzy fabric over my ears. I remember feeling like there was something unnatural about the silence—a sense of impatience.

And then the familiar static and blur of the gray feeling slid into my head, and a creeping darkness shadowed my peripheral vision.

I'm not sure how I knew, but I understood—with one hundred percent certainty—if that darkness somehow managed to reach me, something terrible was going to happen.

I ran back into the building, sprinted through the lobby and hurried up the stairs. I focused all of my attention on looking down and taking one step at a time. I didn't know what was going to happen if the fifth floor wasn't there, but I had the feeling it was something extremely bad.

When I turned the final corner and saw the stairs leading up to the fifth floor, I tumbled forward, convinced they were going to disappear any second.

But they didn't.

I took those stairs two at a time, and when I finally burst into my therapist's office and had a seat in one of the small leather chairs in her waiting room, I was breathing like I'd been chased for miles by a chain saw maniac in a horror movie.

Everything appeared to be the same—the magazines on the table, the art on the walls, the view out the window.

Slowly, I began to relax.

I flipped through a couple of the magazines, but nothing held my interest.

I looked over at the high-rise office tower directly across the street.

The building I was sitting in was perfectly reflected in the mirrorlike glass of the office tower, and I began thinking about the way the old brick appeared reflected in the modern glass. I found the dichotomy between the old and the new comforting, and it momentarily made me feel like I was glimpsing something profound— some kind of deep insight into the connectedness and impermanence of all things. And yet, something wasn't right. I felt a nagging tug on a thread somewhere deep in the back of my mind.

Then I saw it—and everything changed.

The old brick building reflected in that office tower across the street—the building I was currently sitting in, waiting for my therapist to see me—had only four floors.

I was completely frozen in place, unable to move.

At that moment, the dark gray shadows poured into the room from beneath the door and oozed into my mind from the screaming black cracks of another world, and tiny wiggling things crept up from my stomach and took over my body.

And everything went black.

I woke up in the hospital with two sprained wrists and several bruised ribs. Chloe was there. Apparently I'd called her at some point after I'd been arrested. She told me I'd been accosting people on the street, wild-eyed and manic, demanding they count the floors of the building and tell me how many there were.

I couldn't remember anything after I'd seen the reflection of the building with four floors.

The doctors explained that I'd experienced a complete mental break. Chloe helped me hire a lawyer, and he managed to persuade an overworked judge to release me under my own recognizance.

Chloe made me promise to stop playing the game immediately, and I reluctantly agreed.

I made it almost three months.

What if Chloe was right? What if it was happening again?

I knew that The Kingfish Cafe had closed six years earlier, but when I grabbed my phone and looked it up, I couldn't find any of the articles I'd read back then that detailed the closure. All I could find were glowing Yelp reviews—most of them written by people who'd visited the restaurant at some point during the past six years.

That night, Chloe stayed at my place until two in the morning. She told me it was because she'd had a bit too much to drink, but I know Chloe, and two glasses of wine definitely didn't qualify as too much of anything. She was clearly worried that I was headed for some kind of mental break. And, if I'm being honest, I was worried right along with her.

11

HANG IN THERE, TIGER

"Something big is going on over at WorGames," Baron said, waggling his spoon in my direction like an orchestra conductor setting the tempo of an extremely odd time signature.

He'd shown up at my place around eight thirty in the morning. I'd done my best to ignore the buzzer, but Baron was persistent. He burst into my kitchen carrying a bag of groceries that contained a bowl of chia pudding, six Gala apples, a tub of vanilla ice cream, beef jerky, and a Diet Coke. He was either stoned out of his mind or completely sober; it was impossible to tell with him.

"What do you mean?" I asked, unable to stifle a yawn. I'd barely managed two hours of sleep the night before.

"I was talking to my friend Valentine. She's a project manager over there."

"And?"

"And last year they brought in Sidney Farrow."

"Holy shit," I said. "For real?"

"For realz, but nobody could talk about it."

"Damn."

"Yeah. Val told me they made everyone sign an NDA as thick as a New York City phone book from 1986."

"That's very specific."

"You know what this means?"

"No idea."

"I'm going to be working with Sidney Farrow."

"How? What the fuck are you talking about?"

"Valentine got me a job at WorGames."

"Doing what?"

"Testing a new bleeding-edge title that runs on some high-tech augmented reality game engine."

"I'm jealous," I said as I started making myself a cup of heart-stoppingly strong coffee.

Jealous was an understatement. Sidney Farrow's games meant everything to me when I was growing up. While other kids had pictures of boy bands and motorcycles on their walls, I was all about Shigeru Miyamoto and Sidney Farrow.

Sidney Farrow's story was remarkably similar to Hawk Worricker's.

Sidney had entered the world of videogame design a month before she was set to graduate from Stanford, but unlike most people hired directly out of college, Sidney Farrow had already achieved significant real-world success.

While still in school, she'd created one of the most popular on-line games in the world. It was something called Targetta— a MMORPG. Sidney's game was one of the first MMORPGs created outside of a corporate environment. She'd financed her entire vision by licensing her original platform to two large gaming companies.

Sidney's work in artificial intelligence and self-generating world-building was groundbreaking, and a number of her initial open-source engine and narrative design concepts are still being used today.

"You know, Sidney Farrow was raised in a cult," Baron said.

"It was a communal EST group, not a cult."

"What the fuck is EST?"

"Erhard Seminars Training. It was big in the seventies and early eighties. Transform yourself by realizing you're responsible for everything in your life."

"So, pretty much exactly a cult."

I shrugged. I didn't have the energy to argue—especially considering the fact that he wasn't wrong. I was only taking the other side of the argument because it was Sidney Farrow.

"How do you know that shit?" Baron asked, as he moved from the kitchen into the living room.

"I read books."

"Those mind cults practice thought control, NLP 2.0 shit; some even brand each other," Baron said as he went through a stack of magazines and papers on my coffee table, looking for something to amuse him as he ate his chia pudding.

"There's no evidence any of that happened with Sidney Farrow's group."

Baron picked up an old copy of *Games and Gamers* magazine from the coffee table—an issue from sometime in the late nineties.

"She's cool," Baron said.

Sidney Farrow was on the cover, and he was right; she was super cool.

She had wavy red hair, bright green eyes, and a knowing smirk that slightly turned up one side of her mouth. She was wearing Super Mario coveralls over a worn white vintage Atari T-shirt. There was a black anarchy symbol pinned onto one side of the coverall's straps and a yellow X-Men logo button on the other.

Sidney Farrow was the one person in the world I most wanted to meet—although a certain reclusive billionaire with whom I'd recently had coffee ran a pretty close second.

Chloe came over to my place an hour or so after Baron showed up, and the three of us spent the rest of the day trying to dig up information on Alan Scarpio. Unsurprisingly, we were unable to find anyone connected to Scarpio who was willing to speak with us.

"What the hell do we do now?" Chloe asked.

"Dinner?" I suggested. We hadn't eaten much of anything all day.

"I don't know about you guys," Baron said, "but I haven't slept, and I've gotta get up early for Sidney Farrow tomorrow."

"Lucky bastard," Chloe said. She was a huge Farrow fan too.

"Why don't the three of us touch base sometime tomorrow?" I said as I followed Baron to the door.

"Sounds good," Baron said.

I shut the door and walked back into the living room, closed my eyes, and sank into the couch beside Chloe.

The lack of sleep was starting to catch up with me as well.

I jumped a little when Chloe gently placed her hands on my shoulders, but my reaction didn't scare her away. She just squeezed harder.

"It's gonna be okay, tiger," she said. "Hang in there."

Chloe and I often sent each other two memes. One was the infamous photograph of the little "hang in there" kitten dangling from a rope, and the other was a picture of a single white towel hanging on a rack. Towel was our panic signal—a nod to Douglas Adams.

In case of emergency, if one of us really needed to speak to the other, we sent the towel. The kitten was reserved for situations that warranted some light absurd commentary. It was a kind of visual tone poem to general fucked-uppery. "Hang in there" never actually required a response. Towel was another story.

Towel always required a response.

Chloe and I sat side by side on my couch and shared an enormous caprese salad while we looked into the current status of the game. If Rabbits really was broken, and Alan Scarpio felt like I might be able to help fix it somehow, we needed to find out exactly what the hell was going on.

Chloe was scrolling through a couple of references in the comments section of a weird YouTube video when she uncovered a website she thought might be something.

Like *Fight Club,* the number one rule when it comes to Rabbits is: You don't talk about Rabbits. Period. The result of this intense secrecy is that it's fairly difficult to find information about the game online, and even if you're experienced at seeking out Rabbits-related material, most of what you dig up will be either untrue or distorted enough to be completely useless.

There are whispers of severe retribution for players who talk about Rabbits publicly—retribution that includes extreme hacking, swatting, doxxing, and worse. According to the rumors, marriages have been destroyed, people sent to prison, and immense fortunes lost.

Chloe was the best online researcher I knew. From breaking into her high school's computer system and "adjusting" grades in order to make a little extra lunch money to helping her college friends hack their significant others' passwords to see if they'd been cheating, Chloe had a remarkable knack for navigating the hidden corners of the virtual world. If there was Rabbits information hidden out there between the cracks, Chloe had a pretty good chance of unearthing it—*and* covering our tracks after the fact.

It didn't take her long to find something.

"Check it out," she said, flipping her laptop around to show me the screen.

The title of the website was: Rabbits Players X.

"What is it?" I asked.

"Not sure. Looks like random pictures."

She was right. The website was just the title and a group of seemingly unrelated photographs. Directly below the photographs was a blank input form with a send button.

"Is this legit?" I asked.

"A bunch of people on YouTube and Reddit have been trying to put together a full list of players officially involved in the last iteration of the game. This is their latest lead, but so far they haven't been able to crack it."

I took a look at the pictures. There was a flower in the middle of a field, some kind of old Bavarian or other German town, a looped rope, and a photograph of a smiling thirtysomething Black man holding a Canadian flag.

Apparently the Reddit folks had tried to endsource both the Web page's form and send buttons, and then they'd put every image on that Web page through a number of queries, reverse image searches, and a process Chloe referred to as a social media combthrough, but they hadn't been able to find any obvious link between the images.

I found it in less than a minute.

There *was* a connection between the photographs—but a tenuous, distant connection that most people would miss. The flower was a Collie rose. The town was located in central Thuringia, Germany: Apolda, the birthplace of the Doberman pinscher. The looped rope was a bit trickier. "Looped" is an anagram for "poodle." The image of the man holding the Canadian flag might have been tough, but with the other clues already trending in such an obvious direction, it was easy. The man was a professional boxer named Trevor Berbick.

Boxer, collie, Doberman, poodle. The key was dogs.

We tried a few things, but in the end it was the word "canine" that led us to another Web page. That page displayed an image, what appeared to be some kind of screen capture of a list of usernames.

It didn't feel like we were any closer to figuring out what was going on with Alan Scarpio, but it was still exciting to see the names (or pseudonyms) of official Rabbits players up there on the screen. If we hadn't opened a door into the world of Rabbits, we might have at least lifted up the corner of a rug.

There were a few names that would have been familiar to anybody with even a passing interest in Rabbits: Intrepid23, Sadie Palomino, The Wrecking Crew, and the controversial player who had allegedly almost won both Nine and Ten—the merciless clue hunter known only as Murmur.

While I was writing all of the names from that list down in a journal so we might refer to it later, I noticed another handle I recognized: *MorganaLaPhazer69.*

I stared at that username for a long time, but there was no mistaking the handle and its unique spelling. I knew exactly who it was, although I couldn't imagine him having anything to do with Rabbits.

12

DEATH AND VIDEOGAMES

"Hey, K," Russell Milligan said, smiling up at me from behind a pair of thick black designer glasses. "What's up?"

"Not much. Just living, I guess."

"Aren't we all?" he said. An impossibly high wave of thick black hair atop his head barely moved as he stood up for a quick embrace.

"Can I sit?" I asked.

He motioned to the empty chair across from him.

The day after Chloe and I had discovered Russell's unique pseudonym on that website, I'd tracked him down to the Suzzallo Library on the University of Washington campus. He was sitting in the Reading Room—a huge Gothic hall, something right out of Harry Potter.

"When was the last time I saw you?" he asked.

"I don't know. A long time ago, maybe at Monty's place?"

"Yeah, Monty's place. Wow." He nodded, probably doing his best to remember who Monty was. I'd grown up around Russell's younger brother, Luke, but I didn't know Russell very well. We'd spent a grand total of a few hours together, spread out over five or six years, a hell of a long time ago.

"Yeah, so listen," I said. "I need to ask you a question."

"What is it?"

I lowered my voice a little. "What do you know about Rabbits?"

Russell's face twisted up and changed before he'd even heard the last syllable. He shot out of his chair, yanked me up, and dragged me through the Reading Room, outside, and onto the front steps of the library.

"Whatever you're doing, you need to stop," he said, looking around nervously as he spoke.

"What do you mean?"

"The game isn't what you think. You're not going to get rich or become a secret agent, K."

"What are you talking about?"

"I'm talking about real people actually dying while playing."

All of the color had drained from his face and his eyes were wild. I suddenly felt scared, exposed.

"Jesus, Russ, did something happen?"

"Look, it's not a game—or, at least, it's not *only* a game. It's something else. Terrible shit has been happening around that thing. It took me a long time to get my life back, and I'm not getting pulled in again. It's nice to see that you still exist, K, but please, leave me the fuck alone."

And with that, Russell Milligan turned and made his way back into the library while I stood outside on the steps, trying to work out exactly what the hell had just happened.

"So, how freaked out was this guy?" Chloe asked, sitting cross-legged on my couch.

"On a scale of 'who gives a shit' to 'totally freaked out,' I'd put him somewhere just shy of '*Scanners*-style exploding head,'" I said, handing Chloe a cup of tea.

"Thanks," she said.

"I don't get it. I mean, I barely knew him, but he always seemed cool—not the kind of guy who'd lose his shit at the mention of a game."

"He told you to stay away from Rabbits, that people had died while playing," Chloe said.

I nodded.

Chloe took a sip of her tea, then added one more packet of sugar.

"He's right, you know," I said.

"About what?"

"That people have died while playing Rabbits." I did my best to judge Chloe's reaction to my statement. She didn't even blink.

"People die playing all kinds of games, K."

"Yeah, but what if this is . . . different?"

She stared at me for a moment. "Did you read that thing on death and videogames I sent you from *VICE* last year?"

"I don't remember."

"I sent it to you twice."

"Maybe?"

Chloe shook her head, unimpressed. "So, that article talks about how game addiction creates the same changes in your brain as drug addiction."

"Really?"

"Yeah. A kid actually died just this year from playing Diablo for forty hours straight without eating."

"That's messed up."

"It's fucking horrifying is what it is. I love Diablo. I'll send you the article. Again."

Chloe toyed with the handle of her mug for a moment before she looked up. "K . . ."

"Yeah?"

"Did you know somebody who died?"

I'd told Chloe that I'd been in a car accident as a kid, but I never mentioned the fact that the accident had anything to do with Rabbits.

"Yes," I said.

"Playing the game?"

"I think so, maybe."

"What makes you think it was Rabbits?"

"I don't know. I'm probably just seeing connections that aren't there," I lied. I didn't want to get into what had happened in that truck with the Connors sisters. I noticed my mouth was a bit dry, and I was starting to feel a familiar buzzing in my head.

I looked down at my hands and realized I'd been tapping out an Australian Open match between Andre Agassi and Michael Chang.

I casually slipped my hands beneath my thighs. I didn't think Chloe noticed.

"You know Rabbits is all about connections," Chloe said.

She could tell I was hiding something, and I got the feeling she was thinking about asking me a direct question I most likely wasn't prepared to answer.

She put her hand on my thigh and looked into my eyes.

She was worried.

Maybe she had noticed my weird thigh-tapping ritual, after all.

13

PROPERTY OF SHIRLEY BOOTH

A COUPLE OF WEEKS AFTER I'd spoken with Russell Milligan, Chloe and I met up at my place to go over everything we had so far. We invited Baron, but he didn't show. We tried calling, but it went straight to voicemail.

"When's the last time you heard from him?" I asked.

Chloe scrolled through the messages on her phone. "Nothing since right after he started working at WorGames."

"Really?"

"Yeah. You?"

I shook my head. "Same."

"I'd probably go AWOL for a while if I got to spend time living in Sidney Farrow's latest digital dreamscape."

"Me too," I said, "but it's been over two weeks." Sidney Farrow aside, I couldn't remember going more than a couple of days without some kind of text message or phone call from Baron Corduroy.

"Should we maybe send him a towel?" Chloe suggested.

Baron knew Chloe and I used the towel meme in emergencies, so he would understand it was important.

"Let's give him until the end of the day."

"Sounds good," Chloe said.

"What's going on with the Magician?" He'd also told us he was going to look into what was happening with the game. That was close to three weeks ago.

"I don't know," Chloe said. "Ever since we discovered the Wor-Games connection on Scarpio's phone, he's been a bit . . . off."

"What do you mean?"

"I've only seen him at the arcade once since then, and he wasn't all that open to conversation. He just kind of wandered in muttering about a band called Toto, and then went upstairs and locked himself in his office."

"Do you think he's still trying to figure out what's going on with the game?"

Chloe shrugged.

"Do you know if he ended up getting in touch with anyone at WorGames?"

"No idea. You sure got a lotta questions."

"We need to sit down with the Magician as soon as possible."

Chloe nodded. "Can you stop pacing? You're making me nervous."

"Sorry," I said, and sat down on the couch.

Alan Scarpio had gone out of his way to tell me that something was wrong with the game—that if the next iteration started up before that something was fixed, we were well and truly fucked. Then he'd gotten a call from WorGames and vanished.

I kept picturing the look on his face while he was telling me that. He'd been smiling, speaking somewhat flippantly, but there was something behind his eyes.

Something I recognized.

Fear.

"I'll try to pin him down," Chloe said. "In the meantime, I think we should talk to your friend who freaked out when you mentioned Rabbits. It sounds like he might know something useful."

"Maybe, but he made it pretty clear he wasn't interested in talking about it."

"Yeah, well, you didn't have me."

I was pretty sure having Chloe tag along wouldn't make the least bit of difference, but Russell Milligan clearly knew a lot about Rabbits, including something that had freaked him way the hell out.

"We could try," I said, "but he'll most likely tell us to fuck off."

"Let's go collect our 'fuck off' then."

I got back in touch with Russell and he agreed to meet two hours later at a coffee shop a few blocks away from the University of Washington campus.

"Hey," I said, sitting down across from him. "This is Chloe."

Chloe sat down beside me and shook hands with Russell.

"Hey, Chloe. K tells me you're looking for a UX designer?"

So, yeah, I'd kind of lied to Russell about why we wanted to meet.

"Not exactly," Chloe said.

Russell's face darkened a little as he realized what was happening.

"I told you to stay away from that thing," he said as he stood up and started to leave.

"Alan Scarpio said something was wrong with the game and asked for my help," I said. "I'm not sure what's happening."

Russell stopped walking and turned around.

Even though he'd clearly experienced something horrible related to the game, I could tell he was intrigued—excited, even—by the mention of Alan Scarpio. Then, just as quickly as that flash of excitement had appeared, it was gone.

He took a few steps back toward our table and lowered his voice. "What's happening is stay away from the game if you want to stay alive."

"Is there anything you can tell us about what's going on? Anything at all?" Chloe asked.

"Just leave it alone. It's nothing but trouble, I promise you."

"Please," I said. "It's important."

"You're really not going to stop, are you?" he asked, resigned.

"I don't think we can," I said.

Russell looked at Chloe, then over at me.

"You could try the phone number."

"What phone number?" I asked.

"Hazel's phone number."

"Hazel has a phone number?"

"Yeah, an 800 number. Like Bill Murray."

"Bill Murray the actor?"

Russell sighed. "Bill Murray doesn't have an agent or a manager, so the only way to get in touch with him if you want him in your movie is to track down his 800 number and leave a message."

"You're fucking with us," I said.

"Nope," he said. "That's the rumor."

I looked over at Chloe. She just shrugged.

"There was a Rabbits player in Bali who claimed they'd set up a meeting with Hazel using some kind of 800 number," Russell continued. "Most people believe the number's nothing but an unsubstantiated myth, but I heard it from a couple of sources I trust. The phone number is real."

"Do you have the number?" I asked.

"No. I never went looking for Hazel, but I can point you in the direction of somebody who might know how to get in touch."

"Who?"

"No offense, K, but if I give you this, do you *promise* I'll never see you again?"

"I promise," I said.

He nodded at Chloe. "You too."

"But we just met."

He stared at her, unimpressed.

"Fine," Chloe said.

Russell looked at me, then Chloe, and finally back to me. After shaking his head one last time, he grabbed my phone and entered the name "Amanda Obscura" along with a number.

"Text her and tell her you're playing," he said, then he got up and left.

Chloe took a sip of her coffee. "Fun guy."

Per Russell's instructions, I sent a text message to Amanda Obscura.

I received an answer a few minutes later. It was an address and a time. The address was about twenty minutes away, and we had fifteen minutes to get there.

—

Amanda Obscura's place was a thrift store called Bloom Vintage. I'd actually been there a few times before. They had great prices on used vinyl.

The front of the store was filled with vintage clothing, including a huge selection of genuine rock T-shirts from the seventies and eighties. The back section was a combination used-record store and junk shop. There was a sixtysomething-year-old man with thick silver hair that had been roughly pulled back into a long ponytail sitting behind the front counter reading a novel called *Elf* when we arrived. We told him we were there to speak with Amanda. Without looking up from his book, he pointed toward the back of the store.

We found her sitting behind a desk, working on a crossword puzzle.

"What's an eight-letter word for 'know-it-all'?" she asked without looking up.

Amanda Obscura appeared to be in her midthirties. She wore round pink-tinted sunglasses and a tight blue jean pantsuit from the seventies. Her untamed bleached-blond hair was wrapped up in a pink-and-blue paisley scarf.

She held a pen between her teeth as she spoke.

"'Polymath'?" I suggested.

"Shit," she said. "I messed it up."

"I could be wrong." I looked over at Chloe. She shrugged.

"No, yours makes more sense. I should be using a pencil." She tossed the crossword into a nearby trash can and smiled. "What do you need?"

"We're looking for a phone number," I said.

Amanda smiled. "I mean, what do you need from the store?" She motioned around the room. There were dozens of bins filled with vinyl records, and the back wall was covered in floor-to-ceiling shelves of books, CDs, cassette tapes, and all kinds of old electronics.

"Oh," Chloe said. "We don't really need anything. We're just looking for Hazel's number."

Amanda nodded and smiled, but didn't say anything.

I could tell by her face that we were missing something.

"Well, I could certainly use some new records," I said.

Amanda smiled yet again. "That's great. We have a terrific selection. Just let me know if you need help finding anything."

I ended up picking out three albums: Neil Young's *On the Beach,* *Let It Be* by the Beatles, and *Arthur* by the Kinks. I took those back to Amanda, but she wasn't quite ready to help. When Chloe added a jade necklace and a Posies concert T-shirt to the pile, Amanda walked over to the back wall and dug something out of a box on a high shelf.

"Here you go," she said.

She handed Chloe a small green cardboard box that contained a handheld game by Coleco from 1978 called Electronic Quarterback.

Chloe and I looked over the box. It was well-worn, with crooked strips of yellowed masking tape running up two of the four sides. It claimed to contain "all the action of a real football game."

"What is this?" I asked, but Amanda had stepped away to help another customer.

Chloe pulled the game out of the box. It looked like any other handheld sports game from the seventies. It was green-and-cream colored. The top half was a little football field, and the bottom contained the switches and buttons that would have controlled the tiny red lights that represented the players, had the thing been equipped with batteries.

I was looking for the battery compartment when Amanda came back over. "What are you doing?"

"I assume we're supposed to play this game to find the phone number somehow?"

"Sometimes a cigar is just a cigar, kid," Amanda said. She grabbed the game and pointed to something carved into the plastic on the back. It was a name and a phone number.

Property of Shirley Booth

1-425-224-6685

Amanda wouldn't let us take a picture of the game itself, but she did let Chloe write down the phone number once we promised we wouldn't post it anywhere online.

"Shirley Booth?" I asked.

"Google it," Amanda said, then she boxed up the game and slipped it up onto a nearby shelf.

Chloe and I left Bloom Vintage and made our way back to my place to call the number.

A quick search for Shirley Booth revealed she was an actress who'd passed away in the nineties. She'd played the title character in an American sitcom called *Hazel* that ran from 1961 to 1966. That series was based on the comic strip *Hazel* by Ted Key.

"Shirley Booth was Hazel," I said. "Clever."

"Are you ready?" Chloe had predialed the number, and her finger was poised over the call button on her phone.

"Let's do it," I said.

Chloe pressed the button.

We were calling Hazel.

The phone started ringing. It sounded kind of rough and distorted, like an old analog line from the eighties. After three rings there was a click and a woman's voice relayed the following message:

Hi, you've reached Golden Seal Carpet Cleaning. We're currently out of the office. Please leave your name, contact information, and a brief message, and we'll get back to you when time allows. If you're applying for the advertised position, please visit the stationery room on the second floor. Thank you.

"My name is K. I'm here with my friend Chloe. We'd like to speak to you about . . . well, about a lot of things, but I suppose most pressing is the fact that Alan Scarpio told me something was wrong with the game, and that I needed to help him fix it before the next iteration began. Now Scarpio's missing and we're not sure where to turn. Please call me back."

I left my number and hung up.

"What now?" I asked.

"I'm starving," Chloe said. "Let's grab something on our way."

"On our way where?"

"Where do you think? Golden Seal Carpet Cleaning."

14

SECOND FLOOR STATIONERY

WE GRABBED PIZZA and salad at the market, then made our way over to the address Chloe had dug up for Golden Seal Carpet Cleaning.

It was a four-story building on a quiet street in Georgetown.

Georgetown is one of the oldest neighborhoods in Seattle, where industrial commercial–meets–contemporary boho art chic. You can walk past a busy steampunk brew pub set next to a clown school, and a block later you're standing in the middle of a quiet street staring at a low red-brick building from another age.

Vertical Art Deco lines running up the elevated corners of the building reminded me of the power station on the cover of Pink Floyd's *Animals* (minus the enormous white smokestacks). The front doors were locked and there were no company names listed on the directory. We took a quick look around. Every uncovered window we were able to peek through revealed an empty room. There were no people, no cars, and no sounds of life at all. I've seen a lot of empty buildings. This was definitely one of them.

"There's nobody here," Chloe said, using her hand to shield her eyes from the daylight as she stared up at the top floor.

"No For Lease sign either," I said. "Are you sure this is the right place?"

"It's the only address listed anywhere."

I walked up the stairs and tried the door again.

Still locked.

I took another look at the directory. There were small white but-tons next to two rows of empty name plates. "Should we maybe try to buzz?"

"Let's do it," Chloe said.

"Which one?" I asked.

Chloe mashed her way down all twenty of the buttons, each of them releasing a sharp buzzing sound as she made contact.

"Or we could just press them all," I said.

Chloe shrugged.

We waited, but nothing happened. As we started walking down the stairs toward the sidewalk, however, we heard the familiar buzz and clack of a door being unlocked electronically.

We shared a look. Somebody was letting us in.

We sprinted back up the stairs, and I managed to catch the handle of the door a split second before the lock started to reengage. I yanked it open, and Chloe and I tumbled forward into the lobby.

We exhaled in unison as the door closed behind us with a heavy clunk—a sound that echoed through the empty space, underlining the unsettling silence.

We were in.

The floor of the lobby was checkered with well-worn beige and white linoleum tiles. An empty building directory hung on the wall directly in front of us. To the right was an old gray elevator and just left of that, a set of stairs leading up.

"What do you think?" Chloe stared up at the blank directory.

I walked over and pressed the call button next to the elevator. "The outgoing message said that if you wanted to apply for the job to visit the stationery room on the second floor."

Chloe came over and pressed the call button again, three times in a row.

"What are you doing?"

"I'm excited," she said, and punched my shoulder.

I was pretty excited myself, but I was doing my best to keep it together.

On our way here, I'd started noticing the number twenty-three. Twenty-three flowers on a billboard advertising a local florist, twenty-three steps to cross the street, a kid in a LeBron James jersey (23) stepping onto a number twenty-three bus. And now, we were going up to the second floor and Chloe had just pressed the elevator button three times. Twenty-three.

I could feel the wild exhilaration that often accompanied my obsession with patterns and connections and I took a deep breath. One of my many therapists had told me that the best thing I could do when I felt overwhelmed like this was to recognize the remarkable coincidence, marvel at the random chance, then simply let it pass. So I took another deep breath and waited for the number twenty-three to wash over me and disappear.

I couldn't afford to lose control again. Not now.

We stepped off the elevator and into a long hallway that featured the same scuffed beige-and-white checkerboard linoleum.

The second floor was just as quiet as the lobby. If there was anybody inside the building, they were completely silent.

Our footsteps echoed off the floor and the walls as we made our way slowly down the hall. Most of the office doors had been left open, and as we passed by, we could see that the rooms were empty—no furniture, no phones, nothing at all. The dust we kicked up into the air as we walked led me to believe that nobody had been there in a very long time.

When we reached the end of the hall, we turned right into an almost identical hallway—same linoleum, same empty offices on either side, but there was one significant difference.

At the end of this hallway was a closed door.

It looked exactly like a private investigator's door from an old noir detective film. The word STATIONERY had been stenciled or glued onto it using some variation of the Futura font. Directly below the word STATIONERY was the suite number. Twenty-three. Of course.

Chloe and I looked at each other. She raised her eyebrows and smiled, and then she tried the door. It was unlocked.

We entered the room and turned on the lights.

The room was small, about twenty-five feet square. Two large windows filled the wall to the left of the door. There were a number of things inside, but stationery definitely wasn't one of them. The wall to our right, directly opposite the large windows, was covered by three dented gunmetal-gray bookshelves filled with old books, most on the subject of industrial design. In between the books were a number of small potted plants, which were all still alive.

Whatever was going on up there, someone had been watering the plants.

There was a small, low teak desk with matching chair positioned in the exact center of the room. Sitting on top of the desk was an old computer. There was no logo visible, but it looked like a machine from the 1970s, an 8-bit computer called a Commodore VIC-20. Beside the old computer on the left was a cassette tape recorder, and just to the right of everything was an ancient cream-colored cathode-ray monitor.

Chloe sat down in front of the computer, and I switched everything on.

The recorder was something called a Datasette—an archaic system that used cassette tapes to store data. I'd seen something similar in a vintage computer store in New York City, but this setup was different, the keyboard in particular.

From above it appeared normal, just regular letters and numbers, but there were two tiny symbols on the front face of each of the keys: One was a symbol in a language I'd never seen before, and the other was geometric. The VIC-20 had symbols on the front of the keys as well, but not like these. These looked like symbols you might find in a book on alchemy or the occult, but maybe they were simply part of an old computer-programming language; I had no idea.

Once the computer was up and running, I knelt down on the

floor beside Chloe and the two of us were faced with a flashing cursor and the word "Ready."

We tried typing the handful of BASIC programming language commands that we could remember, but nothing happened.

I decided to try a different approach. I typed in one word—"Hazel"—and hit return.

Nothing.

Then I tried the word "Rabbits."

After a momentary flicker and hum, followed by a bright flash and jumble of images, the screen entered a boot sequence, and the tiny speaker atop the cassette player crackled to life.

Suddenly, the monitor was displaying full-color video, and we were looking at a press conference or something similar.

In the center of the screen was a lectern set on a low stage. A crowd of reporters were milling around, waiting for whoever was going to be speaking to arrive.

After a few seconds, a tall, thin thirtysomething woman wearing a white skirt suit waded through the throng of reporters and made her way up and onto the stage. She purposefully stepped up to the lectern, and her amplified voice, strong and clear with a thick British accent, filled the room.

"Minister Jesselman is going to make a brief statement, but we're not going to be taking any questions at this time. We will, however, brief you again after tomorrow's session. Everybody clear?" The assembled press grumbled and moaned; clearly they had some questions about whatever was going on.

For a moment, with everyone milling around, it wasn't clear exactly what was happening or where to focus your attention. Was Minister Jesselman involved in some sort of personal or political scandal? Was he going to announce a run for office? Or were we waiting on something else entirely?

Finally, as if in response to those questions, a distinguished-looking gray-haired man in a blue designer suit stepped up to the lectern and cleared his throat.

"Good morning, everyone. I came here today to address the clean energy initiative bill's initial failure and our desperate need to keep it alive in parliament, but I'm afraid I'm going to have to deliver another message instead."

And with those words, Minister Jesselman calmly reached into the inside pocket of his jacket and removed a snub-nosed silver revolver.

The crowd erupted in a flurry of chaotic movement, yelling and climbing over one another in an attempt to get as far away from the front of the stage as possible, but Jesselman wasn't concerned with them. He just looked directly into the camera, smiled a strange, sad smile, and delivered his message:

"The door is open."

Then he calmly set the gun directly beneath his chin, drew back the hammer with an audible click, and pulled the trigger.

Blood exploded in a dark red wave from behind his head, splashing everything nearby. Then the video cut to black and the tiny cassette player's speaker went quiet.

"Jesus," Chloe said.

I tried to respond, but I couldn't speak. My mouth was dry, my field of vision suddenly tunneled and blurred. The sound of static roared into my head, and I felt the familiar humming and tingling filling me up, like blood rushing to a limb that had fallen asleep.

The gray feeling was back.

Chloe pulled out her phone and did a quick online search for Minister Jesselman. Dozens of articles sprang up immediately. This video wasn't some relic of the past, stored in the magnetic tape of an ancient computer system. This was all over the news.

This had just happened. The video we'd been watching was live.

Then, suddenly the monitor flickered on again.

Instead of that press conference footage, there was something new on the monitor. It was a list of Roman numerals followed by a series of names.

It was The Circle.

But this version of The Circle was different. Instead of ending with the Roman numeral for ten, like the most recent versions, here XI flashed at the bottom of the screen.

I looked over at Chloe and then pulled out my phone and texted Baron. I sent him two words and an image. The image was a towel hanging on a rack. The words were: *Call. Now.*

It looked like the eleventh iteration of the game had officially begun.

NOTES ON THE GAME:
MISSIVE BY HAZEL
(AUTHENTICATED BY BLOCKCHAIN)

How do you play the game? Find the discrepancies, follow the clues; follow the clues and find the discrepancies. Playing is the easy part; what's harder is knowing if you're playing or not. There's no entry fee, application form, or guidebook, and whoever's in charge isn't talking. So how do you know if you're playing the game?

The good news is that if you're playing Rabbits—actually playing the game, for better or worse—you'll eventually know it. Something will be off. Something will be different. Something will be wrong.

And everything will be dangerous.

—HAZEL 8

15

WE HAVE A LITTLE FUCKED-UP SOMETHING TO DEAL WITH HERE

"I'm worried about Baron," I said.

It was ten thirty p.m. and Chloe was locking up the arcade. It had been over twenty-four hours, and Baron still hadn't responded to our emergency towel text.

"Yeah," Chloe said as she grabbed her backpack and flipped it over her shoulder. "He's gonna lose his shit when we tell him about Golden Seal Carpet Cleaning. Maybe he can help us figure out how the hell that ancient computer tape was playing a live video, and then how it managed to wipe itself clean."

"I think we should head over there," I said.

"Good call."

It took us fifteen minutes to get to Baron's building.

We stepped out of Chloe's car, and I shivered a little. I'm not sure if it was due to the fact that it was cold outside, or because two of the streetlights in front of Baron's place had burned out, giving the building a serious retro-horror-movie vibe. It didn't help that the place used to be a nunnery in the fifties, and as a result, there were some Gothic-style flourishes in the masonry that seriously amplified the *Rosemary's Baby* of it all.

We ran across the street and I buzzed his unit.

"No answer," I said.

"He's still not answering his phone, either." Chloe had been call-ing him repeatedly while I buzzed.

Baron's apartment was on the ground floor. We tried knocking on his window, calling, and buzzing a few more times, but there was still no answer.

Chloe and I looked toward the side of the building at exactly the same time.

"I don't know," I said.

Chloe smiled.

We made our way around the side of the building and stepped through a small wooden gate into the narrow lane that ran along the side of Baron's place. The lane was maybe four feet wide and over-grown with weeds and wildflowers.

We walked between the buildings past a rusted tricycle, a few old plastic toys, and a patio chair that must have been white at some point but was now covered in an uneven layer of filth.

The weeds eventually gave way to mud and brown grass. Our shoes made almost no sound as we walked, as if the canopy of dark starlit sky above was somehow absorbing all of the sound from the world.

Somebody had left their blinds open in the building next door, and as we passed by I could see directly into their apartment. There was a small fish tank sitting on a water-stained black Ikea table di-rectly in front of the window. The dark greenish-gray algae run-ning up the side of the tank was so thick that I couldn't tell if there was anything left alive on the other side.

For just a second, I thought I saw a flash of something slither behind the wall of brackish green, but then it was gone.

If there was something in there, swimming around in the briny darkness, trying to catch a glimpse of another world through the sludge, I definitely understood how it felt.

Baron's curtains were closed but his window was open.

He smoked a lot of weed, so he always kept this window cracked a few inches.

I knocked on the glass and called his name. No answer.

"He must be out," I said.

"Let's take a look," Chloe said, and she lifted the window another couple of inches and pushed the curtains aside.

Baron was there, sitting at his desk in the middle of his living room in front of his computer. He was wearing a set of huge white vintage-style headphones and just staring at the screen.

We knocked and yelled a few more times, but he didn't budge.

Chloe lifted the old wooden window up as high as it could go, which was just enough room for the two of us to fit through.

"I'm climbing in," she said.

"I don't know . . ."

"What? He's not jerking off or anything," she said as she jumped up and pushed her head and shoulders through the small opening.

"Okay, but—"

"He'd totally climb into your house," Chloe said, then she slid headfirst through the window and into Baron's apartment.

She was right; Baron would totally climb into my house. I took a look around. Our B&E appeared to be going unnoticed.

"Fuck," I said, to nobody in particular, and followed Chloe inside.

Chloe gently removed Baron's headphones and waved in his face.

"Hey," Baron said, blinking. "What's up?"

He didn't appear angry that we'd just broken into his place. He was completely out of it. For a moment, I wasn't even sure if he recognized me.

Then, "K-mart, what's happening?" he said, his eyes working to focus.

It was as if he'd been looking at me through some kind of thick fog from someplace far away, kind of like whatever had been swimming around behind the algae in that tank.

There was a small black wooden box on Baron's lap, which I assumed had to be filled with weed. He picked up the box and set it gently down on the floor next to his desk as he shook his head and tried to focus his eyes.

"What's going on?" he said, still dazed.

It took about a minute or so for us to notice the smell. I thought maybe there was a dead badger rotting in his sink or something, but it quickly became clear it was Baron himself. He smelled terrible—and it wasn't just that he hadn't showered in days, which he clearly hadn't. It looked like he'd peed himself—and possibly more than once.

"Not much," I said. "What's up with you?"

"I think maybe I lost track of time a little," he said, slowly coming out of whatever weird state he was in.

"Do you think maybe you lost track of a bit more than that?" Chloe said as she looked around the room.

Baron's place was a complete disaster.

There were dishes piled everywhere. Stacks of documents covered his desk and side tables. Dozens of ripped bits of paper and Post-it notes littered with messily scribbled words and symbols had been pinned to a huge corkboard. Aside from the names of a few famous Rabbits players like Hazel, Murmur, and The Dark Thane, there was nothing in any of the photographs and images accompanying the notes that made any sense. It looked like a murder wall from the lead detective's office in a serial killer movie, minus the cinematic red threads that were always connecting things.

Nothing appeared to be connected here.

"When's the last time you showered?" Chloe asked.

"Fuck, is that me?" Baron said. His nose scrunched up suddenly, as he finally noticed the smell.

"What are you doing?" I asked, leaning into the screen.

"I don't remember," he said, still clearly dazed. "Watching a movie, I think?"

Chloe led Baron into his bathroom, turned on his shower, and shut the door behind him.

The video Baron had been watching was just a few minutes long. It was playing in a browser window on some kind of darknet website.

The video reminded me of that demonic student film that made the girl crawl out of the television in *The Ring* and *Ringu,* but this thing Baron had been watching felt much worse, darker, and more weirdly lo-fi.

The video begins with an impossibly tall shadowy figure hunched over a second figure seated on a metal chair. They're in the middle of a small room. The walls are covered in countless thousands of tiny arcane markings. Every once in a while, the light flickers a certain way and the markings suddenly look alive, like so many tiny insects crawling the walls to try to escape the sudden unwelcome illumination.

A minute or so into the video, the tall shadowy figure leans down farther and whispers something into the seated figure's ear.

Slowly, almost imperceptibly, the seated figure begins sinking into the chair. At first it looks like they're simply sliding down, trying to escape the tall shadowy thing, but that isn't the case. The seated figure isn't sliding down at all—they're actually disappearing into the chair.

They're disappearing from the world.

This scene felt murky, dark, and far creepier than anything I'd seen in a movie or television show. Something terrible was happening to that person in the chair, and that something was real.

I heard a sound, distant at first, but as I focused my attention, the sound intensified. It was a kind of low whispering voice, and soon it was vibrating in my skull, a warm pleasant tickling feeling. I looked down. The sound was coming from Baron's headphones, sitting on the floor at the foot of his chair.

I picked up the headphones and was about to slip them on when Chloe pressed the space bar and the video stopped playing.

"Are you fucking crazy?" she demanded. "You wanna end up peeing yourself too?"

The second Chloe pressed the space bar, the video and the link vanished.

I tried to refresh the page, but there was nothing there.

"It's gone," I said. The pleasant tingling sensation in my head was suddenly gone as well.

"Good." Chloe closed the lid of Baron's computer. "Because we have a little fucked-up something to deal with here."

———

As soon as Baron got out of the shower, we sat him down at the table and fed him chicken soup and crackers.

"What's happening? We've been calling and texting," I said.

"Sorry, I've been busy. Working from home a bit."

"What's all . . . this?" Chloe said, pointing at his wall of photographs and ripped bits of paper.

"Work," Baron said. "I can't talk about it."

"Why not?" I asked.

"They made me sign an NDA."

Chloe took a closer look at the murder wall while I did the dishes.

"So, how's working with Sidney Farrow?" I asked. "Is she amazing?"

He smiled and nodded. "She is. I'll introduce you."

"Cool."

"You'd better introduce me too, fucker," Chloe said.

"Of course."

"Dude," I said. "Seriously, I've been worried."

"I've been working on something . . ." His voice trailed off. I could tell he'd completely lost his train of thought.

"What?" I asked.

But Baron could barely keep his eyes open. I had the feeling he might not even remember having this conversation tomorrow.

"I'm kind of tired," he said. "Can we talk in the morning?"

"You promise?" I asked.

He nodded.

"Because we really need to talk about Rabbits," I said. "We found some crazy shit. Things are getting . . . wild."

"We'll talk tomorrow, Scout's honor."

"You weren't a Scout," I said.

"What do you want, a fucking pinkie swear?"

I smiled and relaxed a little. He seemed a bit more like himself.

"We're talking about all of this shit in the morning," I said.

I heard him yell out "Scout's honor, muthafuckas" as he locked the door behind us.

Chloe and I left Baron's place and started walking to her car.

Chloe handed me her phone. "What the fuck, K?"

She'd taken pictures of Baron's murder wall. The scribbles that covered the scraps of paper and Post-it notes were almost completely illegible, and the photographs were just as confusing.

"Is this even English?" I asked, zooming in and pointing to a couple of scraps of paper.

"It's complete fucking nonsense," Chloe said. "Something is way the fuck off with him."

She was right. It was complete nonsense. And something had been way off.

The next morning, Baron Corduroy was dead.

16

NO PLAYING THE GAME!

BARON'S OFFICIAL CAUSE OF DEATH was listed as cardiorespiratory collapse due to a faulty valve.

Natural causes.

His sister had shown up to take him to brunch the morning after Chloe and I found him watching that weird video. She'd discovered Baron sitting on his bed, back against the headboard, empty eyes staring straight ahead.

A few days later, a memorial service was held at a church downtown.

Chloe and I spent the week following the ceremony doing nothing but playing videogames and drinking. We did everything we could to take our minds off one of our closest friends dropping dead from heart failure before the age of forty.

Because of what had happened with Baron, Chloe and I were doubly worried about the Magician. It had been forever since we'd discovered the WorGames connection, and he still hadn't sat down with us to discuss what, if anything, he'd been able to dig up about what was happening with the game.

Not long after Baron's memorial, Chloe and I were eating lunch together in the arcade when the Magician—barefoot and wild-eyed—burst out of his office, practically slid down the stairs, and shuffled across the room to the Robotron: 2084 machine. He pulled a folded old journal of some kind out of his back pocket and made a couple

of notes. After muttering incoherently for a few seconds, he nodded in our direction and then scuttled back through the arcade and
up the stairs.

"The Magician still seems a bit . . . off," I said.

"Yeah, it's getting worse. I don't think he's been home for days."

"Do you think he's playing the game?"

"Um . . . yeah. I sure do. Don't you?"

I nodded. Chloe was doing her best to hide it, but I could tell she
was worried.

"Maybe we should try to talk to him?" I asked.

"I don't know . . ." Chloe said.

"Come on." I started walking up to the Magician's office. "If he
doesn't want to talk, he'll just tell us to fuck off."

"You're probably right," Chloe said as she followed me upstairs.

"I'm definitely right," I said, then knocked on the door.

No response.

We stood there for almost a full minute before I knocked again.

"I said come in." The Magician's voice was muted, barely audible.

Chloe opened the door, and the two of us entered his office.

All of the blinds were closed. The Magician was working solely
by the light of a small lamp and the soft bluish glow emanating
from the screens of two ancient briefcase-style computers running
some kind of operating system I'd never seen before.

It took my eyes a moment to adjust to the near-darkness before I
was able to take a good look around the room.

His office was much messier than the last time I'd seen it. Stacks
of random documents and bits of computing equipment still covered most of the tables and shelves, but now the floor surrounding
his desk was a sea of paper scraps, computer cables, and take-out
containers.

"Holy shit, is that an Amiga?" Chloe asked, pointing to the screen
of the computer on the left.

"What is it?" The Magician spoke without looking at us as he
rushed over to another desk and hit the space bars on two beat-up
old laptops, pulling them out of sleep mode with a whirring sound,

his head now bobbing frantically back and forth between the two screens. "I don't have much time."

Chloe continued to look around the room. I could tell by the expression on her face that she was shocked by the state of the Magician's office.

When he finally turned to face us, I could see why Chloe was so worried. His eyes were wild and distant, his face gaunt and worn.

"How are you?" I asked.

"How *am* I?" the Magician repeated, then stared at me. I couldn't tell if he wanted to embrace me or push me in front of a train. But, after a second or two, he just nodded absently. "I'm fine. Sorry about . . . Baron."

"Thank you," I said.

The Magician turned his attention back to whatever it was he'd been doing on his two laptops, muttering to himself as he glanced frantically from screen to screen.

I looked over at Chloe. She gave me a sign to keep talking.

"Umm . . . so, do you think that Minister Jesselman's suicide means that the eleventh iteration of the game has started?" I asked.

"You saw The Circle and heard The Phrase, 'The Door Is Open'?"

"Yes," I said.

"Then it's started," he said, and kicked a pair of rolling chairs over in our direction. "Maybe you two could take a look at something for me."

We practically fell over each other on our way to him. The Magician didn't normally ask for help looking into anything.

He had identical websites loaded on the two computers. The site was something called Abbey's Skirt.

"What is it?" I asked as Chloe and I sat down on either side of the Magician.

"It's a website," he said, then leaned back in his chair and rubbed his eyes.

"How long have you been working?" Chloe asked.

"I don't know," the Magician said, still rubbing his eyes, "not long enough."

"What is it that you're trying to find?" I couldn't see any difference between the two sites. They appeared to be identical.

The website was simple—an Art Deco image of a woman in a skirt, hands crossed in front of her waist, the title Abbey's Skirt below the graphic, and a long blank form field with an enter button.

"Why Abbey's Skirt?" Chloe asked.

"Abbey's Skirt is an anagram for 'Rabbits keys,'" the Magician said. "There was a discrepancy here when I looked earlier."

"What kind of discrepancy?"

"I don't know . . . but it was there."

"They look the same now," Chloe said.

"Yes, they are. Same URL. Same company. Same source code."

"So—" I said. "Is Abbey's Skirt something important?"

"This site used to be the gateway to a bulletin board, a place we'd come to discuss the game," the Magician said as he stood up and stretched. Then he slowly looked around the room as if he hadn't seen it for a long time. "This place is a mess," he declared, shaking his head as he walked across to the window, lifted the bottom of the wooden frame about six inches or so, and lit a cigarette.

I took another look around the room. Like the Magician said, it was messy, but it was a very familiar kind of messy. It reminded me of something. I looked over at Chloe and wondered if she was thinking the same thing.

It looked almost exactly like Baron's place the night before he died.

"If you know where to look," the Magician said, "there have always been bulletin and message boards where people gather and talk about the game." He exhaled a cloud of smoke and stared out at the city.

I looked over at Chloe, unsure if I should say something.

She shook her head.

Eventually, the Magician continued. "This particular bulletin board was very active in the midnineties. A lot of us came here to discuss developments with the game, but there was one participant in particular—somebody who went by the name Neuromancer—who always knew a lot more than the rest of us. He would only post sporadically, but it was always something helpful or insightful."

"Like what?" I asked.

"Well, for one thing, it was Neuromancer who suggested we consider the game outside of its existence in the form most of us refer to as the modern version—the version that began in 1959. He was convinced that the game had existed for much longer."

"How much longer?" Chloe asked.

"Perhaps as long as humanity, life, or the Earth itself. Neuromancer believed that Rabbits was extremely dangerous and powerful—that it was a game, but so much more. He hinted that there might be something . . . otherworldly connected to it."

I experienced a sudden chill. It was probably the fact that the Magician had recently opened a window. I crossed my arms to try to keep warm.

"I was very interested in what Neuromancer had to say," the Magician continued, "not only about the historical version of the game, but the danger surrounding the modern version as well. He came at everything from a new angle, told us he was searching for something 'behind the game,' something . . ." The Magician trailed off, seemingly lost in thought for a moment.

"Something otherworldly?" I suggested.

The Magician took a long drag from his cigarette and closed his eyes.

I didn't move. I didn't want to do anything to startle the Magician, to make him stop talking.

"Neuromancer believed," the Magician said, "that if you were willing to look hard enough, you'd eventually find direct connections between the game and significant world events: wars, market collapses, assassinations, mass suicides, and many other global occurrences."

He fell silent again, and this time, I felt like if we didn't keep the conversation moving, we were going to lose him.

"But couldn't connections to events on that scale just as easily fall into the world of conspiracy theorists and other nut jobs?" I asked.

"Maybe," he said as he extinguished his cigarette in a small glass jar.

"What happened to Neuromancer?" Chloe asked. She clearly wasn't ready to let this information session end either.

"One day, just as suddenly as he appeared, he stopped posting."

"When was this?" I asked.

"Sometime near the end of the eighth iteration of the game."

"Do you think this Neuromancer could have been Hazel?" I asked.

"I don't think so . . . but it's possible, I suppose."

We sat there in awkward silence for a moment before we were startled by a loud ringing. The old yellow analog phone on the Magician's desk rang once and then stopped.

The Magician ignored the phone and walked over to an old wooden filing cabinet that stood beside the door to the bathroom. He opened the bottom drawer and pulled out a gray metal box. He lifted the lid of the box, removed an ancient Motorola flip phone, and dialed a number.

I looked over at Chloe. She shrugged.

The Magician held the phone to his ear and listened. He didn't say a thing. After a minute or so, he hung up, put the phone back into the box, and slid it back into the drawer.

"The Jesselman suicide has everybody freaked out," he said, shaking his head.

"Who's everybody?" Chloe asked.

The Magician ignored her question. "Eleven has started, and something is wrong."

"What does that mean?" I asked.

"It means you have to stop," he said.

"Stop what?"

"Playing the game."

"But it just started," I said.

"A significant number of players are disappearing . . . and worse," the Magician said as he pressed his fingers against the bridge of his nose and closed his eyes.

"Who was that?" I asked.

"Hmmm?" the Magician replied.

"On the phone."

"A friend," he said.

The Magician clearly wasn't going to give us any more details.

"What about Neuromancer? Any idea who he is . . . or was?" I asked.

The Magician exhaled and pressed his fingers to his temples. "How the fuck do I know? It's the name of a William Gibson novel. Could be anybody."

"How does your friend on the phone know that players are disappearing, or whatever?" Chloe asked.

The Magician stood up and started digging through a mess of printed pages on his desk. Eventually he found what he was looking for and handed it to Chloe.

"That is a list of people who were playing the game and then went missing. I recognize most of the names on this list. These are experienced players. Very careful people."

"Are you sure they're actually missing?" Chloe asked.

"Are you sure you want to keep asking stupid fucking questions?" he spat, his voice loud and strained.

The Magician wasn't himself.

He'd always been quick to anger if you came at him with any theory or question that he deemed lazy or half-baked, and he could shut you down easily with a partially raised eyebrow or a well-placed sigh, but in all the years I'd known him, I'd never seen him like this. He'd never once raised his voice with Chloe.

"Here are some more from Germany and Canada," he said, lifting up another printed page.

"What do you think it means?" I asked.

"The game has become corrupt. These people are gone. And if you two keep playing, the same thing is going to happen to you."

He grabbed Chloe and me by our shoulders, held us together, and did his best to focus his wild, bloodshot eyes. "From now on, the game is off-limits. You understand?"

We nodded.

"I have to get back to work," he said, and with that, the Magician kicked us out of his office.

As I was closing his office door behind us, I heard him yell out: "I mean it. No playing the game!"

The Magician's warning was sobering. His had been by far the most knowledgeable and encouraging voice when it came to the game.

It was right after I'd met the Magician that my interest in Rabbits became a lifelong obsession.

From that point forward, I did almost nothing but try to uncover the strange anomalies, patterns, and connections that might lead me into the game. I had almost as much fun uncovering secret Rabbits chat groups filled with similarly obsessed people as I had trying to figure out how to play.

The entire experience felt like coming home.

I'd spend days combing through clues online, talking to other players, trying to find out information about the next iteration.

One day, shortly before the ninth iteration ended, I was out following a clue.

I'd uncovered an anomaly in a scanned photograph of the top *Billboard* hits from 1979 that I'd found online. A misprint in a certain artist's chart position led me to an independent art show in a gallery in San Francisco. At the gallery, I discovered something in one of the paintings that led me to a small theater in Portland, Oregon, where I met with a bunch of musicians who told me about a secret exclusive event—a performance that was being held at the home of the owner of a local boutique record label. There was supposed to be a clue of some kind hidden in the band's set list, something potentially relevant to winning the current iteration of the game.

It turned out there was no clue—at least nothing I was able to uncover at the time—but it was a really great show.

On the way back to my hotel, however, something strange happened.

The night was overcast and cool, the moon and stars hidden

somewhere deep behind the dark gray clouds that had been threatening rain all day. I'd been going over some recent clues in my mind, trying to find a connection between a Blue Oyster Cult album, a Kundera short story, and a gas plant in northern Russia.

As I walked through the quiet streets of an upscale residential neighborhood mulling all of this stuff over, I was struck by an overwhelming feeling that somebody was following me.

I spun around, but nobody was there.

I started walking a bit faster, but no matter how fast I walked, I could still feel somebody or something back there not only matching my speed, but accelerating. I turned around again.

Nothing.

As I continued to walk through that neighborhood, I could feel whatever it was behind me getting closer, slowly sucking the air and light out of the world as it moved.

I felt a sudden windless chill and turned around again.

This time I saw something—or rather, a lack of something.

There was a kind of darkness hanging way up in the sky—a pool of thick inky murk, blacker than the rest of the night—and it was moving toward me, slowly sinking into the world from somewhere else. I could feel its hunger. Not only did I understand that this thing was invading our physical world from someplace far away, I knew that it was coming for me specifically.

I doubled my speed in an effort to get farther away from it, even as I told myself there was no way that thing could be real. I was simply experiencing a mental break of some kind. I just needed to relax and let it pass.

But it didn't pass.

And at that point I felt something moving forward from within the swirling darkness like a wave. This wave was darker than everything around it—and I understood that, whatever this thing was, it was going to completely erase me from the world.

I felt the temperature drop again, and a dampness filled my nostrils. It smelled like moldy grass and sludge from the shore of a rotten lake.

I tried to run, but my feet were stuck.

As I stood there, a wet cold entered my body from somewhere deep beneath the ground and moved slowly up my legs, eventually clouding its way into my head. I tried to call out for help, but my mouth was suddenly filled with coarse black hair that tasted like the sour musk of an oily animal from the sea.

I tried everything to shake it off and get away, but I couldn't move. I was frozen in place as the darkness rose up into the night sky and poured forward to devour me completely.

Then I woke up.

I was incredibly hungover, with no memory of how I'd made it back to the hotel.

I suppose I probably should have have mentioned the fact that I'd consumed what one might call a shit ton of bathtub gin at the show, but what took place later wasn't related to alcohol. No way.

It had happened. It was real.

And it had happened before.

I'd experienced something similar when I played Connections with my parents, and again in the truck with Annie and Emily Connors.

The return of what I used to call the gray feeling felt not only familiar, but strangely inevitable. It was as if my body were saying: *Aha, you forgot this was something that happens to you, didn't you?*

Well, buckle up, fucker. It's back.

NOTES ON THE GAME:
MISSIVE BY HAZEL
(AUTHENTICATED BY BLOCKCHAIN)

A coincidence is defined as a remarkable concurrence of events or circumstances without apparent causal connection.

When you move through the game, you begin to notice things that people outside it would never notice—the title of the song playing on the radio is a combination of the name of the restaurant you're walking past followed by the name of the street you're walking on. Or maybe you receive two wrong number calls four minutes and forty-four seconds apart. And maybe those two numbers are identical except for the area code, or maybe the numbers are completely different but the two unrelated callers have the exact same name.

Carl Jung referred to meaningful coincidences as synchronicities.

What if I told you that just as I was typing those words, the song "Synchronicity II" by the Police started streaming from the speakers in the random restaurant I'd chosen to sit and drink coffee in while I composed this note?

Just because there is no apparent causal connection, doesn't mean a connection isn't there.

—HAZEL 8

17

IT SMELLS A LITTLE
BOOZY IN HERE

A MONTH OR SO AFTER Baron's death, Chloe and I got together to celebrate his birthday. The Magician had agreed to close for the day in Baron's memory, so I picked up some sandwiches, a case of beer, and a bottle of Baron's favorite Icelandic vodka and made my way over to the arcade, where Chloe and I had decided to spend the afternoon day-drinking and playing Baron's favorite games.

We were doing our best to follow the Magician's edict and avoid Rabbits.

It wasn't all that hard. Baron's death had left us both pretty shaken, and digging into the mystery surrounding the game didn't feel quite as important or exciting after losing our friend.

The Magician was supposed to meet us at the arcade for dinner, but he didn't show. Chloe was worried. She hadn't seen him since the night he'd demanded the two of us stop playing the game.

We played every single pinball machine in the arcade at least once, but reserved most of our time for videogames like Galaga, Gauntlet, Joust, and Wonder Boy. It was nice to relax and spend some quality game time together. No Minister Jesselman suicide. No impossible attacks on famous actors.

And no Rabbits.

Halfway through the bottle of vodka, about an hour after we'd polished off a large pizza, we heard banging coming from the front door of the arcade.

"What time is it?" Chloe asked.

"Almost midnight."

"We're closed," Chloe yelled in the direction of the door.

Immediately, the banging became louder and more insistent.

"What the fuck?" Chloe said. "I'm close to my high score."

Chloe was in the middle of an intense game of Missile Command.

"I'll check it out," I said.

As I turned the corner, I could see that somebody was standing outside, but I couldn't see them clearly.

"I'm sorry, but the arcade is closed," I yelled.

"Please, I need to talk to you." It was a woman's voice. She sounded desperate.

I slowly approached the door and leaned forward to see who it was.

Fuck me.

I unlocked and opened the door, and a slender redheaded woman slipped out of the rain and into the arcade. She was wearing faded blue jeans, a light gray T-shirt, and a dark blue hoodie. She brushed aside a mop of wet hair and held out her hand.

"You don't know me, but my name is Sidney Farrow," she said.

"I know you," I replied. "I mean . . . I'm sorry, I'm K." I shook her hand.

"I wanted to stop by earlier," she said, "but things got a bit crazy at work."

"Oh . . . okay." I didn't know what to say. "So what's . . . going on?"

"I'd like to talk to you about Baron."

"Baron? What about him?" The vodka suddenly seemed to have left my system.

"Who the fuck is this?" Chloe threatened, suddenly beside me. The vodka clearly hadn't left *her* system.

"Chloe, this is Sidney Farrow."

Chloe leaned forward for a closer look. "Holy shit, it *is* you."

"She wants to talk about Baron."

"What? Why?"

Sidney Farrow looked down at the mostly empty bottle of vodka in Chloe's hand.

Chloe followed Sidney's eyes and then slowly extended the bottle.

Sidney took a sip of vodka, exhaled, and shook her head. "Have you guys ever heard of a game called Rabbits?"

I looked at Chloe.

Was this shit really happening?

Those of us who have spent countless hours playing her games know Sidney Farrow not only as the greatest architect of game-engine dynamics to ever work in the industry, but also as an extremely creative builder of characters and story. I've spent so much time living with her characters that I'll occasionally find myself remembering situations and conversations I've had while playing her games more vividly than events that took place in my real life.

Sidney Farrow was directly responsible for four of my top-five favorite gaming experiences of all time.

And she was standing right in front of me.

"Why are you asking about Rabbits? If you don't mind my . . . asking?" I felt like a complete idiot. I'd suddenly lost the ability to speak in coherent sentences.

"Something had been bothering me about the technology Wor-Games was using to playtest my newest game," Sidney said. "When I started asking questions, I felt like I was being handled."

"What do you mean?" I asked.

"As soon as I started poking around, I noticed that I was being watched, very carefully, by certain people in my department. So, I decided to try another approach. I asked somebody completely unconnected to look into it."

"Baron," I said.

Sidney nodded. "I work fairly closely with his friend Valentine. She told me Baron was a fan of my games."

"That's an understatement," I said. "We're all huge . . . fans."

"Thanks," she said. "I'm so sorry about what happened to your friend. He was cool."

"Thank you," I said. Chloe nodded and took a respectful sip of vodka.

"So," I said, "you're interested in Rabbits because of Baron?"

Sidney nodded and pointed at the vodka bottle. It was empty.

"Hey, you guys wanna grab a drink somewhere?"

I looked over at Chloe and then back to Sidney. We couldn't possibly let Sidney Farrow leave without telling us everything she knew about what had happened with Baron.

"We could go to K's place," Chloe said, pulling a wild tangle of keys from her pocket. "It's not far."

"Sounds good, but maybe I should drive," Sidney said. "It smells a little boozy in here."

"I hope you can drive a stick," Chloe said, tossing Sidney the keys.

"Of course," Sidney replied. "I'm not some kind of monster."

Back at my place, Chloe opened a bottle of wine and we sat down with Sidney Farrow.

"So, what can you tell us about what happened with Baron?" I asked.

Sidney explained that Baron's team had been playtesting her game using WorGames' proprietary high-tech cutting-edge system—something called the Byzantine Game Engine. She said they'd been running the game on the new platform for about a week when one of the women on the testing team was injured. Worried her game might be responsible in some way, Sidney confronted the executive in charge and demanded to know what happened. She was told that the woman, a game tester named Mary, had experienced a minor seizure, but that WorGames had been cleared of all liability due to the fact that the woman had some kind of preexisting condition.

Sidney pressed for more information, but they told her, now that this proprietary technology was in play, Sidney—unfortunately— no longer had sufficient security clearance to access anything connected to her game.

Sidney told them to fuck off, said they couldn't do that, then called her lawyer—who took a look over her contract and told her that, sadly, legally, they could.

Sidney had been completely shut out of her own creation.

"I started asking around," Sidney said, "and apparently, right after they'd started testing, some of the players began experiencing headaches, nausea, and intense vomiting."

"And you think their reactions may have had something to do with your game?" Chloe asked.

"I had no idea. Baron had been assigned the testing module right beside the woman who'd experienced the seizure, so I asked him what happened. He told me he'd heard banging coming from the pod next to his, and that he rushed in to discover a woman convulsing on the floor. He said he did his best to try to stop her from swallowing her tongue, and then the emergency medical staff intervened and took her away."

"Any idea what happened to her?" Chloe asked.

"They told me that she was fine, but when I looked into it later on, I discovered that she'd actually died in the hospital a couple of hours after they admitted her."

"Shit," I said.

Sidney nodded and then looked around, seemingly unsure if she should continue.

"What?" Chloe asked.

"Baron told me something else about that incident. He said he'd seen something on the woman's monitor, just before the paramedics arrived and security eventually escorted him out."

"What was it?" Chloe asked. "What did he see?"

"I don't know, but he told me that whatever he'd found reminded him of a game called Rabbits."

I felt a chill.

Sidney continued. "Almost immediately after I'd started asking questions, I was told that all testing connected to my new game was being moved to The Tower and that I would no longer have security access. That's when I asked Baron if he'd help me look into what was happening. He agreed, and promised he'd send me something as soon as he could. At this point he also mentioned you guys, and promised to introduce us."

"Did he find anything?" I asked.

"I don't know. I never heard from him again. I assumed he'd

changed his mind about helping me. But when I heard he'd . . . passed away, I checked his file. It turns out that Baron had been caught trying to access one of WorGames' behind-the-scenes servers and was sent home, suspended without pay."

"Shit," Chloe said.

"Less than a week later, he was . . . gone. I'm sorry."

I nodded. "Thanks."

"So," Sidney continued, "it looks like Baron may have been trying to help me after all. I felt terrible about what happened already, but if what happened to him was somehow my fault, I . . ."

"I'm sure it wasn't your fault," Chloe said.

I nodded in agreement. "Did Baron mention anything specific about what he saw on that woman's screen before she had that seizure?"

Sidney shook her head. "Just that whatever he'd seen reminded him of Rabbits."

I looked over at Chloe. I was pretty sure she was thinking exactly the same thing I was.

What the hell had Baron seen?

"Did he say anything to you guys about what he was doing . . . before he died?" Sidney asked.

We explained how we'd found Baron sitting in front of his computer watching that weird video, about his murder wall, and how we'd lost touch with him for a while shortly before that night.

"I think something is happening in The Tower," Sidney said. "Something fucked-up and dangerous."

"What's The Tower?" Chloe asked.

Sidney explained that The Tower was one of the newer buildings at WorGames. The Scandinavian construction team brought over exclusively to work on the building were flown back overseas the day they completed their work. The Tower was where WorGames kept everything connected to the Byzantine Game Engine.

"What's so special about this Byzantine thing that it needs its own building?" Chloe asked.

"It's what made me take the job," Sidney said. "The BGE produces virtual reality that looks, sounds, and feels exactly like real life. All that's missing is smell. I have no idea how it works, but it's amazing. Putting somebody's face on another person's body and using available online voice samples to create a deepfake version of a scene that never took place is one thing, but what the BGE technology is capable of doing is game-changing, literally. It's fucking breathtaking. When this goes mainstream, it's going to require regulations and oversight on par with complex genetic splicing and manipulation. The BGE will force governments to completely remodel digital ethics and corporations to revamp their intellectual property rules, and players will have to redefine what it means to play a game. It's also going to make WorGames a shitload of money."

"That sounds pretty . . . out there," Chloe said.

Sidney nodded. "Yeah, it's an ethical shitshow, but it's still really fucking awesome. It became Hawk Worricker's final project. He'd started working on the Byzantine Game Engine shortly before his death. He called it the most important thing he'd ever created."

"Really?"

"Yeah. Apparently he discovered the key to his new technology while combining quantum field theory with something called the Baader-Meinhof phenomenon."

"Is that confirmation bias or something?" I said.

"That's part of it, yes—although the term 'frequency illusion' is probably more accurate. It's about how something you've recently been told, experienced, or noticed suddenly crops up everywhere. What Baader-Meinhof suggests is that you're seeing this thing constantly because of selective attention in your brain."

"You're thinking about it, so you see it."

"Exactly."

"And what does that have to do with Byzantine?" I asked.

"I have no idea," Sidney said. "But apparently Worricker was also obsessed with advanced pattern recognition toward the end of his life. He thought everything was preordained—that certain patterns were everywhere, but we didn't notice them because we had no idea how to look for them."

"Sounds like he might have been losing it a little," Chloe said.

"Maybe," Sidney said as she refilled our wineglasses.

"So what's your new game about?" I asked. "Any reason to believe the content might be . . . dangerous somehow?"

Sidney shook her head. "I think it's a super-fun game, but it's not all that different from what I normally do. Character-first action, try to tell a cool story."

"Anything else you can tell us?" I asked.

"Sadly, the NDA I signed was insane. I think I may have given them permission to inject me with a microchip capable of recording anything and everything I say."

"Really?" Chloe asked, raising an eyebrow.

"Yeah," she said. "I can't share specifics. Sorry."

"I understand," I said—and it was true, but damn, I really wanted to hear about Sidney Farrow's new game.

"Did you and Baron talk about anything else?" I asked.

"He asked a lot of questions," she said, "but nothing stands out. Although . . . come to think of it, there was one thing he asked that did feel a little bit odd."

"What was it?" I asked.

"Baron asked if I knew Alan Scarpio, or if I was working with him on a game."

"And?" Chloe asked.

"I told him I didn't know Scarpio, not really. I met him once, at a Sundance party. We had a long talk about Richard Linklater movies. Alan told me *Before Sunset* was his favorite, and that he thought they'd eventually end up making a third film, but that was the entirety of our conversation. I told Baron I'd never seen Scarpio at WorGames—and, as far as I know, he wasn't working on anything for the company."

"*Before Sunset* is my favorite of the three Before films as well," I said.

"Three?" Sidney asked.

"Yeah," I said. "*Before Sunrise* and *Before Midnight*."

"*Before Midnight*." Sidney nodded. "That's the perfect title."

"Yeah, it is . . . but—"

"So," Chloe interrupted, "you don't know if Baron discovered anything while he was digging around your servers?"

Sidney shook her head. "No idea."

We sat there in silence for a moment before Sidney turned to face us. "Do you guys mind if I ask you a really serious fucking question?"

"Go ahead," I said.

"What the fuck *is* Rabbits, really?"

Chloe poured us all another glass of wine, and then we sat down and told Sidney Farrow everything we knew about the game.

After Chloe and I had answered Sidney's questions to the best of our abilities, our conversation moved away from Rabbits and Wor-Games into other areas.

Sidney told us how she'd grown up writing stories. *Dune* was her favorite novel. She told her parents and anyone who would listen that she was going to be the next Frank Herbert.

"I never share this with anybody," she said, "you know, outside of certain intimate moments where sharing is unavoidable." She unbuttoned her jeans and showed us a tattoo on the front of her right hip. It was a graphic of a tiny red hawk with its wings spread.

"Do you recognize it?" she asked.

Chloe and I shook our heads.

"It's the symbol of House Atreides, from *Dune*."

I thought I was a nerd, but Sidney Farrow had a tattoo of a fictional hero's family crest hidden on her body.

Sidney went on to explain how she'd given up writing prose fiction as soon as she met Nintendo's Zelda. From that point forward, all she did was write games.

The three of us compared notes on some of our favorite games and debated the merits and flaws of the movies and comic books that inspired us growing up.

It was amazing sitting across from Sidney Farrow talking about this stuff. I didn't want our conversation to end, but I was exhausted. I hadn't been sleeping very much lately, and had been drinking semi-heavily all day. I kept trying to fight it, but I eventually fell asleep sometime after Chloe opened the second bottle of wine.

When I awoke, it was just after ten o'clock in the morning and I'd somehow ended up in my bed. I did a hangover status check, mentally going over my body one muscle at a time. I was definitely dehydrated, and my stomach felt like a ball of loose wires, but it was nothing a fried egg sandwich and eleven cups of coffee couldn't handle.

I walked out into the living room. Chloe was asleep on the couch, and Sidney was sitting at my dining room table putting on her shoes.

"Hey," I said.

"Hey. Did you get some sleep?"

"I think maybe, but it doesn't really feel like it."

Sidney smiled. "I know what you mean."

Chloe sat up and rubbed her eyes. "What time is it?"

"Ten," I said.

"I'm off to work," Sidney said. "I'll see if I can dig up anything else about what Baron was into at WorGames."

"That would be amazing," I said. "And if there's anything we can do on this side, let us know."

"Will do."

Sidney left, and I took a seat next to Chloe on the couch. She stretched her arms up to the ceiling and we sat there in silence for a moment.

"We just had a sleepover with Sidney fucking Farrow," Chloe said, and the two of us started laughing.

"I'm glad Baron got to meet her," I said. "Before he . . . you know."

Chloe nodded.

Sometimes Baron could be a pain in the ass, but I really missed his boundless energy. It wasn't that he was especially optimistic or anything, but Baron Corduroy was an enthusiast. And Sidney Farrow's work had meant as much to Baron as it did to me.

I really wished he were still alive.

"Who's going to make coffee?" Chloe asked.

"Rock, paper, scissors?" I suggested.

"I'll do it," Chloe said, but she didn't move.

"Maybe we should go out? Eggs?"

"Eggs sound good."

"So good," I said.

"Do you really think Richard Linklater is going to do another *Before* movie?" Chloe asked.

"I hope so," I said. "But *Before Midnight* was a pretty perfect way to end the trilogy."

"Trilogy?" Chloe said. "Since when are two movies a trilogy?"

"Um . . . there are three movies, *Before Sunrise, Before Sunset,* and *Before Midnight.* You know this. I'm pretty sure we actually saw *Before Midnight* together at the Cinerama."

"What the fuck are you talking about, K?"

Chloe pulled out her phone and searched Richard Linklater's filmography to prove her point. *Before Midnight* wasn't listed. She showed me a list featuring a dozen websites. There was no mention of the third film in Richard Linklater's Before series.

"That has to be a mistake," I said, and searched the title myself.

There was nothing.

"What the hell is happening?" I said. I felt a lightness in my head and the room started to dim. I tried to stand, but I could feel the walls and ceiling closing in. I sat back down.

"Are you okay?" Chloe sounded worried.

"I don't know," I said. "I remember that film. This doesn't make any sense."

There was a knock at the door.

"Come in," Chloe and I yelled in unison.

"What did you forget?" Chloe added, as the person both of us expected would be Sidney Farrow entered my living room.

"It looks like somebody forgot to lock the door," said a voice that sounded nothing like Sidney Farrow's.

We spun around to see who'd spoken.

It was the mystery woman I'd met at the diner, the woman who claimed she worked for Alan Scarpio.

"I hope we're not interrupting?" she added.

"We?" I asked, just as two women in their late twenties or early thirties trailed her into the room. They were identical twins, dressed in matching black leather jackets, white T-shirts with dark red stars in the center, denim shorts, and black motorcycle boots. They had cropped bleached-blond hair, wide green eyes, and matching tattoos of two machine guns crossed in the shape of a long X on their right thighs. There was no difference in their hair, expressions, and movements, and—outside of the matching tattoos—there wasn't a single visible beauty mark or scar visible on either one of them.

They were absolutely alike. Perfect copies.

The missing Richard Linklater film was suddenly the furthest thing from my mind.

"Have you spoken with Alan Scarpio?" I asked.

The woman ignored my question and began exploring the room. "Who's your girlfriend?" she asked, as she ran her finger along a row of books on one of my three floor-to-ceiling bookshelves.

"I'm Chloe," Chloe replied. "Who the fuck are you?"

Although we were confronted by all kinds of threatening weirdness, I couldn't help but smile a little when Chloe didn't flinch at this strange woman referring to her as my girlfriend.

The mystery woman smiled. "I'm a brand-new friend. You can call me Swan, if you like."

"Okay, Swan, what's with the suicide girls over there?" Chloe nodded toward the twins leaning against the wall near the kitchen. They looked alert, but there was an air of boredom as well, as if they'd seen this conversation play out a million times before.

"They're with me," Swan said. Clearly that was all we were going to get by way of explanation.

"Scarpio?" I asked again.

"I haven't heard from Alan," she said as she went through a stack of vinyl sitting next to my turntable. "But we do need to find out what happened to him. It's important."

"We?" I asked.

"Yes," she said. "You and me." She slipped Bob Dylan's *Bringing It All Back Home* back where she'd found it and sat down between

Chloe and me on the couch. "I need you to tell me what you found on his phone."

"We didn't find anything," Chloe said—probably a bit too quickly.

"Is that right?" Swan asked, as she picked up my Patti (from *The Leftovers*) Funko toy from the coffee table and looked it over. "Which one of you has Scarpio's phone?"

I looked at Chloe, then back over at Swan. I was torn. Part of me wanted to tell her about the rhubarb, the weird video, Tabitha Henry, and Jeff Goldblum, but there was another part of me—the suspicious part currently watching the two oddly dangerous-looking identical twins leaning against the wall outside my kitchen—that won out.

I handed Swan Scarpio's phone, but didn't tell her anything. I was pretty sure they'd eventually find the video, but, whoever Swan was, I didn't think she was police, which meant we didn't legally have to give her anything.

"Thank you," Swan said as she stood up and tossed the phone to one of the twins. Then she just stood there, staring at me for a long time before finally shaking her head and smiling.

"What?" I asked.

"Are you two playing the game?"

Chloe and I did our best to keep our expressions neutral.

"Well then," Swan said, "you'd better hurry."

"Why is that?" I asked.

"Because you're running out of time." Swan followed the twins out into the hallway and shut the door behind her.

As soon as I heard the door click into place, I ran over and locked it.

I turned around to find Chloe standing in the hallway behind me.

"What the fuck, K?" Chloe asked.

"Yeah." What the fuck was right.

Chloe pulled out her phone. "Come on, come on," she said, urging whatever app she had activated to hurry up and load as she sat down and started putting on her shoes.

"What are you doing?"

She looked up with a grin. "Putting on my shoes."

"I can see that, but why? Where are you going?"

"*We* are going to follow them."

"They could be anywhere by now."

"They're right here," she said, and held up her phone to reveal a blinking green dot on a map.

"You're *tracking* them?"

"Yep."

"How?"

"We're living in the twenty-first century, K. It's a free tracking app. I connected Scarpio's phone."

She finished putting on her shoes, grabbed her coat, and stepped out of my apartment. I heard her yell out "You drive" as she hurried down the hallway toward the elevator.

I grabbed my coat and followed her, even though I was pretty sure the whole thing was a terrible idea.

18

NOW ONWARD GOES

WE FOLLOWED THE BLINKING GREEN DOT on the map as it moved away from my apartment in Capitol Hill and down toward the water. We had no idea what kind of vehicle they were driving, so I did my best to stay a couple of blocks behind the dot on the map as it blinked its way through the city.

They eventually stopped moving, right in the middle of a parking garage off Union Street.

I guided Chloe's car into in the parking garage and waited. It didn't take long before the dot started moving again, much slower this time.

They had to be on foot.

We parked the car and followed until the dot stopped again. It looked like they'd reached their location. They were somewhere inside the Seattle Art Museum.

On the weekend, clerks would be busily swiping credit cards and slipping purchases into shiny museum gift bags, but it was a Wednesday and the museum had only been open for about an hour, so things were fairly quiet.

"Where are they, exactly?" I asked as we moved slowly past the gift shop along a wide white concourse.

"There's a lot of concrete. Sketchy Wi-Fi. The app can't get properly connected."

"Well, it shouldn't be hard to pick out those weird Matrix twins."

"My thoughts exactly," Chloe said, and then the two of us began a methodical section-by-section sweep of the museum.

There was a lot of open space, so we were able to move through the building fairly quickly. There was no sign of Swan or the twins.

"We lost them," Chloe said, and sat down on a bench next to an exhibit guide.

"Yeah," I said, "but how? They have to be here. It doesn't make any sense."

I started looking over the exhibit guide, mentally checking off everything we'd seen, when I noticed something.

"*An Exploration of Heaven and Hell*?" I said. "I don't remember that one."

"We saw the sign upstairs. That display isn't open."

I smiled and shook my head. "Now onward goes," I said.

"What are you talking about?"

"It's something that Alan Scarpio said to me in the diner."

"What does it mean?"

"It says here that the *Exploration of Heaven and Hell* exhibit contains some parchments on loan from the Museum of Prints and Drawings in Berlin, and a handful of works from the Vatican library."

"Great. We'll have to stop by when it's open."

"Some of the parchments are Sandro Botticelli drawings."

"And that's important because?"

"Because Sandro Botticelli was responsible for creating almost a hundred works of art on parchment related to Dante's *Inferno*."

"I'm afraid we're back to who gives a shit."

"The first three words of the tenth canto of Dante's *Inferno* are 'Now onward goes.'"

"Fuck," Chloe said. "Way to bury the lede." She jumped up, grabbed my hand, and yanked me back toward the escalators.

As we carefully approached the cordoned-off area that contained the *Exploration of Heaven and Hell* exhibit, we noticed a number of small No Entry signs on stands set up around the perimeter. About five feet or so behind the signs, two extremely wide pieces of thick, dark gray canvas about the size of theatrical stage curtains hung from the ceiling like the wings of a giant moth.

Chloe pulled the closest piece of canvas aside and peeked into the exhibit area.

"Yahtzee," she said.

"What are they doing?" I whispered.

"It looks like they're taking pictures."

"Of what?"

"Of everything."

"What's in there?"

"I don't know. Museum shit," she said.

"What kind of—"

Chloe yanked her head back. "They're coming out." She grabbed my hand and dragged me around the corner and into the bathroom.

We waited in the bathroom for five minutes or so, and then we carefully and quietly made our way back to the exhibit area that had been roped off.

We took another peek inside.

Swan and the twins were nowhere to be seen.

We stepped carefully through the canvas curtains and entered the exhibit area. The main portion of the exhibit was held within an enormous glass case that covered the entire back wall of the room. Arranged behind the thick glass were works of art in a wide variety of media, including a tapestry called *Glimpsing Hell* from the Vank Cathedral in Iran that depicted, among other things, a circle of demons beheading a copulating couple; a brief but terrifying poem by a Japanese writer called "Yushimo's Hell"; and, sitting on a vintage turntable just below eye level, a copy of *Heaven and Hell,* the ninth studio album by Black Sabbath. Everything on display appeared to be related in some way to the concept of heaven and hell.

I started taking pictures immediately. If museum workers discovered what we were doing and kicked us out, I wanted to have as many images as possible of whatever Swan and those twins had been looking at.

The whole experience—following them here from my place,

hiding in the bathroom, taking pictures of an exhibit that wasn't yet open to the public—was both scary and exhilarating. This feeling was exactly what I'd been after when I picked up my first set of Dungeons & Dragons dice as a kid, and what I'd felt years later, when I'd heard Emily Connors mention the name Rabbits in connection with a mysterious real-world game.

This kind of intrigue and adventure was everything.

The summer before my parents died, and two months before our world would be changed forever by September 11, I climbed up onto the roof of our high school for the first time.

It's amazing how many ways you can find to reach the top of something if you're firmly committed. I chose a wide rusted metal drainpipe and a window ledge, but there were at least five other ways I could have made it up onto that roof.

I stood up there for a long time, staring out at the lights of the city.

The world felt smaller from that vantage point, and much easier to understand. Life was messy and complicated when you were in the middle of it, while it was rushing toward you from all angles, close-up and in full color. Up there on that roof, I felt like I could breathe a little better, zoom out just enough to feel myself situated in the cosmos. From up there I could make out the gridlike arrangement of the houses, streets, and lights and listen to the calming symphony of mundane sounds rising up from the neighborhood. Staring out at the shapes and patterns that made up the city, I felt like I was a bit more in control of my environment.

That summer I began climbing onto all kinds of roofs: houses, apartment buildings, a shopping mall, and countless others. I found looking out at the world from a higher vantage point meditative. It calmed me down, made it easier to think.

One night, while I was up on the roof of my high school, I discovered a hatch. It was clearly supposed to be locked, but the worn old padlock was just looped over its housing, unsecured. Whoever used it probably got tired of locking and unlocking it whenever they needed access.

I opened the hatch and found myself looking down a set of gun-metal gray stairs that led to part of the school I didn't recognize.

I knew that it was wrong, but I didn't hesitate for more than a second or two before I climbed down and entered the forbidden world.

And I was suddenly somewhere else.

It felt like magic.

Walking through the halls of school after hours was like descending into a shadow version of my own world. In this new place, things existed in a different state of being. It was as if everything was suspended there somehow, inactive until the bells rang at the start of September.

Wandering those halls at night alone in a place I wasn't supposed to be felt special, and dangerous—which was exactly the way I felt as Chloe and I slipped between those huge sheets of canvas and rushed across that room to examine the exhibition called *An Exploration of Heaven and Hell*.

There had to be a specific reason Swan and the twins had visited this exhibit, maybe the same reason Alan Scarpio had quoted Dante to me in the diner.

There had to be something connected to the game.

As we explored the myriad works of art that made up that exhibit, we saw terrifying things, including some images by Gustave Doré and a number of truly bizarre religious sculptures and drawings, but one piece grabbed our attention immediately, an oil painting by an unknown artist.

It was harrowing.

Near the bottom of the canvas, hundreds of small figures poured from burning cracks in the earth in tiny rows as a dozen or so grotesque demons with animal heads stood poised to yank them up and consume them. There was one demon, much larger than the rest, towering over the proceedings like a twisted puppet master, its mouth wide and bloody, waiting to devour its next victims.

That demon had the head of a large hare.

Printed on the image, beginning directly beneath the bloody mouth of the enormous hare-headed demon, was the opening of the tenth canto of Dante's *Inferno,* which began with the three words Alan Scarpio had said to me in the diner: *Now onward goes.*

Right at that moment, similar to what had happened to me in that high school when I was a kid exploring someplace I didn't belong, the museum's security personnel arrived and kicked us out.

"What do you think?" Chloe asked.

We were back at my place. Chloe was staring over my shoulder as I examined one of the photographs I'd taken of the giant demon rabbit painting.

"I think these might be significant," I said, pointing to a group of tiny Roman numerals on some rocks near the bottom of the painting. There were four numbers in total.

Chloe leaned forward. "Why are there tiny numbers in that painting?"

"Not sure," I said, "but there are four more numbers on the hands of these demons."

"Holy shit," Chloe said, leaning in. "You're right."

Those numbers were also incredibly small, but they were there.

I booted up my laptop and pulled up a Web page featuring Dante's *Inferno.* Chloe helped me count the stanzas and compare them to the numbers.

It took us a few tries to match everything up, but a few minutes later, we found it.

The Roman numerals on the rocks gave us the lines, and the numbers on the demon's hands gave us the words. Those clues led us to the following from the tenth canto:

7 (the) 108 (portal) 81 (is) 93 (open)

"The door is open," Chloe said. "We already know that, though, right?"

"Yeah," I said. "There has to be something else."

The two of us spent the next couple of hours staring at the photos we'd taken in the museum and trying to figure out our next steps.

"There's nothing else here," Chloe said, rubbing her eyes.

"There has to be," I said, pointing to a section of the painting that featured a whole bunch of people, some of them almost microscopic, spilling out of a large crack in the earth. "Maybe it has something to do with the number of figures."

I counted the figures in every single row until I came up with the same number three times. I made a note of the resulting digits and handed it to Chloe. She grabbed my laptop and I read the numbers while Chloe typed.

We put those numbers through every kind of alphanumeric code and puzzle algorithm we could find, but nothing came up.

Then, as I was reorganizing the photos we'd taken on my desktop, I noticed something.

"Holy shit," I said.

"What?" Chloe leaned forward to check out my screen.

"Look at this." I grabbed four photographs of etchings from various parts of the exhibit and pulled them together to form one square image.

"What is it?" Chloe asked. "It's geometrically pretty but it's just—"

Then she saw it.

"That's impossible," she said.

But it wasn't impossible. It was right in front of us.

Those four separate illustrations, created by Gustave Doré in the mid-1860s, when combined into a square, formed a perfect QR code—technology that wouldn't be created until 1994.

Chloe pulled up a QR code reader on her phone and took a picture. The resulting URL brought us to a Web page.

"Shit," Chloe said as she flipped her laptop around to show me her screen.

Below the image of a spinning ball were the words "404 error. Page not found."

"Defunct link," I said.

Chloe slowly closed her screen.

"What are you doing?" I said. "We need to keep digging."

"Maybe," Chloe said, "but first we need to figure out what's going on with you."

"What are you talking about?"

"I'm talking about you missing six hours of your life, forgetting we go to The Kingfish Cafe all the time, and remembering Richard Linklater movies that don't exist."

"I know how it sounds." I exhaled.

I was just about to tell Chloe that I must have misremembered that movie and the rest of it, and that this wasn't really a big deal, but I couldn't lie to her. "Okay," I said, "please try to keep an open mind."

Chloe nodded.

"I remember everything about that movie," I said. "It exists—or existed—and The Kingfish Cafe *was* closed permanently more than five years ago. I understand that, for you, *Before Midnight* was never made or released and The Kingfish Cafe is open for business as usual, but—and this is going to sound crazy—I think that, not that long ago, things may have existed in a . . . different state, for both of us."

"You're kind of freaking me out right now, K."

"I understand, believe me. I'm more than a little freaked out myself."

"A different state? What the hell does that mean?"

"I'm not sure quite yet. All I'm asking is that you give me a bit of time to figure it out. Just don't . . . lose faith."

Chloe stared at me for a moment, and then she grabbed my hand.

"I'm not going to lose faith, I promise, but you have to tell me if anything else . . ."

"Out of the ordinary?" I suggested.

"Fucked-up beyond imagining happens," Chloe finished.

"I promise I'll let you know," I said.

"You'd better," she said as she packed up her laptop. "I'm going to work, but if you find anything else like that weird demon rabbit QR code bullshit, you call me right away."

I nodded.

"We're going to figure this shit out, K."

"Are we?"

"You're goddamn right we are."

19

FOURS

I WALKED DOWN THE STREET toward the arcade, a thin hooded sweatshirt my only protection against the pouring rain. I could feel the tiny rocks and pebbles on the wet asphalt through the thin soles of my favorite brown leather boots as I ignored the Don't Walk sign and jogged across the street.

I was about half a block away from the arcade when I felt the familiar sensation.

It began, like it always did, with a deep tingling in the pit of my stomach—a deep tingling would soon turn into a fuzzy thick vibration. And then the worst of it would begin.

Fuck. It was happening again.

I lunged for a nearby lamppost in an attempt to avoid what I knew was going to happen next. What happened next was the end of the world.

Gravity was the first thing that went.

Everything that wasn't tied down left the surface of the Earth at once and began moving slowly upward. The screaming and crying of people and animals was deafening as we all began our inevitable ascent toward oblivion.

It must have been a comet or asteroid strike of some kind that had knocked our planet out of orbit, or perhaps our galaxy had bumped into another larger system out in space. Whatever had happened, one thing was perfectly clear: Everything was over, and all that was left was the dying.

No matter what we're doing—sitting still on our couches or lying in our beds—every single one of us is moving through the universe at somewhere around 1.3 million miles per hour. We have no idea just how terrifyingly exposed we are—tiny things on a tiny world stuck inside a relatively small galaxy whipping through deep space at an alarming rate of speed. Anything apocalyptic could happen at any time.

And now it finally had.

My fingers missed the lamppost I'd lunged for by inches, and I continued my ascent up into a cool, seemingly endless blue that would eventually become a thick, infinite, inky black.

Just as I left the atmosphere and entered the darkness that marked the edge of deep space, I spotted the tower, soaring up from below.

Babel. Babylon. Ziggurat.

These were the names that popped into my mind when I first saw it, rising up from the blue-green surface of the Earth into the cool black nothingness of space.

I wondered why we couldn't see this thing from Earth. How had we never discovered it? I tried to see the bottom, to figure out its geographic location, but I wasn't able to see enough of the Earth's surface to place the tower among the familiar shapes of the continents.

As I continued speeding upward I wondered what it was going to feel like to inhale the empty vacuum of space. Then, as if on cue, everything dimmed and I began drifting away from consciousness. At that moment, my outstretched hand brushed against the wall of the monolithic thing, and some kind of panel or door opened.

In that split second, just before I'd completely moved past the tower and into the permanent darkness, I was somehow able to grab on to the edge of the doorway and pull myself into the enormous black structure.

Once inside, the door slid shut behind me, and I found myself standing in what appeared to be an elevator made out of the same material as the exterior surface.

The elevator was completely empty except for a symbol set into the wall at eye level: a small circle balanced on the tip of a triangle.

It reminded me of a keyhole someone might peep through in an old movie. There was a soft white glow emanating from the circle.

It was a button.

I had no idea if it would take me up or down. I pressed it, and after a moment, the elevator began ascending.

I'd been going up for what felt like a minute or so when the light coming from the circle began to change color, slowly morphing from a soft white to a bright red. At that point, the elevator sped up and began shaking violently, then we changed direction with a force-ful lurch and I was thrown to the ground.

I was now moving horizontally, pinned to the side wall as the elevator continued to accelerate.

After what felt like an eternity, the elevator eventually slowed down, finally coming to a complete stop.

I stood up, leaned against the side to catch my breath, and waited for the doors to open.

Then, without warning, the elevator was descending.

It felt like a controlled descent at first, but the elevator began gathering more and more speed, finally accelerating into a terrify-ing, high-powered thrust toward oblivion. I was slammed into the ceiling, a sharp pain radiating from my neck and back, and still the elevator's speed continued to increase.

Looking down at the smooth black floor as I sped toward extinc-tion, I thought about my parents in that capsized ferry.

I always imagined them together at the end, holding hands, float-ing in the ferry's dining area, breathing their last breaths from that final inch of air along what would have been the floor of the boat. I pictured them staring up at the tiles of that floor, at the scuff marks made by hundreds of people's shoes as those people had waited im-patiently in line to get food or maybe buy a magazine. What would my parents have given in that moment to have been stuck in traffic, or in a long supermarket line behind some asshole trying to use ex-pired coupons again?

Then suddenly I was sitting with Annie and Emily Connors, back in that truck on that lonely country road, the fuzzy static of the radio the only sound.

I opened my mouth to warn Emily about what was going to happen, but before I could speak, the world ended in an explosion of wild light, heat, and rumble.

I woke up covered in sweat, with no air in my lungs.

I'd forgotten how to breathe.

It was like that feeling you get when your mind tricks you into believing you've momentarily forgotten how to swallow.

I jumped up and smashed my knee against the glass corner of my coffee table as I rushed through my living room. The sharp sudden pain in my knee forced an involuntary scream from my lips, and my lungs were suddenly working again.

I yanked open the sliding door and stepped out onto the balcony, filling my chest with crisp rainy air in enormous panicked gulps.

The cool bracing wind and wet concrete beneath my feet slowly brought me back to reality.

Of course it had been a dream—a recurring dream I'd been having, off and on, for as long as I could remember.

Aside from the beginning of the dream, which was always slightly different, once the world lost all gravity and I began to float it was the same: outer space, the black monolith, the elevator, everything.

I looked into the kitchen at the clock on my microwave. It read 4:44 A.M.

There's a theory among those of us interested in (read: obsessed with) the game of Rabbits—something we call *fours*.

The theory goes like this: Rabbits players, and perhaps also would-be Rabbits players, notice one specific time on the clock, 4:44 (afternoon and/or morning), more often than people not connected to or interested in the game. This has to be complete nonsense, of course—an example of nothing more than confirmation bias—but I do notice that specific time constantly, and can't help but think of Rabbits whenever it happens.

The first thing I did after I noticed the time was compose a text to Baron. Whenever one of us sees that specific time on a clock, we text each other: 444.

Once the fog left my brain, and I remembered that Baron was gone, I deleted the text message and crawled back under the covers.

I missed my friend.

After a few minutes of tossing and turning, I realized I wasn't going to be able to get back to sleep, so I got up to make coffee, and then started looking into Minister Jesselman's suicide.

The incident had taken place on the Cardiff University campus in Wales. Nobody interviewed could agree about what Jesselman had meant by "the door is open"—although most people believed it was related either to his open-border immigration policy (his campaign had used the phrase in their election materials a couple of years back) or to a personal scandal he'd been involved in featuring some kind of English sex cult.

Outside of The Phrase, there was nothing that appeared to connect the incident to Rabbits—but it had to be connected. There was no way our discovering that video was a coincidence.

I closed my laptop and started digging around to see what I might make for breakfast. I had my choice of expired watery yogurt, questionable homemade granola with way too many raisins, or bananas, some too green, the others too black. While I was trying to decide, Chloe called and told me to meet her at a restaurant downtown for brunch. I told her I'd be right there.

"I found something this morning," Chloe said in between bites of overcooked home fries and undercooked pancakes.

The restaurant was an old pub that served greasy spoon–style food during the day. Chloe and I had been there a few times before. The dark wooden walls and sticky floors always made me nostalgic for college. Outside of the eggs Benedict, the food was uniformly terrible. I always had one of their Benedicts, but Chloe clung to the futile hope that she'd eventually find something else on the menu that might pass as edible.

The place was almost completely empty. Most of the morning regulars had already passed through on their way to work.

"What is it?" I asked.

"Remember when the Magician handed me those pages with the names of players who'd died or went missing?"

"Yeah."

"Well, I remembered seeing one of those names in a couple of Rabbits forums recently, so I looked her up."

"And?"

"She was a player from Cameroon who died under mysterious circumstances, bitten by a spider that wasn't indigenous to the area. Her best friend was raising hell about how something was fishy, and then one day, she just disappeared."

"That's weird," I said, "but it might just be coincidence."

"It's not good, K. Girl dies, friend goes missing. Shit like this is happening all over the world."

I grabbed my coffee and moved over to Chloe's side of the booth. "You sure?"

Chloe nodded.

"How?"

"A couple of legit Rabbits obsessives I know run a popular dark-net forum called TuringLeft."

"Isn't that site in Spanish?"

"Yeah, they're based in Madrid. My friend helps moderate. I asked her if she'd heard anything about people connected to Rabbits going missing and maybe even dying. She told me that players are worried something's wrong with the game. This morning, when I logged in, there was a message splashed across the front page of that forum in ten languages."

"What message?"

"This one," she said as she pulled up a screen capture on her computer. Sprawled across the forum's home page in a bright red spray paint font was a message that read:

STOP. PLAYING.

"Shit," I said.

Chloe closed her computer and took a sip of my coffee (she'd finished hers a while ago).

"This is it, isn't it?" I said.

"What do you mean?"

"What Scarpio warned me about. He said if we don't fix the game before it starts, we're all truly fucked. What if this is just the beginning of us getting well and truly fucked?"

"Maybe," Chloe said.

She sat there thinking for a moment.

"But . . . what if this is all part of it?" she asked.

"What do you mean?"

"I mean, false corruption of the game, people disappearing. That doesn't feel out of line with Rabbits, does it?"

"Maybe not . . . but this stuff still feels different."

"Well, didn't you say different iterations of the game had different . . . vibes or something?"

"I said that?"

"During one of your sessions, you explained how each version of the game teaches you how to play it as you're playing, like the novel *Gravity's Rainbow* teaches you how to read it *as* you're reading. You went on to use Pynchon's novels to describe some clue from the sixth iteration of the game."

This was starting to sound familiar. Maybe Chloe really had been paying attention during my information sessions.

"Jesus, I sound pretentious. I haven't even read *Gravity's Rainbow*."

"For real?"

"I've tried a bunch of times. I'm saving it for the old-age home, along with Proust."

"Sometimes you are so fucking on the nose," Chloe said.

I smiled. She had me there.

"Still, I'm worried about the Magician," Chloe said. "I haven't seen him since he told us not to play the game."

"Isn't there anybody you can ask?"

Chloe shook her head.

"I'm sure he's fine," I said, doing my best to sound like I believed what I was saying. "He's probably just out shopping for a new Asteroids cabinet or something."

"Maybe." Chloe nodded, but she wasn't convinced.

I took a sip of coffee and looked out the window. Something had caught my eye—something was off—but I couldn't figure out what it was.

"Next time I see him, I'm going to tag him with a fucking tracking device."

"Good idea," I said, and laughed.

As I was laughing, I noticed the sky darken, and felt a familiar buzzing up through the lower half of my body.

I realized what had been bothering me.

In the distance, visible across the street and towering over a section of Seattle I knew like the back of my hand, was an enormous green glass skyscraper I'd never seen before in my life.

Seattle is in a perpetual state of construction, but even though the skyline is a forest of cranes atop buildings in various stages of completion, there was no way I could have missed this thing. It was huge.

"What is it?" Chloe asked.

"Nothing," I said. "Where the hell is our server with the check?"

I was startled awake by my phone. I must have fallen asleep sometime after I got home from the restaurant. I stumbled around in the dark trying to track down the source of the blaring Pink Floyd song I'd chosen as my ringtone.

"Hello?"

"What the fuck, K?"

It was Chloe.

"What the fuck what?"

"You forgot."

"Forgot what?"

"What do you think?"

"This conversation is starting to feel like a test I'm failing. What's going on?"

"Your horde of misfits is here at the arcade waiting for you."

"Shit," I said, jumping out of bed, "I'll be right over."

"Hurry up," she said. "These animals are getting unruly."

20

AN ASSHOLE IN A JOURNEY T-SHIRT

"WHAT DO YOU KNOW about the game?" I asked as I leaned back against a racing game by Namco (via Atari) called Pole Position, and crossed my arms.

The group was mostly composed of the usual suspects, but there were a dozen or so new faces, which was always nice to see.

"It's a dangerous thing. They sweep this shit under the fucking rug, man, but the government knows everything." It was a thin man in his early thirties who'd spoken. He'd grown a spotty orange goatee since I'd seen him last.

"There are rumors about deaths connected to the game, yes," I said. "Anybody else?"

"It's been going on for centuries." It was Sally Berkman, our resident Advanced Dungeons & Dragons librarian. She'd been here last time, along with Orange Goatee.

"There are many who believe that's possible," I said.

"What do you believe?" Sally asked.

"I think it's probably true. There's a consensus that the modern game began in 1959, but there's growing evidence that Rabbits itself might be much older, going back centuries, millennia—or perhaps even longer."

It felt good to have something familiar to focus on in light of recent events. Standing in the arcade surrounded by the sights and sounds of the old machines made me feel better—not back to normal by any stretch, but as close to it as I'd felt for quite some time.

"What I don't understand, is . . . what makes you an expert?" A young man in a Journey T-shirt had spoken. He looked to be in his early twenties. I'd never seen him here before.

It was nice when the new blood was engaged this early, but I had the feeling this guy was going to be a problem.

"That's a great question," I said, "but it's a question with a very complicated answer. Phones and other electronics into the box, please," I said as I opened the large cedar chest with the graphic of the weird hunting scene stamped onto the top of it.

Once everybody had relinquished their devices, I closed the chest, placed my hands on top of it, and leaned forward dramatically.

"This is a game unlike any other," I said, then stepped out from behind the chest and began to pace around the room.

"What does it mean to play a game? Is it possible to play without knowing all the rules? Is it possible to play and not even know you're playing, to be unaware of the potential danger you're facing?" I let that last sentence hang in the air for a moment before I walked over and put my hands on two game cabinets sitting next to each other: Space Ace and Donkey Kong Jr.

"Can anybody tell me the primary difference between these two games?" I said as I slipped a quarter into Space Ace and pressed the Player One Start button.

"One's a cartoon, obviously," said Orange Goatee, which resulted in a smattering of laughter.

"Yes, one is a cartoon, and that is important." I let that linger, momentarily forgetting Baron wasn't there. He'd been my plant for so long that I'd become accustomed to him stepping in to add flavor and drama when required.

"It's a closed system, LaserDisc," Chloe called out from somewhere near the back of the room.

"That's right," I said as I started playing the game. "Although Donkey Kong Jr.'s narrative is certainly not unlimited," I continued, "there are far more potential outcomes and variables in that game compared to Don Bluth's LaserDisc classic."

I stepped away from the Space Ace machine and allowed the first of my lives to expire.

I could feel the unease from everybody assembled. I was standing in an arcade full of gamers. Watching a character die on the screen when you could simply run up and start playing was maddening.

It was hard for me too—and I was the one responsible for it.

"In Space Ace, everything is binary," I continued. "Each series of moves you make has only two possible outcomes: You make the correct moves in the correct order and you continue; you get it wrong, you die."

I let that hang there ominously as I let my second life expire on-screen.

"These days, we have vast open-world narrative experiences, games that don't follow prescribed quests or storylines, seemingly endless virtual lands and expansive storyworlds that we can move through and explore for months without experiencing the same encounter twice. But what if there was something bigger? What if there was an open-world experience so enormous and complex that its canvas for gameplay was the world itself? Perhaps even the entire universe?"

On the Space Ace machine, just before I was about to surrender the last of my three lives, I took control of my onscreen character (Dexter, who prefers to be called Ace) and guided him through what was left of the game.

Once I'd completed Dexter's quest (defeat the villainous Commander Borf), a brief victory movie played and then the credits began to roll. "This," I said, timed perfectly with the reveal of the list of names on the screen, "is The Circle, circa the seventh iteration of the game."

Everybody gathered around the machine for a closer look.

It was at this point that a couple of the newer attendees asked for their phones back so they could take a picture. I told them they could play Space Ace and take as many photos as they liked, but they had to wait until after the session.

"You didn't answer my question," Journey T-shirt said, raising his voice above the din of 8-bit audio that made up the sonic back-drop of the arcade.

I knew this guy was trouble.

Every once in a while I'd get somebody like this, a YouTube comment section complaint in human form, whose only reason for coming was to stir shit up.

Normally I'd try to impress him with *The Prescott Competition Manifesto,* but I had the feeling if I didn't give this guy a little something extra, and soon, there was a risk he was going to get seriously unruly. With this kind of conspiracy-hungry crowd, one dissenting voice with imagination could result in an angry mob quicker than suggesting the Kennedy assassination wasn't anything other than one mentally damaged man in a tower.

"You're not really supposed to talk about Rabbits," I said, lowering my voice a little.

Everyone stopped talking at the word "Rabbits." I rarely referred to the game by its unofficial name during these sessions.

"Of course," I continued, "speaking about the game in general terms is widely accepted—necessary, even—to attract new blood, but talking about specifics is out of bounds. Today, however, we're going to shake things up a little."

They were all paying attention now—even Journey T-shirt.

"The very nature of the game is secrecy, and the complex series of rules uncertain, but you can discover a great deal if you know where to look. An unexplained hacking challenge appears on a website that previously didn't exist; a weird series of unnerving videos begins popping up on YouTube; the events of a short fictional horror story on Reddit are starting to come true in real life. Some or all of these things might be related to the game. How do we know? We don't. We can only draw connections and hope we're finding a way in."

I pulled out my phone and a small portable projector box I'd purchased online for fifteen bucks. I was on my way toward the back of the room to switch off the lights when the room went dark. Chloe had been here for my presentations many times in the past, but I had no idea she'd been paying attention. So far, she'd hit every one of

Baron's cues flawlessly. I wondered how she was feeling. Had she been looking around the room for Baron's stupid grin every ten minutes or so like me?

I dug through the images in my phone's photo library and eventually found what I was looking for. Then I slipped my phone into the projector box, adjusted a small black slider, and two images of a painting appeared in sharp focus, side by side, on the back wall of the arcade.

"This is a well-known painting called *Christina's World* by Andrew Wyeth," I said. "I've seen the original hanging in the Museum of Modern Art in New York. It's beautiful—one of my favorite works of art on Earth."

There were mumbles of recognition.

"If you look carefully at these images, however, you'll notice a slight discrepancy," I continued. "The image on the left features two windows in the farmhouse in the top-right corner, and the image on the right features three."

More murmurs from the group.

Half were most likely surprised and excited at the prospect of some unknown mystery I was about to unfurl, and the rest were probably murmuring in recognition because they'd heard rumors that some kind of puzzle or quest involving *Christina's World* had been part of the ninth iteration of the game.

"The farmhouse in what we consider the authentic, original version of *Christina's World* features two dormer windows, just like the photograph on the left. The version in the photograph on the right, with three windows, is incorrect, so it has to be a fake. There is one significant problem with that theory, however . . ."

I let that hang there dramatically for a moment.

"You see, the photograph on the right—the impossible photograph featuring three dormer windows in the farmhouse—was taken at the Museum of Modern Art in New York, sometime near the end of the ninth iteration of the game."

There was genuine excitement, even among the regulars. This was more concrete detail regarding actual gameplay than I'd ever given in the past.

"That's impossible," said Orange Goatee. "It has to be photoshopped."

"Maybe," I said. "But what if it wasn't?"

This felt like a moment when Baron might normally yell something out to add to the drama, but Chloe was silent.

I took a deep breath and continued. "What if a top secret organization had existed for millennia? And what if that organization had more resources than the Vatican and the U.S. government combined?" I didn't give anybody a chance to interrupt and answer my rhetorical question; I was on a roll. "And what if that organization was powerful enough to not only rent out the Museum of Modern Art, but also hire actors to fill the space for an entire day, create a fake version of *Christina's World,* and hang it in place of the original?"

"Sounds like something a wealthy and extremely resourceful person named James Moriarty might be able to pull off," Sally Berkman said.

"Exactly," I replied. Sally was, of course, referring to the "Moriarty Factor," a term Rabbits players used to describe some of the more elaborate and expensive scenes and situations attributed to whatever organization was behind the game. Secretly renting out MoMA and hiring a flood of actors to fill it up was just one of many rumored examples.

"This is all wonderful, but how do we know you've actually played the game?" Journey T-shirt asked.

"It sounds like you may have missed the 'you don't talk about Rabbits' part of the presentation," I said.

A few people laughed.

"If you really did play the game, prove it." Journey T-Shirt really wasn't going to stop.

There were a few murmurs from the group.

I started to speak, but a sudden sharp stab of static and pain took my breath away. My ears began ringing and my eyes began to blur. A warm tingly panic crawled up my body, and the room began to sway. I reached down and grabbed ahold of the desk to steady myself as I tried to calm my breathing. The tunnel vision would be next, and if that happened, there was no way I'd be able to continue.

I was really starting to hate this asshole and his Journey T-shirt.

"Is it true you have a copy of the *PCM*?" Chloe yelled out from somewhere in the back of the room.

"It's true," I said as I scrambled to dig my reel-to-reel recorder out of the old cedar chest. His disruptive spell clearly broken, Journey T-shirt shook his head and walked out of the arcade.

"How many of you are familiar with *The Prescott Competition Manifesto*?" I asked.

There were nods and words of recognition before I pressed play, and the familiar sound of Dr. Abigail Prescott's voice filled the arcade.

"You looked a little freaked out back there."

"I'm fine."

Chloe and I were sitting in the diner across from the arcade, in the same booth I'd sat in watching Alan Scarpio eat rhubarb pie.

"Really? You told them about *Christina's World*."

"I felt like I needed something to push them over the edge. Besides, Nine ended a long time ago."

"In 2017. Not that long ago, K."

"It's fine," I snapped. "Who fucking cares." I leaned back in my chair and crossed my arms.

I knew what Chloe was saying, and she was right; I should never have revealed game-specific details related to *Christina's World* in front of that group. There are certain things, like The Circle and *The Prescott Competition Manifesto,* that are generally considered acceptable topics of conversations among civilians (i.e., nonplayers). But to speak in detailed terms about part of a puzzle related to a recent iteration of the game? It wasn't something people seriously interested in Rabbits did. It was considered disrespectful—and out of bounds.

I unfolded my arms and put my head down on the table. "I don't know what got into me," I said. "I'm tired."

"I think you need to stop," Chloe said.

I looked up from the table.

Chloe was staring at me, and in the entire time I've known her, I don't remember ever seeing her this serious about anything.

"Stop what?"

"I'm not kidding, K. No more Rabbits."

Even though the Magician had demanded we stop playing, hearing Chloe say the same thing was sobering.

"You're really suggesting we give up now, when we've just started making some progress?"

"I'm worried about you."

"I'll be fine," I said. "No more talking about *Christina's World,* I promise."

"It's not just *Christina's World,* K. Baron's dead. Players are going missing. You're making up movies that don't exist, and you saw how the Magician looked the last time we saw him. Something bad is happening."

Chloe was right, of course. Baron was gone, and I'd been experiencing events that were . . . deeply out of the ordinary. Crazy shit was definitely happening, but I felt like that was precisely why we needed to keep going.

"Alan Scarpio told me something was wrong with the game," I said. "Now that the eleventh iteration has started, we need to figure out what he meant before it's too late."

"K . . ." Chloe said as she clasped her hands together on the table.

"What?"

"Don't freak out."

"Okay . . ."

"Promise?"

"I promise," I said.

"You know, you're the only person who saw Alan Scarpio."

"Yeah, so?"

"So . . . maybe it was like the Richard Linklater movie or The Kingfish Cafe."

"What are you saying, Chloe?"

But I knew exactly what she was saying.

"I'm worried you might be experiencing some kind of . . . relapse. I don't want to have to visit you in that section of the hospital again. I'm not going to let what happened to my sister happen to you."

I shook my head. "That's not going to happen."

She raised her eyebrows.

"I'm serious. No way. I'm fine."

"No, you're not fucking fine," Chloe said. "And if you don't respect me enough to be honest, then I'm out."

And with that, Chloe walked out and left me sitting alone in the diner.

21

TENSPEED AND BROWN SHOE

I NEEDED SOMETHING to take my mind off the game and the conversation I'd just had with Chloe at the diner, so I went back to my apartment and put on Jean-Michel Jarre's 1976 masterpiece *Oxygène*.

I listen to *Oxygène* often, not only because it's a perfect blend of some of my favorite analog synthesizers, but also because Jean-Michel Jarre recorded that album himself at home in a makeshift studio. I love early records by Todd Rundgren, Guided by Voices, and Lenny Kravitz for the same reason. There's just something about having the freedom to do whatever you want—combined with the reality of limited physical and financial resources—that allows for transcendent works of art.

But the music wasn't working.

I couldn't stop thinking about Chloe or Rabbits.

There was nothing I could do about Chloe at the moment, so I turned my attention to the game.

Everything had started with Alan Scarpio in that diner.

I opened my laptop and dug up the video we'd discovered on his phone.

What was I missing?

I ran through everything we'd found on Tabitha Henry and wondered if somewhere else in the city, Swan and her pet twins were doing the same thing.

After I'd rewatched the video three times, I fell down a social media clickhole that began with my looking into anybody connected to Tabitha, and ended with me checking out a series of photographs on a popular Jeff Goldblum fan page.

I was scrolling through pictures of Jeff Goldblum from some of my favorite movies, including *Nashville, The Fly, The Player,* and *The Big Chill* when I stumbled onto something new.

Someone had recently uploaded some behind-the-scenes photos from a 1980 TV show starring Goldblum called *Tenspeed and Brown Shoe.*

I'd seen clips of Jeff Goldblum in some older movies like *Death Wish* and *California Split,* but I'd never heard of *Tenspeed and Brown Shoe.*

After that series of photographs ended, I found myself clicking through another recently added group of pictures related to a disaster movie from a couple of years ago. That movie was better than it had any right to be, but it was all due to Jeff Goldblum. He played an eccentric geologist concerned with global warming. He stole every scene he was in.

I was two or three photos into this new series when I noticed a familiar face.

It was the blond publicity assistant from the Tabitha Henry video.

She was standing in the background of a photograph that had been taken on a red carpet somewhere in Italy. I wasn't surprised to see her—after all, the studio she worked for had made a bunch of films with Jeff Goldblum—but, because she was such a huge part of that disturbing video, I moved over to the studio's Facebook page and continued clicking through images.

I started by looking through the publicity photographs from their most recent movies, but I wasn't able to find the tall blond woman anywhere. Then, I went back and started looking through photographs taken the year after the Tabitha Henry incident.

I was clicking through the press tour photographs of a blockbuster comedy film that had premiered at the Toronto International Film Festival when I found her.

She was standing in the background of a few of the pictures featuring the female lead of that movie. I was about to shut down my computer and make something to eat when one of the photographs caught my eye.

It looked like this particular picture had been taken in some kind of on-set makeup trailer. The female lead of the movie, a well-known A-list actress, was leaning back in her chair. Her eyes were wide and she was clearly laughing about something. The blond assistant was leaning forward, facing the camera, her left arm resting on the actress's left shoulder, her right hand reaching down and grabbing the arm of the actress's chair. It was an energetic and beautifully candid moment caught on camera. The composition and the lighting were perfect; so perfect, in fact, that it took me a second to notice something was off.

On the blond publicity woman's right arm, just above the wrist, was a long, thick scar, in the exact place she'd been cut in that Tabitha Henry video.

I called Chloe, and immediately hung up when I noticed the time.

It was the middle of the night.

I went back to searching.

It took me a few minutes to dig up the blond publicity woman's name. Some additional photographs led to a few leads on social media, and a comment posted by one of her online friends eventually led me to a LinkedIn profile.

The scar woman was Silvana Kulig. She no longer worked for the studio, and currently lived in Romania with her husband.

I sent a message to the email listed on her profile. I lied and told her that I was researching an article on contemporary movie studio publicity and its effect on Hollywood blockbusters.

About forty-five minutes later, I received a response. It included a phone number.

I did a quick online search to figure out what time it was in Romania. It was midafternoon, so I opened WhatsApp and called the number.

"Hello?" It was a woman's voice.

"Hi. Is this Silvana?"

"Yes."

"My name is K. I'm sorry to bother you, but I was hoping to ask you a couple of questions. Do you mind if we switch over to video?"

"Sure," she said, "just a sec."

Silvana's hair was much shorter, her face a bit fuller, but she was clearly the woman from the photographs.

"I was wondering if you could take a quick look at something for me?" I asked.

"Okay," she said.

I sent her a copy of the photograph with the scar.

"I'm sure it was traumatic, and I apologize in advance if I'm being insensitive for asking," I said, "but I was wondering if you could tell me how you got this scar on your arm?"

"What the fuck is going on?"

"What do you mean?"

"Why are you people doing this?"

"Doing what?"

"Photoshopping scars on my fucking arm and then calling to talk to me about it."

"Are you saying something has been altered in the picture?"

"No shit," she said. "I just took a screen capture by the way. I have your face."

"What do you mean 'you people'? Did somebody else ask about your scar?"

"I'm hanging up now."

"Please." I pulled out my driver's license and held it up to the camera. "I promise I'm not trying to scam you or pull some kind of prank. I'm just trying to solve a mystery."

She stared at me for a moment, and then asked me to hold up my license again while she took a screen cap.

"You have two minutes," she said.

"Who asked you about this photograph?"

"He didn't give me his name, said he needed to remain anonymous for security purposes."

"Did he say anything else? Maybe something about a game?"

"No. What the fuck is going on?"

"I promise I'm not crazy," I said, "and I'm not doing this to bother you. I really just need to know what happened to your arm. It's hard to explain, but—like I said—I think it might be really important."

Silvana stood up and moved into another room. It was a large foyer. She flipped her camera around and pointed it at a huge photograph that covered the entire back wall of the room. It was the image of Silvana leaning over the famous actress. However, in this version of the image, there was no scar on Silvana's arm.

She turned the camera back around and held up her right arm. Her skin was perfectly smooth and clear. No scar.

"I don't have a scar. I've never had a scar. You need to tell me what the hell is going on."

I described the event with Jeff Goldblum in detail, but left out the fact that I had a copy of that video. A weird photograph was one thing, but if I sent her a potentially fake and extremely violent video featuring her likeness, I had the feeling she was probably going to hang up and call the police. I certainly would.

Silvana told me she remembered working on the movie, but that no attack like the one I'd described had taken place. She said if I wanted a better look at that particular image, it had been included in a book the photographer had released earlier this year. She gave me the photographer's information and told me that back then she went by her maiden name, Silvana Mitchell.

Just as she was about to hang up, I thought of something.

"After I sent you that picture, you took a screen capture of my face."

"You're damn right."

"I understand completely. Did you happen to do the same thing with the other person who called about that photograph with the scar?"

"Of course," she said.

"Would you be willing to send me that image?"

"If I still have it."

I thanked her for her time and hung up.

It wasn't hard to find the book of photographs Silvana was talking about. I typed the photographer's name into Google, and that picture was suddenly everywhere. Silvana didn't have a scar in any of the images of that photograph that came up.

I saved the highest-resolution image of the photograph to my computer and compared it side by side with the version I'd found online earlier.

They were identical except for the scar.

As I leaned forward to double-check those images, I felt something shift in my living room. It was as if the shape of the room had suddenly changed, and the quality or consistency of the air had been altered somehow—like the cabin of an airliner pressurizing, or that moment of silence in a horror film just before a black cat jumps out from behind a trash can and scares the shit out of the audience.

That's when a text alert shattered the silence and I almost fell off my chair.

It was from Silvana. She'd forwarded a picture of the man who'd called her asking about that video.

It was the Magician.

I waited until seven A.M. and then called Chloe again. She eventually picked up.

"What?"

"I need to show you something."

"It had better not have anything to do with Rabbits."

"Are you coming, or what?"

Nothing from Chloe.

"Hello?"

"I'll come by tonight after work. We can order food."

She hung up.

Chloe showed up at five thirty.

"Don't get mad," I said, "but I found Silvana, and she told me something about the Magician."

"Who the hell is Silvana?"

"Promise you won't be mad."

"I promise I'm already mad," she said.

The two of us sat down and I told her about the photograph I'd discovered, and what Silvana had to say about it.

Chloe took a look at the photos with and without the scar.

"Holy shit, this is so weird."

"The Magician must have found the same pictures I did, and called Silvana about the scar on her arm."

"I still haven't heard from him," Chloe said.

"It looks like he's out there somewhere following the same clues we are. I'm sure he'll be in touch soon."

Chloe nodded, but she looked unconvinced.

"I wanted to say sorry for earlier," I said. "I hate to see you stressed out, and it's so much worse when it's my fault."

"It's not your fault. It's just . . . everything with Baron and the Magician, and you missing time and stuff . . . I don't wanna lose you too."

I smiled. "Thanks," I said. "I don't wanna lose me either."

The two of us ordered some food and watched a French thriller from 2003 called *Swimming Pool*. Chloe picked it. I didn't tell her that I'd seen it already. I was happy to watch it again with her. Anything to take my mind off things for a little while.

"Should we open a bottle of wine?" Chloe asked, after the movie ended.

"Maybe in a bit," I said.

Chloe shifted and stretched, and as she was stretching, she sank into the middle of the couch, into the soft spot between the two cushions. I had to grab her to stop her from falling over. Our faces were suddenly less than an inch apart.

"You seem a little tense," Chloe said, moving even closer.

"I'm fine," I said, which wasn't completely true. I'd started shaking.

And then, we were kissing.

Chloe tasted like summer, her lips full and soft, her skin warm against my face.

The two of us pulled away at exactly the same time.

"Holy shit," Chloe said.

"Yeah."

Chloe snatched the remote control from my lap. "Wanna watch another movie?"

"Sounds good," I said.

22

THE BYZANTINE GAME ENGINE

CHLOE AND I WERE STARTLED AWAKE at eight thirty the next morning by my phone vibrating on the coffee table. The two of us had fallen asleep on the couch.

I answered the phone and put it on speaker. It was Sidney Farrow.

"Hey," I said, doing my best to sound like I'd been up for a while.

"Do you have time to meet later today?"

"Sure, anytime."

"I'll be there in an hour. I think I found something."

"Great."

"Can you tell Chloe?" Sidney said.

"Um . . . yeah. No problem."

I hung up the phone and rolled over to find Chloe staring at me with a concerned look on her face.

"What happened last night can never happen again," she said, deadly serious.

I opened my mouth to speak when she burst into laughter.

"Oh my god," she said. "Your face." Then she jumped up. "I'm going home to take a shower and change. I'll be back."

Sidney Farrow showed up at my place about an hour after she'd called. Chloe walked through the door a few minutes later.

"I did a lot of digging," Sidney said, "but I wasn't able to find anything on any of the testing module servers, the design database, or any of the machines running bytes for my new game. But then, yesterday morning, a technician I asked to flag anything connected to Baron's ID code found some files that had been uploaded by somebody using that code."

"What files?" Chloe asked.

"It looks like Baron uploaded a few things to the company's internal general folder on the day the woman who'd had the seizure was taken to the hospital. An encryption protocol is automatically activated whenever someone using a Byzantine ID uploads something, so I needed to get them decrypted."

"What were they?" I asked.

Sidney handed me her phone.

The first file was a screen capture. It looked like it had been taken from some kind of news show. There were two talking heads: standard anchorwoman and her male counterpart. Running along the bottom third of the screen was a crawl displaying headlines covering the news of the day, most of them related to a hurricane building somewhere off the coast of Florida.

"That's a scene from my game," Sidney said.

"No way that's computer generated," Chloe said, leaning in for a closer look. "It's too . . . real."

"I told you the Byzantine Game Engine was amazing."

Chloe was right. The image was photorealistic. But aside from the fact that the game looked exactly like real life, nothing stood out. It was just two news anchors talking and smiling into the camera while the day's headlines ran along the bottom of the screen. Nothing appeared to be Rabbits-related.

"Do you have another version of this scene anywhere, or a copy of the scripted dialogue?" I asked. "There might be something in there that's relevant."

"The BGE doesn't work like that," Sidney said. "Those news anchors could be talking about almost anything."

"But somebody must have written and recorded the dialogue," Chloe said.

Sidney shook her head. "The key to Byzantine is Hawk Worricker's advanced AI. The characters learn as the players play. The

BGE's voice synthesis engine sounds completely human. It's uncanny, literally. No two people playing the game will ever have the same experience."

"That sounds . . . impossible," Chloe said.

"I know. It's my game, and I have no idea how it works. Byzantine is . . . truly next level."

"Is it some kind of random world generator like No Man's Sky?" I asked.

"No Man's Sky is a cave painting compared to Worricker's game engine."

"How do they make it look so . . . real?" Chloe asked.

"Outside of the initial world-building and developing my half of the original AI's programming and learning matrix, I have no idea," Sidney said. "There are whispers about quantum computers, but I've never seen anything like that."

"I can't believe they locked you out of your own game," Chloe said.

Sidney shrugged. "That was part of the deal. I was put in charge of creative, and they got my code. The Byzantine Game Engine—and whatever else they're doing up in The Tower—is strictly off-limits. How the BGE does that magic shit is a proprietary WorGames secret."

"What about the other files Baron uploaded?" Chloe asked.

Sidney picked up her phone and opened the next file.

It appeared to be a frame grab from a security camera, taken at night in a modern office building lobby. The time stamp read: 12:34 A.M.

The image was dark, but I could make out two figures moving away from the lobby entrance toward a bank of elevators. The figure farthest from the camera didn't look familiar, but I recognized the other person immediately.

It was Alan Scarpio.

Above the video's time stamp was a date. That security camera footage had been recorded the night Alan Scarpio met me at the arcade.

"Any idea what Scarpio was doing at WorGames?" I asked.

Sidney shook her head. "No, but the bigger question might be: What was Scarpio doing in The Tower?"

"Wait," I said. "That footage was taken in The Tower?"

Sidney nodded.

This was starting to feel like some kind of crazy dream.

Sidney Farrow.

Alan Scarpio.

What the fuck was happening?

"Can we get up there and check it out?" Chloe asked.

"My deal gives me access to everything *but* The Tower. They were extremely clear about that. In retrospect, kind of terrifyingly clear."

"And that's what they're doing up there?" Chloe asked. "Working on their super-high-tech game engine?"

"That's what I was told."

"What about the other files Baron uploaded to the WorGames folder?" I asked.

"Four more pictures," Sidney said and handed me her phone.

They were all screen caps of that news program. The talking heads were the same two generic male and female news anchors, but the story running along the ticker at the bottom of the screen was different.

In three of the screen captures, the text was related to the hurricane story we'd seen in the first image, but the text in the fourth screen capture was different.

I zoomed in.

"Holy shit," Chloe said. She was looking over my shoulder. "I still can't believe this resolution."

"What are you looking at?" Sidney asked.

"The story scroll along the bottom of the screen."

"Looks like they're complaining about immigration. It makes sense. This show is supposed to be a right-wing broadcast."

"Notice the headline above that news ticker?"

"What about it?"

"Holy shit," Chloe said, leaning forward as I zoomed in until the headline filled the screen. The headline was four words: *The Door Is Open*.

"What does it mean?" Sidney asked.

"It's a key phrase in the game," Chloe said.

"It looks like somebody at WorGames was either playing or looking into Rabbits," I said.

"Okay." Sidney stood up. "Fuck it. Come on."

"Where are we going?" I asked.

"We're going to visit The Tower."

NOTES ON THE GAME: MISSIVE BY HAZEL

(AUTHENTICATED BY BLOCKCHAIN)

The metaphor of the house.

The key to playing the game is to avoid thinking too big.

Just take a look at what's in front of you and start to build. Eventually, you'll discover that you've created a foundation you can stand on. Once you have your foundation, you'll be able to build faster, eventually adding scaffolding, then framing, and finally, if you've done the work—if you've followed the clues in the proper order—you'll step back and see that you've built an entire house.

At that point, once you've built your house, you'll see so much more. At that point, you'll discover a secret.

At that point, you'll learn you're actually going to have to build an entire city.

—HAZEL 8

23

THE MEECHUM RADIANTS

In 2005, DECADES AFTER Hawk Worricker had disappeared completely from public life, WorGames began construction on the building that would eventually become known as The Tower.

Sidney told us there were countless rumors whispered among WorGames employees about what was "really" going on up there. Depending on who you asked, The Tower was either some kind of high-level experimental (and perhaps illegal) genetics laboratory, a corporate multinational gaming think tank, the U.S. home base for something called alternative astronomy, or a secret society so secret that nobody had ever heard of them.

The fact that there were no interior photos of The Tower available anywhere online, and Google Earth revealed nothing but a bunch of blurry rectangles, only deepened the mystery. Sidney told us she'd heard whispers that the top floor of The Tower had been sold as residential space in order to help finance the structure: Madonna, Leonardo DiCaprio, and William Shatner were just some of the names she'd heard connected to it.

We parked in the employee parking structure—which was relatively deserted on a Saturday—and made our way onto the campus proper.

Everything was top-of-the-line, from the irrigation system that took care of the exotic trees and plants, to the high-speed glass elevators gliding silently up some of the taller buildings. If it was new and exciting—and expensive—they had it at WorGames.

As we walked along the wide, polished micro-cobblestone path known colloquially among WorGames employees as Main Street, we passed a few workers—hoods and umbrellas up against the rain, headphones in against the world—but other than that, the campus was fairly quiet. We walked for a few more minutes before we rounded a corner and entered a small park. At that point, we got our first full glimpse of The Tower.

Rising up and out of the back corner of a low red-brick structure called Building A, The Tower loomed over the WorGames campus like some kind of brutalist glass-eyed sentinel. It was tall, at least twenty stories, but it was hard to tell exactly how many floors there were due to the heavily tinted windows.

As we moved closer, we could see that most of the visible bricks of both Building A and The Tower were vertical rather than horizontal, giving both structures a unique look and feel—like contemporary science fiction crossed with Antonioni-esque Italian noir.

We slowed as we approached the entrance to Building A, and I looked up at The Tower.

The way it was slightly backlit, dark and foreboding against the dusty gray sky, reminded me of the monolithic structure from my elevator dream and a sudden ominous dread came over me like a shadow slowly blocking out the sun. Perhaps sensing my discomfort, Chloe grabbed my hand, and the two of us followed Sidney inside.

Like all of the buildings on the WorGames campus, Building A was almost as green inside as it was out. The wide glass entryway was filled with a large collection of small trees and hanging plants.

As we entered the lobby area, Sidney smiled and waved at the lone receptionist seated behind a long polished wooden counter that ran the length of the entire room. The wall behind the counter was covered in some kind of bluish-green ivy or moss. It reminded me of the check-in counter at a high-end Las Vegas casino.

Sidney wasn't able to access The Tower because her security clearance didn't allow it, but she had a plan.

We were going to walk right in like we owned the place.

Sidney led us through the lobby, down a wide staircase and into a long corridor. The sound of our shoes echoed off the smooth walls and polished dark red floor as we walked.

As we approached the end of the corridor, a security guard waved at us from a nearby bench. He looked to be about sixty-five, bald, with an easy smile.

"Hey, Albert," Sidney called out.

"Hiya, Sid."

Visible through a series of floor-to-ceiling windows on our left was an enormous courtyard—a dense world of deep green. As we passed by, I pictured myself employed at WorGames, sitting on a bench out there, eating lunch with my co-workers, breathing in oxygen-rich air and dreaming about the worlds we'd be creating together—worlds pulled directly from Sidney Farrow's imagination. What would my life have been like working at a place like WorGames? Would that have helped me forget about Rabbits?

It didn't help Baron.

I was snapped out of my reverie as we left the courtyard behind us and entered what Sidney referred to as The Tower atrium.

The atrium was spacious and circular, with an incredibly high, slightly domed ceiling. The floor appeared to be made of the same dark red polished stone as the hallway, but where the hallway floor was unadorned, the floor of the atrium was covered in a mosaic of intricate, swirling designs. Those designs were centered around a specific point in the middle of the room: a small white circle located directly beneath a giant pendulum. The pendulum hung from the ceiling by a long thin wire, and at first, its slow, hypnotic movement lent the room a sense of peaceful calm, but I could feel it up there, fighting its way through the space, doing its best—against the spinning axis of the planet—to trace a perfect line in the air.

As I thought about the pendulum, struggling in vain against vast universal forces outside its control, I shivered, and couldn't help but feel the weight of everything we were up against.

I actually did a double take to make sure the Earth was spinning in the right direction.

There were two reception desks on our left as we entered, and a number of long low wooden benches to the right. The lobby appeared to be unoccupied except for a tall black-haired woman with a narrow face standing behind the desk closest to us on the left.

"Good morning, Ms. Farrow. How can I help you?"

"We need to go upstairs," Sidney said.

"I'm sorry?"

Sidney pointed. "We're going up."

"I'm afraid you don't have security clearance to access The Tower." I could tell by her expression that she clearly didn't want to say no to Sidney. "I hate to do this, but is there maybe somebody you can call for additional clearance?"

Sidney ignored her and led us between the two reception desks, down a short hallway, and into a long foyer. On our right was another wall covered in ivy, on our left two sets of tall elevator doors.

Sidney walked over and pressed the call button.

Both sets of elevator doors opened, and the three of us stepped into the elevator closest to the reception area. The doors closed behind us.

Inside there were two rows of twelve buttons set beneath a wider button marked with the letters PH.

Sidney mashed every single button immediately, but none of them stayed lit.

A few seconds later, the doors opened.

We were still on the ground floor, but now the security guard was standing in front of us.

"Sid," he said, "what's going on?"

"Don't get in the middle of this, Albert. I need to go upstairs."

"Sure," Albert said. "That's fine, but you have to wait for clearance."

"This is bullshit," Sidney said, stepping out of the elevator with Chloe behind her.

"Your clearance is coming," Albert said.

Sidney was clearly surprised. "It is?"

Albert nodded. "Ten minutes."

As I stepped out of the elevator behind Sidney and Chloe, something changed. The air was different suddenly, heavier, charged somehow.

Something was coming.

The back of the foyer, directly across from the elevators, started filling up with dark swirling shapes, and the familiar thick tingling of the gray feeling began gnawing its way into my skull.

But something was different.

I had no idea what this thing was, this gray emptiness that had become such a large part of my life, but I eventually realized what it was that felt different. It was excited.

It wanted me to step back into the elevator.

So I did.

As soon as I started moving backward, the shadows surged forward and slammed me into the back of the elevator.

As I hit the wall, I heard Chloe yell my name. The sound of her voice snapped me out of whatever spell the gray things had cast and I lunged for the open door button. But I was too late. The elevator was rising.

I looked up at the numbers. I hadn't pressed anything, but the wide PH button was illuminated.

The elevator ascended at a remarkably high speed. My ears popped after a few seconds and I could feel what was left of the buzzing and tingling sensations leaving my brain.

And then the doors opened and I stepped out.

The floor was smooth black marble and the walls were finished with some kind of polished metal. A large abstract painting filled the wall at the end of the wide hallway to my left, and a set of glass double doors were visible at the other end of the hall in the distance.

Nothing stood out about the shapes and colors of the painting, although part of me thought I'd seen it in an art history textbook during my first year of college.

I turned away from the painting and walked toward the double doors. The air was cool and clean, the humidity high and refreshing. Somebody had clearly spared no expense to make the atmosphere perfect.

I pushed through the doors and entered a small lobby. There was a high reception desk to my right and a few chairs and small tables to my left. Behind the reception desk was a set of dark wooden doors. They were a few feet taller than normal, and almost completely covered in intricately carved symbols.

There was nobody around, no phone to call or bell to ring, so I walked over to the wooden doors and knocked.

No answer.

There was a small security panel to the right of the doors, which led me to believe I'd need some kind of access code to get in, but when I turned the handle and pulled, the door opened easily, with a barely audible click.

I stepped through the door and onto the thick glass floor of a mezzanine of some kind. In front of me and to the right, a floating staircase—with wide steps made of the same thick glass—led down to the main level.

The room was a bit dark, so it took my eyes a moment to adjust, but once they did, I couldn't stop looking around.

I felt like I'd stepped into a library from another world.

The walls were three or four times the height of a standard office, and the ceiling featured three extremely wide skylights that looked like giant backlit canvas paintings of an overcast gray sky.

The wall on the left was covered with antique floor-to-ceiling bookshelves. Bisecting the bookshelves was a thick glass walkway accessible by two additional floating glass staircases. There were Victorian-era chairs and tables up there where someone could sit and read, and a number of old-style wooden rolling ladders on both the main and mezzanine walkway levels that could easily be used to reach the books on the top shelves of either section. Two huge lighting fixtures hanging from the ornate ceiling reminded me of the midcentury–meets–Native American décor of the Overlook Hotel in *The Shining*. If you'd told me this was the Victorian headquarters of the National Geographic Society, that would have made perfect sense.

The wall to my right, which ran adjacent to the bookshelves, was covered by the biggest screen I'd ever seen outside of a football stadium, and the wall directly in front of me was nothing but windows covered with what appeared to be electronically adjustable neutral-density filters. I'd seen those filters in *Wired* recently, and if the skylights featured the same technology, this entire floor could go from bright sunlight to total darkness with the simple press of a button.

The expansive view of the city visible through the windows grounded me a little. Although I'd clearly entered some kind of bizarre H. G. Wells dreamscape, at least that dreamscape appeared to be located in Seattle. And even though the room was enormous, it didn't feel empty. An impressive collection of art covered the myriad desks and tables, and everything, from the furniture to the area rugs, had been arranged in a way that made perfect use of the space.

On the floor, the antique-meets-cool-glass aesthetic turned slightly midcentury modern. Facing the enormous screen were two black-and-brown Eames lounge chairs on a large worn Persian carpet. There was loud music playing from a modern vertical-style turntable mounted on a nearby wall.

I made my way down the stairs and approached the turntable. The song currently playing was jazzy and busy, with deep strings, shuffling drums, and wild guitar. It was kind of terrifyingly beautiful as it moved from delicate vibraphone sections to insane organ breaks to monumental auditory mountains of strings.

"Have you heard this recording before?"

I spun around at the sound of a man's voice.

"I'm sorry," I said, "the door was open."

"Well, technically, the door was unlocked, but it was closed." The man was middle-aged or maybe a bit older, Caucasian, with long, wavy gray hair. He wore thick-framed black glasses, a long-sleeve white cotton shirt, and plain blue jeans. He didn't seem angry that I'd entered without permission. More like . . . amused.

"This album is called *Song of Innocence* by a man named David Axelrod," he said. "It should have been far more popular than it was."

"It's interesting music," I said.

"It certainly is." The man nodded. His hawkish face was well-lined and clearly life-worn, but his eyes, which were two slightly different shades of blue, held a bright youthful sparkle.

We stood facing each other for a moment, before something changed in the man's expression. The smile slowly faded from his lips, and a kind of recognition passed over his face.

"Hello, K," he said.

"How do you know my name?"

"I knew your parents."

"Who are you?" I asked.

He laughed. "Well, that's a complicated question. But everyone just calls me Crow."

"Crow?"

"That's right," he said.

"What is this place?"

"Well, that's an even more complicated question, I'm afraid, but I'll do my best to answer it in as satisfactory a manner as possible."

He smiled again, wider this time, as if he'd just remembered something amusing.

"What is it?" I asked.

"I'm sorry. It's just that you remind me of your mother."

"How did you know my parents?"

"We did some work together, a long time ago."

I took another look around the place. This was some serious Bruce Wayne–level shit. What the hell was this guy doing working with my parents?

"What is this place? Do you . . . live here?"

"My living quarters are located on the floor below us," he said. "This is where I spend most of my time, however. We call it The Terminal." He pulled out his phone, hit a few virtual buttons, and the giant video screen lit up.

After a few seconds, the screen became a giant map of the world.

The man called Crow made a series of short waving motions with his hands, and that movement caused the image to zoom in closer to North America. He was manipulating the screen using some kind of advanced kinetic control system. It was extremely cool, but it felt like something out of a near-future sci-fi movie, not technology that was currently available.

"There are facts, lines, patterns, and laws beneath the world you recognize, K."

That sounded more like the beginning of a speech than a statement requiring some kind of response, so I waited for him to continue.

"Numbers are significant," Crow continued. "For example, there is a number representing all of the women in the entire world who have given birth within the past hour."

The camera's slow zoom continued into the United States.

"There is an exact number of people who were married this week, and a number who have dropped out of high school over that same period. These are specific numbers, precise numbers. Do you understand?"

"I'm not sure that I do."

He smiled, motioned again, and the camera continued its zoom into the West Coast of the United States.

"There's one number representing the amount of people who currently hold a winning national lottery ticket, and another for the number of unfortunate folks currently locked in the trunk of a car while being transported to another location."

"Jesus," I said. That took a bit of a dark turn.

Whatever app was manipulating the images on Crow's giant screen zoomed toward the city of Seattle, as he turned away from the screen to face me.

"All of these numbers exist. They are exact, and they are knowable."

"That's obvious—logically speaking," I said. "But the fact that those numbers are knowable in theory doesn't mean they're at all knowable in practice."

"Ah, but with respect, K, that is exactly what it means."

"Again, conceptually, I understand everything you're saying," I said, "but it still feels a lot more like a thought experiment than an actual possibility."

"Why?"

"Although I'm willing to concede those numbers exist, they would be essentially impossible to know, and certainly impossible to check for accuracy."

"Maybe not," he said.

I watched as Crow's satellite or whatever it was completed its task. It turns out it hadn't been zooming into Seattle, but rather Olympia. We were looking directly down at the house I'd grown up in. I had no idea where this conversation was going. Why the hell was he showing me my childhood home?

Suddenly, a numbing buzz started moving through my stomach and up into my chest. I could feel my lungs tightening and my throat constricting. I did my best to concentrate, to try to slow my breathing, as Crow continued speaking.

"What if there were equations and computations connected to these numbers—effective ways to figure out not only how to calculate these things, but also influence and perhaps even change the outcomes of certain events?"

"Sorry, but that sounds unlikely."

"The world is run on systems, K—traffic, sanitation, electricity, the Internet . . . even children's elementary school admissions. Influencing and adjusting these systems for the better is one of the things we're working on here."

This guy was clear and confident as he spoke, but what he was saying was crazy. Kidnapped people in a trunk being taken to another location? Elementary school admissions? What the fuck?

"Okay, so how are you . . . influencing and adjusting these events, exactly?" I asked.

Crow did something on his phone and the room grew darker still (definitely the high-tech neutral density filters).

Suddenly the gigantic screen was split into dozens of smaller squares, each displaying something completely different.

"That's the Nikkei, the Toronto Stock Exchange, and the Dow Jones Industrial," he said, pointing to distinct sections of the screen. "Over there: Sports Scores and Salaries; that's Social Structures and

Education Systems; those two screens are Rare Earth Elements and Industrial Minerals. And down in the bottom-right corner: Music, Art, and Weather."

"What's all of this for?"

"For doing what we do here."

"Which is?"

"Making adjustments, in order to change the things that need to be changed. Cause and effect."

He performed another motion with his hand and suddenly the screen was filled with hundreds of people's faces. Another wave and those hundreds became thousands. A series of brief movements and there was audio—thousands of voices talking at once.

"What are they doing?"

"They're working."

"What kind of work?"

He didn't answer my question, just zoomed in to one section of the screen. "This person is the head of international development for a Beijing-based company that's working on a very promising clean energy alternative."

The screen was suddenly filled with an image of an older Chinese man walking down a hallway. "He's going to be late for work today, and that's going to set off a series of events culminating in his being arrested for solicitation."

He waved his hand again, and we were looking at an attractive Japanese woman in her midthirties. She appeared to be running some kind of meeting in a large boardroom somewhere.

"This woman's name is Nuri Tamaka. She's next in line as the head of international development for the company. The biggest difference between Nuri Tamaka and the man she will be replacing is that Ms. Tamaka isn't in the pocket of a large American oil and gas corporation."

He waved again and another woman's profile filled the screen. She looked very similar to Nuri Tamaka, but a bit younger. "This is Ms. Tamaka's sister. What if, two nights from today, Nuri Tamaka—after sneaking into her sister's apartment to prepare a surprise birthday party—walks in on her fiancé and her sister having sex? Based on our research, we believe this would effectively end Ms. Tamaka's engagement, which would be significant because Nuri Tamaka and her fiancé have been trying to get pregnant. If Nuri Tamaka remains oblivious of this affair, it's possible she might plan to have a child and turn down the job, opening the door for another man in the pocket of big oil and gas to step in."

"Isn't it also possible," I said, "and perhaps even more likely, that this woman has a baby and balances her family and career? It happens all the time."

"Of course," he said, "but based on a significant number of recorded conversations and recent behavioral trends related to Ms. Tamaka and her fiancé, that outcome is statistically very unlikely. We wouldn't be employing this level of attention if we weren't fairly certain about the outcome."

"So, what, you're manipulating people's lives?"

"I was just asking a question, K."

"These people who work for you, who are they?"

"I've found that people drawn to complex games and game theory often have a highly developed sense of pattern recognition and an innate ability to see connections—or, more importantly, possible future connections."

He waved again and the giant screen went dark.

"This is just a small sample of what we do here. There's so much more going on beneath the surface—so many systems and events to monitor and influence."

"What's happening on the other floors of The Tower?"

"Eighty percent of the building is nothing more than an enormous server farm, I'm afraid."

"Computers?"

"A whole bunch of them." He smiled again.

I tried to imagine exactly how much computational power that might be, then gave up. I had no way to comprehend those types of numbers, and I had something else on my mind in that moment.

"How did you know my mother?"

"I met your parents in San Francisco. We worked together for a long time. This"—he motioned around the room—"is the end result of some of that work."

"I'm not sure I understand. What kind of work are you talking about?"

Crow took a moment, as if he was considering whether or not I was ready to hear the answer. "Are you familiar with Kellan Meechum?" he asked, finally.

"A little," I said. "Wasn't his thing other dimensions and ley lines?"

"That was part of it, yes, but there was so much more."

Crow leaned back against a table and continued. "While working with a group of scientists that would eventually make up a large part of the MKUltra team, Kellan Meechum discovered something incredible—and quite by accident. He'd spent his early life focused on proving the existence of ley lines—a bunch of pseudoscientific nonsense focused on the importance of perceived alignments of landmarks, religious sites, and manmade structures. But in 1945, Meechum stumbled upon something else. While trying to connect ley lines to patterns and anomalies in Fibonacci numbers and Benford's Law, he uncovered something he referred to as Radiants—theoretical lines running through the world, lines of energy Meechum believed would morph and change as the world changed around them. It's difficult to explain, this morphing or migration of energy—and Meechum himself admitted he wasn't completely up to the task. But investigating the cause wasn't what Meechum was interested in. He was interested in investigating the *effect*. You see, near the end of his life, Meechum had converted to Christianity. At that point, he believed God had long abandoned this world, and that as a result, humanity was denied access to the afterlife. Meechum was looking for . . . the other side. He'd become convinced that the Radiants were leading him somewhere. He believed he'd discovered a map to heaven and hell."

Like his precise numbers theory from earlier, I got the sense Crow believed everything he was saying, but that didn't make it sound any more believable.

"What if I told you that Kellan Meechum was right?" he continued. "And, although the heaven-and-hell aspect of his theory was nothing more than the religious ramblings of a man approaching the end of his life, his Radiants actually exist?"

"I don't know," I said. "That's pretty out there."

Crow smiled. "I understand your skepticism. I think you'll find it much easier to grasp if you compare the Meechum Radiants to Earth's magnetic field."

"Okay . . ."

"Pigeons, foxes, and turtles use Earth's magnetic field to navigate the world. Cattle align themselves in accordance with it, and dogs as well, when they defecate."

"I'm sorry, but what do defecating dogs have to do with magical pathways to heaven and hell?"

He forced a smile and continued. "Many scientists believe humankind hasn't fully lost the power of magnetoreception that we had millions of years ago. As part of Earth's magnetic biosphere, humans—like those other animals—have always had the ability to detect the magnetic field subconsciously. Before he became obsessed with the religious nonsense, Meechum described his Radiants as a similar, unseeable source of energy—no more magical or strange than Earth's magnetic field. He believed that if we were somehow able to understand the movements and uncover the language of these Radiants, we might be able to use them to shift or slip between dimensions."

"Between *dimensions*?"

"I know. It's a lot to digest," he said.

"So you're telling me my parents believed in the Meechum Radiants?"

"Oh, definitely. That's one of the reasons they moved up here to Washington State."

"What does Washington have to do with it?"

"Washington State is home to one of Meechum's most powerful Radiants: Radiant twenty-three. Meechum often referred to it as the Terminal Line."

"That's why you call this place The Terminal?"

"Yes."

My parents told me they'd moved to Olympia because my mother got a new job. What if this guy was telling the truth? It sounded impossible. My mother worked for a bank.

"I really enjoyed working with your parents, K. I only wish it had been under better circumstances."

"What does that mean?"

"There were certain restrictions we had to deal with back then—restrictions I've since managed to clear up. Now we have the freedom and technology to do so much of what we'd planned back then. I only wish your parents were here now to share this experience."

"That's what you were working on with my parents? The Meechum Radiants?"

"That was a big part of it, yes." He motioned around the room. "I'd like to think we're honoring their tragic deaths in some small way by continuing to do this work."

He looked pensive for a moment. "Had I known you were here," he continued, "I would have made certain we'd met much sooner."

A slow darkness crept across the room like someone was dimming the lights.

"What does that mean? Had you known I was here?"

"Well, that's a long story, and I'm afraid I don't have time to get into it at the moment." He pulled out his phone and hit a few buttons. "I'll bet you're wondering why there's nobody else working with me here, in such a large space."

"It does feel a bit . . . excessive for one person," I said. "Although there were a lot of people on that giant screen."

"The number of remote operatives we have working for us is significant, but there are also people working directly with me here in the building."

I heard the sound of the elevator doors opening from somewhere nearby.

"Including somebody I believe you know," he said.

I turned at the sound of footsteps.

A woman in her late thirties or early forties walked toward us from the double doors that led back to the elevators. She was about five foot seven with thick, shiny auburn hair. She wore a brown pencil skirt, a cream-colored top, and tortoiseshell Ray-Ban glasses.

Her eyes widened and her mouth fell open when she saw me. For a brief moment, it looked like she was going to pass out.

"K?" she said, then turned to Crow. "What the fuck is going on?"

It was Emily Connors.

The man called Crow took Emily aside, and the two of them spoke in hushed tones for about a minute. Then, after a sharp glance in my direction, Emily turned around and stalked back out the way she'd come in.

"What's wrong?" I asked Crow.

I hadn't seen Emily Connors for years, so why had she gotten so upset? Did seeing my face again remind her of that night in the truck with Annie?

"She's just a bit annoyed with me, I'm afraid," Crow said. "She'll be fine."

"Can I talk to her?" I asked.

"I'm not sure that's such a good idea just now, but we'll see what we can do." There was something almost threatening in his tone as he spoke.

"Sure," I said, but I was still thinking about Emily. What the hell was she doing here? What was going on?

Crow started walking me back to the double doors that led to the elevator.

It was clear our conversation was over.

I had no idea what had happened to Sidney and Chloe after the elevator had taken me upstairs. Maybe they were still down in the lobby waiting for security clearance.

"I'll be in touch," Crow said as he pressed the call button for the elevator.

I took the elevator back down, feeling stunned. Crow? Emily Connors? What the hell had just happened?

The doors opened and Chloe yanked me out and into the foyer. "What the fuck are you doing? We're getting security passes."

I opened my mouth to speak, but Sidney shushed me with her hand. "I've been able to get us access to the upper floors of the building," she said.

At that moment, Albert from security arrived holding three laminated security passes. "Sorry for the wait," he said.

Sidney grabbed the passes from Albert's outstretched hand and dragged us into the elevator.

Once inside, she scanned her security pass and then pressed the PH button.

"Let's start at the top and work our way down," she said.

I nodded. I thought about telling them what was waiting up there, but they'd find out soon enough.

I hoped I'd see Emily Connors again. I had a lot of questions.

Once we reached the penthouse level, the doors opened and we stepped out of the elevator. Sidney led us down the long hallway, through the glass doors, and into the small empty lobby. She took a quick look around, and, just like I'd done earlier, went directly for the wooden doors with the security panel. Something had been bothering me since we'd arrived at the penthouse, but I couldn't put my finger on it.

Before I could tell her that the doors were unlocked, Sidney waved her pass in front of the panel, there was a click, and she yanked open the door.

At that moment, I figured out what had been bothering me. It was the air. The atmosphere was different. The temperature and humidity had changed, and as the three of us stepped through into the penthouse proper, it was clear that something else had changed as well.

We were standing on the same mezzanine looking over the same room, but it was completely different.

The high ceiling was there, along with the three skylights, and the view through the windows was identical. But there was nothing left of Crow's high-tech lair—no bookshelves, no furniture, no rugs, and no obscure music from the 1960s.

The entire room was filled from floor to ceiling with computers—each machine much larger than the regular black server boxes that filled those mysterious top secret government buildings in Hollywood movies.

A few minutes ago, this room had been a beautifully furnished high-tech–meets–steampunk James Bond–villain library, and now it was nothing more than some kind of generic server farm.

As I stood there staring at wall after wall of black computers where bookshelves had been just minutes earlier, the gray feeling hit me like a wave of cement, and I passed out.

24

YOU LOOK LIKE YOU MIGHT
NEED MORE THAN A COOKIE

I WOKE UP IN THE LOBBY of The Tower staring into the eyes of Sidney Farrow.

"Welcome back," she said.

"Are you okay?" Chloe asked.

"I'm fine. Low blood sugar," I lied.

"Are you sure?" Sidney asked. "You look like you might need more than a cookie."

"No, really, I'm good," I said, sitting up.

I took a look around. They'd laid me down on one of the wooden benches. Sidney and Chloe knelt on the floor in front of me.

"Sidney checked it out," Chloe said. "From the sixth floor to the penthouse, there's nothing but endless rows of stacked servers."

"That's a lot of computing power," I said.

I was having a hard time focusing on Chloe's words. I was still coming to terms with what had just happened. Did I really just meet a man named Crow? Was Emily Connors there? As I continued to gather my senses, I looked past the two reception desks, through the windows, and into the courtyard. There was a circular fountain out there that I couldn't remember seeing earlier. Surrounding the fountain was a group of large stone birds, all staring up at the sky, wings spread, waiting to take flight. I found myself wondering what had been going on in the mind of the sculptor. Why were those birds poised to escape such a beautiful place?

"Hey," Chloe said softly, snapping me out of my reverie. "Are you sure you're okay?"

"I'm good," I said.

"You don't look so good," Sidney said.

"That's an insane amount of computing power for gaming," Chloe said as the three of us stepped outside.

"What do you think is going on up there?" I asked.

"I don't know," Sidney said. "Floors one through five are dedicated to Byzantine Game Engine personnel. The elevator won't stop at any of those floors, and security says they don't have access. There's no way we're getting in there."

"Security doesn't have access?" I asked.

Sidney shrugged. "That's what they told me."

"Do you know a man named Crow who works here?"

Sidney shook her head. "Doesn't ring a bell."

"Do you think you could check?" I asked.

"Sure. Is that his last name? Like the bird?"

"I'm not sure."

"I'll look into it," Sidney said and then glanced over at Chloe. "You should probably go home and get some rest."

"Could you maybe call your boss and try to get access to the rest of the floors?" I asked.

"I don't have a boss."

"So who do you call if you need something from the top?"

"Lawyers. I'm going to put in a formal request to stop my creative team from delivering assets until I see what the hell they're doing with the Byzantine Game Engine."

"Do you think that's going to work?" Chloe asked.

Sidney shrugged. "I have no idea, but it's worth a shot. I don't want anybody else having seizures, dying, or passing out." She turned back to me. "Are you *sure* you're okay?"

I nodded.

In the Uber on our way back to my place, I stared at a series of stuffed animals glued to the dashboard of the older model Prius. I was trying to ascertain the species of each of the animals while simultaneously trying to work out a way to tell Chloe what had happened with Crow. But how was I supposed to talk about what had happened without including the part about my returning to that penthouse to discover everything had miraculously changed? And of course, I'd also have to include the fact that my close childhood friend Emily Connors had shown up for some reason.

I was tired. My head was filled with static and fuzz, and sitting there, in the back of a car with Chloe, I was starting to question whether or not *I* believed any of that stuff had actually happened. The stuffed animals were some kind of generic Pokémonlike creatures. I couldn't decide if they were mice or rabbits. The one in the middle had big green eyes and long reddish ears and had come partly unglued from the dashboard. It appeared slightly off-balance, and every time we went over a bump, it shook and swayed like a haunted bobblehead.

"Are you sure you're okay?" Chloe asked. She could tell something was bothering me.

"You were there," I said. "I just kind of passed out."

Chloe grabbed my hand and squeezed.

"Can you believe all of those servers?" I asked, changing the subject.

"I know," Chloe said, shaking her head. "Whatever they're doing up there, they're doing it with a shit ton of computer power."

The car dropped us off at my place, and I took a long shower.

After I'd finished washing my hair, I stood there with the window open and listened to the sound of the rain outside as it merged with the steady splash of the water hitting the tiles. I went back over what Crow had said about my parents and the Meechum Radiants—about his army of operatives working to butterfly-effect the world—but my mind kept going back to Emily Connors. What the hell was she doing there?

Had she really been there?

Was it possible Chloe was right about what she'd said earlier?

Was I losing it?

Had I imagined the whole thing?

———

After I'd used up what had to be most of the building's hot water supply, I dried off, slipped on my most comfortable jeans and a promotional T-shirt from a newish HBO Max sci-fi show I'd never seen, and sat down next to Chloe on the couch. She turned and smiled, and I felt my body relax. We still hadn't spoken about our make-out session the other night.

"Feeling better?" she asked.

I nodded.

"Shit," she said.

"What?"

Chloe jumped up and started putting on her shoes.

"You're leaving?"

"I have to go home and get some clothes, and cover a shift at the arcade," she said as she grabbed her hoodie and left my apartment.

A few seconds later, she came back in, ran over, and kissed me. "I'll come by right after," she said. "And, K?"

"Yeah?"

"We're not going to do anything Rabbits-related for a while, okay?"

"You keep saying this."

"I'm fucking serious this time."

"You're fucking serious every time."

Chloe just stared.

"I'm fine," I said.

"I'm not kidding. No Rabbits."

"I'm not kidding either. I'm totally fine."

"You passed out."

"I'm sure it was just low blood sugar."

"Please don't treat me like an asshole. I'm growing kind of fond of you."

"I'm sorry," I said. "I'm kind of fond of you too."

"That means no Alan Scarpio, no Tabitha Henry, no Sidney Farrow—at least for a while. I mean it. Promise me."

I nodded, and then Chloe left my apartment again, this time for real.

I meant what I'd said to Chloe. I *was* fond of her. In truth, I'd been crazy about her for quite a while, but I wasn't being quite as honest when I'd agreed to avoid the game.

Rabbits had opened up something within me the night that Annie Connors died, something that needed to be fed—a hunger that would eventually lead me to the Magician's arcade, and, finally, to playing the game myself.

I couldn't let it go.

After Chloe left, I went online and looked up the album Crow had been listening to when I'd arrived, *Song of Innocence* by David Axelrod. That album had been released on Capitol Records, and the image of the record's label I was looking at on my screen was identical to the label on the record that had been spinning on Crow's turntable.

I hadn't imagined it.

I'd never heard of David Axelrod before in my life, which meant that, barring some weird blocked memory from my childhood that included information about that album, what I'd experienced up there in the penthouse of The Tower wasn't a dream or some kind of mental break.

It had happened. It was real.

Next, I looked up Emily Connors.

There was nothing. No information online about the girl I'd grown up with. No Facebook, no LinkedIn, and no White Pages.

Emily Connors was what hackers referred to as a ghost.

Crow had also mentioned Kellan Meechum, so I searched his name as well. One of the first things that popped up was an article that had been published a few months before Meechum's death. The article was titled "Invisible Lines."

Imagine there is an enormous fingerprint beneath the surface of the world—a web of channels or grooves or something similar. Now, imagine that by traversing, crossing, or manipulating those invisible lines in very specific ways, one is able to effect material changes in the fabric of our universe. I believe there is another level of reality—or perhaps multiple levels—and that understanding and mapping these channels or grooves—these lines that I refer to as Radiants—is the key to understanding not only those other worlds, but our own world as well.

The scientific community believed that Kellan Meechum's later work—most of which had been focused on the existence of these Radiants—was simply the product of a man slowly losing his mental faculties. Like Nikola Tesla's research near the end of his life where he'd claimed to have created a perpetual motion machine, nobody took Kellan Meechum or his Radiants seriously.

But I wasn't so sure.

What if Meechum was right? What if his Radiants were the key to understanding Rabbits? What if they were the key to understanding something about my parents?

25

WHAT ELSE ARE WE GONNA DO, PLAY TETRIS?

I woke up to the sound of buzzing in my head.

I must have fallen asleep at some point while looking into Kellan Meechum and his Radiants. It was pitch-black in my bedroom.

I checked the time. It was just after five in the morning.

At first I thought the sound might be the familiar gray feeling creeping around the corners of my skull, but it wasn't that.

It was somebody buzzing my apartment.

I pressed the talk button of my intercom. "Hello?"

No answer.

Whoever it was didn't buzz again.

I checked my phone. Three missed calls from Chloe. There was no way I was going to be able to get back to sleep, so I decided to go for a run.

Morning near the water in Seattle feels primal. The breeze moving over the ocean delivers a constant salty brine that wraps around your senses like a blanket. When that scent hits, it almost always brings me back to weekends in Seattle with my parents. I can hear the voices at the market yelling over the distant roar of the waves, and I can see the ubiquitous posters advertising bands playing venues like the Off Ramp and the Showbox—local bands that would soon be filling arenas.

I ran along the seawall, doing my best to forget what had happened at WorGames, focusing my attention instead on the smells of the early morning and the sounds of my feet as they hit the wet concrete and grass. But I eventually found myself thinking about my parents. I'd always imagined the two of them up there in my mother's office, working on ledgers and calculating expense account deductions. But what if Crow was telling the truth? What if they weren't accountants after all? What if they were up there working on something completely different?

When I got home, I took a shower and avoided another call from Chloe.

I'd come to a decision during my run.

A stranger named Crow had painted an entirely different portrait of my parents. I needed to find a way to speak with him again, and hopefully Emily Connors as well, but before I could speak with either of them, I needed to find a way to get back up to The Tower.

I sent Sidney Farrow a text asking if she'd be able to meet me.

It was Sunday, so I suggested a brunch place that had good food but was never busy for some reason. She said she was in the office working all weekend, but I could just come by whenever.

I arrived at WorGames an hour or so later.

A few minutes after I'd stepped back onto the campus, I started to feel the familiar anxious humming and throbbing in the back of my head. I did my best to push that feeling out of my mind and kept walking toward the low brick building that housed Sidney Farrow's game design team.

I didn't have time for the gray feeling. Not now.

As I made my way along the concourse, I passed a handful of WorGames staffers on their way to work. I was surprised to see so many here on a Sunday. In fact, the entire campus was alive with movement. I was passed by a bunch of people riding bikes and scooters, and there was a group of a dozen or so incredibly bendy bodies practicing morning yoga in the grass, just a few yards off the paved pathway.

As I walked past the longhaired yogi leading the session, I almost bumped into a middle-aged woman yelling and tugging on a black-

and-white dog's leash. The dog had started pooping in the middle of the wide path, and the woman was begging the dog to stop.

I smiled and slowed down as I reached the last major intersection before Sidney's building, a four-way stop.

I ended up standing next to another WorGames staffer who was also walking a dog. This guy was in his early thirties, about five foot six with dark wavy hair and a light beard. He wore a wool hat, a green plaid jacket, and Dr. Martens boots. His dog was a Dalmatian, the same breed as the pooping dog I'd just passed.

I smiled and had just bent down to pet the dog when I noticed a strange look on the man's face. He wasn't moving. He just kept staring around the intersection as if he couldn't believe what he was seeing. I followed his eyes and saw what he was reacting to.

There were people standing at every one of the other three stop signs.

This wasn't surprising, as the campus was fairly busy. What was surprising, however, was that every single one of those people had a dog. And what was even more surprising was the fact that every single one of those dogs was a Dalmatian.

I felt a chill pass through my body as the gray feeling started to cloud my mind. I hurried through that intersection and quickened my pace. I had the sense that the gray feeling was pushing me forward, guiding me toward something inevitable.

I didn't like it.

I felt exposed and alone, and I suddenly wanted to get to Sidney as soon as possible. I needed to see a friendly face.

I kept my eyes forward, focused on the path ahead, and I didn't encounter any other dogs between that intersection and Sidney's building.

About ten minutes after I'd entered the lobby area and checked in with the receptionist, Sidney Farrow stepped out of an elevator, into the lobby, and walked over to the reception area. After a brief conversation, the receptionist pointed to where I was sitting, and Sidney approached.

"Hi," she said. "I'm sorry to keep you waiting. I'm Sidney."

I just stared.

"Farrow." She held out her hand.

"Um . . . I'm K."

"K? K-A-Y, or just the one letter?"

"Just the letter. I mean . . . it doesn't really matter . . . Are you okay?"

She smiled, awkwardly. "What do you mean?"

"Are you . . ." I leaned in and whispered, "Am I supposed to act like I don't know you or something?"

"I'm sorry," she said. "I've been seeing a lot of people these days. Have we met before?"

The expression on Sidney's face in that moment left room for two possibilities: one, she was the greatest actor in the history of the world, or two, she firmly believed that we had never met.

"I'm pretty busy today. What can I do for you?" she continued.

"Do you really not remember me? Or Chloe? Drinking wine, talking about my friend Baron?"

"I'm sorry, I don't remember the two of us meeting at any point. Are you talking about Baron Corduroy?"

I nodded.

"You were friends with Baron?"

"Yeah . . ."

"I'm so sorry," she said. "We really miss having him on the team."

"You don't remember texting with me earlier this morning?"

"Definitely not, no."

I pulled out my phone to show Sidney our text exchange, but something was wrong. There was nothing there, and Sidney's number no longer existed as a contact. And there was something else. My phone said it was Monday. It was Sunday when I woke up and left the house. I started to sway, and stars sparkled in my peripheral vision.

"We've met," I said. "We drank wine, you showed us your tattoo—House Atreides, from *Dune*."

"Okay," Sidney said. At the mention of her hidden tattoo, her tone changed completely. She lowered her voice. "I don't know who the fuck you are, but if you don't turn around and leave right now, I'm calling security."

"My name is K. You came to the arcade because of something that happened with Baron, because of the Byzantine Game Engine."

Sidney pulled out her phone and started dialing.

"Please," I said. "I really need to get back up to The Tower."

Sidney spoke into her phone. "Albert, I need you in the lobby immediately."

I turned away from Sidney and hurried out of the building.

I stepped out into a light rain and called an Uber.

I waited around for a couple of minutes for the driver to show, but I was pretty freaked out by what had just happened, so I eventually canceled the ride and just started walking.

I walked for hours.

The rain had completely soaked my hoodie and jeans, but I just kept walking, doing my best to put one foot in front of the other, working to keep the gray feeling at bay and pushing all Rabbits-related thoughts away as quickly as they popped into my head. I couldn't have lost an entire day. There had to be some kind of logical explanation.

It was at this point that I noticed a car following me.

A yellow Prius had been driving behind me for about ten minutes, maintaining its distance while other cars sped up and passed. I could tell it was the same car because it had a decal on the passenger-side door that featured a tree floating above the words: ASK ME ABOUT NATURE-X. I tried to get a look at whoever was inside the car, but the windows were tinted.

The person behind the wheel may have had a perfectly good reason for driving slowly, and perhaps the fact that they'd been traveling the exact same route as me was a coincidence, but just in case, I crossed the street and left the Prius at an intersection in the far lane, unable to follow. Then, to make certain they wouldn't be able to find me again, I turned down a random alley half a block down.

Unless they had some kind of drone or stealth helicopter technology, I'd definitely lost them.

But I saw the Prius again a few blocks later, and once again, it was following me, keeping its distance a few cars back. I thought about turning around, running up to the car and knocking on the driver's-side window, but something about the entire situation didn't feel right.

That's when the floodgates finally opened, and the familiar wave of anxiety poured into my mind and body. Suddenly, I had the feeling I was walking alongside myself, my body completely untethered from my mind. In that moment, I had one thought: *If I could just lose that yellow car, everything would return to normal.*

I pulled out my phone to take a picture of the car's license plate, but the rain kept interfering with the touch screen. I was eventually able to open my phone's voice recorder application, so rather than write it down, I simply dictated the license plate number into my phone.

I walked for another block or so and then turned around. The car was still there.

After another half block, I pulled the same trick that had momentarily worked before. I left the yellow car stopped at a red light, but this time, instead of turning down a random alley, I stepped directly onto a bus that had conveniently just pulled over. There was no way they could possibly follow me now.

The bus was packed with people. I paid the fare, made my way through the crowd, and found a seat near the back. I stared out at the street through the windows. The yellow Prius was nowhere to be seen. I tried to relax, but I was feeling strange.

I took a deep breath. The car was gone. Everything was fine.

So why was there an unpleasant warm buzzing feeling moving through my body? Why was my heart racing, and why were my eyes unfocused and blurry? I started running through a deep-breathing exercise as I looked around.

The bus was filled with a mix of genders, ages, races, and socioeconomic classes. I'd taken the only available seat, between two older Eastern European women who were holding at least seven Target shopping bags between them.

As I was looking around the bus, I saw a face I recognized, near the back. He was seated next to a young South Asian couple with a baby.

It was Crow.

He smiled and nodded.

I forced myself to smile back as I watched him reach up and pull the cord. A loud bell rang, and the bus pulled over at the next stop.

But instead of Crow exiting the bus, everybody else got up and walked off, leaving the two of us alone.

At that point, the bus started moving again, and Crow came over and took a seat directly across from me.

We were now the only two people on the bus except for the driver.

"Hello again," he said.

"Hi," I said. "I was hoping I might be able to speak with you."

"And here we are."

I nodded. What the fuck was happening?

"You were surprised that Sidney Farrow didn't recognize you."

"Yes." I was just about to ask him how he knew that, but I stopped myself; I wasn't sure I was ready to handle the answer.

"I have some questions about you and my parents, and I'd like to speak with Emily Connors," I said.

"I'm afraid that's not going to be possible."

"Why not?"

"I'm going to ask you to do something, K—but please understand that I'm not asking you to do this for me. This is for you. I'm giving you this . . . opportunity out of respect for your parents. If you were anyone else, this conversation would be much different."

"Okay . . . can you please just tell me what's happening? The last time we met you said that had you known I was here, you would have made sure we'd met much sooner. What did you mean?"

"You're not supposed to be here," he said. "Or at least, that's what I had been led to believe."

I sat there for a moment, staring down at my hand gripping the edge of the sharp plastic seat. Was I dreaming? This couldn't be real. Why did all of those people get off the bus?

"What the hell does that mean?" I asked.

"If you don't stop playing the game you're calling Rabbits immediately, everything you know is going to either change or disappear, and everybody you know is going to forget you exist. This includes that girl Chloe from the arcade, I'm afraid."

"What . . . ?"

He smiled. "I'm sorry it has to be like this. I really am."

"Why are you doing this? Saying these things?"

"Like I said, this has nothing to do with you personally, K, but you need to stop playing Rabbits—and that means no looking into anything related to anything else that might be even remotely connected to the game. Do you understand?"

"I'm not even sure I am playing. Not really."

"Well, then," he said, "what I'm asking shouldn't be difficult." He rang the bell, and the bus pulled over and stopped.

And then the man called Crow stood up and stepped off the bus.

After a moment, I leapt up to follow him, but the doors had already closed. As the driver guided the bus slowly back out into the traffic, I rang the bell repeatedly.

"Pull over!" I yelled, but the driver just kept driving.

He finally pulled the bus over two blocks later, at the next scheduled stop.

I hurled myself off the bus, pushed past a group of people trying to get on, and rushed out onto the sidewalk.

I ran the two blocks back to where Crow had exited the bus, but he was gone.

I walked the rest of the way home.

I'd been inside my apartment for about five minutes when somebody buzzed.

I pressed the talk button of my intercom. "Hello?"

"I'm outside. Let me in."

I was trying to come up with some way to tell Chloe about the missing Sunday, Crow, and Emily Connors that didn't make me sound like a lunatic when Chloe burst into my apartment and handed me her phone.

"This guy," she said.

There was a pale, thin man with a skinny black mustache on Chloe's screen. He was standing in front of a bank of computer monitors.

"Who is he?"

"He's Fatman."

"Fatman?" I asked.

"Yeah."

"He's not fat."

"I guess it's ironic or something."

"Must be," I said.

"So I'm cashing out around ten thirty last night when I hear a sound coming from the Magician's office. I rush up there because I think he's finally back. I'm about to knock and give him shit for making us worry when I hear a voice coming from behind the door."

"Fatman?"

"Let me finish."

"Sorry."

"At first, I thought the Magician must have come in through the back, so I knock again, and then I open the door. And suddenly I'm on a video call with some guy."

"Fatman."

"That was the handle listed on the screen. He didn't give me his real name."

"He's a friend of the Magician?"

"He says they had a regular weekly call. It wasn't Skype or Face-Time, though. It looked like homemade software, or maybe something military."

"Really?"

"Yeah. There was a standard video window, but the rest of the interface was text-based, kind of like DOS. It was either really low-tech or bleeding-edge. It was hard to tell."

"So who was this guy?"

"I have no idea. He asked me if something had happened to the Magician, if he'd been acting strange lately."

"What did you say?"

"I didn't say anything. I had no idea who this guy was; he was just a face on a screen talking to me through some weird-ass software."

"So what happened next?"

"I asked him how he knew the Magician, but he was kind of cagey. And when I came right out and asked him if he'd ever heard of Rabbits, he disconnected the call."

"Shit."

"I tried calling back, but the user account called Fatman had been deactivated. I tried again and the computer froze. When I booted it back up, the entire program was gone."

"That's . . . weird," I said.

"No shit," Chloe said as she pulled one of the Magician's old Windows laptops out of her backpack.

"Wait, you stole the Magician's laptop?"

"No, I borrowed a computer from my absentee boss, just in case he needed saving from the consequences of playing an ancient and potentially deadly game."

"You know it's called a personal computer for a reason."

"Don't be so dramatic, K."

"Holy shit. You think *I'm* the one being dramatic here?"

"I do," she said as she hit enter on the old laptop and the password screen gave way to the familiar launch logo of Windows 95.

"What happened to not playing the game for a while?" I asked.

"I wasn't playing the game. This guy was just . . . on the screen."

Suddenly I thought about Crow's warning. What if he made Chloe forget I existed? Or what if he did something worse than that? I pictured the look on Baron's face when we'd climbed through his window and found him sitting in front of his computer. I didn't think I could handle seeing Chloe like that.

"Are you sure we should be doing this?" I asked.

"What else are we gonna do, play Tetris?"

26

IS THAT A FUCKING CROSSBOW?

ALONG WITH THE OUTER SPACE ELEVATOR scenario, there's another dream I've been having for as long as I can remember.

It begins with me staring at a sheet of ice, what appears to be the surface of a frozen lake. It takes me a moment to realize that my body is freezing, but then I'm shivering as I examine the cracks, colors, and shapes in the ice. The cold is intense, but the mosaic of the ice is so beautiful that I'm able to momentarily forget about the pain and just trace the artistic perfection in the surface of the lake with my eyes.

It's at this point that I suddenly realize I'm not above the ice but beneath it.

And I can no longer breathe.

This is when I understand that I'm about to die. Panic sets in, and I begin to thrash wildly beneath the freezing blue water, clawing, kicking, and screaming at the surface. But every action does nothing but push me farther down into the icy darkness.

While I'm stuck there beneath the ice, thrashing and dying, I can see everyone up on the surface skating and walking hand in hand, laughing and having fun, and beyond that the blur of families on the grass, laughing at their barbecues and playing Frisbee.

And behind all of that, I can see the sun shining beautifully, way high up in the sky.

Then, just as I'm about to succumb to some weird Leonardo

DiCaprio—esque *Titanic* trip to the unforgiving bottom of that cold wet world, the ice becomes something else.

It becomes glass.

A windshield, to be more specific.

And then I'm speeding along that dark country road in the truck with Annie and Emily Connors. I can hear the sharp crackle of static on the radio, and I can smell the Body Shop Dewberry perfume oil that Annie had been wearing.

The snowy static from the radio feels electric as it fills my ears, my head starts to shake, and a loud screaming pain slowly begins to tear my mind apart.

Then, as the world around me blurs and begins to fade away and the pain from the static in my head becomes too much to bear, I sense the dark thing coming toward me from somewhere outside my reality.

I realize the world is about to end.

And that's when I wake up.

"Are you okay?"

I was looking into Chloe's face, my kitchen ceiling visible behind her in the distance.

I was lying on the floor.

I sat up and the world slowly slipped into focus. "What happened?"

"You had another . . . episode," Chloe said.

"What time is it?" I asked, as I did my best to remember what had happened, how I'd ended up on the floor of my kitchen looking up at Chloe.

"It's seven forty-five," she said, helping me up. "What's the last thing you remember?"

"You stole the Magician's laptop," I said, "we looked over a few things, and then I was here."

"I borrowed his computer. We've been through that bit. That was two hours ago."

"It was?"

"I'm taking you to urgent care."

"I'm fine," I said as I scrambled to stand.

"Oh, well then," she said, "as long as *you* say you're fine."

I gave her the finger—along with what I hoped looked like a carefree smirk—and sank into one of the white plastic chairs at the dining room table.

What the hell was happening to me?

The last thing I remembered was worrying about Chloe for some reason. And then it came flooding back—not the missing two hours, but the reason I'd been so concerned.

Crow.

I'd been thinking about his warning, the fact that he'd mentioned Chloe specifically. That must have been when I passed out.

Did my concern for Chloe have something to do with my losing time? I've heard that stress can do crazy things to our minds and bodies. Could it be that simple? Did I just need to download a meditation app and book an hour of hot yoga?

Chloe sat down across from me and folded her arms.

I was just about to try to explain away my losing time, again, but there was something in the way Chloe was looking at me.

This was it.

If I didn't come completely clean, Chloe was going to know it, and I was going to lose her. Whatever happened, whether she believed me or not, I needed to be honest.

But more than that, I *wanted* to be honest.

Chloe was scared, probably picturing me in an MRI machine with wide-eyed technicians staring at a brain tumor the size of a small grapefruit.

I was pretty sure I didn't have a tumor—although when I started running over the wild story I was about to tell Chloe, I began to suspect I might be a bit overconfident about the tumor-free nature of my brain.

I told her everything.

I started with the mysterious man named Crow, how I'd originally met him in The Tower and how he'd gone on to pull a serious Moriarty move on a city bus filled with people he must have paid off. Then I explained how I'd been feeling recently—how the sensation

I called the gray feeling had flared up again after being dormant for most of my adult life. Chloe sat there expressionless. Her eyes didn't offer shock, worry, scorn, or support. She just nodded and listened.

Okay, so technically I didn't actually tell Chloe everything.

I left out the fact that I'd seen my childhood friend Emily Connors. I did this because what had happened with Crow was crazy, but adding a childhood friend showing up out of nowhere just felt a little . . . unhinged.

When I'd finished, I leaned back in my chair and waited. A few seconds later, Chloe exhaled and ran her hands through her hair.

"Crow?" she asked, clearly still trying to come to terms with everything I'd told her.

"That's what he told me," I said.

"You and I met Sidney Farrow?"

I nodded.

"And we drank wine with her late into the morning?"

"Yeah."

Chloe sighed. "That would have been amazing," she said.

"It was."

Gradually, I began building a picture. Chloe remembered Swan and the twins, but she had no memory of anything involving Sidney Farrow—including our visit to WorGames and the three of us examining the files Baron had uploaded. I didn't have the guts to ask if she remembered our kiss. I couldn't bear to lose that as well— though I'm sure we'd have to confront the issue eventually.

"K . . . ?"

"Yes?"

"Promise you won't get mad?"

"I know it's . . . impossible to believe. I just wanted to be completely honest."

"And I appreciate that," she said. "But you have to understand how all of this sounds to me."

I nodded. "I do."

The two of us sat there in silence for a moment, then I remembered something. I pulled out my phone. "I got the plate number of the car that was following me."

"Really?"

"Yeah. Do you think we might be able to find the owner?"

"Um . . . you're a part-time day trader and I'm living off royalties from a song I wrote more than a decade ago. Who the hell do we know who can run a plate?"

"Fair point," I said, staring at a blank screen on my phone. "It's dead."

I dug up a charger and plugged my phone into the wall. A few seconds later, the phone booted up and I opened the voice recorder application.

"What is it?" Chloe asked.

"I couldn't open my camera, so I recorded the plate number using my voice recorder." I showed her my phone.

Something didn't make sense. The most recent file was thirty-five minutes long.

"That's a pretty big file for a license plate."

"My fingers were wet. I probably didn't turn it off properly."

"Wait," Chloe said, excited. "When did you start recording?"

"Just before I met Crow on that bus."

Chloe jumped up, her eyes were huge. "Fuck, K, play it!"

I positioned the cursor near the end of the file and pressed play. The sound of Crow's voice warning me not to play the game spilled from my phone's tiny speakers.

I pressed stop and looked up at Chloe.

"Play the whole thing," she said.

Once we'd finished listening to the recording, Chloe sat back down across from me at the table. "That's insane," she said.

"I know."

"Really, though . . . I mean, do you have any idea how much money and planning something like that stunt on the bus would take?"

I nodded. It was true—although I hadn't really thought about it in those terms. There was something about the man called Crow, however, that made me feel like pulling that kind of stunt wouldn't actually be difficult for him.

"You asked him about somebody named Emily. Who's that?"

"A friend of my parents," I said, which wasn't exactly a lie.

"What if this guy is really dangerous, K?"

"I think he definitely falls into the dangerous category," I said.

"He warned you not to play the game."

"Or look into anything even remotely connected to Rabbits," I added.

"So what the fuck are we doing?"

Ever since I'd met Crow, I couldn't stop thinking about my parents. Was my entire childhood a lie? What were they really doing when they told me they were working on balance sheets and ledgers? Mapping fucking Meechum Radiants with Crow?

"I need to know what this guy knows about my parents, and I'd like to know if any of this stuff is connected to the game, but I'm not sure I want you . . . mixed up in this stuff anymore."

"Yeah, well, we're in this shit together, I'm afraid. I'm not going anywhere." She jumped up, grabbed the Magician's laptop, and brought it over to the dining room table. "Let's start with everything on this computer." Then she pulled her chair close to mine and gave me a huge kiss.

"What was that for?" I asked.

"Felt like it."

So, whatever was going on in this reality, Chloe and I were still involved in some kind of romantic relationship. I was relieved, but felt kind of unsteady. Were we at the same point emotionally? What about sex? Had we slept together in *this* reality?

"What are you thinking about?" Chloe asked.

"What do you mean?"

"You're looking at me like a fucking weirdo."

"You're a fucking weirdo," I said, and smiled.

"That's better," she said, and then the two of us sat down and went over everything we'd found in the Magician's bookmarks and browser history.

So, against the dire warnings of pretty much everybody, Chloe and I were back digging into the world of Rabbits.

We found a lot of really cool stuff in the Magician's bookmarks—including some code-breaking application links, veiled historical references to an ancient game, and interesting examples of alternate reality game puzzles—but we didn't find anything that pointed toward anybody called Fatman who matched the description of the guy Chloe had spoken with earlier.

After we'd finished, Chloe grabbed the Magician's computer and started to close it.

"Wait," I said.

"What?"

"If we're going to invade the Magician's private digital world, we should probably go all the way."

"I'm listening," Chloe said.

"I haven't used a Windows-based machine in a while, but there has to be a way to access library and application file data, right?"

"Sure is," Chloe said.

She performed a series of searches using the file explorer, but wasn't able to come up with anything. Then she tried a couple of hidden image file searches. One of those searches uncovered some thumbnail image files located inside a hidden library folder at the root level of the Magician's computer.

Chloe found Fatman right away. He was smiling back at us from one of the images. Chloe said it was a thumbnail screen capture generated by whatever video chat program the Magician had been using, probably created automatically during a system crash or similar disconnection situation.

"What the hell are HD video chat images doing on a computer running Windows 95?"

"Ninety-five is just a skin he's using for some old software. There's a proper OS on here as well."

Chloe navigated to a hidden subfolder and found a bunch of other thumbnails related to the same video chat program; three of them featured Fatman. Most of those screen captures featured the room Fatman had been standing in when he'd spoken with Chloe in the arcade, but one of the images was slightly different from the rest.

Fatman must have changed the position of his computer's camera at some point, because this particular screen cap provided a wider view of the room. Deep in the background of this image was a warm pink glow. The glow was coming from a neon sign that read: YALP.

"What the hell is yalp?" I said.

"Look at this," Chloe said as she changed the view from regular to mirror image horizontal.

"Holy shit," I said.

The word "yalp" had now become the word "play."

"How many Seattle businesses have the word 'play' in the title?"

"A lot," Chloe said, and the two of us sat down to look for neon signs.

We'd spent more than an hour combing through pictures featuring neon signs in Seattle when Chloe finally flipped her laptop around to reveal the website of a strip mall sex shop called Sinplay. The pink neon sign in the window matched the image from the Magician's computer exactly.

Chloe stood up. "Get your shit. We're going."

"It's almost midnight, is it even open?" I said as I stood up and stretched.

"Don't know. Hours aren't listed."

Chloe called the number on the website, but there was no answer.

"Are you sure it's the right place?" I asked, but Chloe was already putting on her shoes.

We found parking a couple of blocks away and walked over to the address Chloe had dug up online. As we made our way up the street toward the glowing pink neon sign, I thought I heard someone following us. I spun around, but there was nobody there. Chloe said she hadn't heard anything, but I was positive I'd heard footsteps and shuffling at some point, about half a block behind us.

Sinplay was located in a low brick building between a bicycle repair shop and a dry cleaner. The building's bricks had been painted black at some point, but so much of that paint had weathered away that it was almost impossible to come up with a word to describe the building's color.

There were no cars parked out front, and apart from the pink neon sign, there were no lights on inside or outside the store.

Sinplay appeared to be closed.

We tried calling again, but—just like before—there was no answer.

As we approached the glass door to knock, Chloe noticed something. "There's a basement," she said, pointing toward the bottom of the neon sign.

The building had an additional section directly below street level that was accessible only by a small staircase located behind a wrought iron gate. The lower section looked like it used to be a retail space, but now it appeared to be some kind of office or storage area. A significant portion of the window had been plastered with posters advertising various adult products.

"Locked," Chloe said, rattling the padlock on the gate.

"We should come back tomorrow," I said.

"Sounds good," Chloe agreed. "Let's eat. I'm starving." She turned around and started walking back toward the car.

Just as I was about to join her, I saw something moving through the basement window. "Wait," I said.

Chloe spun back to face me. "What?"

"There's somebody there."

"Don't fuck with me, K."

"I'm serious."

Chloe walked back over to the gate and the two of us stared through the bars into the basement.

Through gaps in the posters, we were able to make out parts of a black-and-white harlequin-patterned tile floor, and numerous stacks of books and filing boxes. There was light, coming from a source located somewhere in the back of the room, that dimly illuminated the front section of the store.

Something moved in the far-right-hand corner of the window.

"It's a cat, K," Chloe said.

"It definitely wasn't a cat," I insisted—just as a black-and-white cat jumped up onto one of the stacks of books that lined the other side of the window and began licking its paws.

Chloe shook her head. "Let's go."

"I swear, it was bigger than a cat," I said and leaned forward to get a better look into the dimly lit basement.

"Fine. I'll hop over and knock," Chloe said as she started climbing up the iron gate.

"That's not a great idea," said a disembodied voice.

"Fuck," Chloe exclaimed, so startled by the sudden sound that she almost fell.

"What are you doing?" the voice asked.

I followed the sound to a small speaker located next to the basement door.

"I know it sounds ridiculous," I said, "but we're looking for somebody named Fatman."

There was a long silence before a door opened behind the gate and a thin middle-aged man wearing a pink-and-blue faded *Beverly Hills, 90210* T-shirt and gray sweatpants—not the kind that one might acceptably wear out in the world—stepped outside. He was holding a large medieval-looking crossbow, which was locked and loaded and pointed directly at my chest.

"It's not ridiculous, it's ironic," he said, looking up at Chloe dangling precariously from the top of the metal gate.

"Is that a fucking *crossbow*?" Chloe asked.

"We come in peace," I added as Fatman lowered his crossbow and unlocked the gate, which swung open with a slow comedic creak, Chloe still attached.

I helped Chloe down and the two of us followed Fatman inside.

Fatman's office wasn't exactly messy, but it was definitely filled to capacity. Narrow makeshift paths had been fashioned between countless rows of bookshelves, cabinets, and desks. A closer look at the shelves, however, revealed order beneath the chaos. Although each shelf had been crammed full of books and printed materials of all kinds, everything appeared to be arranged in alphabetical order.

The ceiling was low, and the fluorescent lights gave the place the vibe of an old newsroom from the seventies. Movie posters covered a couple of the walls: *The Usual Suspects, Pulp Fiction,* and *The Rescuers Down Under,* to name just a few.

Enormous tattered blood-red curtains, which looked like they'd been taken from the set of a late-night talk show from the sixties, covered the entire back wall.

Whatever the hell this guy was doing down here, it looked like he'd been doing it for a very long time.

"You're the girl from the Magician's office," Fatman said as he closed and locked the door behind us.

"That sounds like a Lisbeth Salander vehicle," Chloe said, smiling.

Fatman ignored her joke. "How did you find me?"

Either he wasn't familiar with Stieg Larsson or he didn't think Chloe was all that funny. I thought her line was actually pretty good.

"The sign," I said.

He looked over at the bottom of the neon sign visible in the window and smiled. "Smart," he said. "That's smart."

He led us deeper into the large office, and as he maneuvered around a couple of narrow bookshelves, I noticed he limped a little.

"Fell off a camel," he said, as if that was the most mundane way in the world to injure your leg.

"Really?" I asked.

Fatman ignored my question and sat down in an old wooden rolling chair across from an unfortunate brownish-green couch. With the crossbow on his lap, he motioned for the two of us to sit. Then he looked at us over his thick black-framed glasses. "So, who are you people?"

"I'm K," I said, sinking deeper into the old sofa with a long creak.

He slowly nodded and turned to Chloe.

"Chloe," she said.

"You're the one Alan Scarpio came to see," he said as he turned back to face me. I noticed it wasn't a question.

"How did you know that?"

"Wild guess," he said, with a faint half smile.

"Did the Magician tell you that?"

He ignored my question and posed one of his own. "Have you heard from the Magician?"

"No," Chloe said. "Have you?"

He shook his head. "You"—he pointed at Chloe—"asked me about something before."

"Rabbits," Chloe said.

He carefully set his crossbow down onto a side table, angled it away from us, and leaned forward in his chair. "What do you two know about the game?"

"We know you're not supposed to talk about it, for one thing." I said. I wasn't sure if we should trust this guy. We had no idea who he was.

"For people concerned about not talking about something, you sure have a shitload of questions." He stood up and walked over to a nearby table where he plugged in an electric kettle. "Tea?" he asked.

Chloe and I nodded.

As he boiled the water and prepared the tea, he told us that his real name was Neil. And then he just started talking. And talking. His initially cool and distant demeanor was quickly displaced by a torrent of words and fragmented sentences. I got the feeling Fatman Neil didn't get a lot of visitors.

"Okay, so John Lennon from the Beatles, right?"

"Yeah?" I said, looking over at Chloe, who appeared just as confused as I was.

"He was supposed to be in the film *WarGames,* but he was assassinated before that could happen. And I don't mean he was killed roughly *around that time,* I mean they took him out *immediately before* that shit was about to go down."

"What does that have to do with anything?" I asked.

"Everything has to do with *everything,*" he said. "That's the thing you can never forget. That's the thing *behind* the thing."

Chloe looked over at me, and I could tell she was thinking this guy might just be a little bit out of his fucking mind.

"The last thing the Magician and I spoke about was you," Neil said, finally, nodding in my direction.

"Me?"

"Yes. He said Alan Scarpio came to see you and told you something was wrong with the game, that something needed to be fixed before the next iteration began. Does that sound about right?"

I nodded.

"Did he say anything else?"

"Just that we'd be well and truly fucked if the next iteration began before the game was fixed."

"Well," Neil said, leaning forward in his chair, "that doesn't sound good, does it."

"No," I said. "It doesn't."

"Why do you think Scarpio came to see you that night?"

"That's exactly what we're trying to figure out."

"Are you?"

"What do you mean?"

"I mean: How hard have you been trying to figure out why Alan Scarpio asked you—and I mean *you specifically*—to help him?"

I blinked. "I don't know. I mean, that part definitely doesn't make any sense."

"What if it did?"

"What do you mean?"

"I mean, what if Rabbits isn't what you think? What if it isn't just a game?"

"If it's not a game, then what is it?" Chloe asked.

"Oh, it's definitely a game," Fatman Neil said. "But what if it was more than that?"

I looked at Chloe. She just shrugged, and Fatman continued.

"Would you notice thirty dollars less in your bank account? What if the bookmark you were using was suddenly stuck between different pages than it had been when you left for work that morning? What if you woke up one day and some of the pictures in an old family photo album were different than you remembered?"

Chloe shook her head. "What are you talking about?"

Chloe was clearly confused, but I knew exactly what Fatman Neil was talking about. He was describing pretty much everything I'd been experiencing (minus the gray feeling and the freaky swirling things hovering just outside the edges of reality).

He ignored Chloe's question, stood up, and grabbed his phone. "I think it's time I introduced you to Mother."

"You want to introduce us to . . . your mother?" I asked.

"Not my mother—just Mother." Neil opened some kind of application on his phone and pressed a button. The enormous red curtains that covered the back wall of the room slowly parted to reveal a huge bank of video monitors of various sizes, shapes, and resolutions. There were more than a hundred screens covering the wall. It was beautiful in a "desert junk collector building an entire house out of old compact discs or soda bottles" kind of way.

Below the giant bank of monitors was a comfortable-looking, well-worn brown leather easy chair, and a long table covered in a variety of different colored computer keyboards. Hanging above the monitors was a banner that read: WE WANT THE FUTURE WE WERE PROMISED, NOT THE FUTURE WE DESERVE.

"*This* is Mother," Neil said, and took a seat in the chair.

"Holy shit," Chloe said, staring up at the wall of screens.

"How many monitors do you have hooked up here?" I asked, coming over to stand beside Neil.

"A lot," he said.

"What is all of this?" Chloe asked as she joined us.

"Mother is an elaborate citywide network of battery-operated and solar-powered cameras, portable microphones, and switch relays. If the other side is watching and listening to us—and you'd better believe they are," he continued, "then we need to be watching and listening right back."

"This is incredible," Chloe said.

"They have grocery store cards collecting our data, smart speakers tracking every word, drug store and transit loyalty points cards, gym memberships, key fobs, and black strips on the back of your driver's license. They have GPS-capable computers in our hands and pockets at all times. They know who we are and what we're doing. We needed something to fight back."

"To fight back? Who are you fighting?"

"The system," he said, as he pressed a few buttons on a keyboard—what appeared to be some kind of boot sequence. "The bad guys."

"These cameras are citywide?" Chloe asked.

"Yes, although in order to achieve full coverage, a portion of our network is audio only."

"So you watch and listen to the entire city of Seattle?"

"Pretty much, yes."

"That has to be an *enormous* amount of data," I said.

"It is."

"How can you possibly parse it all?"

"I can't. That's Mother's job."

"Your computer?"

"Not exactly. Mother's an algorithm."

"What does it do, exactly?"

"*She* does this," he said, then reached over and pressed a few buttons on one of the keyboards positioned along the long table.

The images on the wall of screens suddenly shifted, morphing into a single, very large map of the city covered with a variety of small color-coded numbers and symbols—the latter reminded me of something you'd find in an ancient alchemy textbook. The map appeared to be centered around a section of downtown Seattle. I wanted to pull out my phone and take a picture, but something told me Fatman Neil wasn't going to be cool with that.

"What does all this mean?" Chloe said, leaning forward—as if getting slightly closer might help her make sense of the visual chaos contained in those multiple screens.

"She notifies us when something out of the ordinary happens. Mother's a mix of pattern discovery, facial recognition, speech interpretation, traffic monitoring, and fractal modeling software."

"Holy shit." I couldn't think of anything else to say.

"Just wait until quantum computers hit the mainstream. The possibilities are endless."

"Aren't quantum computers still decades away?" Chloe asked.

"They're coming. But like Andersen Cheng from Post-Quantum said—and I'm paraphrasing here—the first working quantum machine will never be announced, because whoever gets it will become the master of the universe."

"That's a bold claim," I said.

"It's a fact. They'll be able to crack Bitcoin and intercept any global communication setup in existence. They'll become a superpower overnight."

"Quantum or not, this setup is impressive," I said, and I meant it, although I couldn't help thinking Mother felt like the indie version of whatever the hell Crow had built up in The Tower at WorGames. Was Fatman using Mother to mess with people's lives in a similar way?

"Thanks," he said.

"And you're using all of this to play Rabbits?" Chloe asked.

"Me? No, I never play the game."

"So what's all this for?" I asked.

"During the last two iterations of the game, we noticed that something was off, that things were . . . changing. Mother was designed to monitor those changes."

"Things were changing . . . how?" I asked.

"There were more . . . incidents of alteration, coincidences that fell outside the usual parameters, changes in the intensity in the game—or, more specifically, in the way the game was affecting the world."

"Incidents of alteration?"

"It's technical," he said.

"How does Mother work, exactly?" Chloe asked.

"She was designed to monitor and track systems."

"What kind of systems?" I asked, experiencing a sense of déjà vu as I spoke. Hadn't I asked Crow the same thing?

"All of them," he said. "Or at least all of the systems designed to keep a major North American city operational: sanitation, transportation, food and beverage, and many more."

"And if something breaks down in one of these systems, you fix it?" I asked.

"Mother wasn't designed to help us interfere or manipulate; we're strictly observation only."

I was extremely uneasy about the thought of privatized citywide surveillance, but at least Fatman didn't appear to be manipulating people's lives the way Crow was doing up in his Tower.

"And you work here, all alone?" Chloe asked.

"We've created something similar in San Francisco, Los Angeles, Cleveland, Prague, London, New York, and a bunch of other cities."

"We?"

"Those of us concerned about changes in the game."

"So you're not playing Rabbits? Not at all?" I asked.

Neil turned very serious suddenly. "No, and neither are you—unless you're stupid, suicidal, or both."

"Because players are disappearing," I said.

"No," he replied. "Because *so many* players are disappearing . . . and worse."

I wasn't sure Fatman knew about Baron, but he clearly understood that people connected to Rabbits were dying.

"Do you have any idea why this is happening?" Chloe asked.

Neil shook his head. "That's what we've been trying to find out."

"What happened to Alan Scarpio?" I asked.

He shook his head. "Mother couldn't find anything, and that's very concerning."

"What do you mean?"

"Even though he is notoriously reclusive, Scarpio remains a fairly recognizable public figure. The day he disappeared, he *completely* disappeared. There was nothing on any of the dozens of cameras and microphones that had picked up Scarpio's activity regularly in the past. He just . . . vanished."

"Vanished . . . like the Magician," I said.

Fatman nodded.

"What are those?" Chloe asked, pointing to a few glowing yellow stars that had popped up on various locations on the map of the city while we were talking.

"AILs," he said. "Alteration incident locations. Those stars mark the locations where players reported potential incidents of alteration."

"What are you talking about?" Chloe asked.

"Incidents of alteration are when things appear different than expected."

"You mean like the Mandela effect and the Berenstein Bears? False memories?" Chloe asked.

"Exactly," Neil said. "Except what if they're not false?"

"Other dimensions? Multiple worlds?" Chloe asked, but I could tell he wasn't talking about that. He was talking about something else entirely.

"You're talking about the Moriarty Factor," I said.

Fatman smiled.

"But isn't the Moriarty Factor just whatever trillion-dollar multinational conglomerate is behind the game guiding the experience and leading the players to clues?" Chloe asked.

"That's one theory," Neil said. "Somebody behind the game spending a whole bunch of money to make things happen."

"What do you think's happening?" I asked.

"I'm not sure, but I do know one thing."

"What's that?" Chloe asked.

"Moriarty was a bad guy."

Neil let the last bit of that sentence hang in the air as he stared at me, and I thought back to the man named Crow and what he'd said to me after he staged that elaborate scene on the bus.

"What are you saying?" I asked.

"There are many of us who believe that somebody or something has been working to . . . compromise the game."

"Is that possible?" Chloe asked.

"Think about what happened with that politician in London. Look how public that was," Fatman said.

"So?" I asked.

" 'The door is open'? You do know that's a key phrase in the game, right?"

"Sure," I said, "but it's also just four words."

"You don't believe it's a coincidence," he said.

"Maybe not, but those four words were used in connection with Jesselman's take on immigration during his campaign two election cycles back. We can't be sure his suicide was connected to Rabbits."

"He was involved with a group called The Children of the Gray God—a pagan-based cult in England. He was busted having sex with three of their younger female members on Glastonbury Tor. It was a bit of a scandal."

"The Children of the Gray God?"

"Yep. The very same secretive group that has been mentioned in connection with Rabbits in the past. The group that—"

Just as Neil was about to say something more, his computer screens lit up with activity. He pressed a few keys and suddenly a text alert popped up on his phone. "Sorry, I have to get back to work."

"Can we meet again sometime this week? Maybe tomorrow?" I asked.

"Nope," Neil said as he led us out of his office and back up through the gate.

"What?" Chloe asked. "Why not?"

"Whatever you do, stay away from the game," he said as he closed and locked the gate behind us.

Our interview was clearly over.

We left Fatman Neil working on the makeshift citywide computer matrix he kept in his strange porn shop basement, and made our way back to Chloe's car. The moment she closed her door, she turned to face me. "What the fuck is up with the Berenstein Bears and the homemade super-spy computer bullshit?"

"Berenstain," I said.

"You're not funny," Chloe said.

"I'm actually serious."

"It's fucking Berenstein, and I'm not arguing with you."

For those who might be unfamiliar with the Berenstain multiverse conundrum, there's a popular series of children's books called The Berenstain Bears. But, interestingly, just like Chloe, most people remember it as The *Berenstein* Bears. This belief in an alternate pronunciation actually runs much deeper than a simple argument that can be addressed with a Google search. The people who remember The Berenstein Bears insist their spelling and pronunciation are correct, and refuse to believe that name had ever been written or pronounced any other way.

So, what happened?

The most prevalent theory goes like this: At some point in our history, two (or more) dimensions or streams of time diverged. Our world somehow hopped tracks—slipped streams into a parallel reality. There now exists an alternate reality—which is actually our previous reality, or one of our previous realities—where that series of books is still called The Berenstein Bears and Berenstain never existed.

There are similar theories surrounding a nonexistent film from the 1990s called *Shazaam,* which allegedly starred the comedian Sinbad as a genie, and the Mandela effect, a phrase coined by self-described "paranormal consultant" Fiona Broome. Broome claimed that she remembered South African leader Nelson Mandela dying in prison in the 1980s, while in reality Mandela lived until December 2013.

The most logical explanation for all of these competing memories is perhaps best illustrated by the following example. The belief people share that a film from the 1990s called *Shazaam* starring Sinbad existed is most likely due to a number of factors, including the following: Sinbad the comedian presented a number of *Sinbad the Sailor* movies in 1994. While presenting the films, Sinbad wore a genielike costume. In 1996, a similarly named film, *Kazaam,* was released starring basketball player Shaquille O'Neal as a genie.

So, we're either misremembering similar things en masse, or we're living in slightly different dimensional streams that branched off at some point in the past.

As an interesting aside, Fatman Neil had a *Kazaam* poster up in his lair.

"Neil seems like a fairly well-adjusted guy," I said.

Chloe held up her hands. "I can't even."

We drove for a few minutes in silence.

"What are we gonna do now?" Chloe said.

Something about her voice sounded strained. I looked down at her hands on the steering wheel. She was squeezing hard, her knuckles tight and shiny. It didn't happen often, but I could tell that Chloe was overtired and heading into a kind of light manic state.

I'd seen her like this before. I wasn't the only one with an obsessive personality issue connected to the game.

———

A few years after we met, there were rumors that something big was happening with Rabbits, and we were all trying to figure out if the next iteration of the game had started.

Chloe had been chasing some clues related to a missing coast guard officer, and had somehow ended up stranded on the northern anchor of the Aurora Bridge. While she was up there looking for something that was supposed to be carved into the stone, she'd slipped and almost fallen to her death.

When I finally caught up with her and helped her off the bridge, she was severely dehydrated and hadn't slept for days. I had to track down and pay Chloe's alcoholic mother fifty dollars in order to get her to call the hospital and have her daughter taken off the hospital's involuntary hold list.

Like most of us consumed by the game, Rabbits was a way for Chloe to temporarily enter another realm—a place where everything wasn't exactly the way it was in real life.

We each had our reasons for wanting the fantastical world promised by Rabbits to replace the flawed emotional narrative of our real lives. For Chloe, escaping into a mysterious world meant that she was able to forget her family for a while and focus on something exciting that she was really good at.

For me, Rabbits was a way to try and hang on to the sense of mystery and wonder I'd been obsessed with as a kid. But it was more than that. I'd always imagined my obsession with the game was somehow helping me get over the loss of my parents.

But what if the opposite were true?

I'd always believed I was following patterns and looking for connections related to the game because I was trying to stop thinking about my parents, but what if I'd been drawn into the world of Rabbits specifically because I wasn't ready to let them go?

"What are we going to do now?" Chloe asked.

"Now, it's bedtime," I said.

"For real?"

"It's almost two in the morning."

"So? Don't two in the morning me. What about The Children of the Gray God? We need to know all the fuck about that."

I wanted to know all the fuck about that too, but I was worried about Chloe. She needed to sleep. *I* needed to sleep.

Fatman Neil's porn store basement wasn't more than fifteen minutes from my place, but Chloe was distracted, and after missing a couple of turns, she'd managed to turn it into a half-hour drive.

"We've been warned off Rabbits by Russell Milligan, the Magician, Crow, and now Fatman Neil," I said. "Maybe we need to take a step back, just to regroup."

"Wait, so you're the voice of fucking reason now?" Chloe snapped.

"Hey, we 'voice of reason' each other. It's what we do."

"I can't believe you can just go to sleep with all that's happening."

"You're going to go to sleep too, okay?"

"Fine."

We drove in silence for a few blocks.

"Sorry, I'm a bit . . . edgy. It's just that I've been thinking a lot about Baron," Chloe said. "It's so fucked-up. What if we can figure out what happened?"

"We know what happened."

"I mean what *really* happened."

"I don't know," I said.

"Come on, K. Baron's dead."

"Exactly," I said. "Baron's dead and I don't want you to be next."

We drove in silence for another block.

"It's because you dig me so hard, isn't it?" Chloe said.

"Maybe," I said.

I did dig Chloe, a whole lot, but at the moment, I had no idea what was going on with the two of us. I had a bunch of questions like: Would this version of Chloe's interpretation of events over the past couple of months match my own? Was the strange shit I'd been experiencing some kind of weird dimensional flux, or was it something far more mundane?

What if I was in the middle of some kind of mental or emotional breakdown?

Chloe dropped me off at home, and although my body was exhausted, my mind was too wired to sleep. I turned on the television for the first time in ages (I kept my cable subscription for the Seahawks). I thought I'd try to find something that might help unwind my brain enough to let me fall asleep.

I laid down on the couch and started watching a black-and-white movie from the fifties called *The Night of the Hunter*. I'd chosen that movie not only because I knew it was a great film, but also because I'd actually fallen asleep watching it once before.

I was nine years old. My parents were hosting their monthly film-noir evening with their closest friends, Bill and Madeline Connors—Annie and Emily's parents. As always, after they'd put me to bed, they made popcorn and the four of them settled in to watch their movie.

I've always loved movies, and whenever my parents had these film nights, I'd sneak out of my bedroom and hide upstairs behind the banister. I was able to see the television clearly from up there, but because of the angle, my parents couldn't see me. As long as I stayed quiet, I was able to watch whatever they were watching.

The previous month they'd chosen something about a guy looking for murderous androids (a film I'd learn years later was *Blade Runner*), and before that it had been something about a boat and a sea creature that I couldn't clearly recall.

But I remember exactly what it was about *The Night of the Hunter* that had made it impossible for me to turn away. It was the fact that the man in the movie—the preacher character played by Robert Mitchum—had two words written across his knuckles: "love" and "hate."

"Would you like me to tell you the little story of right-hand/left-hand?" he'd said, just before he went on to mime an intense struggle between love and hate using only his hands, his fingers intertwined as if he were battling for the souls of all mankind.

The scene was mesmerizing.

The Night of the Hunter felt different from the other black-and-white movies I'd seen—more real somehow. More grown-up. There was something about the way *The Night of the Hunter* made me feel—as if there was something going on beneath the surface of that film, something deeply authentic and moving. It was the same way I would come to feel about Rabbits, later.

My parents found me asleep in the hallway sometime after *The Night of the Hunter* had ended and carried me to bed. They never mentioned anything about my cinematic transgressions, and I continued to spy on their movies from behind that banister for as long as we lived in that house.

But this time, as I was nodding off, I realized something.

I jumped up from the couch, opened my computer, and loaded a clip from *The Night of the Hunter* on YouTube. I pressed play.

The scene with Robert Mitchum unfolded just as I remembered, with the two hands, love and hate battling for supremacy, but something was wrong. In the version I remembered, "love" had been written across the knuckles on Mitchum's right hand and "hate" across his left. In the version I was looking at now, the words were reversed.

I performed a search and took a look at a dozen or so images. They were all the same. "Hate" on the right, "love" on the left.

I felt a wave of panic wash over me, and the world went black.

I was jarred violently awake by a beeping and blaring Klaxon followed by an announcement.

It was a test of the Washington Emergency Alert System.

I jumped up and switched off the television. The room was suddenly dark and completely silent. The only light came from the clock on the DVR: 4:44 A.M.

NOTES ON THE GAME:
MISSIVE BY HAZEL
(AUTHENTICATED BY BLOCKCHAIN)

Find the game. Play the game.

Once you discover the entry point phrase, "The Door Is Open," it's time to follow the clues and find your path.

Once The Door Is Open, the game begins to focus on those players who are making progress. The game will guide them.

As the clues get deeper and more complex, the players begin to fall away. Eventually, if you make it far enough, you will be one of the few remaining who know something is different. You will be one of the few who understand. You will be one of the few who may have touched another world.

—HAZEL 8

27

THE CHILDREN OF
THE GRAY GOD

I MUST HAVE FALLEN BACK ASLEEP, because when I woke up to the sound of somebody buzzing my apartment, it was after noon.

I stumbled into the living room and hit the button that would let whoever it was into the building. I didn't have the energy to ask. If it was Swan and her twins, so be it. I unlocked my door and started the process of making coffee.

As I was pressing the lever down on my electric kettle, Chloe rushed into my apartment and shoved open my living room curtains.

"What's with the darkness, K?"

"It's Seattle. It's always dark."

"That's why we need as much light as we can get," Chloe said as she moved through my apartment and switched on all of the lights. "Cousin Johnny's going to call as soon as he gets a break on set."

"Johnny from England?"

"Obviously."

"Didn't you guys have a fight?"

"His mother and mine hate each other, but we're cool."

"When's the last time you spoke with him?"

"His dad's funeral, I think."

"Okay, so . . . why is he calling?"

"I texted him last night. He said he might know somebody who was in that sex cult."

"Really?"

"Yeah, he knows way too many people."

Chloe pulled her laptop out of her backpack.

"I found something else," Chloe continued.

"What is it?"

"Minister Jesselman was working on an Internet privacy bill on behalf of a number of lobbyists at the time of his death."

"And?"

"And, one of the companies connected to that bill is Chronicler Enterprises."

Chloe opened up her computer.

"Wait," I said. "Isn't that the company behind Tabitha Henry's escape rooms?"

"It sure is."

"Shit. Were you able to dig up anything else on them?"

"There's nothing online but a defunct URL."

Chloe loaded a Web page, which displayed the following text.

Page not found (404 error).

Below the text was the ubiquitous error 404 graphic of an exclamation point inside a yellow triangle.

It was a dead site, but something about it looked familiar. It took me a few seconds to figure it out.

"The font," I said.

"What about it?"

"It's the same."

"The same as what?"

"As the error message page the QR code led us to from those Gustave Doré drawings we found in the museum."

I loaded that website on my laptop and we compared the page from the QR code that featured the 404 error message below the graphic of a spinning ball, with the new site that Chloe had found featuring the same error message above a triangle with an exclamation point.

The style of the pages and the font were exactly the same.

"They look identical except for the graphic," Chloe said.

We took a look at the HTML source code using the developer tab in our browser, but we couldn't find anything in the code.

"What is this stuff?" Chloe pointed to a line of text that appeared at the bottom of each of the two pages. There were a bunch of seemingly random numbers, spaces, and letters followed by the message: *Request failed with HTTP status 404.*

"Looks like nonsense," I said.

Chloe nodded.

"But . . . what if it isn't?" I leaned in for a closer look.

"What do you mean?"

"I have a theory," I said as I sent the pages to my printer.

"You wanna share?"

I rushed across the room and waited for the printer to finish.

"What are you doing?"

I pulled the two pages out of the printer, pressed them together, and held them up to my dining room chandelier.

"This," I said, and motioned Chloe over.

"Holy shit," she said.

Set amidst the random numbers and letters that ran along the bottom of the page was one section of comprehensible text. A URL: *gatewickinstitute.com*

"What the hell is the Gatewick Insitute?" I asked.

The two of us sat down to try to figure that out.

"Gatewick is linked to a number of obscure experimental medical research studies that took place in the seventies and eighties," Chloe said as she scrolled through what she'd been able to dig up.

I couldn't find anything, so I closed my computer and moved over to sit beside Chloe on the couch.

"Anything else?" I asked.

"A little."

The last physical address Chloe had been able to find was a cluster of buildings in San Francisco, but that was way back in 1987. There was nothing current.

It looked like the Gatewick Institute had sold itself as some kind of medical research facility–slash–self-help spa retreat, promising peace of mind and body for a very reasonable price.

Along with the cluster of buildings in San Francisco, Chloe managed to uncover a handful of newspaper and magazine ads from around that time that shared a now-defunct telephone number with the Gatewick Institute. The ads were mysterious and vague. They were looking for research subjects for some kind of medical study that appeared to straddle the line between pharmaceutical well-being and new-age enlightenment.

The handful of people Chloe had been able to find connected to the institute were either dead, completely detached from the world of social media, or both.

We were just about to take a break and get something to eat when Chloe showed me a photo on her phone—a picture of a narrow red-brick-and-glass building with long uniform rows of birch trees running along concrete pathways on either side of it.

"Where is this?" I asked, my mouth suddenly dry, my breathing slightly shallow and labored.

"San Francisco. One of a small cluster of buildings that belonged to the Gatewick Institute in 1982."

"Where did you get it?"

"Darknet forum."

"Is there any other information?" I tried to focus on the moment, to anchor myself next to Chloe on the couch, but I could feel my heart beginning to race in my chest. I took a deep breath and held it for a few seconds before exhaling.

"You recognize this place," she said.

Forty-thirty.

"Maybe," I lied. "I'm not sure." I was having trouble keeping my voice level.

"Are you okay?"

Deuce.

"I'm fine."

But my stomach felt light and empty. A few glittering stars danced around the edges of my eyes as my peripheral vision threatened to tunnel.

Advantage, McEnroe.

I looked at Chloe and followed her eyes. She was staring down at my legs where I'd been tapping out the 1992 U.S. Open fourth-round match between John McEnroe and Jim Courier.

"K, you need to tell me what the hell is going on."

I tried to force a smile, act like everything was fine. I took four or five slow deep breaths, then got up and walked over to the closet. I reached up and removed a black-and-brown banker's box from the top shelf.

"I've seen that building before," I said as I sat back down on the couch beside Chloe and opened the box.

"What is this?" she asked.

"It's everything I have left of my parents."

Chloe and I had spoken about our families countless times over the years. She was aware of the ferry accident that had killed my parents, and I knew about her experiences with an alcoholic mother and a sister who was constantly on the verge of being institutionalized for an extreme personality disorder. But I'd never taken Chloe through the contents of the box. It was one thing to talk about this stuff; it was quite another to see it staring back at you in full color.

Although I hadn't opened the box in years, my mind had cataloged everything in significant detail.

Chloe's eyes scanned each item as I pulled it out and set it down on the coffee table. There were a number of worn, old file folders filled with papers—including birth, marriage, and death certificates—a couple of baseball and hockey trophies, Ruby's leash and collar, a large stack of old photographs, and a bunch of other distant memories in physical form.

"Oh my god. You dress exactly the same." She held up a picture of me in jeans and a David Bowie T-shirt.

"Settle down," I said. I was starting to feel a bit better. Having Chloe with me as I went through this stuff helped a lot.

I opened one of the folders and flipped through a bunch of pages until I found what I was looking for. It was a picture that had been paper-clipped to a photocopy of the deed to our old house in Olympia.

"Holy shit," Chloe said.

"Yeah. I don't know what's happening."

The photograph Chloe had picked up featured my parents and their best friends, Bill and Madeline Connors, standing with a few other people in front of a brick building. She held up that picture and the photo from the darknet forum, side by side. The buildings were identical. The birch trees, the concrete paths, everything.

"It's the same place," Chloe said.

Even though the angles were slightly different, it was clearly the same building. I knew it the moment I'd seen it on Chloe's phone earlier.

Maybe Crow was right.

Maybe my parents hadn't actually been accountants after all.

"I have something else," Chloe said as she swiped away the image and started searching through the darknet forum again.

"Wait," I said, "go back."

She returned to the photograph. "What?"

"Can you zoom in on the doorway?"

Chloe zoomed in, framing the door of the building in the center of her screen.

There on the wall, just next to the door, was a thin, dusty silver sign. A small circle atop a triangle—the symbol from my elevator dream.

An image from my recurring nightmares was the logo of the Gatewick Institute.

"Do you recognize that symbol?" Chloe asked.

"I'm not sure," I lied.

Chloe pulled up some other documents from that darknet site: three scanned pages. The headers on top of all three featured the logo of the circle atop the triangle.

"Look at this shit," Chloe said, handing me her phone.

I read through the contents of the first page. There were a bunch of questions that appeared to be related to mental and physical fitness, followed by a checklist of activities designed to "counter the negative" and "enhance the positive." "Looks like part of an outline for a treatment plan, maybe?"

"Do you think your parents really *were* involved in this stuff?"

"I don't know," I said.

Chloe was shaking her head as she read over my shoulder. "What does all this shit mean?"

"Probably nothing," I said, hoping Chloe would concur.

"Oh, it's definitely not nothing." She pointed at the second of the three pages. "Medication and meditation, float tanks, DMT? This is some MKUltra bullshit right here, K."

"What if it was just some kind of intense self-help retreat thing?"

"Strobe light treatment, hypnosis . . . Jesus, K, the medication panel includes ayahuasca." She held up the page.

"Lots of people do ayahuasca these days," I said. "The nouveau new age set take that shit like it's vitamin C."

"Not back then," she said.

I shrugged.

"And the rest of the ingredients have been redacted."

"So?"

"So, if ayahuasca is the mildest ingredient in your psychotropic stew, you're in serious fucking trouble. You had no idea your parents were into this stuff?"

"No way. As far as I knew, they were accountants. I mean, I guess I knew they were involved in some kind of spiritual community with most of their friends, but I was an only child. Whenever our families got together, I was focused on hanging out with the other kids."

"Are you still in touch with any of those family friends?"

I thought about the Connors sisters, and the accident came flooding back.

The sound of the static on the radio. The smell of the cab of the truck.

"Hey," Chloe said. "K?"

"What?"

Chloe put her hand over mine. At some point I'd begun tapping on my thigh again. "Are you okay?"

"No," I said, "I mean, yes, I'm fine. No, I'm not in touch with any of those childhood friends."

This was true. I'd tried to look a few of them up on social media over the years, but there wasn't much there. Once again, I left out the fact that I'd recently seen one very close family friend named Emily Connors in Crow's office.

Chloe's hand on top of mine was comforting, and I found myself able to relax a little while she did another darknet search on the Gatewick Institute.

There was nothing we hadn't seen already.

Then Chloe's phone rang. It was her cousin in England. She answered and put it on speaker.

"Hey, Johnny."

"Chloe, how are you?"

"I'm good. I'm here with my friend K. You're on speaker, so don't say anything fucking weird."

"So nothing family-related?"

"Definitely not," she said.

Johnny laughed. "Okay. So, I spoke to a woman I know about your cult thing. She says she'll be up until midnight your time and you can give her a ring if you like."

"Was she part of the cult?"

"Not sure, but she seems to know quite a lot about it."

A bunch of other voices started speaking on the other end of the line.

"Sorry, kid, I've gotta run back to set. Good luck."

"Thanks, Johnny," Chloe said.

A second after her cousin had hung up, Chloe received a text with a name and phone number. The woman's name was Carlotta Blake.

"You wanna call or wait until the morning?" I asked.

"What do you think?" Chloe said as she dialed the number.

Carlotta picked up on the first ring.

"Hi, Carlotta, my name is Chloe and I'm here with my friend K."

"Hi, it's nice to meet you. Johnny said you'd be calling."

"Cool," Chloe said. "He told us you'd be okay with answering a few questions about the Gray God people?"

"No worries. Ask away."

"Okay, so, first thing," Chloe said. "Have you ever heard of Rabbits?"

"Um . . . I'm sorry, what?"

"Not the animals. We're talking about an obscure underground alternate reality game," I added.

Nothing from Carlotta.

"Carlotta? Are you still there?"

"I'm here. Yes. Sorry, no, I haven't heard of anything called Rabbits specifically, but the cult was definitely involved with some kind of weird game."

"How so?" Chloe asked.

"Well, it was this thing that the elders would do with some of the adepts—a ceremony that was supposed to guide them to what they called the sacred path. I remember hearing a couple of them refer to that process as 'the game' at some point."

"Do you know what they meant by the sacred path?"

"Not really, but they also referred to it as the path to the Gray God."

"How long were you part of the group?"

"Oh, it's definitely a cult, not a group, and I wasn't really part of it. I was there for less than forty-eight hours. My friend was a journalist who'd been embedded with those weirdos for a year. She was writing a long-form article for a national newspaper. Near the end of her time with the cult, she began feeling like something was off, like she might be in danger, so she asked me if I'd be willing to join the group for her last week, you know, to keep an eye on her."

"You weren't worried about the fact that it was a cult?" I asked.

"I mean, I was only there for a short time, but I was worried about my friend. I'd tried to convince her to leave, multiple times, but she told me she'd put in way too much effort, and that she was close to discovering something big. I suppose I would have been more concerned had I known what was going to happen to those two girls."

"The girls who were caught having sex with the minister on Glastonbury Tor?" I asked.

"No, the girls who disappeared."

"What girls?" Chloe asked.

"The two girls who met the Gray God, if you believe those lunatics."

"What happened?" I asked.

"Okay, so my friend was pretty high up in the cult at this point, and she was able to persuade the elders to let me come along on what they call pathfinding."

"What's that?" Chloe asked.

"It was bloody nuts is what it was. First the adepts, including my friend, would get together in a room filled with all kinds of really strange old computers, do a boatload of drugs, and then they would somehow try to find the path to the Gray God. This was part of the thing I heard a couple of them refer to as 'the game.'"

"And you don't recall them using the term 'Rabbits' at any point?"

"No, not that I remember, sorry."

"What happened to the girls?" Chloe asked.

"Okay, so after they did whatever crazy shit they did in that room, the rest of us joined them, and we went out pathfinding."

"What does that mean, pathfinding?" I asked.

"Apparently, during their session they'd discovered some kind of clue, and we were all going out to Whitechapel to find it."

"What was the clue?"

"They'd discovered a street that didn't exist."

"What does that mean?" I asked. But I knew exactly what she meant.

I felt a deep thrumming building in my chest. A street that didn't exist. This was Emily Connors's impossible woodpecker, this was that version of Andrew Wyeth's *Christina's World* with too many windows in the farmhouse. This was Sidney Farrow forgetting who I was.

This was Rabbits.

"All we were told was that it was a street that didn't or shouldn't exist," Carlotta continued. "They didn't know exactly where it was, so we were split into three groups of four. My friend and I were part of a group that included two young women, barely into their twenties."

Carlotta stopped talking for a moment. She was clearly upset.

"Take your time," Chloe said.

Carlotta took a few deep breaths and then continued.

"Right. Okay, so the two young women were really excited. They kept referring to a page covered in wild scribbles. I think they were using it as some kind of map to guide us through Whitechapel."

"Do you have an idea where they found that map?"

"Apparently the drugs they'd taken during the first stage of the process helped them enter a trance, and they'd just write down whatever popped into their heads, like automatic writing or whatever. They scribbled all kinds of words, crazy symbols, and patterns. Somebody was in charge of looking at everybody's scribbled nonsense and picking out repeating words and patterns. They took those repeating bits and apparently that's what they used to build their map. At least, that's what my friend told me."

"Did that page of words and scribbles guide you to a street that didn't exist?" Chloe asked.

"Yeah, it actually did," she said. "But right before that, something else happened. The girls got excited. They kept whispering to each other that they could feel him, that he was coming."

"Who?"

"They said that the Gray God was calling them, and they started to run. My friend and I followed, but it was hard to keep up. We ended up running for three or four blocks until we came to the entrance of a narrow old cobblestone alleyway, but when I looked down at the GPS on my phone, there was no alley. As far as Google Maps was concerned, we were standing in front of a solid building. And something else was strange."

"What?" Chloe asked.

"There was nobody around. Somehow we'd ended up alone on a Friday night in London."

"So?" Chloe said. "Maybe it was just a lull or something."

"No. That doesn't happen. This is London, mate. There are always people everywhere."

Carlotta was silent for a moment, possibly reliving the weirdness of those vacant streets.

"What happened next?" I prompted.

"My friend told the girls that we were supposed to wait for the others and enter the alley as a group, but they weren't having it. They said that the Gray God was calling to them, and that he wanted them to hurry. Then the two girls held hands and stepped into the alley. I can still hear the sound of their heels clicking against the cobblestones as they moved forward, hand in hand, into the darkness. My friend texted the others our location, and then we followed the girls."

Carlotta paused for a moment to take a sip of something, and then continued.

"Now, this is when things start to get extra weird," she said.

"What do you mean?" Chloe asked.

"Well, it's kind of hard to explain but . . . something started to change in the alley, near the back."

"Change how?" I asked.

"Well, it started like some kind of smudge in the distance . . . a smudge that soon became something else. It was like a horror film. The darkness was . . . folding around the alley somehow, and we could no longer see the two girls ahead of us. Suddenly I felt an irresistible urge to run away. Something was coming. I could feel it."

"You felt like this thing was coming for you?" Chloe asked.

"It was worse than that," Carlotta said.

"What do you mean?" I asked. My mouth was suddenly dry, and I felt the deep heat slowly rising from my chest to fill my head.

"It was coming for everyone," she said.

I took a deep breath and did my best to calm down. I looked over at Chloe. She was staring back, worried, hands clasped between her knees, her knuckles white.

Carlotta continued. "Anyway, at that point, I grabbed my friend's hand and the two of us sprinted away from there as fast as we could manage."

"And the girls who'd entered the alley?" I asked, although I already knew the answer.

"Gone," she said.

"Was there a door or something somewhere that they might have used to leave the alley?" Chloe asked.

"There was nothing. It was a dead end. No doors or fences. We caught up with the rest of the group on the next street over and breathlessly explained what had happened. They were excited and demanded we take them back to the alley immediately. We ran back over to where we'd last seen the girls, but the alley wasn't there. The street was the same, but where the alley had been mere minutes ago, there was now nothing but solid building."

"And you're sure you had the right street?" Chloe asked.

"Positive. Everything else was exactly the same—but no alley. I don't know what it was, but something happened to those girls. I didn't sleep at all that night. The next morning, I called my friend to ask her about the alley and to let her know that she was leaving that cult no matter what. But she was gone."

"She disappeared?"

"No. She was dead."

"What happened?" I asked.

"They told us she'd suffered a heart attack—but she was only twenty-eight."

Chloe and I shared another look.

Baron was only thirty-nine.

28

ROCKET

"Now entering Westlake Station," a lightly distorted robot voice declared as the mostly empty Link train car slowed and finally came to a stop inside the tunnel.

Chloe had to work for a few hours, so I decided to go downtown to Pike Place Market and grab some groceries for dinner.

I stepped out of the transit tunnel and looked up into the dark gray sky. It wasn't raining, but there was a pretty good chance that was about to change. I pulled my hood up against the cool briny ocean air, and hurried down toward Third Avenue.

I was running over a few of the recipes that I could pull off in my mind (I was thinking fish and pasta) when I noticed a few things in quick succession: First, I saw a black sports car—some new model of Audi maybe—run a red light, turn, and start speeding in my direction. Next, I saw Swan and her bleached-blond twins walking toward me from about fifty yards up the street. Then, as if one onrushing car and the Swan/twins situation wasn't enough, two other cars abruptly changed direction, tires squealing, and started speeding toward me against the traffic on either side of the Audi.

Suddenly, three cars were coming straight for me.

I turned and started to run as fast as I could, but I wasn't sure I'd be able to avoid getting hit if at least one of them didn't stop.

Just before those three cars were about to hit me or hit the brakes, a white van roared through the intersection and came to a screeching halt directly in front of them. The cars swerved out of the way like they were in a videogame, and I was left staring at the passenger-side panel door of a white van. The magnetic logo on the door read: GOLDEN SEAL CARPET CLEANING. That was the name of the company tied to the number Russell Milligan told us might belong to Hazel.

The side panel door slid open.

"Get in."

I jumped inside and the man who'd spoken closed the sliding door behind me.

The van sped away from the intersection.

The interior was finished more like some kind of modern high-end camper than a carpet cleaning company's equipment van. In fact, there *was* no equipment inside, just two small cream-and-teak Danish Modern sofas with a rectangular coffee table set between them.

The man who'd opened the door for me took a seat on the small sofa to my right. He had brown eyes and jet-black hair.

"I got your message," he said, and motioned for me to take a seat across from him.

He spoke with a slight British accent and looked to be in his early forties. His ethnicity was hard to place, maybe Turkish or Italian. He was wearing a black suit, clearly tailored to fit his thin athletic frame.

"What message?" I asked.

"This one," he said, and then pressed play on his phone. Suddenly my voice filled the car.

My name is K. I'm here with my friend Chloe. We'd like to speak to you about . . . well, about a lot of things, but I suppose most pressing is the fact that Alan Scarpio told me something was wrong with the game, and that I needed to help him fix it before the next iteration began. Now Scarpio's missing and we're not sure where to turn. Please call me back.

"Hazel?" I asked.

The man just smiled.

"Where are we going?"

"I'm supposed to drop you off," he said as he received a text alert on his phone.

"You're supposed to drop me off?" I echoed.

He nodded.

"Where?"

"Please excuse me for just a moment," he said as he started composing a message to somebody.

Was I actually taking a van ride with the legendary Rabbits player known as Hazel right now? Should I ask him about Alan Scarpio? I thought about it for a moment. No. Even though he may have just saved my life, I had no way of knowing who this guy really was.

Hazel or not, Chloe was going to be so pissed that she missed this.

As I was thinking about Chloe and how mad she was going to be, I noticed something for the first time.

There was nobody driving.

I'd never been inside a driverless car before, but the ride itself didn't feel all that different. The way the steering wheel moved reminded me of an amusement park ride. I was fully prepared to be freaked out when I'd noticed nobody was driving, but actually, I found it oddly comforting.

A few minutes later, the van pulled over, and the mysterious man who may have been Hazel opened the side door and stepped outside.

"This is where I leave you," he said.

"Where are we?"

"Seattle," he said.

"Thanks a lot."

He smiled.

"What am I supposed to do now?" I asked.

"I have no idea," he said as he walked around the van and peeled off the magnetic sign that read GOLDEN SEAL CARPET CLEANING.

"Who sent you?" I asked.

"You called," he said, and then he stepped into the driver's seat, and guided the van away from the curb and out into traffic.

How did the call Chloe and I had placed to Golden Seal Carpet Cleaning almost two months earlier result in this guy and his driverless van coming to my rescue?

I took a look around. The van had dropped me off in the middle of the Fremont neighborhood, on Evanston Avenue, right in front of a coffee shop I used to frequent when Baron lived in the area.

Connected to the building that housed the coffee shop was something called The Fremont Rocket—a Cold War relic turned community totem that towered above the area. No actual rocket parts had been used to create the enormous work of art, but the bits of old airplane parts they'd used had been assembled in a perfect Art Deco interpretation of outer space, à la *Barbarella* or *Flash Gordon*.

As I stood looking up at the rocket, a red Volkswagen bug pulled up. Blasting from the windows of the vintage car was a song from the late 1980s by the band Def Leppard. I recognized the lyric "I can take you through the center of the dark" as it blared out of the bug's powerful stereo.

The song was called "Rocket."

Standing beneath a statue of a giant rocket listening to a song called "Rocket" would be an interesting coincidence on its own, but what if, at exactly the same time, a couple walked by—two women in their midforties, one wearing a light blue NASA T-shirt and the other an original 1988 Love and Rockets Sorted Tour jacket? At that point, you might take it as a sign—and if you were the kind of person who was obsessed with patterns and coincidences, you'd have to follow them to see where they were going.

So I did.

I tailed the couple up Evanston to North 36th, where they turned right. I tried to stay about half a block behind them as they walked. They looked happy, laughing and holding hands. Seeing them like that—so completely together and so seemingly unburdened—made me smile.

I couldn't remember a time when I'd felt that free.

As the two women walked by the little walkway that led into Troll's Knoll Park, I started to feel a familiar vibration at the base of my skull, and by the time they'd passed the narrow set of stairs that led up to Aurora Avenue, the gray feeling had firmly taken hold of my brain.

Every step I took felt labored, like I was pushing my way through sludge at the bottom of a lake. I forced myself to concentrate on my breath, and looked down as I walked, counting the lines on the sidewalk to calm myself. By the time the two women had stopped moving and were standing in front of the enormous cement troll that lurked beneath the bridge, the gray feeling had been tamped down enough for me to function, and I was able to move normally. But it was still there, somewhere in the back of my mind. I could feel it.

It was waiting for something.

The Fremont Troll is an eighteen-foot ferroconcrete troll that lives under the Aurora Avenue Bridge (officially known as the George Washington Memorial Bridge). Somebody won an art contest or something in the late eighties, and the Fremont Troll was the result. It's a colossal, weirdly beautiful monument that I absolutely love. Sadly, people tag and otherwise vandalize the sculpture quite often, and layer after layer of cement has to be constantly applied to bring the troll back to something close to its original appearance.

One of the most interesting aspects of the Fremont Troll is that he (or she) is clutching a car in his (or her) left hand. In 1990, when the troll was being constructed, the artists included a red Volkswagen bug with a California license plate in the sculpture. Over the years, the appearance of the Volkswagen has changed. After decades of abuse at the hands of graffiti artists, vandals, and middle school kids playing truth or dare, the color of the car is no longer discernible and the license plate is long gone.

One fact remains indisputable, however, and that's the fact that the troll is holding an original Volkswagen Beetle from the 1960s or '70s.

Except it wasn't. Not anymore.

There, clutched in the troll's hand, in place of the Volkswagen bug, was an Austin Mini Cooper.

———

The two women took a selfie with the troll in the background, then continued their walk, moving leisurely along North 36th Street.

I was trying to decide whether to follow them—while also working to come to terms with the revelation about the new model of car in the troll's hand—when I noticed some posters glued to one of the stanchions that held up the base of the bridge.

There were four identical posters, one on each side of the stanchion, advertising an upcoming music festival in Oregon. The genre was apparently something called space rock, and the festival was taking place about two and a half hours southwest of Portland in the area surrounding the Yaquina Head Lighthouse. The reason I'd found the posters so compelling was the fact that they featured an image of a lighthouse that had been converted into a rocket.

Another rocket.

I looked for significance in the date of the event, in the names of the bands (all local Pacific Northwest indie rock), but there was nothing.

Just the rocket-lighthouse.

Was I actually considering driving hours down the coast following clues related to rockets? What if the next clue pointed to Uganda?

If I hurried, I'd be able to catch up with the couple who'd led me here, but I was pretty sure that their connection to the clues I'd been following (whether real or imagined) was over. If I wanted to keep going, the rocket-lighthouse posters were the next clue. They had to be.

But I couldn't drive three hours on a hunch—at least not at the moment. So I did the next best thing. I pulled out my phone and used Google Street View to take a closer look at the area surrounding the lighthouse.

The lighthouse sits on a bluff overlooking the Pacific Ocean. There are a few small outbuildings connected via a winding concrete pathway that bisects the wide rocky area.

I looked over everything—zoomed in to each building, explored the surrounding geography as closely as I could using Google's images—but nothing stood out. At least, nothing obviously Rabbits or rocket-related.

I was getting hungry, so I made my way back to the coffee shop beneath the rocket. I ordered the avocado salad and grilled cheese sandwich that I'd always eaten when Baron and I used to frequent the place. I considered asking the clerk who served me about the model of the car in the Fremont Troll's hand, but I was pretty sure he'd tell me exactly what I didn't want to hear—that the car was now and had always been an Austin Mini Cooper.

While I ate, I zoomed in and around the area surrounding that lighthouse. I had no idea what I was expecting to find, but it gave me something to focus on while I was doing my best to avoid thinking about the implications of that car in the troll's hand, and what this additional change in the nature of my reality might mean moving forward.

I was exploring the coastline and looking at a winding set of weatherworn wooden stairs that led from the lighthouse parking area down to the beach, when I noticed something strange. It wasn't immediately clear what I was looking at, until I zoomed in to get a better look.

There in the countless smooth gray stones that made up the beach, written using scraps of ubiquitous golden-colored driftwood, was a message comprised of one word and one letter: *Monorail K*.

For just a moment I couldn't remember how to breathe. I took a sip of water and looked around the coffee shop. What the fuck was happening?

I looked down at my phone again. Nothing had changed.

Monorail K.

I took a look at the date the picture had been taken by Google. June 2018.

Is it possible that this image, taken three years ago, might have something to do with me, sitting in this coffee shop staring at it three years later? If I wanted an answer to that question, I suspected all I had to do was call an Uber and ride ten minutes south to the monorail.

———

The car dropped me off at Seattle Center Station, and I took the escalator up to the monorail. I slipped my card into the machine and was just about to buy a one-way ticket back to Westlake Station when I noticed something strange about the screen.

I had two choices.

I've lived in Seattle since I was a kid, and in all of that time, the monorail has consisted of only two stops, roughly a mile apart: Seattle Center Station and Westlake Center Station. Those are the only two stations. No matter which station you board at, the monorail has only one stop to make. But now I was presented with two choices: Westlake and Sea-Tac.

Suddenly, the monorail had a station at the Seattle-Tacoma International Airport?

This was impossible. There was no Sea-Tac Station.

I bought a one-way ticket to the airport.

I could tell things had changed from the moment I stepped into the car.

Because the monorail has only two stations, there's no need for a map of the route. Instead, there are drawings and photographs featuring the historic train throughout the years.

But now, in place of the historical drawings and photographs I'd been looking at my entire adult life, there was a map that included three stations: Center, Westlake, and Sea-Tac.

I sat down and rode the monorail to the third station on the map.

If there was any question I was following the correct path, there was a newspaper sitting facedown on the seat beside me. I picked it up and flipped it over. The date of publication was a few days ago, which was just as impossible as a third station on the monorail, because the newspaper had shut down ages ago, publishing its last issue sometime in the fall of 2000.

It was a free biweekly called *The Rocket*.

"Welcome to Sea-Tac Station," said a woman's voice on the loudspeaker as the train pulled into the station. I'd spent the fifteen minutes it took to reach the airport alternating between scanning the train and the faces of the six other people riding it, and looking through *The Rocket* for clues.

I couldn't find anything.

But there had to be something.

It turns out that something was actually a someone.

She was standing on the platform when I stepped off the train at Sea-Tac Station.

It was Emily Connors.

"Come on," she said, grabbing my arm. "I don't have much time."

"What the hell are you doing here?"

"Wasting my time looking for you when I should be figuring out a way to save the world," she said, leading me down to the street.

"I'm sorry?"

"You don't need to be sorry. Just get in the fucking car."

Emily pressed a button on her fob and the gull-wing doors of a nearby black Tesla X opened with a distant whir and click.

"What's going on?" I asked. "Is reality somehow . . . changing?"

"I'm guessing you noticed a few . . . discrepancies on your way here?"

"Yeah. Is this . . ."

"Another dimension?"

"I didn't wanna say it," I admitted. "But . . . *is* it?"

"It's kind of complicated. But right now, I really just need you to get into the fucking car."

The two of us got into the car and Emily started driving. Fast.

As we merged onto the freeway, I looked out the window at downtown. The building that had appeared out of nowhere earlier was gone and the skyline was back to the way it had been before all of this stuff started. Sure, the Fremont Troll was holding a different car, and the monorail had three stations, but if I didn't look too closely, I was almost able to imagine that everything was back to normal.

Emily pulled off the freeway one exit later.

I had a million questions, but I couldn't decide what to ask first, so I sat silent in the passenger seat as Emily guided us through the city.

She eventually pulled into a small concrete carport just off Lake Washington Boulevard. We stepped out of the car and onto what I'd assumed was a stone pathway treated with some kind of rubber, but as soon as our feet touched the surface, the path started moving. It was a conveyer belt, kind of like you might find in an airport—what they call a people mover.

The conveyor belt eventually dropped us off in front of a small white concrete structure that housed an elevator. There was no call button, but Emily did something on her phone, the doors opened, and the two of us stepped inside. As soon as the doors shut behind us, the elevator started moving up.

We stepped out of the elevator into a marvel of open-concept design.

Directly across from us as we entered, facing the lake, were enormous floor-to-ceiling windows. The view was impressive. It felt as if somebody had removed everything that wasn't water, trees, and distant mountains. The dark gray clouds hanging above the lake gave the place a sad but cinematic feel, like a wealthy murderer's house in a Nordic thriller.

Through a sliding-glass door that opened onto a wide deck, I could see a set of stairs leading down to the conveyer belt we'd just taken to the elevator. Beyond that was nothing but grass and trees.

The interior was perfectly appointed, from the Florence Knoll sofa, Noguchi table, and Nelson ball pendant lamps to the built-in, floor-to-ceiling bookshelves and light cork floors.

"Your place is amazing," I said.

"Me?" Emily laughed a little. "No way. It belongs to a friend."

"They must be some friend," I said.

Emily's smile disappeared and she nodded toward the sofa. "I don't have much time, so if you have a lot of questions, you'll want to start asking."

I took a seat on the sofa. Emily grabbed a nearby molded plywood chair, slid it across the floor, and sat down directly across from me.

For the first time since she'd picked me up at the monorail station, I could see Emily clearly. She looked tired—nothing that a few good nights' sleep wouldn't clear up—but there was something else: a look in her eyes, a kind of distance, a sadness.

"The last time I saw you, in that penthouse at WorGames . . . was that real?" I asked. I figured why not start with a big one.

She didn't answer me. Instead, she just stared.

I had the feeling she was looking for something behind my eyes, but I had no idea what it was.

"Emily?"

"I'm sorry," she said. "You remind me of somebody else."

"Who?"

She shook her head and answered my earlier question instead. "It was real," she said. "The penthouse, Crow."

"What happened? When I went back up there, everything was gone. It was completely different."

"Everything was gone because Crow moved it."

"He moved a *building*?"

"Well, mainly just the top floor, and it's more like he kind of . . . changed it."

"How does that work?"

"It's similar to the method I used to bring you here."

"Where is . . . here?"

"It's complicated," Emily said.

"Fine, then. Let me ask you this. *Are* we in another dimension?"

Emily ran her hands through her hair and exhaled before ignoring my question and asking one of her own.

"How much do you know about quantum physics?"

"Not a lot," I said. "I mean, I know particles can also be waves, and that in a two-slit experiment, observation affects the outcome, but I've always found the probability stuff daunting."

"Okay, so I'm going to do my best to explain the mechanism behind what's happening to the best of my ability. Just stop me when you don't understand."

I nodded. I had the feeling there was a whole lot I wasn't going to understand.

"What do you know about the Meechum Radiants?" Emily asked.

"Only what Crow told me, and what you can find online."

"What did Crow say?"

"He said Kellan Meechum had discovered something he'd likened to ley lines—veins in the fabric of the world—and that Meechum called them Radiants."

"Good so far," Emily said.

"He also told me that my parents believed in these Radiants, and that these mysterious lines of energy could be used to somehow manipulate travel between dimensions."

"A lot of this is going to sound a bit . . . out there, but . . . there's something going on beneath the world, something that you and I take for granted."

"Some magical multiverse type of thing?"

"Quantum mechanics isn't magic, K. It's science."

"What the hell are the Meechum Radiants?"

"We don't know exactly, but back in 1945, while Meechum was leading an experiment connected to strange attractors and the butterfly effect, he believed he'd stumbled upon something. He discovered that certain cause-and-effect manipulations, coincidences, and chance encounters were . . . enhanced in very specific parts of the world—amplified somehow."

"And this amplification was connected to his Radiants?"

"Yes. By performing certain . . . movements or patterns, or by following connections and tracking coincidences, Meechum claimed he was able to . . . manipulate the butterfly effect, that he could perform a series of seemingly unconnected moves and facilitate an effect based on a completely unrelated cause."

"A series of moves?"

"Okay, the story goes that Meechum had spent years mapping out a number of ostensibly random coincidences and anomalies in and around the city of Seattle. He eventually discovered that, along certain pathways, these anomalies weren't as random as they appeared. He began noticing groups of highly improbable coincidences the closer he came to successfully engaging certain pathways—what he called Radiants. Meechum believed that these Radiants might be used to facilitate changes in the world, and that the ability to move back and forth between universes was not only possible, but probable. He said that, in one case, he'd been able to successfully manipulate a bank's interest rate by simply preventing a data analyst in an unrelated field from buying her morning coffee."

"And you seriously believe this stuff?"

"Yes. And our parents believed it too."

"So that's what we're dealing with here? Magical lines?"

"I already told you, it's not magic, K. It's science."

"We are in another dimension, aren't we?"

She stared at me for a long moment, like she'd been describing something completely obvious and couldn't believe I wasn't getting it.

"Have you noticed anything strange about your life? A terrible feeling comes over you and the world is suddenly . . . different somehow?"

"Like déjà vu?" I asked, but I knew Emily wasn't talking about déjà vu.

She was talking about the gray feeling.

"Déjà vu is most likely a brief glimpse into being awake in another dimension. I'm talking about something else. Have you ever experienced missing time, or an obsession with patterns or coincidences? Or maybe you notice that part of your reality has suddenly changed? Normally it's nothing huge, like the South won the Civil War or the Beatles never existed. It's something small, but significant to you in that moment. Maybe a company's logo looks different from the logo you remember as a kid, a children's book no longer has the same name, or a farmhouse in a famous painting has a different number of windows."

"You're talking about the Mandela effect," I said.

"What I'm talking about is feeling like the world around you is slowly forgetting the world you know, one tiny piece at a time."

"I've felt all of those things," I admitted.

Emily nodded, and I noticed something in her eyes. The exhaustion I'd noticed earlier was still there, but there was something else.

She had the look of somebody ready to give up after treading water alone in the deep ocean for days waiting for help that was never going to arrive.

"How does it work?" I asked.

"In order to find me, you had to follow coincidences, find a pattern. And on your way here, I'm sure you noticed certain . . . discrepancies."

"The Fremont Troll was holding a Mini Cooper instead of a Volkswagen."

"Interesting," Emily said.

"You remember that troll holding a Volkswagen, don't you?" I asked.

"I do," she said.

"Thank god."

"But I've forgotten so many other things."

"What do you mean?"

"Most of the discrepancies—those things that you notice are different in your new world—will soon fade. You can write them down on scraps of paper, compose intricate stories to yourself, use audio and video, but none of that will matter. Because, in the end, you'll never believe yourself, never remember. Those things will always seem like a fiction."

It sounded impossible, but I felt like I was already losing the plot of the Richard Linklater movie *Before Midnight*. I still understood that it had existed, and knew that I'd seen it at least three times, but I could no longer remember any of the details.

"I'm sorry," she said, checking the time on her phone, "but I'm going to have to speed things up. Where was I?"

"You'd just finished with the Meechum Radiants."

"Right, so, a few years after Kellan Meechum published his final paper on the Radiants, a computer scientist named Hawk Worricker picked up the baton, so to speak, and started digging deeper into Meechum's work."

"WorGames's Hawk Worricker?" I asked.

"Yes. WorGames is a lot more than it appears to be," Emily said.

"What is it?"

"I'm getting to that."

"Sorry."

"It's fine. Just stop talking."

I opened my mouth to apologize again, but quickly shut it.

"Worricker was a genius—a total savant when it came to mathematics and statistical analysis. He was brilliant at forecasting strategic outcomes. He would collect as much data as he could and then extrapolate certain results involving clusters of people and industries over time. He was amazingly accurate and made millions by betting on changes in the market. But it wasn't until Worricker discovered Meechum's Radiants that he found his own life's work. That's when everything changed.

"Worricker became obsessed with figuring out what the Radiants were, how they worked, and why they existed. Eventually, he'd collected enough data to run some models and projections, and he discovered something incredible. Meechum's Radiants were real. He was astounded and excited . . . until he discovered something else—something terrifying."

"What was it?"

"Worricker discovered that Meechum's Radiants were decaying, and that they would soon lose their efficacy."

"Their efficacy? What were they doing?"

"Worricker believed what Meechum had discovered was more than simply invisible lines of manipulatable energy beneath the world. Worricker believed that these Radiants existed for a reason, that they functioned as a kind of multiuniversal insurance policy."

"What?"

"Okay, I don't have much time, so I'm going to explain it to you the way it was first explained to me. The Radiants serve as a kind of universal reset mechanism—a way to release a little steam, so to speak. They exist to help maintain the integrity and health of the individual streams of the multiverse."

"The multiverse? That's where quantum physics comes in?"

"Yes. We live in a multiverse, K."

"So there are endless Emilys and Ks out there, having thousands of variations of this conversation right now?"

"As far as I know, it doesn't work like that. A new universe isn't created based on every minor decision point in a person's life. It requires a significant output of energy to create an inflection point."

"Are we talking planetary events?"

"That would qualify, sure, but even a single human being *can* create enough of this type of energy—more than enough to create an inflection point, given the right set of circumstances. And it turns out there are . . . other ways to manipulate the Radiants as well."

"What kind of ways?"

"It's something our parents were into."

"You're talking about the Gatewick Institute."

"Yes," Emily said, "but we're not there yet."

"Sorry."

"First, Worricker needed to work out a way to fix what he believed was a decaying universal repair mechanism. This would take time, and countless failed attempts, but he would eventually figure it out."

"Rabbits."

Emily nodded. "At first it was simply an evolving artificial intelligence engine—a way to perform certain adjustments at certain times. It would take Worricker a decade to figure out that the framework of a game was the most effective method of manipulating the Radiants worldwide."

"This was in 1959, the beginning of the modern version of Rabbits?"

"Exactly."

"So, okay, Worricker created Rabbits to, essentially, patch a multidimensional repair mechanism. What happens if, one day, Rabbits fails to do its job?"

"Then that day will be the first day of the end of the world."

"Am I really in a different dimension than the one I woke up in this morning?"

"Right now? Technically, yes."

"So is there another version of me sitting in my apartment right now?"

"No."

"Why not?"

"Full disclosure, I don't know exactly how everything works, but from what I've been able to figure out, people's . . . let's call them souls, for lack of a better word, exist in a kind of cosmic pool. Each person in every dimension is a unique individual, but they all draw from that particular soul's multidimensional pool."

"Okay . . ."

"Only one iteration of a person can exist in each dimension at any given time, and—in the extremely rare case that a person switches dimensional streams—the version of the person that now exists in a new stream merges with or replaces that stream's original instance. The resultant memory retained from the prior incarnation depends on something we call dimensional drift. It's the same if an iteration of that person remains behind after the drift or slip."

"*If* a person remains behind? *If* a version merges or replaces?"

"Like I said, we're not sure exactly how it all works." Emily checked the time on her phone again. "I'm sorry, K, but I really have to get going."

"What about the Gatewick Institute?"

"Hawk Worricker created the institute to study Meechum's Radiants further. His intention was to find out if the Radiants might be manipulated for good, to help bring economic and social prosperity to all. Gatewick was all about trying to discover new ways to safely manipulate the Radiants."

"So the Gatewick Institute was never about playing Rabbits?"

"No. The game was completely separate. Worricker created the Gatewick Institute as a kind of augmentation, as a way to understand the Radiants and to do good in the world without interfering with Rabbits. Worricker understood that the game was the key to keeping the multiverse healthy, so he would never have intentionally allowed anything they did at Gatewick to adversely affect Rabbits."

"Gatewick was working to do good?"

"Yes. The altruistic nature of that research was what eventually brought our parents to Gatewick, along with a bunch of others—

including a man named Edward Crawford. Everybody just called him Crow."

"So Crow really did work with our parents?"

"Yes."

"How did you end up working with him in The Tower?"

"When I was a teenager," Emily said, "I found a bunch of crazy shit in my parents' closet—stuff that led me to believe they weren't actually real estate agents. The thing that immediately captured my imagination took the form of a complicated underground game—a game that I quickly became obsessed with figuring out how to play."

"Rabbits." I could almost hear the crackle of the static on the radio and feel the hum of the truck's wheels as she spoke.

"Cut to later. My obsession with the game resulted in the death of my sister."

"It was an accident."

"An accident that was pretty quickly followed by the death of my parents. And, if I'm being honest, I didn't really handle either of those events all that well. By the time Crow found me, I was making ends meet as a kind of online bounty hunter–slash–collections officer in New York City. I was an easy recruit. Crow explained what he had in mind, how he was planning on putting my particular set of skills to use, and I started working for him."

"Your particular set of skills? That sounds like a Liam Neeson movie."

"You know how I asked you about feeling strange, noticing patterns and coincidences, or missing time?"

"Yeah . . ."

"Well, that's because the research our parents were doing at the Gatewick Institute involved them taking a large number of experimental drugs—including a prenatal cocktail our mothers were instructed to continue taking through all three trimesters of their pregnancies."

"You're saying these drugs are somehow connected to my experiencing missing time and obsessive behavior around coincidences and patterns?"

"That's exactly what I'm saying, K. My mother took those drugs as well. All of the Gatewick parents did."

"Wait . . . so you've experienced these things?"

She nodded.

"Does that have anything to do with how you were able to bring me here? To this . . . dimension, or whatever it is?"

"It has everything to do with that, yes."

"How does it work?"

"Something happened at Gatewick—something completely unintentional."

"Which was what?"

"A few of the children born to Gatewick parents who'd been taking part in the prenatal drug study presented with certain . . . unique abilities."

"Like what?"

"Under very special circumstances, these children were able to manipulate Meechum's Radiants without using the advanced mapping techniques and computer systems normally required."

"What sort of special circumstances?"

"Moments of extreme emotional distress."

I swallowed hard, my mouth suddenly dry.

"So, you have these . . . unique abilities?"

"I do—a little."

"What does that mean?"

"My mother stopped the drug therapy early in her first trimester, so I didn't end up with very much Gatewick sauce."

"But you had enough to manipulate Meechum's Radiants, to bring me here, to this dimension?"

"What I did is like a . . . trick. I created a kind of temporary bubble that's going to compress soon—and when that compression happens, I need to be somewhere else."

"What about me?"

"The compression should take you back to where you began. Or at least, to where you were when you began following this trail."

"Should?"

"I'm sorry, none of this stuff is . . . absolute."

"What about me?"

"What about you?"

"How much . . . Gatewick sauce do I have?"

"Do you know how long your mother was taking the Gatewick drugs?"

I shook my head.

"Well, then," Emily said as she stood up and started walking over to the elevator, "it's a mystery."

"When I met Crow in The Tower, he told me I wasn't supposed to be *here*. Do you know what he meant?"

"Your parents used your ability to hide you from him."

"My Gatewick sauce."

"Exactly."

"Is that why he tracked me down and threatened me?"

"I'm not sure, but he was surprised when you showed up in The Tower, and Crow *really* doesn't like surprises."

"What's he doing up there?"

"What did he tell you he was doing?"

"Making adjustments for the good of mankind, or something like that."

Emily shook her head. "When I first started working with him, he genuinely seemed to be trying to continue Worricker's legacy, working to change the world for the good. But after a while, I started noticing strange patterns and anomalies in Crow's work."

"What was happening?"

"It turns out he'd been working on something else in tandem with our work in The Tower."

"What?"

"A long time ago, something terrible happened while Crow was manipulating the Radiants."

"What?"

"His daughter disappeared, and ever since, he's been trying to find a way to use the Radiants to bring her back."

"Is that possible? Bringing her back?"

"I have no idea, but whatever he's been doing to try to find his daughter has had an increasingly destabilizing effect on the Radiants. Looking back now, I can see how everything was slowly twisting up his mind. But he'd changed so slowly I almost didn't notice it happen, the way a frog sitting in cold water doesn't notice that the water has gradually turned to a boil until it's too late."

"Does he know that what he's doing is messing with the mechanism that stabilizes the multiverse?"

"He knows. I'm just not sure he's capable of understanding . . . or caring. Not anymore."

"And there's nothing we can do?"

"Rabbits is the only system that can counter what he's been doing and stabilize the Radiants."

"So, what, winning Rabbits would help?"

"Win the game, save the world."

"How the hell are we supposed to do that?"

"I don't think we can."

"Why not?"

"Aside from the fact that he's been killing and terrorizing players, Crow's manipulations have messed up the mechanics of Rabbits so badly that it's pretty much impossible for anybody to even find the game right now, never mind win it."

Emily pressed the call button on the elevator.

"Please, I have so many more questions . . ."

"Believe me, K, I'd love nothing more than to talk for hours. I've missed you—I really have—but I have to leave right now, or I won't make it back."

"Can't we have a few more minutes?"

Emily checked the time on her phone. "In about thirty seconds, my manipulation is going to end, and things will go back to the way they were when you woke up this morning."

"So what am I supposed to do now?"

"You could wish me luck," she said.

"Why? Where are you going?"

"To kill Crow," she said, "and try to find a way to win the game."

And with that, Emily stepped into the elevator and the doors closed behind her.

After a moment, I jumped up, opened the sliding door that led outside, and ran down the stairs to the first floor. I turned the corner and sprinted toward the elevator structure at the end of the conveyer belt. There was no way I was going to let Emily Connors out of my sight again.

I easily beat the elevator down and was standing in front of the doors when they opened. But the elevator was empty.

Emily Connors had disappeared.

29

SO IT'S FUTILE AND POTENTIALLY DEADLY. WHAT THE HELL ELSE YOU GOT GOING ON RIGHT NOW?

THE FIRST THING I DID after leaving Emily's friend's midcentury mansion on the lake was stop by the Fremont Troll.

He (or she) was holding a Volkswagen bug, not an Austin Mini.

A quick online search in the Uber on my way home revealed that there was still no third movie in Richard Linklater's Before trilogy, the weird skyscraper was back where it didn't belong, and those bears were still called Berenstain and not Berenstein.

It looked like I was back in the world I'd left behind after a day spent following Emily's series of clues and coincidences. I checked the time on my phone. I was supposed to meet Chloe at my place for dinner in half an hour.

"What are we cooking?" Chloe said as she entered my apartment and kicked off a pair of beat-up black-and-white checkered Vans.

"Cacio e pepe," I said.

"Ooooh. You know I love your fancy spaghetti," Chloe said as she reached around and kissed me on her way over to the fridge.

"Are you getting wine?" I asked.

"You know I am."

"Good, because I think we might need it."

She turned back to me with a concerned look. "Why? What's up?"

"Oh, for one thing, I spent the afternoon in another dimension."

Chloe laughed as she pulled a chilled bottle of white out of the fridge and set it down on the counter. "Well, if that's the case, we might need more than sauvignon blanc."

I set the wooden spoon I'd been using to stir the butter, cheese, and pepper into the pasta, and turned to face Chloe.

"What? You're kidding, right?" she asked.

I shook my head. "I have had one fuck of a day."

Chloe poured us each a glass of wine and sat down at the dining room table.

"Start at the beginning," she said, "and don't leave anything out."

I plated our dinner, took a sip of wine, and told Chloe about my day—about Emily and everything she'd said regarding my parents, Gatewick, Meechum, Crow, that Rabbits had most likely been created to repair and maintain a much older interdimensional multiverse repair mechanism, and all the rest of it.

When I was finished, Chloe leaned back in her chair and exhaled. "Holy shit," she said. "I don't even wanna tell you about my day now."

I pulled out my phone to show Chloe the photograph I'd taken of the poster advertising the music festival, and a picture I'd snapped of the Fremont Troll holding a Mini Cooper instead of a Volkswagen. Obviously, the music festival poster didn't mean much out of context, and the troll photo could have very easily been faked, but I could tell Chloe believed me, even without further scientific examination of the evidence.

"Does this mean you have some kind of . . . super Gatewick powers?"

"I don't think so," I said. "I think it just means I'm a little fucked-up because my parents took drugs and made me play weird games as a kid."

"You're not fucked-up, K. You're complicated. Huge difference."

"Thanks . . . I think."

Chloe nodded, then topped up our glasses of wine. "So, after hearing you describe your day of wild adventures, I think there's only one thing to do."

"I'm listening," I said, and folded my arms.

"We have to do what your friend Emily told you."

"And what is that?"

"Win the game, save the world."

"Okay. But as much as I appreciate your enthusiasm, Emily also told me that Crow has been terrorizing and killing players, and that his manipulations have messed up the mechanics of Rabbits so badly that it's become pretty much impossible to play the game, never mind win it."

"Sounds like a challenge to me."

"Really? Because, to me, it sounds like a futile and potentially deadly enterprise."

"So it's futile and potentially deadly. What the hell else you got going on right now?"

We finished eating, loaded the dishwasher, then sat back down at the table.

"What if we're not safe here?" I asked.

"In your apartment?"

I nodded. I wasn't worried about myself. I was thinking about Chloe. Crow had made it clear. If anything happened to Chloe, it would be on me.

"You're thinking about the Swan lady and her suicide twins?"

"Or anybody else Crow decides to send," I said.

"If somebody was coming to get us, wouldn't they be here already?"

"Maybe. I don't know. What if they're waiting to see if we start trying to play the game again?"

"Haven't we been playing the game ever since we saw Minister Jesselman blow his brains out on live TV?"

"I don't know. I suppose so."

"Do you believe there's something fucked-up going on and that our multiverse is in genuine danger?"

I thought about her question for a few seconds. Did I believe all of this was real? I was losing a lot of the details, but I knew I'd seen the movie *Before Midnight*. I could no longer recall much of the plot, but I remembered where we'd sat in the theater. Something was definitely happening.

"Yes, I think the multiverse might be in danger," I said, finally.

"Well, then?"

"What I can't believe is that it's somehow up to you and me to fix it."

"Let's avoid the Chosen One bullshit and just go back to the beginning to see if there's something we missed. And if we happen to find something, we can decide at that point whether or not to pursue it. Deal?"

"Deal," I said.

"Great." Chloe grabbed her laptop, I opened mine, and the two of us went back to the beginning.

We started at the arcade, then moved on to Scarpio's phone, the attack on Jeff Goldblum, Silvana's disappearing scar, and finally, Russell Milligan and Golden Seal Carpet Cleaning.

We didn't find anything new, but we were surprised by the sheer volume of crazy shit we'd been through over the past couple of months.

It was after midnight by the time we shut it down. We decided we'd continue our reexamination of everything in the morning, starting with Baron's death.

I had just copied the images Chloe had taken of Baron's murder wall to my computer, and I was about to shut my laptop for the night, when Chloe noticed something.

"Wait," Chloe said.

"What?"

"There." She pointed to three Post-it notes in the middle of Baron's wall of nonsense.

Baron had written three names: Hazel, Murmur, and The Dark Thane.

"What is it?" I asked.

"Those are three really famous Rabbits players."

"They sure are," I said. "Do you think that means something?"

"Why did Baron write down their names?"

"No idea."

"And look at this," Chloe said as she leaned closer. "Here they are again."

Chloe had zoomed in on a small scrap of paper featuring the same three names. Only here, Hazel and The Dark Thane's names had a line through them, and Murmur's name was circled. "Why is Murmur circled and the other two names crossed out?"

I shook my head. "Baron wasn't in the most . . . logical frame of mind. It's probably just nonsense."

"Maybe," Chloe said, "but what if he was looking for help?"

"From Hazel, Murmur, and The Dark Thane?"

"Why not? They've all played the game at the highest level. If Baron was looking into something specific about the game, any one of those players would be a great place to start."

"What does it say here?" Chloe zoomed in on another scrap of paper.

"Where?"

"Baron's drawn an arrow from Murmur to this printout. It's titled: 'Rabbits Groups: Seattle.' This one is circled."

I leaned forward. "The Navidsonians?"

"*House of Leaves* reference?" Chloe asked.

"Probably . . . but you don't really think this is some kind of clue, do you?"

"Well, K, it is *some* kind of clue. But what kind of clue it is sort of depends on your perspective, and maybe your attitude."

"What is that supposed to mean?"

"Well, it's not *supposed* to mean anything, but what it *does* mean is that I think you need to get up off your ass and help me find these fucking Navidsonians so we can ask a famous Rabbits player a couple of questions."

"You think we're actually going to be able to find Murmur? Why not just try to track down Oprah or Bono?"

"Baron left us a clue to find Murmur, not Oprah or Bono. Don't be a smart-ass. Didn't Hazel pick you up in a van earlier?"

I was pretty sure that guy wasn't actually Hazel, but Chloe had a point. We had called a number that allegedly belonged to Hazel, and somebody (perhaps it actually was Hazel himself) showed up in a van and saved me from getting squashed by three cars simultaneously.

"Fine. Let's say this does lead us to Murmur, which is incredibly unlikely."

"Agree to disagree."

"What about the rumors?"

"I think the rumors are probably overstating things."

"When you say *things,* you're talking about pesky little *things* like ruthless and dangerous behavior, betrayal, and most likely murder?"

"That stuff has to be exaggerated," Chloe said.

"Does it though?" I asked.

"Those three names mean something, and we're looking into it." She loaded a popular Rabbits chatroom in a Tor Browser and angled her screen away from me.

I sat there for a moment while Chloe typed away, her fingers hitting the keys a little bit harder than normal.

I shook my head. "Fine," I said.

I could see Chloe smile a little from behind her screen.

"We'll look into it in the morning, but right now the two of us are going to get some sleep."

30

ZOMPOCALYPSO AND THE BEAR

The next morning, we ate croissants and eggs while we scoured all of the Rabbits darknet websites we could find for any information on past or present players tied to a Seattle-based Rabbits-related group called the Navidsonians. We cross-referenced every mention and rumor until we had ten names we'd seen listed at least four times in four completely separate and seemingly unconnected instances. Then, we stuck those ten names up on the wall of my dining room using color-coded Post-it notes and began compiling all the information we could find.

Five hours later, after looking into every mention we could dig up and eliminating as many questionable pseudonyms as possible, we had our list of potential members down to four names:

1. Karl Yasserman
2. Darla Chung
3. Carla Yu
4. Trenton Hall

Could one of those four people be the infamous Rabbits player known as Murmur?

All four of the names had been mentioned in connection with the Navidsonians at some point or another, although we couldn't find anything that connected any of them to Murmur.

We decided to focus on Trenton Hall from Vancouver, British

Columbia, and Darla Chung from Tacoma, Washington. Both Chung and Hall were rumored to have taken part in more than one iteration of the game, so there was a bit more speculation online surrounding their participation in Rabbits and potential membership in the Navidsonian group.

We were unable to find any current geographic information on Trenton Hall, but Darla Chung had a Facebook page that included a number of photographs. Darla was slight, about five feet tall with a bright photogenic smile. She was definitely not what I had in mind when I pictured the infamous—potentially murderous—Rabbits player known as Murmur.

As with Hazel—the most famous Rabbits player of all time—nobody really knew all that much about Murmur. There were certain "higher-level" players we'd heard rumors about like Californiac (allegedly billionaire Alan Scarpio), Vampire Billy (might be a well-known actor from a long-canceled television series), and Sadie Palomino (rumored to be Silicon Valley venture capital legend Vera Spiotta). But Murmur, like Hazel—by design or otherwise—had always been surrounded by an air of mystery and danger.

Everyone seriously interested in the game had heard stories about Murmur. That they had purchased four hundred tickets to a concert rumored to contain a clue, just to make sure nobody else could attend, or that they had turned a close friend in to the police in order to gain an advantage during the ninth iteration.

But the most common (and alarming) rumor by far was that Murmur once threw another player off a nine-story roof to prevent them from finding a clue connected to Rabbits. That player was also, allegedly, Murmur's spouse.

I was pretty sure Darla Chung wasn't Murmur. Judging by the photos on her Facebook page, there was no way Darla was capable of throwing anybody off a roof.

A number of Darla's photos included a close friend named Alison, a real estate agent who'd recently sold a condo that had been featured on Zillow.

Alison's professional website featured photographs of her sales. Those photos included that condo: a nicely renovated two-bedroom located about fifteen minutes from my place. Alison was smiling in the picture, her arm around the buyer.

The buyer was Darla Chung.

According to everything we'd been able to dig up, the Navidsonians met on Thursdays and Sundays.

It was Wednesday. Chloe and I decided that the two of us would head over to Darla Chung's condo first thing in the morning.

We were going on a stakeout.

Early the next morning, we parked outside Darla's building, drank coffee, and rewatched all three episodes of the first season of *Sherlock* on my laptop as we waited.

Darla finally stepped out of the front door around two P.M.

We got out of the car and followed her on foot.

Darla led us up her street, through Volunteer Park, and into a quiet residential area. After we'd been walking for about fifteen minutes, she stepped off the sidewalk and jogged up the stairs of a midsize craftsman-style house. She knocked, and somebody we couldn't see clearly from where we were standing opened the door and let her in.

The moment Darla was through the door, Chloe yanked me up the stairs and knocked.

Two seconds later, Darla opened the door. She'd barely had time to step inside.

"Hi," Chloe said.

"Hi," Darla replied, surprised. "Who are you?"

"I'm Chloe, and this is K."

I waved hello.

"We're playing Rabbits and we need some help," Chloe said.

"Who is it?" a voice called out from inside the house.

"It's Chloe and K. They say they're playing the game."

There was a long pause and then we heard a woman's voice.

"Well, don't just stand in the doorway, take your shoes off and get your asses in here."

———

The woman who'd spoken was Easton Paruth. She was South Asian, around fifty years old. She had short gray hair with bangs that reminded me of the window in a prison cell door. She was sitting at the head of a long rectangular table in a narrow dining room. There were four other people sitting around the table with Easton: the Colonel, a man who looked to be about sixty-five with wild white hair and round wire-rimmed glasses; Alberto, a Brazilian who had probably been some kind of athlete a decade ago; and a young married couple from Ireland named Jenny and Hugh. Jenny was aggressively tattooed from her wrists to her neck with bleached-blond pink-tipped hair, and Hugh was thin and pale, with extremely short-cropped red hair and sharp green eyes. The house belonged to the two of them. Chloe and I shared a look.

Could one of these people actually be Murmur?

"You know you're not supposed to talk about the game," Easton said in a very slight Indian accent. She had a mischievous twinkle in her eye.

I liked her immediately.

"Is that what you're doing here? Playing the game?" I asked.

Darla took a seat at the table and looked nervously over at Easton and Hugh.

"Oh, we're not playing," Darla said. "We're a kind of . . . a support group, for those who used to play."

"Darla, what are you doing?" Hugh demanded.

"It's okay. We're among friends," Easton said.

"Are you sure?" the Colonel asked.

Easton stared at Chloe like she was trying to make up her mind. "You two *are* friends, aren't you?"

"We are, yes," Chloe said.

Easton turned her attention to me.

I nodded. "Friends," I said.

The Colonel and Alberto grumbled their displeasure.

"Well, you see," Easton continued, "the game has a way of swallowing your life, and what we're doing here is trying to keep our explorations . . . contained. Supporting one another and making sure we don't . . ."

"Spiral out of control," Jenny added.

"Exactly," Easton said. "The game has become far too dangerous. So we meet here to keep one another . . . safe."

Judging by the way the others looked to her before they spoke, I had the feeling Easton might be the leader of the group.

"But you *are* playing?" I looked directly at Easton as I asked this question, but her eyes betrayed nothing.

"No," Hugh said. "We're just . . . comparing possibilities."

"We get together to discuss a few rabbit holes and try to figure out one or two puzzles. We solved quite a few during the ninth iteration," Darla said.

I continued to look over at Easton Paruth, but her face remained expressionless. Was it possible this woman was actually Murmur? She seemed so . . . nice.

"What are you working on now?" I asked, turning my attention to Darla.

She smiled as she spoke, clearly excited. "It's pretty cool, actually. A new video was just released on YouTube and we found a hidden—"

"Darla!" Jenny interjected. "What the fuck?"

"It's okay," Easton said, glancing over at Jenny, who quickly averted her gaze. I was right. Clearly, Easton was in charge here.

"Somebody found a hidden level in a videogame called Zompocalypso," Easton said. "We're just trying to ascertain whether it's safe to explore that mystery, or if it might be a trailhead connected to Rabbits."

"So if it was connected to Rabbits, you'd want to avoid it?" I asked.

Easton just smiled.

"Zompocalypso? Isn't that the Fortnite rip-off?" Chloe asked.

"Well, that description is a bit reductive," Hugh said, clearly a fan of what was definitely a shitty derivative version of Fortnite. There was no way Hugh was Murmur.

"What's special about this hidden level?" I asked.

"It contains an image—a collage of symbols and numbers, obviously clues of some kind, but we've been unable to figure out exactly what it all means," Easton continued.

"Can we see it?" I said.

"I don't see why not," said Easton, "if the entire group is in agreement."

There were whispers around the table.

"We could step outside for a moment, if that would be better," I offered.

"That might be for the best," Easton said. "We'll call you back in."

Chloe and I stepped outside, onto the front porch.

"You wanna take off?" she asked, once the door had closed behind us.

"What? Why would we do that?"

"We can just play Zompocalypso ourselves. We can easily find that secret level," Chloe said.

I'd been thinking the same thing. We would almost certainly be able to find that hidden level on our own, especially now that we knew it existed.

"Come on," Chloe said as she started walking down the steps. "There's no way any of those people are Murmur."

But I wasn't so sure. "I don't feel like Easton's being completely honest," I said.

"You think she's playing the game," Chloe said.

"I do," I said as the door behind us opened with a slow wooden creak.

"You guys can come back in now," Darla said.

Chloe came back up the stairs, and the two of us reentered the house.

We were guided to a couple of seats that had been set up for us at the far end of the dining room table. There, visible on a laptop, was the hidden screen from Zompocalypso.

It was exactly as Easton had described it: light-colored numbers and symbols atop a dark blue background.

Everything was arranged around one symbol that was much

larger than the rest. That symbol sat in what appeared to be the geometric center of the screen.

It was a triangle with a small circle on top—the symbol from my elevator dream and the front door of the Gatewick Institute.

What were the odds that a symbol from a recurring dream I'd been having since childhood was just randomly part of this thing? I'd never played Zompocalypso in my life.

"What do you think?" Easton said.

I leaned forward and touched the screen, checking out the tiny symbols and numbers. "It's kind of beautiful," I said, which was true. The graphics were extremely sophisticated and detailed—completely different from the cheap patchwork graphic design of Zompocalypso.

"What can you tell us about these?" I asked, pointing to the tiny symbols.

"We think the little ones are meaningless, just creepy for creepy's sake. The same arcane background art is available online for ninety-nine cents."

I nodded. "What about that?" I asked, pointing to the middle of the screen. "Any significance to that symbol, the circle and the tri-angle?" I asked.

"Not that we know about," Jenny said, but I thought I may have seen a brief flash of something pass across Easton's face.

"How did you find the hidden screen?" Chloe asked; there was no point in us spending time solving the game-within-the-game ourselves if these people had already figured it out.

There were rumblings from the table.

"Should we step outside again?" I asked.

"You have to bring the golden war hammer to the blacksmith's shed in the lower quadrant, and then you can walk through the back wall into a hidden room," Darla said. Jenny and Hugh gasped, clearly upset Darla was sharing this information with us.

"What?" Darla said. Jenny and Hugh shook their heads.

Easton smiled a tiny, bemused smile. "It's okay," she said. "We're a group of like-minded people, all interested in learning more. And if we can help one another in some small way"—Easton looked over at me—"well then, where's the harm in that?"

"We found this screen of symbols on the back wall of that room." Darla zoomed out and revealed that what we'd been looking at was indeed the back wall of a hidden room.

"Cool," I said.

"What do you make of it?" Easton asked.

"No idea," I said. "Do you guys have any theories?"

"We do have some thoughts," Darla said.

"Thoughts that we're not prepared to share," the Colonel added, the tone of his voice suggesting that perhaps Darla should stop talking.

Alberto nodded in agreement with the Colonel. He also appeared to have had just about enough of the sharing.

Maybe Alberto or the Colonel was Murmur?

I looked over at Chloe and she nodded. It was time to ask.

"Have any of you heard of the Rabbits player known as Murmur?"

As I asked the question, Chloe and I scanned the faces of everybody at the table. We were looking for any kind of reaction.

But there was nothing.

They'd all heard of Murmur of course, but—according to them—they didn't know any more than we did.

We stayed there for about an hour and a half, swapping anecdotes about the game. We told stories about the puzzles we'd encountered and compared notes on *The Prescott Competition Manifesto*. I offered to share the version of the *PCM* that I played during the informal Rabbits information sessions I ran in the arcade, but they'd all heard that version already.

Darla walked us to the door, and on our way out, she made us promise to let her know if we found anything Rabbits-related in that hidden screen from Zompocalypso.

"For a support group working to help one another avoid playing a dangerous game, you all seem really interested in everything related to that game," I said.

"We find that talking about it in a safe environment is helpful," she said. "We think of it like methadone for heroin addicts. It's better than the alternative. We've all had a pretty rough time playing the game."

I nodded. "I understand."

"Plus," she said, lowering her voice to a whisper, "we need to make sure the game isn't . . . following us."

"What does that mean?" I asked.

But just then, Easton called Darla back into the house.

"Sorry," she said. "Gotta run."

Chloe had to work, so she dropped me off at home and the two of us agreed we'd reconnect in the morning. She said she'd try to look into Zompocalypso during her shift if the arcade wasn't busy.

I put some water on the stove for pasta and chopped up some garlic. While I was waiting for the water to boil, I thought about what had happened with Easton Paruth and her group. Had they actually retired from the game, or was something else going on? The possibility that we'd just met an infamous player was exciting, but if one of those people really was Murmur, we had no idea which one.

Sitting around talking about the game with like-minded humans felt good, and even a little bit inspiring, but we were no closer to figuring out what to do next.

After I'd finished eating (spaghetti aglio e olio with tiger prawns and a glass of California Zinfandel), I sat down to take a look at the strange numbers and symbols that Darla and her friends had found hidden in that secret level of Zompocalypso.

I turned on my console, downloaded the game, and quickly navigated my character to the hidden level, per Darla's instructions.

After hours staring at those images and getting nowhere, I went into my bedroom and flopped down onto my bed face-first.

It didn't take more than a few minutes to fall into a deep and dreamless sleep.

When I woke up, it was completely black.

I sat up and reached for my phone to find out how long I'd been sleeping, but it wasn't there. I must have left it in the living room.

As I sat there in my bed, I began to feel strange.

I knew that I was in my bedroom, but something felt different.

There was enough ambient light coming in through the windows to illuminate the familiar shapes and shadows of my stuff. I could see the back of the old wood-and-leather chair I picked up from the side of the road the week I'd moved in, the overstuffed clothes hamper leaning out of my closet, and the crack of moonlight beneath the blinds that didn't reach far enough down to properly cover the window. I was definitely still in my bedroom. But something wasn't quite right. Was it the quality of the air or the humidity again?

As the sleepy feeling slowly left my brain and my senses became sharper and more focused, I knew it wasn't the humidity. It was more than that.

I had the very distinct feeling I was somewhere else entirely. And as strange as it might sound, I didn't want to turn on the lights.

It felt scary, but it was also exhilarating, and I really didn't want to lose that feeling.

As a kid I'd been interested in (read: obsessed with) things that fell outside of our normal human experiences—not only paranormal and supernatural things like ghosts, ESP, and UFOs, but also stuff like religion, astrology, and mythology. I tried Ouija boards, séances, even whispering "Bloody Mary" into a mirror, but I was never able to conjure anything paranormal.

I would have given anything to have seen a ghost. That would have been confirmation there was something else out there.

As I grew older and my experiences led me to believe that things like ghosts and ESP were almost certainly fictional, my obsession with uncovering real-life mystery and weirdness in the world slowly began to fade.

But it never disappeared completely.

That night in the truck with Annie and Emily, the world felt different.

Something had changed.

Now I was feeling something eerily similar as I made my way slowly down my hallway in pitch-blackness.

My eyes gradually adjusted to the darkness as I entered the living room. The cool soft glow from the lights of the city coming through the large window dimly illuminated everything. Nothing appeared to be out of place.

I was in my living room, but still, something felt off.

I couldn't see my clock from where I was standing, but something told me, if I could have seen it, it would have read 4:44 A.M.

I stood in front of the window and looked out over the city. I could see a young couple stumbling along the sidewalk below. They were arguing about something that seemed extremely important to him but meaningless to her.

I could tell by the weird buzzing and fluttering in my upper stomach that there was no way I'd be getting back to sleep—at least, not for quite a while. So I decided I'd make some coffee and do my best to get ready for the day.

While I was waiting for the water to boil, I stared out my windows at the slowly waking city. The arguing couple had been replaced by the first trickle of cars and pedestrians leaving their homes and straight-lining their way to another world. The world of work. The office.

The feeling that I'd somehow woken up in another world was still with me, but the muted sounds of the distant traffic and the slight hum as the compressor in my refrigerator kicked on slowly brought me back to reality. I was probably just dehydrated, or maybe I'd woken up at a weird time during a deep REM cycle. I grabbed a bottle of water from the fridge and drank the whole thing.

I was halfway up the stairs before I actually realized I was on my way to the roof.

I'd spent a little time up there in the mornings the previous summer, sipping coffee and staring out at the city, but I'd never been there in the dark.

As I stepped out onto the roof and looked up into the night sky, the otherworldly feeling that had been bothering me since I woke up disappeared into the back of my mind. All I could think about was the stars. I'd never seen the sky this cloudless and clear in Seattle.

I'd spent some time up in northern British Columbia, and this reminded me of the wide, bright starlit skies I'd experienced out there in the middle of the forest, far away from the lights of any town or city.

I stood there staring up at the sky for a long time.

Even with the light of the moon and the wild shine emanating from the lights of the city below, I could clearly see the stars.

I was looking up at the Big Dipper when it came to me.

The hidden level from Zompocalypso.

While I was rearranging the placement of everything in my mind, I began to see a pattern. Those seemingly random scribbles of numbers and symbols suddenly weren't random at all.

I ran back downstairs, turned off the kettle (which had boiled dry), loaded a map of current constellations onto my laptop, and navigated my way back to the hidden level in Zompocalypso.

It took me about five minutes to find the secret hidden within that mess of scribbles and symbols.

There were yellow numbers on the Zompocalypso screen that corresponded to the specific locations of each star that made up the constellations of the night sky.

I began with Polaris, the brightest star that makes up the Little Dipper, or Ursa Minor, and quickly mapped out the numbers on the hidden screen that matched the locations of each of the seven main stars that comprised that constellation.

When I combined those numbers, I had sixteen digits.

I'd played enough alternate reality games and studied Rabbits for long enough to suspect that these numbers were most likely some kind of code. I tried every alphanumeric, hexadecimal, and binary combination I could think of, but there was nothing. I stared at the screen again. Something was bothering me, but I couldn't put my finger on it. What was I missing?

After going back and forth over every pattern and number combination I could think of, I eventually found it. It wasn't the numbers that had been bothering me. It was something else entirely.

There was an extra constellation.

I was aware of Ophiuchus, the large constellation represented by a man holding a serpent that people occasionally (and incorrectly) refer to as the thirteenth sign of the zodiac, but this was different.

I couldn't believe I'd missed it. It was smaller than the others, hidden in a mess of numbers and symbols I'd initially thought were just part of the background.

It was composed of twelve stars in the shape of a triangle and circle—the symbol from my elevator dream.

Once again, I went through every combination of possible clues and patterns I could think of that might connect those stars and numbers, but still couldn't find anything that looked even remotely like a clue.

But there was no way I was going to give up now.

I made some coffee for real this time, and went back to work.

I combined the numbers and letters associated with the twelve stars that made up the thirteenth constellation in the image on the hidden Zompocalypso screen, and then typed that enormously long string of alphanumeric characters into the address bar of a Web browser, added dot com, and pressed enter.

Nothing.

But when I typed those same characters into the address bar of a Tor Browser and added .onion (a darknet URL suffix), something happened.

A website loaded, and what appeared to be a video started playing.

But it wasn't a video. It was the Earth, and the way the camera was zooming closer was familiar. I was looking at some kind of satellite application.

I sat back and watched as the application zoomed forward into North America, up to Washington State, and finally came to a stop, right above a back alley in downtown Seattle.

31

NOBODY SAID IT WAS GOING TO BE EASY

WHEN I DISCOVERED the satellite footage or video or whatever it was that had zoomed in to that back alley on my laptop screen, it was just after six in the morning.

I called Chloe, but she didn't answer, her phone most likely on her nightstand, on silent.

I was on my own.

I stepped out of my building into a light rain. The sky was monochromatic, a layer of dark, gloomy gray covered the city from the horizon to the Space Needle. I zipped up my hoodie and hurried across the street into the waiting Uber.

We drove in silence through the city toward the Pike Place Market, the rhythmic clunking of the wipers and the wet glimmer of lights reflected in the streets hypnotic and comforting.

When we were a block or so away from the alley, I asked the driver to pull over and I hopped out of the car.

I double-checked the exact location on my phone, and then started walking.

I didn't notice the rain at all as I hurried between the towering buildings toward whatever was waiting for me at that spot on the map.

I was close.

The camera had zoomed in to the middle of the alley between Western and First. This area would soon be filled with the hum and bustle of the waking city, but at that moment it was peaceful and still. I could hear the distant cries of seagulls waking in anticipation of another day spent scavenging around the waterfront.

I stepped off the street and into the alley. This was it.

I took a deep breath and readied myself. If there was something waiting in there, I really hoped that something wasn't a murderous back-alley-dwelling human.

I walked past the rusted fire escapes and barred windows looking for anything related to that hidden screen in Zompocalypso, anything that might be connected to Rabbits.

But there was nothing.

No pattern hidden in the wet gray-brown cobblestones, no clues in the number of rungs that made up each of the fire escape ladders, no hidden messages in the graffiti spray-painted on the brick walls and dumpsters that lined the alley.

Had I been wrong about the extra constellation?

I was just about to leave when I heard a deep, low scratching sound coming from one of the nearby dumpsters.

I wrapped my hand around my key ring and arranged it so a couple of the keys slid in between my fingers—as if that was going to help me fight off whatever Seattle night terror was waiting behind the dumpster. I shook my head, let go of my keys, and walked slowly and carefully toward the dark green metal container, ready to run for my life if a person (or something worse) suddenly stepped out.

I was about three feet away when a large rat scuttled out from around the bin.

I jumped backward and almost fell over.

I wasn't afraid of rats—Seattle had more than its share of them—but echoes of the strange otherworldly feeling I'd experienced when I woke up remained with me, and no matter how excited I was about following the potential clue I'd uncovered, I was still walking through a long dark alley alone in the rain.

I took a deep breath and pulled the wet dumpster away from the brick wall.

There was nothing there except for another rat.

This one was even bigger than the first. She was lying on her side on a pile of wet newspapers feeding a handful of little pink babies.

I carefully pushed the dumpster back into place and was about to switch my focus to potential connections between the businesses and addresses that made up the streets on either side of the alley, when I noticed another dumpster directly across from the one providing shelter for the brand-new family of rats. The last thing I wanted to do was disturb another rodent family feeding, but I'd come all this way. I knew that if I didn't check everything it would gnaw at me, and I'd have to come back again later.

I took a deep breath, readied myself for any and all types of rat contact, and pulled.

One of the dumpster's casters was missing, which resulted in a deep reverb-y scraping howl as I dragged the large, wet metal box away from the wall.

There were no rats.

But there was something.

The wall behind the dumpster was covered in a mess of numbers, letters, and symbols, all surrounding something familiar.

The circle atop the triangle.

The layout and style of the art were similar to that hidden screen from Zompocalypso. Seeing it here in this context felt like a glimpse into a secret world. My breath quickened and I could suddenly hear my heart beating in my ears.

"What do you think?"

I'm not sure whether I heard her voice before or after I'd taken out my phone and started taking pictures.

I turned around to face the speaker.

It was Easton Paruth.

I hadn't heard her approaching. She must have entered the alley while I'd been moving the dumpster away from the wall.

"You're following me?" I asked.

"I had Darla hide a bit of tracking technology in one of your shoes."

"What?"

She didn't answer my question. "Do you mind if I take a look?"

I stepped aside so she could get a better view.

"It's beautiful," she said as she stepped forward and placed her hand on the triangle in the middle of the wall.

"You've seen this symbol before," I said.

Easton continued to run her hand along the wall.

"A circle atop a pyramid is a familiar sigil in the world of the game. It's something we refer to as The Moonrise," she said.

The strange symbol from my elevator dream suddenly had a name.

"What does it mean?" I asked.

"I'm not sure. But it's deeply connected to the game. It's something that normally appears as a marker—a sign that you're on the right path."

I nodded toward the wall. "Are you going to take a picture?"

"I do believe I will, thank you."

She took about a dozen photographs from a few different angles.

"Why are you following me?" I asked.

Easton finally stopped taking pictures and put away her phone.

"Let me buy you a coffee. I'll tell you all about it."

"Are you Murmur?"

"Coffee," she said.

She helped me push the dumpster back against the wall, and then started walking back toward the entrance to the alley.

I ran after her. There was no way I was going to let her out of my sight without some kind of explanation.

Easton took off her jacket and placed it over the back of her chair. She was wearing an elegant orange-and-blue top cut at an angle across her shoulders. She had a significant collection of metal bracelets on her wrists and huge golden hoops hanging from her ears.

"So, I'm sure you have some questions for me, and I promise I'll try to answer them to the best of my ability, but do you mind if I ask you a couple of things first?"

We were sitting across from each other at a low table in a coffee shop. It was still fairly early, but the locals were beginning to file in for their morning fix.

"What would you like to know?" I replied, then burned my tongue as I nervously sipped at my coffee, which was still way too hot to drink.

"Is it true that Alan Scarpio asked you for help?"

I stared at Easton for a moment. I couldn't decide what to say. It was clear she already knew or suspected that I'd spoken with Scarpio, but she wanted confirmation for some reason.

"Will you answer one question first?" I asked at last.

She nodded slowly—not an affirmation, but rather, an indication that she was thinking about it. "That depends, I suppose."

"Are you the player known as Murmur?"

She smiled for a moment, then finally nodded.

Shit. Easton Paruth just got a whole lot scarier.

"How long have you been playing the game?"

"That's two questions," she said, "but that's okay. I've been playing the game for a long time."

"That's not exactly what I meant."

She smiled. "You'd like to know how long I've been playing the eleventh iteration?"

"Yes."

"I'd like to tell you about my experiences, K, but lately people affiliated with the game have a habit of . . . disappearing or turning up deceased."

"What do you mean?" I asked. There was no reason for me to share the fact I'd been hearing the same thing—at least, not yet.

"Several players I know personally have recently died or gone missing, and there are rumors that the worldwide numbers are much, much higher."

"What do you think is going on?"

She shrugged. "I know I have something of a . . . reputation for playing a little outside the rules, but it really is getting dangerous out there. You should watch yourself, K. There aren't that many of us left."

"Do Darla and the others have any idea that you're using them to help you play Rabbits?"

"Not talking about the game is still an important part of it. You would do well to remember that."

A threat—or hint of a threat—from Murmur wasn't something that could be taken lightly, but I was tired and, frankly, at this point, I was almost beyond caring. "We're talking about it now, though, aren't we?"

"Well, yes," she said with a wry smile. "I suppose we are."

I blew on my coffee to cool it down.

"You're not angry that I used you to track down this clue, are you?" she said.

I shrugged. "Not really." And it was true. I really didn't care. I was having coffee with Murmur, and she'd used me to help her play the game. It was an honor. Chloe was going to lose her mind.

"We all have our own methods of playing," Easton said. "But the fact you're here and still alive is impressive."

"Thanks," I said, and took another small sip of coffee, careful not to burn myself this time. "It's true," I confessed. "Alan Scarpio did ask me for help. He told me that he believed something was wrong with the game."

Easton leaned across the table. "He was right. The game has always been dangerous, but what's happening now . . . it's different. Players are disappearing and dying at an unprecedented rate."

I nodded.

"If Scarpio really did ask you for help, then you must be connected to whatever's going on."

"I suppose so." I fidgeted with my coffee cup on the table. As excited as I was about speaking with Murmur, there was no way I was going to tell her about Crow and the Gatewick Institute.

"No connection at all between you and Scarpio before this?" she asked.

"None. The first time I met him was just before he disappeared."

Easton took a sip of coffee and leaned back in her chair, metal bracelets jangling around her wrists. I counted them—ten on each wrist. Twenty bracelets, a twenty-dollar bill in a man's hand in line, twenty sugar containers on the servers'-station table. I shook my head. The last thing I wanted to do now was fall into some kind of pattern-recognition sinkhole. There was a fine line between those patterns that were connected to the game and the ones that weren't, and although I felt like I was still operating on the right side of that line, it was getting blurrier every day. I'd grown to depend on Chloe and Baron to keep me focused and on track, but Baron was dead and Chloe wasn't here. I took a slow deep breath.

"Why are you still playing?" I said. "If you don't mind my asking."

She stared at me for a moment, then looked around as if she was worried somebody might be listening. She pulled her chair closer to the table.

"Because I know what happens when you win. I've seen it."

"What do you mean?"

"I was there. I've seen somebody win the game."

"Who?"

She shook her head. I wasn't getting that information.

"I've seen somebody get their heart's desire," she said as she stood up and set a ten-dollar bill on the table. "It was real, and it was amazing, and that's why I'm still playing."

She smiled warmly. "I wish you luck, I really do, but I hope you understand, you're not to attempt to contact me again."

I nodded, and Easton Paruth walked out of the coffee shop.

As soon as Easton was out of sight, I slipped off my sneakers and found a small flat device that had been hidden beneath the insole of my left shoe. It was flat and gray. It looked like one of those Tile things people use to track their keys.

I slipped the tracking device into what was left of my coffee like a secret agent crushing a sim card, and rushed outside to follow Easton.

But by the time I stepped out of the coffee shop, she was nowhere to be seen.

32

THE MOONRISE

CHLOE WAS WAITING OUTSIDE my building when I got home.

"You called me at six in the morning?" she asked.

"I did."

"Where the hell have you been?"

I smiled.

"You got to have pie with Scarpio *and* coffee with Murmur? What's next, bagels with rescue-van Hazel?"

While Chloe made us breakfast, I told her everything that had happened; how I'd figured out the secret astrological code in that hidden level of Zompocalypso, and how Easton Paruth—who'd admitted she was Murmur—had followed me to that wall behind the dumpster.

After breakfast, I pulled up the photographs I'd taken of that wall, and the two of us spent a couple of hours staring at my phone, trying to make sense of the mess of numbers, letters, and symbols.

"That's the symbol from the door at Gatewick," Chloe said, pointing to the small circle atop the triangle sitting in the center of all the other symbols and letters.

"Easton called it The Moonrise," I said.

"What do you think it means?"

I shook my head. "I have no idea."

We sat there in silence for a moment.

"The Magician would know about this," I said, and immediately regretted it.

The Magician was still MIA, and the last thing I wanted to do was remind Chloe about that fact.

"Sorry," I said.

Chloe shook her head. "It's fine. There has to be somebody else we can ask about this thing."

I thought about Russell Milligan, but there was no way he was going to speak with us again.

"I don't know, maybe Fatman?" I said.

Chloe jumped up from the couch. "Fuck, yes. Fatman," she said, as she ran over to the front door and tossed me my shoes.

"Wait," she said.

"What?"

"Check for tracking devices."

The two of us pulled our shoes apart, but we couldn't find any-thing.

33

AN INVISIBLE CITY

WE FOUND PARKING a block and a half away from the porn shop, hopped out of the car, and pulled up our hoods in unison against the rain. As we ran across the street, Chloe reached out and grabbed my hand—and, for just a moment, I felt like I was living in a normal world, like Chloe and I were a regular couple running across a street in the rain toward a warm table in a cozy bistro, not a couple of game-obsessed lunatics rushing toward a porn shop basement in order to ask a crossbow-wielding shut-in to help us win a deadly game that might be the only thing keeping the multiverse together.

While we made our way up the sidewalk toward the store, I imagined what it would be like to do all of this stuff alone. There was no way I would have been able to handle it. I was really happy that Chloe and I were doing this together.

We approached the store, and I could see that the tall wrought iron gate was open and hanging out over the sidewalk.

"What the hell?" Chloe said. She'd clearly noticed the same thing.

As we walked through the gate and down the steps toward the basement door, we heard a distant banging and shuffling coming from somewhere deep inside the office.

"Hello?" Chloe called out.

The banging and shuffling grew louder and then abruptly stopped.

The door that opened into Fatman's office was ajar. I knocked and then pushed it open a bit farther. The slow creak of the door against the silence inside the office was unnerving.

"Fatman?"

"Neil?" Chloe said, right behind me.

There was no answer.

"We're coming in," I said. "Please don't murder us with a crossbow."

We stepped into the room.

The fluorescents were out, but the office was dimly illuminated by a swath of warm light coming from somewhere in the back of the room.

The entire place had been torn apart. What had once been somewhat orderly rows between shelves were now winding rivers of scattered books and papers.

"Hello?" I called out again. I figured it would be worth losing the element of surprise if we could avoid a crossbow bolt through the rib cage.

Still no answer.

"What the hell happened here?" Chloe said as we waded through the mess of books and papers strewn across the floor.

"Looks like the ransack scene in every movie ever," I replied. "Don't touch anything."

"Holy shit." Chloe was staring at the back wall of the office. "Mother's gone."

I followed her eyes. She was right. There was nothing left of the huge makeshift supercomputer that had taken up the entire back wall. Where there had once been more than a hundred monitors and a shit ton of other electronic stuff, there were now only wires and splinters of black spray-painted wood.

While we were standing there staring at the wall, we heard another series of dull scraping sounds coming from the back room—quieter this time.

"Shit," I whispered. "Do you think whoever did this is still here?" I was so floored by the state of the place, I hadn't even considered that possibility.

Chloe picked up a lamp and tested its weight.

"That's probably not gonna help," I said as I unscrewed the metal leg from an old dining room table that used to be covered in boxes.

"Where the fuck did you learn that?" Chloe asked.

"No idea. Saw it in a movie maybe?"

I handed the heavy table leg to Chloe, unscrewed another for myself, and the two of us carefully made our way to the back of the room, toward the source of the light and the dull scraping sounds.

The light was coming from the entrance to a hallway that ran parallel to the main room. As we turned the corner, we could see that the source of the light was a slightly ajar door at the end of the hall.

We approached slowly, and when we finally made it to the end of the hall I used the table leg to gently push open the door.

It was hard to tell what kind of room it was at first, because of all the blood.

It wasn't until we saw the toilet, located on the other side of a metal divider, that we realized it was a bathroom.

There was a man sitting on the floor with his head propped up against the back wall next to the toilet.

It was Fatman Neil.

It looked like he was dead, and had probably been that way for a while.

Chloe pulled out her phone, but just as she was about to dial 911, we heard a banging noise coming from outside.

It sounded like the front gate.

We ran out of the bathroom, back through Fatman's ransacked lair, outside, and up the stairs.

There was nobody there. The street in front of the porn shop was empty.

There was a pretty good chance that whoever was responsible for murdering Neil had been in there with us at some point. I felt a shiver as I wondered just how close Chloe and I had come to ending up with Neil on the floor of that bathroom.

We went back to the bathroom to call the police, but just as Chloe was about to dial, Fatman started gurgling.

We rushed to his side.

"Hang on," I said. "We're calling for help."

Neil grabbed my arm and pulled me close. I could see that he'd been stabbed numerous times. One of those wounds was a jagged open cut along the side of his neck. He was extremely weak and couldn't speak—most likely because something in his throat had been severed. I got the feeling he wasn't going to make it until the ambulance arrived.

He kept trying to talk, but whatever he was trying to say came out as gurgling bubbles of blood. He stretched out a bloody finger and pointed toward one section of the floor that wasn't completely covered in blood.

"What?" I asked. "There's nothing there."

But Neil wasn't using his finger to point, he was using it to write.

It took every ounce of strength he had left, and in the end, he managed just one word, written in his own blood:

Valdrada.

Then Fatman Neil died.

Chloe tried CPR and mouth-to-mouth while I dialed 911, but Neil wasn't coming back.

We leaned against the wall and waited for the ambulance. We were completely freaked out, but relatively calm. I'm pretty sure we were both in shock.

"What the fuck is Valdrada?" Chloe asked.

The exact same question had been rattling around in the back of my mind while Chloe was performing CPR.

It finally came to me.

"It's an invisible city," I said, jumping up.

"What the fuck does that mean?"

"It's a novel by Italo Calvino," I said as I ran back into Fatman's office.

Fatman kept all of his books in alphabetical order, and, although the place had been ransacked, the books remained somewhat alphabetical when they'd landed on the floor. It didn't take me long to find what I was looking for. It was a hardcover book called *Invisible Cities.*

There was a chapter in that book about an invisible city called Valdrada.

Valdrada had been constructed on the shore of a lake so that the entire city would be reflected in the water. This reflection wasn't simply a two-dimensional representation of Valdrada, however, it was a complete manifestation of the city above. The interior of every room, all of the people, and every single action they performed were mirrored in the city below.

I opened the book and turned to a chapter called "Cities & Eyes 1." I was looking for something hidden in the text of the novel or written in the margins, some clue that might help us find out what the hell was going on. I didn't find anything like that, but there was something.

Nestled into the spine of the book, on the first page of that chaper, was a small thin metal key.

I'd been looking for some kind of clue in the text of the novel. I definitely wasn't expecting a literal physical key.

I slipped the key into my pocket just as the paramedics burst through the door. They were followed a minute or so later by the police.

Suddenly, Fatman's office was an extremely active crime scene.

34

THE AMERICAN

WE WERE QUESTIONED for about an hour and a half at the police station.

We told the police we'd gone to that porn shop basement to ask Fatman Neil a question about a game we were playing. We didn't mention Alan Scarpio, the surveillance computer array Neil called Mother, or the fact that the game might be connected to Neil's death.

They asked us all kinds of questions about the game. We told them it was something called Starfire Enterprises, which was an ongoing alternate reality game connected to the marketing surrounding the ninth movie in a popular action movie franchise. Their eyes glazed over when we started explaining what an ARG was and how it worked. They took dutiful notes, but they had no idea. Their takeway was clearly: weird gamers, knew the deceased a little, keep them in mind if anybody else they know gets killed.

Eventually, a tall brunette woman with a scar across the bottom of her mouth who told us her name was Detective Marianne Sanders took down our contact information and told us we were free to go.

The police gave us a ride back to Chloe's car.

Chloe started the car, and the two of us sat together in silence for a few moments.

"What the fuck, K?"

"I know. That was messed up."

"What are we going to do now?" Chloe asked.

I pulled the key from my jacket pocket and handed it to Chloe.

"What is this?"

"Found it in the book."

"*Invisible Cities*?"

"Yeah."

"Look at this," Chloe said, holding the key up to the light.

It was faded, but something had been stamped into the front:

The American

29

"What do you think?" I asked.

"The American Hotel?"

I nodded. "That makes sense. It looks like this key might fit some kind of locker, maybe?"

"I've been to the American," Chloe said. "It's a backpacker kinda place. I'm sure they have lockers."

She typed the address into the GPS app on her phone, put her car into drive, and pulled out into the street.

"What are you doing?" I asked.

"What the fuck do you think? We're going to the American to figure out what that key opens."

On our way over to the hotel, we came up with a plan. We'd ask for a tour, and then, as soon as we found the lockers, I'd ask to use the bathroom while Chloe continued with the tour. Then I'd sneak back to the lockers, open number 29, and grab whatever was inside.

"Welcome. How can I help you?" A twentysomething blond woman, with two long, thick dreadlocked pigtails that made her look like a cantina character from a *Star Wars* movie, smiled as we entered the lobby.

"Hey," Chloe said. "We're looking for a place for a few nights. We were hoping we might be able to take a look around?"

"You bet," she said. "Just a sec." She grabbed a set of keys and came around to our side of the counter. "Follow me," she said.

She took us through the various rooms—the dining area, the communal spaces, and a few of the unoccupied bedrooms. There were a lot of bunk beds and some pretty cool eclectic hostel-style furnishings. There were also a whole bunch of lockers, but they were all secured with combination locks.

It looked like our bathroom ruse wasn't going to be effective.

"Do you have any other lockers?" I asked.

She thought for a moment, then shook her head. "No, I think we've seen them all. If you have something that won't fit, I'm sure we can figure it out, keep it in a secure room or whatever."

"It's not that." I showed her the key. "Is there anything here that this might be able to open?"

She took a look at the key, then back at me. "You're not really looking for a room."

I looked over at Chloe.

"Where did you get that key?" Pigtails put her hands on her hips. I could tell she was ready to shut us down completely. We needed to come up with something fast.

"My brother," Chloe said. "He always kept it around his neck."

I had no idea where this story was headed. Chloe didn't have a brother.

"No matter what," Chloe continued, "swimming, showering, running a marathon, that key was always there. He never talked about the key with any of us, but it was obviously something really important to him." Chloe paused and took a deep shaky breath. "My brother passed away recently."

"Oh my god," Pigtails said. "That's terrible. What happened?"

Chloe shook her head. "He was electrocuted."

"What? I'm so sorry." Pigtails's hands involuntarily covered her mouth in horror.

"Yeah, it was a downed power line. He touched a metal railing, slid down an icy road, and just . . . died."

I shook my head. Chloe and I had rewatched and subsequently reread *The Ice Storm* recently. I can't believe she was using the Elijah Wood character's brutally beautiful death to lie to this poor woman.

"It's this way," Pigtails said as she led us through a narrow hallway and down a set of stairs into a basement.

"Watch your heads on the stairs," she said. "The ceiling is pretty low."

We stepped into a narrow room that smelled like old leather and damp newspaper. There were two short walls of old lockers, numbered 1 to 30, on either side of a long, worn wooden bench sitting on the polished concrete floor. It looked like a compact version of a changing room at a YMCA or a boxing gym circa 1982.

"We use these for the staff. Number 29 is one of the lockers we don't have a key for. I don't think it's been opened the entire time I've worked here. We haven't needed the extra space, so we've never bothered to have a locksmith open it. Do you think there might be something inside?"

I recognized that look in her eyes. She was getting excited about the mystery.

"We're not sure, but we think there might be," I said.

Pigtails nodded, and was about to open the locker when she turned to Chloe.

"*You* should do it," she said. "Your brother would have wanted it this way." She handed Chloe the key.

"Thank you," Chloe said, grabbing the key.

Did I see a tear rolling down her cheek?

I shook my head. We were horrible people.

Chloe opened the locker. There was something small and circular inside.

"What is that?" Pigtails asked.

"Looks like a movie," Chloe said as she pulled out an old film canister, about six inches in diameter.

Chloe opened the canister. Inside was a roll of film. There was a worn label on the inside of the lid that featured a familiar logo.

A small circle atop a triangle.

"Do you think it's a movie of your family?" Pigtails asked, hopeful.

"I'm absolutely sure it is," Chloe said. "My brother loved making old-school home movies. Thank you so much for everything. This means a lot."

"You are so welcome," Pigtails said, and then she led us back upstairs where she asked us to leave our information, just in case. We returned the locker key, and she made us promise to let her know what we found on that film.

"I'll drop you off on my way home," Chloe said as we got into the car. "I promised my neighbor I'd walk her dog. First thing in the morning, I'll dig up a film projector."

"Sounds good," I said.

On our way to my place, I rolled down the window and Chloe put on some music. As we drove through the city, I did my best to let the Belle and Sebastian album *Fold Your Hands Child, You Walk Like a Peasant* take my mind off what had happened to Fatman Neil.

I closed my eyes and leaned back.

I remember hearing the first song from that album—"I Fought in a War"—the evening of the day I'd found out that my parents had died.

I was standing in line at a grocery store.

I suppose I could have asked somebody to bring me some groceries, but I needed milk and just didn't have the emotional energy to start a conversation with anyone I knew.

It wasn't so much that whoever I saw would be feeling pity for me—although that definitely would have been hard to take. It was more the idea that I might have to look at somebody else's face and give a shit what they thought about me, or about the way I presented myself in that moment of grief.

I couldn't handle the idea of being forced to consider somebody else's opinion of my reaction to my parents' death. Was I crying enough? Was I crying too much? I really didn't need anybody else to be sorry for my loss.

It was none of their fucking business.

While I was waiting to pay for my milk and bread, a young woman stepped into line behind me. She was around twenty years old. She was wearing two different-colored flip-flops on dirty feet, ripped jean shorts, a Guns N' Roses T-shirt, and a vintage puka shell necklace. The smell of the watermelon gum she was chewing filled my nostrils as the loud music coming from the huge headphones she'd pulled off her head and left dangling around her neck filled my ears.

The song was "I Fought in a War" by Belle and Sebastian.

When I looked back at that girl, slowly swaying to the music, blissfully unconcerned with anything else in the whole world, I was pretty sure I'd never seen anything so carefree and beautiful in my entire life.

I started crying, and I couldn't stop.

35

NO SPITTING ON STAGE

I CALLED CHLOE the next morning. She was in a thrift store haggling over the price of an old 8 mm projector. She told me to be at her place in fifteen minutes.

I rode my bike over and ran into her just as she was pulling into her parking space.

"Did you end up getting a projector?"

"I actually got two. One's 8 millimeter and the other is Super 8."

"What's the difference?"

"No idea. The guy said something about the size of the sprockets. He told me I could return whichever one doesn't work."

We each carried a projector up from Chloe's car.

I opened the canister we'd found in the locker and took a look at the sprockets while Chloe pulled up images of 8 mm film online. It looked like what was in that canister was Super 8, with a magnetic stripe for sound.

"Does that projector play sound?" I asked.

"Don't know. It's got speakers."

"If whoever recorded this footage had a microphone hooked up to their camera, there could be audio on there."

"It's too bright in here," Chloe said, pointing at the huge windows. "Let's do it in the bedroom."

I set the Super 8 projector down on a cedar chest at the foot of Chloe's bed, closed the thick set of blackout curtains that covered the windows, and switched off the lights. The room was suddenly completely black. It felt impossible to me that someplace this dark could exist in the middle of the day.

"Let's see if the bulb works," Chloe said, startling me.

I'd been so absorbed in cataloging the items in her room, I hadn't noticed she'd entered and was standing beside me.

I felt the skin of her arm brush mine as she reached for the projector, but before she turned it on, she leaned back and kissed me. While we were kissing, she flipped a switch on the projector and the room exploded with light.

"Ouch," I said.

Chloe laughed as she focused the light into a bright rectangle and guided it over to the giant *Howard the Duck* movie poster that filled one of her walls.

I jumped up and started taking down the poster.

"Careful," Chloe said, "that's a rare and valuable piece of cinema history."

"Of course," I said as I gently set the poster aside.

And just like that, we had a place to watch a movie—or whatever the hell was lurking inside that ancient can of Super 8 film.

It turns out this particular projector was a bit tricky to load. It took us about twenty minutes to figure it out. When we finally got it working, I switched off the lights again and Chloe started the projector.

The first thing that popped up on the wall was a name and logo: the Gatewick Institute, and the now familiar symbol of a triangle and circle, The Moonrise.

"Fuck," Chloe said as she grabbed and squeezed my hand.

It was exciting.

The projector was loud, but I could hear what sounded like distant muted music coming from somewhere.

"Can you hear that?" I said.

At first I thought it was coming from a car outside, but it was actually the projector's tiny built-in speakers.

The film had sound.

We turned the volume up as high as it could go. It was much better, but it still wasn't very loud.

———

The movie opens on what appears to be an empty hallway. The muted piano music is coming from somewhere off-screen, probably upstairs.

After a few seconds, the subject of the film, a man in a long dark leather jacket, enters the frame and begins walking down the hall.

Whoever's operating the camera remains behind the subject, keeping him in focus as he moves forward. Leather Jacket Man never turns around completely as he walks down the hall, so we can't see his face. The camera follows as he turns and moves down another hallway to a door. He eventually reaches the door, opens it, steps inside a room, and switches on a light.

A dim bulb hanging from a thin wire in the ceiling illuminates a medium-size room. The walls are almost completely covered with graffiti. There are a few scattered chairs and tables sitting on a filthy gold-colored carpet. All of the furniture has been scratched and carved up with graffiti that matches the walls. There's a framed sign hanging in the middle of the wall directly across from the door that reads: PERFORMERS THAT GO OVER THEIR SET TIMES BY MORE THAN TEN MINUTES WILL NOT BE PAID. NO SPITTING ON STAGE.

It looks like some kind of green room for bands, comedians, or other entertainers, probably located in the back of a sketchy live music venue somewhere.

It's at this point that Leather Jacket Man turns around and we see his face for the first time.

As the man in the movie turned around, Chloe gasped and squeezed my hand really hard.

The man in the leather jacket was the Magician.

He looked similar to the last time we'd seen him, the same worn-out look in his eyes, his hair the same length and style. But there's a calmness to his demeanor in the film. Whatever's about to happen, he appears to be ready for it.

"Go on, now," he says to whoever's operating the camera. "But leave it rolling."

After a few seconds, the Magician pulls out what appears to be a journal. Then he compares something in its pages with some of the graffiti on the wall in front of him, and just as he turns to check out one of the other walls, there's a burst of static and light. It only lasts a millisecond, but in that time, something has happened.

The Magician is no longer alone.

In the corner, behind the Magician, is an impossibly tall figure, maybe seven or eight feet in height—way too tall for the size of the room. The figure is standing incredibly still, its neck bent beneath the ceiling, towering over the Magician, who doesn't seem to realize that he's no longer alone.

When the tall figure finally begins to move, it becomes immediately clear that—whatever this thing is—it's definitely *not* a man.

Its form slowly changes as it begins to fill up the shadows, sucking up what little light remains in the room.

Suddenly, the Magician stops looking at the wall and straightens up.

He understands there's something behind him.

I felt Chloe shudder beside me. She moved closer, hooking her arm around mine.

Back on the screen, the Magician looks down at his journal and then up again. He can see it now, the darkness moving toward him from the corners of the room—a terrible thing made up of smaller dark gray shapes pouring and swirling in from around the edges.

I could feel myself reacting to the familiar gray shapes. My heart was racing, and an unpleasant warmth began seeping into my body.

Then the film itself slowly begins to lose light.

As the darkness moves to take over the frame, the Magician looks up toward the camera and we can see immediately by his expression that something is terribly wrong.

"No," he says, looking down at his journal and then up at one of the graffiti-covered walls. "This isn't right. This can't be right!"

He drops his journal, turns, and bolts toward the camera.

He doesn't make it more than two steps before he runs into part of the darkness that has been slowly seeping into the room.

As he lunges forward, something happens.

The lower part of his body becomes stuck immediately, but the top continues to move, stretching unnaturally as his momentum carries him forward.

For a moment it looks as though he's entered some kind of advanced and beautiful yoga pose. He's stretched thin, like he's made of hot, freshly blown glass, and then his body snaps and pops, slowly breaking in two, right around the middle of his chest.

Dark pink-and-crimson mist sprays the air as his body splits open.

For just a moment, we can see his lungs moving beneath the shining white teeth of his rib cage, and then he's suddenly snapped apart and sucked back into the darkness, and the room is completely black again.

The film ran out with a metallic flapping snarl and Chloe jumped.

I switched off the projector, and everything was silent. I could feel Chloe shaking beside me. She was crying.

"Chloe," I said, but I didn't have the words to continue.

After a minute or so, Chloe got up, switched on the lights, and opened the curtains. Her tears were gone, and the broken expression I'd seen on her face as she'd watched the film had been replaced by a look of resolute focus.

"That wasn't the Magician," she said. "It's impossible."

I nodded, but I wasn't sure. There was something about that movie that felt . . . real.

"It was pretty freaky," I said. I couldn't think of anything else to say.

"Those gray shadow things? Come on, K. Those were clearly visual effects."

I nodded and tried to hide the fact that my heart was pounding and I was having trouble breathing. I'd just seen the Magician torn apart by a deadly, terrifying darkness, but unlike Chloe, I was pretty sure those shadow things weren't special effects.

I'd seen them before.

I saw them coming for me the night I'd spent walking around Portland, outside the elevator in The Tower, with Crow on that city bus, and I'd seen them in a dream, standing in the middle of the road, the night of the accident with Annie and Emily Connors.

I understood something in that moment.

If we didn't stop playing the game, those shadow things were coming, and they were going to keep coming until what had happened to the Magician happened to everyone on Earth.

NOTES ON THE GAME:
MISSIVE BY HAZEL
(AUTHENTICATED BY BLOCKCHAIN)

Who is in charge?

Gameplay dictates that someone or something is guiding the players, pointing us toward potential solutions or possible pitfalls, but are these Wardens of the game capable of conscious thought the way we imagine it? Or are they controlling things based on factors outside of humankind's capacity to understand?

There are some who believe a group of Illuminati-esque secret operatives are out there somewhere, guiding the players from a distance. Others are certain there's a dark alien race—a species so different from our own that we're unable to comprehend any part of them with our basic human senses—working behind the scenes to control the players' movements through the game.

Whatever's really going on, it's become clear that these keepers of the secrets of the game are highly dangerous and extremely complicated. And if they actually do exist, none of them is talking.

—HAZEL 8

36

EAST OF BARN

AFTER WE'D FINISHED watching that Super 8 film, Chloe entered a kind of manic state. She buzzed around her apartment, darting back and forth between her laptop, desktop, and phone, her mind operating in a wild new gear.

The first thing she did was call every single number connected to the Magician that she could find, and ask if anybody had seen or heard from him. (They hadn't.) Then she went over that Super 8 movie frame by frame, looking for something that might reveal a location or any kind of clue at all, but nothing stood out.

After that, she asked me to pull up all of the photos I'd found online featuring Silvana Kulig, and the two of us pored over them for anything we might have missed earlier.

Still nothing.

At one point, Chloe called Silvana herself and asked about the Magician. Did he say anything else? How did he sound? But Silvana didn't have anything new to offer. After that, Chloe asked me to call Russell Milligan, and when I gently suggested we should get something to eat and maybe slow down for a minute, Chloe told me she wasn't hungry and demanded I make the call. When I suggested that maybe we should wait until tomorrow, she asked me to leave.

Chloe was clearly freaked out by what we'd just seen, and, although I wanted to stay there for emotional support, I could tell that she needed some time alone.

———

I went home to finish some laundry I'd started earlier, but I couldn't stop thinking about the Magician. If the woman with the pigtails from the American Hotel was right, and that locker hadn't been opened for years, how the hell was the Magician in that movie? He looked exactly the same age as he was the last time I'd seen him.

Chloe wasn't the only one shaken by watching that film.

After I'd finished folding my clothes, I lay down and tried to clear my mind and relax.

I must have fallen asleep at some point, because I woke up to knocking at my door.

I took a look at the time on my phone. It was just after six thirty. Nobody had buzzed up, so I ignored it. If it was Chloe, she'd call.

A few minutes later, there was another knock, louder this time.

I got up and walked over to the door. There was nobody visible through the peephole. They must have left. I was still looking through the peephole into the empty hall outside my apartment when . . .

Bang! Bang! Bang! Bang! Bang!

Somebody started hammering on my door. It was so sudden that I stumbled and fell backward.

When the banging ended, there was still nobody visible through the peephole. Was somebody crouching on the floor of the hallway, or hiding around the corner while they hammered on my door? It didn't seem possible based on the wide angle of view, but either way I took a couple of steps back, predialed 911, and held my finger above the call button.

"I'm calling the police, asshole!" I yelled.

I waited for a minute or so before I yanked the door open, ready to call, but the hallway was empty.

Whoever had been banging was gone.

I thought about making something to eat but I was full of adrenaline, and there was no way I was going to be able to relax enough to focus on cooking. I decided I'd go for a walk. I could always grab something along the way.

———

I had no idea if whoever had been banging on my door was watching my building, so I decided to leave out the back.

It had recently stopped raining, and the alley behind my building smelled like wet garbage. I started breathing through my mouth as I walked past a row of overflowing dumpsters. At the end of the alley, I jumped a large puddle of rainwater and stepped onto the broken sidewalk that led to a nearby park.

I shoved my hands into my jacket pockets as I walked by the children's playground that marked the beginning of the park. The pinkish-orange light from the setting sun reflecting off the slide and swing set reminded me of the background of an anime movie I'd seen recently. I was thinking about going over to swing for a while, when I heard a familiar sound.

Somewhere behind me, somebody was riding a bicycle.

I decided to skip the swings and turned left at the end of the block.

The bicycle was still back there, following at a distance of about ten yards.

During my freshman year of high school, I'd been followed by a car filled with seniors looking to perform an initiation rite, and I'd recently been followed by a Prius that led to a man called Crow threatening me on a bus, but there was something about being followed by a bicycle that felt intimate, more threatening. It wasn't just the fact that a car was bulkier and therefore more easily outmaneuvered by somebody on foot; it was the sound. If you've never experienced it, the sound of somebody following you on a bicycle—the rhythmic clicks and creaks of the gears and pedals—is just really fucking creepy.

A minute or so after I'd noticed the bicycle, I jogged across the street, cut through the front yard of a low-rise apartment building, and hurried toward the parking area around the back.

The setting sun was hidden by an adjacent tall building, so it was much darker in the parking lot. I was looking behind me for the cyclist as I jogged between a couple of parked cars, and when I turned back around, I almost ran directly into a man wearing a dark gray wool suit. The color of his suit matched the darkness of the late evening almost perfectly.

"I'm sorry," I said instinctively as I twisted to avoid him.

He didn't flinch.

Maybe I was just feeling edgy because of everything that had been happening, but I had the distinct feeling that the man had been waiting there, behind that building, specifically for me.

At that moment, a car pulled into the parking lot, headlights slicing through the dark, and I caught a flash of something shining in the man's hand.

It looked like a gun of some kind, or maybe a Taser.

I started walking away. Fast.

After a few seconds, I turned and risked a look behind me. The man in the wool suit was following, perfectly matching my speed.

I started lightly jogging up the alley toward the street, doing my best to look casual, like I was just a little late for a nice dinner with friends.

The man started jogging behind me. He had a slight hitch in his gait, just enough to make him appear a little bit crooked as he ran.

It made him even more menacing.

I sped up.

I felt like if I could just make it out of the alley, I'd be okay. There would be cars on the street, probably some people out walking. There's no way the man would risk attacking me in such a public setting.

I started to run faster, and I heard the man behind me do the same.

I looked back, and saw him sprinting toward me, loping slightly as he ran, like some kind of comic book villain.

He was moving too fast, I thought, as he suddenly lunged forward, grabbing at my shoulders, his fingers raking my neck and back. At that point, fight-or-flight adrenaline kicked in, and I was able to hit another gear. My lungs burned as I pushed my knees and arms up and forward in a burst of desperate kinetic synchronicity.

After a couple of seconds that felt like minutes, I twisted my head back to check on the man. He was too far behind.

I was going to make it.

About ten yards from the street, as I started to slow down in order to ensure I didn't lose my balance and tumble into the middle of the road, the cyclist from earlier burst into the alley directly in front of me, effectively blocking my way.

I swerved to the left and somehow managed to maneuver myself between two large recycling containers, jump a low gate, and keep my balance as I ran along the narrow pathway between two matching gray brick–and–glass apartment buildings.

I was in the zone now, running for my life.

I had no idea where either of my pursuers was at this point.

I felt nothing but the need to escape.

I didn't stop running until my legs gave out and I stumbled out of a back alley, moving so fast that the front of my body ended up way over my knees, and I slid across the pavement headfirst into a parked car. My body was so full of adrenaline that I didn't feel a thing. I stood up and took a quick look around. I was miles from where I'd encountered the man in the wool suit. No sign of him or the cyclist.

I relaxed a little and took a longer look at my surroundings.

I was standing in the middle of a familiar street.

Without realizing it, I'd run pretty much straight over to Baron's place.

I had no idea if the people who'd been following me were still around. I needed to get out of sight as soon as possible.

I made my way along the narrow corridor between Baron's building and the apartment complex next door, past the plastic chairs and the rest of the familiar junk. Just like the last time I'd been there, Baron's living room window was cracked open.

I took a cursory look around to make sure nobody was watching, and then I pushed opened the window, crawled through, and tumbled inside.

———

I had no idea what the process was when somebody died, how it worked with the mortgage payments or what was done with a person's personal effects, but the place looked pretty much the same as the last time I'd been there, except that the kitchen had been cleaned, all of his food was gone, and the weird makeshift murder wall he'd created had been removed.

I made my way across Baron's living room, past the coffee table with the brass knob that always fell off when you bumped it, and through the dining room that had previously contained the murder wall.

I wasn't searching for anything in particular, but I figured, since I'd taken the time to break and enter, the least I could do was take a quick look around.

I was pretty sure I wasn't going to find anything. If Baron had something he wanted to keep secret or safe, he most likely would have hidden it somewhere on his laptop, which wasn't there.

After a cursory search of the bedroom and kitchen, I sat down on the couch and took another look around.

What was I expecting to find?

Chloe and I had already gone through all of the weird nonsense written on Baron's murder wall, and there wasn't anything out of the ordinary in his drawers, walls, or cupboards.

I swung my legs up onto the couch, leaned back, and rested my head on the armrest.

As I lay there, staring at the ceiling in my dead friend's apartment, I realized that it felt good to be inside his place, surrounded by his things: the clay ashtray he'd made in seventh grade (half a joint still balanced on the side), the original 1963 Mouse Trap game by Ideal Toy Company (sitting in a constant state of half-assembly on his dining room table for more than two years), and the huge framed poster of *Mad* magazine issue number 166 from April 1974 featuring a painting of a giant middle finger (a gift from me for his thirty-fifth birthday).

I could almost feel him there in the room with me.

After I'd been lying on the couch for a few minutes, I started to get the feeling that something was different, like I was missing something obvious, but I couldn't figure out what it was.

A few things had been moved around and his framed *Sword and the Sorcerer* movie poster was on the floor instead of on the wall above the couch, but those things weren't what was bothering me.

And then I finally saw it. His Apple IIe.

Baron's ancient Apple computer sat next to his turntable on a beat-up old brown wicker credenza his grandmother had given him. Everyone just assumed the old computer was decorative, and for the most part it was, but I knew that it actually worked. What I didn't know was why it was plugged in, and why one of Baron's dining room chairs was sitting in front of it.

I switched on the computer and waited for the old machine to boot up. A few seconds later, 8-bit music started playing, and a message appeared on the screen:

```
Your adventure is loading . . .
```

A few seconds after that, the following appeared on the screen:

```
EAST OF BARN

You are standing in a clearing in the middle of a
densely wooded area. Located just to your west, at
the far end of the clearing, is a large rust-colored
barn.

There is a small leather case on the ground near
your feet.
```

It looked like the opening scene of some kind of text-based adventure game like Zork—a Lord of the Rings–style fantasy game written in the late seventies by a couple of MIT students.

In Zork, you'd maneuver through a world of dungeons using simple commands like "take leaflet" or "read leaflet." Zork had been inspired by the original text-based adventure game called, imaginatively, Adventure. Apparently the MIT guys weren't all that impressed with Adventure's limited vocabulary, so instead of "kill orc," they made sure Zork could understand more complete sentences like "kill orc with broadsword."

The lines of text on Baron's computer screen were followed by a blinking cursor.

I stared at the screen for a few seconds and then entered the words "go west." The screen changed, and I was suddenly playing the game.

I did my best to memorize everything about the narrative as it unfolded.

It appeared to be a simple dungeon crawl: Find the golden idol (using the cloak of invisibility), kill the big boss (with the flaming sword of Arioch), and rescue the town from a fire-breathing dragon (imaginatively named Burnie).

I finished it in about twenty minutes. It was a fairly simple quest, but there were quite a few really cool riddles and puzzles along the way.

I stood up and stretched, and, as if on cue, the screen changed.

Your adventure continues in Morlana's Quest II.

An online search for Morlana's Quest brought up a handful of results. The first was an article on classic videogames from 1984 mentioning a trilogy of text-based adventure games that were supposed to be released by an Infocom competitor but were never completed. The other search results were all images—or rather, different versions of the same image.

They were all photographs or scans of a vintage ad from an old videogame magazine. The ad featured a boy, about eleven or so, wearing glasses and a cream-and-brown houndstooth shirt. He was holding a dark brown wooden box covered in arcane symbols. Next to the box on the table were a full color map, a game cartridge, and a floppy disk. The game was called Morlana's Quest. The ad stated that the game was available for both home computers and the Atari 2600.

Morlana's Quest had been created by a fairly new company in the world of videogames. That company was called WorGames.

The visionary mind behind both Morlana's Quest and Wor-Games was, of course, Hawk Worricker. Coincidence? No way.

And there was something else.

I'd seen a wooden box like that before. It had been sitting on Baron's lap the night Chloe and I found him staring at that weird video—the night before he died.

I jumped up and ran over to Baron's desk.

The wooden box was still there, sitting on the floor next to the desk, exactly where Baron had set it down that night.

I picked it up.

Looking at it up close, the first thing I noticed was that one of the symbols on the lid was familiar. It was, of course, a small circle balanced on the tip of a pyramid.

The Moonrise.

I wanted to open the box, but even more than that, I wanted to open the box with Chloe.

I looked at my phone. It was just after eight.

It was time to check in and see if Chloe was ready for company.

37

FUCKING STEELY DAN?

CHLOE CRAWLED INTO BARON'S APARTMENT through the window.

"I would have buzzed you in," I said as her feet hit the floor.

"Where's the fun in that?" she asked, brushing the dirt from her jeans.

"Are you okay?"

Chloe walked over and hugged me for a long time.

"It couldn't be the Magician in that movie. It doesn't make sense," Chloe said, finally pulling away. "That movie is so old and he looks just the same. It has to be fake."

It sounded like Chloe was still trying to rationalize what we'd seen happen to the Magician. I was happy that she was doing better, although I wasn't sure I agreed with her thesis. That movie looked pretty legit to me.

"I don't think we should jump to any conclusions. Let's just try to figure out what's going on. One step at a time."

"I'm sorry I was being a weirdo earlier," she said. "That movie really freaked me out."

"Me too," I said.

I thought about telling Chloe what had happened with the bicycle person and the man in the wool suit, but I didn't want to up her current level of anxiety.

"Is that it?" Chloe pointed to the box.

I nodded and handed it to her.

"Shit. That's the Gatewick symbol."

"Yeah, suddenly this thing is everywhere."

Chloe was just about to open the box when I grabbed it from her hand.

"What?" she asked.

"Nothing," I said as I opened the box.

If there was something horrible inside, I didn't want Chloe exposed to it before I was.

But it wasn't anything horrible. At least, not yet.

There was nothing inside except for a photograph and a cassette tape.

"What is it?" Chloe asked as I handed her the box.

She picked up the cassette tape and looked it over. "Does Baron have a player?"

"I bought him a Sears model on eBay for his birthday. It should be around here somewhere."

People who play the game need to access all kinds of obscure and out-of-date media; you never know where the clues, connections, or inconsistencies are going to pop up. I have two different brands of micro-cassette recorders, three reel-to-reels, two turntables, and a MiniDisc player, and those are just a few of the archaic media formats I've had to use in my search for clues related to Rabbits.

"This looks familiar," I said as I lifted the photograph out of the box.

"What?" Chloe said, handing me Baron's cassette player.

I passed Chloe the photograph. It was a picture of a brick wall in a back alley—the brick wall I'd discovered behind that dumpster.

"It's the same place," I said.

"It has to be connected," Chloe said.

As Chloe was looking for an outlet so she could plug in Baron's cassette player, I heard the sound of footsteps outside the door.

"Sshhh," I said.

"What?"

I pointed toward the front door.

Chloe and I sat in silence staring at the crack between the door and the floor.

Shadows.

Somebody was there.

We heard the muted whisper of voices, followed by the jangle of something that sounded like keys or tools.

I grabbed the cassette tape, photo, and wooden box and the two of us tumbled out the window we'd climbed through earlier.

I heard the door to Baron's apartment open as my feet hit the ground, but I didn't risk sticking around to see who it was.

I ran to catch up with Chloe.

"Did you see who it was?" Chloe asked as the two of us got into her car.

"No," I said.

"Your place?"

"Do you have a cassette player at yours?"

"You don't wanna go home?"

I finally told her about the creepy wool-suit dude and cyclist combo from earlier, and we agreed that my place was probably being watched.

"We need to hear what's on that cassette," I said.

"There's a player at the arcade," Chloe said.

I nodded. "Good idea."

We entered the arcade, said a quick hello to the part-time evening-shift guy named Marcus, and made our way upstairs to the Magician's office.

Chloe stepped over the piles of books and papers with practiced precision as she made her way to a tall wooden filing cabinet filled with a variety of anachronistic electronics. She fished around for a few seconds and finally pulled out a Realistic brand portable cassette player.

"I'm pretty sure this one works," she said as she bent down and plugged it into the wall behind one of the Magician's desks.

I pulled a couple of rolling chairs over and the two of us sat down.

"You ready?" Chloe asked, her finger resting on the play button.

"Ready."

She pressed play.

The recording began with what sounded like somebody opening a door, walking across a room, and putting a vinyl record onto a turntable.

The person walking around on the recording never spoke. They just set the needle down and a jazzy lounge-type song started to play.

I didn't recognize it, so I loaded the world's most popular audio fingerprint app and pressed the button that would activate its "listen and identify" function.

A few seconds later I had the information.

The app told us it was a song called "Third World Man" from the album *Gaucho* by Steely Dan.

The recording ended as soon as the song stopped playing.

"Fucking Steely Dan?" Chloe said.

I shrugged. "Let's listen again," I said.

Just as Chloe was about to press play on the cassette player, we heard a knocking from downstairs.

Chloe pulled out her phone and loaded a security application.

"Fuck," she said, and handed me the phone.

On the screen was a security-camera feed from the front door. There were three people visible.

It was Swan and the twins.

38

R U PLAYING?

WE LEFT THE ARCADE through the back and drove over to Chloe's apartment, checking every few minutes to make sure we weren't being followed.

At Chloe's place, we made a digital copy of the recording and then put the resulting file through a bunch of specialized software to see if there was some kind of clue hidden in the visual wave form depiction of the audio.

There was nothing.

Chloe picked up the photograph of the back alley from the wooden box I'd found in Baron's place. "I think we should go down there and check out the wall."

"What for?"

"This picture had to be in Baron's weird Rabbits box for a reason."

"Okay," I said, "but we should eat at some point. I'm starving."

"Me too, but let's check the alley first."

It took us twenty minutes to get downtown.

It had recently stopped raining, but the streets were still wet. Walking along cracked and crooked sidewalks, looking up at the Lego shapes of overcast black-gray sky visible between the towering buildings, I almost felt like everything was back to normal, like Chloe and I were just moving through downtown enjoying a standard cool dark night in the Pacific Northwest. But then I remembered Baron, sitting in front of his computer wide-eyed and broken, and the Magician being ripped apart by some kind of horrible cosmic darkness. I grabbed Chloe's hand. She squeezed back, and the two of us entered the alley.

We pulled the dumpster away from the wall, and used the flashlights on our phones to reveal the markings surrounding the circle and triangle that I'd discovered earlier.

But something was different.

Splashed across the original symbols and numbers on that brick wall, in thick yellow letters, somebody had painted the following question:

R u PLAYiNG?

"Holy shit," I said.

"Crazy," Chloe whispered. She stepped forward and touched the yellow paint reverently, as if she was worried it was going to disappear the moment she made contact.

"It's dry," she said.

We took pictures of the wall in case we needed to compare it with my original photographs, but I could tell nothing had been changed other than the question that had been painted over everything.

R u PLAYiNG?

Yes, we certainly were.

We'd just gotten into Chloe's car and started driving when I thought of something.

"Can you pull around the other side of the alley?"

"You wanna check out the front of the building with the spray-painted message?"

"We might as well. I think it's the pizza place with the chewy crust."

"No, that's a few doors down. Last week the space we're looking at was a Holy Cow Records pop-up shop, and before that some hipster Pottery Barn thing. That's where I bought those Edison bulbs you wanted to steal from my kitchen."

"Right," I said. "I remember."

Chloe guided her car around the corner and pulled in front of the building. She was right. It was a retail space that had been used by a number of pop-up shops lately. It looked like the record store was still in there.

"Are we going in?"

"Is it open?"

"Looks like it," she said. "You go in. I'll park and order us some pizza."

"Make my half plain cheese, please," I said.

"So basic."

"So perfect."

Chloe drove away and I stepped into the pop-up record store. I thought I'd have to rush through the place, but the sign on the door indicated they'd be open for another forty-five minutes.

A twentysomething woman with orange hair wearing a fifties-style poodle skirt smiled at me from behind an old gray tanker desk as I entered. I smiled back.

I was the only customer.

I took a look around for anything that might be related to the game—messages hidden in the way a bunch of collectible records had been arranged on the walls, some kind of pattern in the décor, or the number of bins, but I couldn't find anything.

If there was something in there related to Rabbits, it wasn't jumping out.

A few minutes later, a young couple came in and I felt comfortable sneaking a few photos of the place. I tried to get shots of everything, including all the walls and bins, so we could go over them in detail later.

Chloe texted. She'd ordered and was sitting at a table in the back.

I waved goodbye to the woman behind the counter on my way

out and hurried up the street to join Chloe. I felt my blood sugar crashing. I'd forgotten I was starving.

"Anything in the record store?" Chloe asked in between bites of pizza.

I shook my head.

As we ate, I tracked a tall blond woman walking by on the sidewalk outside the restaurant and wondered if Swan and the twins were lurking somewhere nearby, watching and waiting to pounce.

"What if your friend Emily's right and Crow really is out there killing Rabbits players?" Chloe asked.

"Well, then, we might be fucked," I said.

"Murdered by a game. What a way to go."

"Yeah, what a way to go."

All of the color suddenly left Chloe's face. "Shit," she said.

"Baron would have said exactly the same thing if he'd been here."

Chloe nodded. She knew I was right. But that didn't make it any easier.

Chloe and I had finished our pizza and were waiting for the check when I thought of something.

"Shit," I said.

"What?"

"I'll be right back." I rushed out of the pizza place and ran the half a block or so down to the pop-up record store. I couldn't believe I hadn't thought of it sooner. I grabbed the handle of the door and pulled.

Locked. Fuck.

I pressed my face against the window. I could see the young woman with the orange hair behind the register. I knocked on the door and waved. She set down a handful of cash she'd been counting, looked up, and saw me. I could tell she was thinking about opening the door.

I made a praying motion with my hands.

It worked. She let me in.

I told her I knew exactly what I wanted to buy, and it would take me less than a minute. I went straight to the vinyl records, flipped to the S section and pulled out Steely Dan's *Gaucho*. I would have bought them all, but they had only one copy.

Chloe was standing in front of the store when I came out.

"What the hell?" she asked. Then she saw the Steely Dan record.

"Damn it. Why didn't we think of that earlier?"

"We were hungry?" I suggested.

We started walking over to where Chloe had parked her car and as we walked, something strange started happening. The streetlights began switching off—going completely dark, one by one, immediately after we passed each of them in turn.

At first we thought it was just a funny coincidence. I mean, what kind of weird power outage could possibly be connected to the location and pace of two people walking? But eventually it started to feel like something else—like somebody or something in the darkness was following us.

As we moved up the sidewalk toward the car, I felt a chill. I grabbed Chloe's hand and the two of us started walking faster.

When we were a few blocks away, I turned and looked behind us. It took a second to make them out but they were there, in the distance—dark shapeless things moving slowly, like large black fish at the bottom of a dark sea.

It was happening again.

The same thing that happened all those years ago in Portland. The same thing that had happened to the Magician in that Super 8 film.

The shadow things were coming.

We ran the remaining two blocks to the car and didn't look back.

I listened to the sound of the rain against the windshield as we drove back to Chloe's place.

Chloe told me that she hadn't actually seen any weird shapes in the darkness, but the streetlights switching off behind us had been more than freaky enough for her.

I was thinking about those streetlights and the strange twisting shapes in the darkness when I received a text alert.

It was an image of a white towel hanging on a rack.

Chloe was beside me and Baron was dead. There was nobody else who knew our secret emergency code.

A few seconds after that message, I received a Google Maps link. There was a yellow pin marking a location.

It was the diner across from the arcade.

39

TOWEL

As we approached the diner, I thought I saw the sky dim for a moment, just a little, like somebody had been adjusting the brightness and then suddenly changed their mind.

"Did you see that?" I asked Chloe.

"What? The billboard?"

I shook my head. I was talking about the sky. But when I took another look up in that direction, I saw the billboard Chloe was referring to, and I noticed something odd.

It was an advertisement for an album by a famous recording artist. At first glance, it didn't seem out of place, but when I looked again, I noticed that the billboard was promoting the artist's brand-new album, not a collection of greatest hits or previously unreleased material.

The artist was David Bowie.

"Okay," I said, grabbing Chloe's hand just as she was about to open the door to the diner, "I'm going to ask you what might sound like a strange question, but . . . is David Bowie alive?"

"Umm . . . yes, I mean, as far as I know. Are you okay?"

"I'm fine," I said.

"Are you sure?"

"Yeah," I said, opening the door to the diner. "Let's go."

The diner wasn't busy. There were five or six other people inside, but none of them looked up as we entered. Maybe whoever had sent the towel wasn't here yet.

We took a seat near the back and ordered coffee. After we'd ordered, Chloe moved over and slid into my side of the booth.

"Why did you ask me if David Bowie was alive? We just saw him with Gram Parsons and Emmylou Harris at the Tacoma Dome."

"Gram Parsons?"

"K, you're really freaking me out right now."

"I'm sorry, it's nothing."

I wanted to ask Chloe a whole bunch of questions about Gram Parsons, but I just forced a smile and turned my attention to the shopkeeper's bell jangling by the front door. Somebody was entering the diner.

It was Swan and the twins.

I felt a wave of anxiety crash through my body, and vertigo hit me like a wave of wet cement. I grabbed Chloe's hand and tried to stand, but I couldn't move.

Swan slid into the booth across from Chloe and me, and the twins stood on either side of the table, blocking any potential escape.

"You got my message," Swan said.

"Why did you kill Fatman Neil?" Chloe asked, glaring at the twin blocking our side of the table.

"We didn't kill him, sweetheart," the twin on the right said.

"Bullshit," Chloe spat.

At that moment I saw something. It was the shadow things again, moving slowly toward us from the back of the diner.

"We have to leave, right now," Swan said, standing up and reaching for my hand.

"We're not going anywhere with you," Chloe said.

I looked back at the shadow things, then at Swan. I could see her yelling, but I couldn't make out what she was saying.

That's when the lights went out.

The diner was completely black and the sounds of people talking had suddenly transformed into a garbled hum that filled my head.

And then I was somewhere I didn't recognize—or rather, I was nowhere.

I had the strange feeling that I was stuck, hovering in between places, straddling some kind of line, and I wasn't able to tell which side of that line was mine, or exactly how many sides of the line there actually were.

I had no idea where I belonged.

It was horrible, feeling completely alone and untethered, but it wasn't a new feeling. I'd felt this way before, a long time ago, as a child.

I had nightmares when I was a kid—night terrors, the doctors called them.

In these dreams, I would find myself lying in a thick inky darkness, paralyzed and unable to wake up. I felt like I was stuck in a dark empty limbo.

I called it the in-between place.

In the beginning of the nightmare, the in-between place was always empty, terrifyingly void of anything but the cool darkness, but if I concentrated extremely hard, I was often able to tune in to something—something I could feel alive and swirling all around me. Then suddenly I'd feel like I was floating, like I'd become part of the thick viscous darkness, and it wouldn't be long before I'd lose my ability to feel where I ended and where the darkness began.

And there was something else there, somewhere deep in the darkness.

There were currents.

Each of these currents led somewhere . . . else . . . every one of them a potential avenue of escape from the way I was feeling. But no matter how hard I tried, I was never able to choose a current and use it to escape. So I'd remain stuck in that dark limbo, feeling like my eyes were open but my body was frozen in place, and eventually, finally, I'd wake up screaming.

It was my mother who taught me how to deal with my nightmares.

One night, after a particularly bad dream, she sat up with me while I tried to calm myself enough to fall back asleep.

She asked me to describe how it felt when I was lying there paralyzed.

I told her everything—how helpless and terrified I felt, stuck in the floating darkness, how I was unable to choose any of the currents that I knew would allow me to escape my paralysis.

My mother told me that the best way to deal with the situation was to follow my instincts and make a choice. First, she said, I needed to bring all of the emotion I could to the surface—think about the love I felt for my family, think about being strong and centered—and then she told me to concentrate as hard as I could on the currents and focus on finding the best path, the one that felt right. And once I'd done that, all I had to do was reach down into that specific current, grab her hand, and she'd be there to help me wake up.

I don't remember ever using that technique my mother taught me, but the night she told me about it, I had the best sleep I'd had in ages. The following week I began seeing a behavioral therapist who put me on some medication and taught me a number of techniques designed to diminish my stress and anxiety.

The night terrors eventually became less frequent, but by that point I had the real-life nightmare of the accident with Annie Connors to deal with, and not long after that, the death of my parents.

As I was sitting there, in that diner, frozen in place in the pitch-blackness, I wondered what it would be like to live there in the in-between place forever. It felt cool and quiet, but it didn't feel evil or scary. It was more . . . indifferent—like, no matter what happened to me or anybody else, the darkness was always going to be there: cold, unfeeling, and constant.

In that moment, I thought back to what my mother had said that night, how I'd be able to choose the correct path. All I had to do was make a choice.

I cleared my mind of everything but Chloe. I thought about the way her eyes lit up when she was excited, the way her lips tasted against mine, her smart-ass smile, and then I was moving, rushing past the currents.

My body soon felt like it was sinking, floating, and flying at the same time. I understood that if I didn't make a choice soon, there was a chance I'd be stuck, lost in that endless darkness forever. So I reached down.

I felt something solid.

It was Chloe's hand.

I pulled her up and away from the booth, and suddenly the two of us were sprinting toward the door.

"Don't turn around," I said as we ran, but Chloe was already looking over her shoulder.

"I think it's okay," she said. "There's nothing there."

"Swan and the twins?" I asked, as the two of us shoved open the front doors of the diner and burst out onto the sidewalk.

"Gone," Chloe said. "I turned back and they weren't there anymore."

We kept running up the street and didn't slow down until we reached Chloe's car.

"Did you see anything . . . strange in the diner?" I asked as I opened the passenger-side door and slipped inside.

Chloe was shaking as she got into the car beside me and started it up. "I didn't really see anything, but I . . . felt something."

"Like what?" I asked.

"Something really fucking scary."

40

THE HORNS OF TERZOS

CHLOE AND I DROVE AROUND for half an hour to make sure nobody was following us, and then we made our way back to her place. We walked up the steps to her building, arms around each other in comfortable but exhausted silence.

Once inside her unit, Chloe flipped on the lights and I tossed my jacket over a dining room chair.

The two of us shared a bag of slightly stale barbecue chips and an enormous can of Japanese beer while we rewatched a horror movie from 1977 called *The Sentinel*. Eventually, we fell asleep in each other's arms, listening to the new album by David Bowie.

Half an hour later, I woke up and bolted upright in bed. "Fuck."

"What?" Chloe said.

"I need your keys."

Chloe held the building's front door open as I ran out to her car and grabbed the copy of Steely Dan's *Gaucho* that I'd purchased in the pop-up record shop. After the chaos at the diner I'd forgotten all about it.

We hurried back upstairs and unwrapped the album.

Chloe dug up what Baron had always referred to as her portable hipster picnic turntable, and the two of us read along with the lyrics while we listened.

There didn't appear to be anything there, no secret message carved into the vinyl, no words hidden in between the lines.

But there was also no song called "Third World Man."

I grabbed the cassette player we'd borrowed from the Magician's office, and we relistened to the track that our song ID app had identified as "Third World Man."

"It's a different song," I said.

"What?" Chloe asked.

"On the vinyl. It's different."

The song "Third World Man" wasn't on the version of the album that we'd just purchased. In its place was another song titled "Were You Blind That Day." The music sounded the same, but there were different lyrics.

It was a different song.

We flipped the album over and checked the track listing. The fourth song on side B was called "Were You Blind That Day," *not* "Third World Man."

Chloe jumped up and asked me to play both versions again.

"That's so weird," she said.

I did an online search and found something immediately.

Our audio fingerprint app had identified both songs as "Third World Man," but it was incorrect.

Apparently, during sessions for their previous album, *Aja,* Steely Dan had recorded an early version of the song that would eventually become "Third World Man." That song was titled "Were You Blind That Day," but because the music was essentially identical, our audio fingerprint app was unable to tell the two songs apart.

The weirdest thing about this "twin song" situation was that it wasn't a rough demo version from the *Aja* recording sessions. It was perfectly polished studio-quality Steely Dan, the kind of pristine recording that audiophiles used to test their speakers.

But this was impossible.

No version of "Were You Blind That Day" had ever been officially released in any form. "Third World Man" was, and had always been, the final song on the *Gaucho* album.

We searched the Internet. Every single image of *Gaucho* contained "Third World Man" as the last song. We checked scans of the album's liner notes online and compared them to the album we'd just purchased. Everything was identical except for that one song.

Like a rare stamp, coin, or baseball card with an error, somehow we'd ended up with a copy of an album that featured a song that never appeared on the official release.

But there was more.

It wasn't just the title; the lyrics of "Were You Blind That Day" were completely different as well, and one of the names of the musicians credited on that song wasn't listed on the official release of the album.

His name was Mordecai Kubler. He was credited as "Horns of Terzos."

"What the fuck kind of instrument is a Horns of Terzos?" Chloe asked.

"No idea," I said. "But neither song has any brass instruments at all."

We did an online search for Mordecai Kubler and Horns of Terzos. Nothing came up.

"Can you try the darknet?" I asked.

"You know that's not how it works, K. You don't just try the darknet."

"Okay, so, how does it work?"

"You can try a blind Torch, but for this kind of thing you need to know where to look," she said.

"So where do we look?"

She flipped her computer around. "I checked everything," she said. "There's nothing."

"You could have led with that."

Chloe suggested we try something else. She had a friend at the university who had access to a number of older education- and library-based intranets. Because the majority of these databases weren't online, she thought we might get some different results.

And we did.

"This could be something," Chloe said. She turned her screen around and revealed an abstract for a graduate thesis written by somebody named Sandra Aikman. Her thesis compared the imagined worlds of Frank Herbert, J. R. R. Tolkien, Fritz Leiber, and Mordecai Kubler to contemporary people and cultures.

"Oh shit," I said. "Can we take a look at that thesis?"

"For six dollars and ninety-nine cents we sure can," she said.

I entered my credit card information, and Chloe downloaded the PDF.

We devoured that thesis in less than an hour.

It was interesting to read Sandra Aikman's political take on the imagined worlds of some of my favorite writers, but sadly, Mordecai Kubler was a minor character. Sandra Aikman had used only one novel by Kubler as reference material. Thankfully, however, that book was *The Horns of Terzos*. She'd included a notes section at the end of her thesis along with a biography of all of the writers mentioned in her work. The entry for Mordecai Kubler was brief:

Mordecai Kubler. Born in 1937 in Chicago, Illinois, Kubler studied science and English at Brown University, publishing his first and only novel, The Horns of Terzos, *in 1973.*

We did one more deep dive online for any mention of Mordecai Kubler or his novel, but we were unable to turn up anything new.

"We've got nothing," Chloe said.

"We have Sandra Aikman."

"We do?"

"It looks like she lives in Portland," I said as I spun my computer around to reveal Sandra Aikman's Facebook profile.

"Please tell me it's not Portland, Maine."

"Oregon," I said. "She hasn't posted in years, but the last time she did, she was teaching English at Portland State."

"Message or visit?" Chloe asked.

"Let's message first and see what she says," I said.

The next morning, we received a return message from Sandra Aikman. We called the number she'd left and she answered on the second ring. We explained how we'd read her thesis and were interested in talking to her about it in person. She said she'd love to meet, but she was no longer living in Portland.

It turned out she'd moved to Seattle a couple of years ago to work on a book. We told her we were also located in Seattle and set up a meeting at a coffee shop near her apartment in an hour.

Sandra Aikman was Black, about five feet tall, with deep brown eyes and a quick, genuine smile that lit up her entire face. She told us about her continued interest and research into the subject of her thesis, and we explained that we were looking for information about something we'd recently discovered using a DNA-mapping service. We told Sandra Aikman that Mordecai Kubler was Chloe's grandfather.

We totally lied.

Sandra seemed surprised that we'd been unable to find a copy of Kubler's novel. She told us she had at least two copies of her own and that we were more than welcome to come back to her apartment to take a look.

It turns out she actually had three copies of the book. I asked if she'd be willing to let us borrow one of them. She handed us a beat-up old paperback, so well-worn that the title was no longer visible on the spine. She told us to keep it, but made us promise to share any information we were able to dig up on Mordecai Kubler, especially if we were able to track down any of his work outside of *The Horns of Terzos*.

The Horns of Terzos was a short novel, barely two hundred pages. Chloe and I took it back to her place, and read it together in just over four hours.

The story was a kind of retelling of the myth of the Minotaur.

In Greek mythology, the Minotaur is a creature with the head of a bull and the body of a man who lives in the center of the labyrinth—an elaborate maze designed by Daedalus for King Minos of Crete. The Minotaur is eventually killed by Theseus after an arduous journey to the center of the labyrinth.

Mordecai Kubler's novel was a contemporary (at the time) fantasy take on the myth. The hero of the book, a young woman named Xana, must pass through the labyrinth, fight the monster, and save the world. There was a map of the fictional land of the story printed on the first page of the book. The mythical land was called Terzos, and its largest continent, Tsippos, looked remarkably similar to another landmass.

It looked like North America.

In addition to the shape, the names of the cities and provinces that made up the magical land of Tsippos were also somewhat familiar. On the far-right coast there was Other Manhattan and Other Providence, down south there was Other Orleans and Other Athens, and on what we'd refer to as the West Coast you had Other Angeles and Other Venus. Above that, what we call the Pacific Northwest was divided into two provinces: Other Poseidon and Other Victoria.

Xana's quest in the book is fairly straightforward. First she must pass three tests: The Cavern, The Gauntlet, and The Gate. Once she's made it through those three challenges, Xana is supposed to enter The Labyrinth and fight her way to the center. There, in the center of The Labyrinth she'll have to battle and defeat her final foe: The Man in The Tower.

Yeah, it was quite a coincidence.

There were a glossary of terms and some additional maps in the back of the book—including a roughly sketched map of the area where the climax of the story takes place, a city in the coastal province of Other Poseidon called Oudwood. This rough map of Oudwood was something that Xana carried with her and included the markings and notes she had made on her quest to find The Tower.

Those markings looked very familiar.

On the map, Xana had traced the three points of the triangle that made up the first part of her quest: The Cavern, The Gauntlet, and The Gate. Up near the top of the map, surrounding the apex of the triangle, she'd drawn a circle representing The Labyrinth. In the center of The Labyrinth, The Tower.

"It's The Moonrise," Chloe said.

Here it was again—the symbol from my elevator dream, and the logo of the Gatewick Institute.

"A man in a tower and The Moonrise symbol; there's no way either of those things can be a coincidence," Chloe said.

"Coincidences are nonexistent in Rabbits."

"You sound like the Magician."

We sat in silence for a moment. I could tell that Chloe was thinking about what had happened to the Magician in that Super 8 movie.

I put my arm around her and she leaned her head against my shoulder.

"What are we going to do?" she asked.

"Shit, I was just going to ask you the same question."

At that moment, all the lights and appliances in Chloe's apartment flickered on and off a few times.

"Does that happen a lot?" I asked.

"Nope," Chloe said. "Glass of wine?"

"Definitely. And I think, while we're drinking, we should probably go over *The Horns of Terzos* again—in detail," I said.

Chloe poured us each a glass of Malbec, and I started going over everything we'd written down the first time we'd read through the novel.

"The editor doesn't exist, and neither does the publishing imprint," Chloe said as she sat back down beside me on the couch.

"There has to be a clue in here somewhere," I said.

"Maybe we should try something else?" Chloe asked. "We've been staring at this stuff for hours."

I looked away from my computer and rubbed my eyes. When I opened them again, I found myself staring up at a gift I'd given to Chloe for her birthday. It was a map of Washington State drawn in the style of the maps of Middle-earth that Christopher Tolkien had illustrated for Lord of the Rings and *The Hobbit*.

"What?" Chloe could tell I was thinking about something.

"In the Mordecai Kubler novel, Other Poseidon is made up mainly of Washington State, right?" I said.

"Yeah, so?"

"So I have an idea," I said. "Is that printer on the network?"

"Yeah, why? What's up?"

I pulled out my phone, took a photo of the map in the back of *The Horns of Terzos,* adjusted the brightness and contrast, then sent that image to Chloe's printer.

"Can you bring up Seattle on Google Earth?" I asked.

Chloe started typing while I jumped up and ran over to the printer. Once the page had finished printing, I pulled a rolling chair over to where Chloe was sitting. She'd loaded a map of Seattle from Google Earth, which I adjusted until it was the size of the fictional city of Oudwood from the novel.

They were a perfect match.

It looked like Mordecai Kubler had used an accurate map of North America for his fictional land of Tsippos, and by extension accurate maps of Washington State for the Province of Other Poseidon, and Seattle for the city Oudwood.

"Up here you have The Labyrinth," I said, pointing to the circle at the top of the triangle on the map of Oudwood, "and there, in the center of The Labyrinth . . ."

"Holy shit," Chloe said as her eyes followed my finger. "It's Wor-Games."

"The Tower," I said.

"Do you think this shit might be real?"

"Look at the bottom-left-hand point of the triangle."

"Is that the building where you found that weird graffiti behind the dumpster?"

"Sure is," I said.

I pulled out my phone and dropped four pins in my map application: the exact locations of the three points that made up the triangle or pyramid, and the point in the center of the labyrinth, then I handed my phone to Chloe.

"What's this?" she asked.

"Our map."

"Fuck me, are we really doing this?"

"Whattaya think?" I said. "Win the game, save the world."

41

AN UNKINDNESS

IN *THE HORNS OF TERZOS*, Xana begins her quest at the bottom-left-hand point of the pyramid, journeys to the right corner, and finally ends up at the top. In the novel, the highest point of the pyramid is known as The Gate.

Passing through The Gate delivers Xana into a world that looks almost identical to her own, but is actually somewhere called The Other Place.

Xana has now entered The Labyrinth.

When she eventually makes it to the center of The Labyrinth, she'll have to find a way to defeat The Man in The Tower.

"You really think if we hit the three points of this pyramid we'll actually find this Crow guy?"

"I don't know. I think we might."

"Okay," Chloe said. "Let's go find your Man in The Tower."

We decided we'd start by following Xana's path in the novel from the beginning, so Chloe drove us back to the alley behind the pop-up record store.

We walked over and took another look at the wall behind the dumpster. It appeared to be unchanged, but I took a picture just in case.

After I hit the button on my phone to take the photograph, the light in the alley dimmed a little, and for a split second I thought I saw the symbols come to life and shimmer against the brick wall, suddenly awash in a swirling darkness.

I shook my head and pressed my palms into my eyes. I smelled something familiar in the air, like wet feathers and fur. I was disoriented by the smell, and I could hear blood suddenly pounding in my ears. I tried to shake it off, but my body felt endless, like there were no borders between me and the world, and I was suddenly extremely cold. I knuckled my hand hard against the wall to both try to steady myself and use the pain to pull me out of whatever weird reverie I was falling into.

The next thing I knew, we were driving down the street in Chloe's car—and judging by our location, we'd been driving for about ten minutes or so.

"I have to pee," Chloe said.

I just stared straight ahead, trying to figure out where we were and how we got there.

"Are you okay?" Chloe was staring at me.

"I'm fine."

"Are you sure?"

"Where are we going?" I asked.

"Oh, you're perfectly fucking fine, are you?"

"Please, just tell me where we're going?"

"We're going where you told me to go." Chloe looked down at my phone, which was sitting on my lap, the map I'd downloaded earlier displayed on the screen.

We were driving toward the point at the bottom-right-hand corner of the pyramid, someplace called Bellevue Downtown Park.

"Stay with me, K," Chloe said.

I could tell she was worried.

I was worried too.

I'd just lost ten minutes of my life.

Bellevue is just across Lake Washington from Seattle. The twenty-one-acre park features a huge circular lawn with a wide waterfall that empties into a beautiful reflecting pond. Near the center of the circular lawn there's a cluster of three large trees. If there was an obvious starting point for exploration, that cluster of trees was definitely it.

"What do you think we should be looking for?" Chloe asked.

"I don't know. Something related to the game," I said. "The Moonrise? Maybe a white rabbit?"

"Oh, thanks. That's super helpful."

As we started walking toward the cluster of trees, I felt something change.

An irresistible sinking sensation rolled over me like a thick slow wave. I looked around for the cold and crawling things I knew had to be out there waiting, but all I saw was a great creeping darkness move across the park, slow and steady, like the shadow of an enormous haunted airship from another age.

"I think we might need to hurry." I grabbed Chloe's hand and we rushed forward into the small grove of trees.

"You sure you're okay to do this?" Chloe asked.

"I'm fine," I said, which was a total lie. I felt terrible. I was feeling completely untethered again, like I was floating at least three feet above my body. I wanted to let go, to relax, but I was worried that if I did, I'd end up passing out or missing time, or both.

I bit the inside of my lip. Hard. The pain and tang of blood brought me back to my body.

I needed to keep it together.

Chloe and I stood in the small clearing with those three large trees. Above us, the leaves and branches came together, forming a high canopy. We took a look around, but aside from a group of enormous ravens perched high in the treetops, there didn't appear to be anything particularly unique or interesting about the area.

I could feel the darkness. It was close. If I shut my eyes, I could sense something inside me reaching out, trying to connect with whatever was out there waiting.

We needed to hurry.

Once again, I looked around for some kind of sign that we'd come to the right place, but nothing appeared significant. No symbols carved into the trunks of the trees, no rogue skywriting in the firmament above, no strange foliage that didn't appear to be indigenous to the area.

I heard a rustling sound and took another look up at the trees. There were more ravens than I'd initially thought—a lot more.

The tops of the trees were now almost completely black.

As I stared up at the huge black birds, my mind went back to a summer vacation with my parents. They were having an animated discussion about whether a group of ravens was called an unkindness or a conspiracy. I couldn't remember which one of them ended up being right.

Then I felt my body growing thick and heavy, and the light of the world dimmed again, or, more accurately, everything became slightly desaturated, the formerly vibrant colors of the park now faded and distant. I grabbed Chloe's hand and started to run. I couldn't risk passing out or missing time again. We would just have to move to the next point on the map and trust that we were following the right path.

As soon as we started to run, the ravens took off into the sky—all of them at once. The sound of their wings as they all rose up together was deafening. There were hundreds, maybe as many as a thousand or more of the enormous black birds. They momentarily blacked out the light as they swirled, cawing and flapping, above the small grove of trees.

We ran as fast as we could through the park, away from the ravens, and as we ran, I could hear sharp hissing and spitting snaps as the sprinklers in the grass behind us began popping up and spraying.

I looked back as we finally stepped off the grass of the park and onto the sidewalk. Only those sprinklers that had been directly behind us as we ran had been switched on. None of the other sprinklers in the park had been activated.

I had no idea if the ravens and the sprinklers were signs that we were on the right path, but they would have to do.

A couple of blocks before we made it back to where we'd parked, Chloe pulled me aside and reminded me that she had to use the bathroom. She pointed to a Starbucks across the street.

———

The coffee shop was pretty busy. Dozens of people were going about their day, looking at their computers, communicating with loved ones and reading articles, books, or magazines on their tiny screens.

They couldn't feel the darkness that was coming.

But I could.

I rubbed my arms nervously as I waited for Chloe. She was taking forever in the bathroom and I wanted to keep moving.

"Harold," the barista called out—the name of the person who had ordered the most recent drink. "Harold."

Six men slowly made their way up to the counter.

"Harold?" the barista said again, clearly freaked out.

All six men held up their hands and looked around.

They were all named Harold, and they were all kind of confused.

"Nonfat latte?" the barista called out, hopefully.

"Is that for Harold?" A man stepped out of the men's bathroom and made his way to the counter.

Harold number seven.

Kellan Meechum believed this type of significant coincidence was an indicator that you were following one of his Radiants, and Hazel had said something similar about the game as it related to these types of occurrences.

Did this mean that we were on the right path?

Or was this maybe a sign of something else? Something terrible? I felt my stomach drop. I looked over at a tower of chocolate espresso beans and artisanal popcorn that was flanked by baskets of bottled water on either side. There was no way the world could possibly end among things like these, was there? I thought back to Crow's weird lecture about being locked in the trunk of a car. At least in that scenario you knew where you stood. There was something about considering an apocalyptic event while standing in the middle of a Starbucks staring at a banana nut muffin that felt sadly unreal.

I knocked on the door to the bathroom. "Everything okay in there?" I asked.

No answer.

I knocked again, and this time I noticed that the little green indicator above the door handle said "vacant." The door was unlocked.

I pulled the door handle down. "I'm coming in," I said, and opened the door.

The bathroom was empty. Chloe was gone.

I checked the other bathroom. Empty as well.

There were only two doors, and I'd been standing in front of them the entire time. There was no way Chloe could be anywhere but inside one of those two bathrooms, and there were no windows in either room.

She was gone.

I ran through the coffee shop, past the Harolds, and out into the street. I could feel the presence of the shadow things out there, like some kind of weird barometric pressure building up behind the fabric of the world.

I looked down at my phone. The point of the pyramid was about twelve miles away. I wondered if I'd blacked out and Chloe had somehow slipped past me, but I definitely hadn't experienced any lost time, and Chloe would have no reason to leave me there alone.

I called her. There was no answer.

I summoned an Uber. Five minutes later, I was on my way to Chloe's place.

I thought about heading directly to the top of the pyramid to complete Xana's quest, but there was no way I was going to leave without making sure Chloe was okay.

I half-expected my driver's name would be Harold, but it was a middle-aged woman named Geneva.

I asked her to wait for me while I ran up to check Chloe's loft.

But I couldn't find it.

Chloe's name wasn't listed anywhere in the directory, and when I buzzed the number of her suite, a man answered. He told me he'd been living in that unit since the building had been converted into a residential property, and nobody named Chloe had ever lived on that floor.

I got back into the car and instructed Geneva to take me to the tip of the pyramid. I had no idea what was happening, but the last time Chloe and I were together, that was where we were headed.

It was up to me to try to finish what we'd started.

The tip of the triangle or pyramid pointed to a strip mall in Northeast Seattle.

I stepped out of Geneva's Prius and looked over the names of the stores in the strip mall. Nothing stood out.

I turned around to see if there was anything nearby that might be connected to the game, and my eyes were immediately drawn to the sky.

At first it looked like storm clouds, but clouds didn't move like that. Something was coming. The darkness was swirling above a four-story building that took up about a quarter of the block directly across from the strip mall. At the top of that building was a neon sign that read: PYRAMID SELF STORAGE.

Their logo was a pyramid beneath a shining sun: a circle above a triangle.

I hurried across the street into the Pyramid Self Storage loading bay and ran up a short set of cement stairs that led to an open service window connected to a small office. There was nobody there, but a handwritten sign on the counter said "Back in fifteen."

I'd been waiting around for a few minutes when I realized I didn't have a plan. What was I going to ask them when they came back? Should I try to bribe them to show me the register, like a detective in a Raymond Chandler novel? Ask to rent a locker myself?

I decided I'd go with option two when I felt a familiar chill.

The shadow things had arrived.

A darkness descended from somewhere and began slowly pooling around the loading bay. Long tenebrous swirls twisted and slid along the smooth gray concrete. It wouldn't be long before they reached the service window.

I wasn't sure if the darkness was pursuing me or if I was moving along one of Meechum's Radiants and this was just part of that process. But, either way, it was coming, and I knew exactly what was going to happen if it reached me.

I would be torn apart like the Magician in that Super 8 movie.

I took off running.

As I ran along the polished concrete corridor between the small reddish-orange garage doors that provided access to the various storage lockers, I could feel the darkness behind me, cold, hungry, and impatient—and closer now than ever before.

I could feel it longing to feed.

I rounded a corner and ran down another hall, speeding past the rows of padlocked metal doors, the darkness close behind.

Eventually, I turned in to a long corridor that ran the length of the entire building. As I ran, I finally felt like I was putting some distance between me and whatever was back there.

But the corridor was coming to an end.

About twenty yards ahead, I could make out the familiar vertical wooden slats of an old freight elevator.

I was moving so fast that I almost slipped and fell when I tried to slow down.

As I crashed into the elevator, stabs of pain from my wrist and shoulder alerted my brain that something was wrong. I ignored the pain, clutched the slats with two hands, yanked up the elevator door, and dived inside.

As I grabbed the rope and pulled the door closed behind me, I could see the gray shapes in the darkness.

Long thin shadows, like dark smoky fingers, slipped through the bars. Just as the darkness was about to reach me, I slammed the green button and the elevator started moving up with a hard lurch.

But I was too late.

The shadow things flooded the elevator and I could feel them sliding into my mind. The world swam and shook, and I felt like my head was being ripped apart. Then I was falling backward into an impossible deep black.

And then I passed out.

42

WIN THE GAME,
SAVE THE WORLD

I WOKE UP in the elevator.

Not the storage company's freight elevator, but the elevator in The Tower that had taken me to the penthouse to meet Crow. The PH button was illuminated and I was moving up. Fast.

I was only in there for about thirty seconds or so before the elevator stopped, the doors opened, and I was staring out at the same wide hallway as before.

I did my best to compose myself. Twice I'd been up here, and twice I'd had completely different experiences. I had no idea what to expect this time.

After I felt calm enough to walk, I stepped off the elevator and into the hallway.

I made my way quickly down the hall, passed through the now-familiar glass double doors, and entered the small lobby.

The last time I'd been here, the lobby was empty. This time, however, there was a man sitting behind a reception desk. He was Persian, in his late twenties, wearing a dark gray sweater and white collared shirt.

"Can I help you?" he asked.

"I'm here to see Crow," I said. No point in messing around.

"Do you have an appointment?"

"I'm not exactly sure."

He nodded and forced a smile. I heard the sound of him hitting a few keys on a keyboard, and then the foyer was completely silent.

I took a seat in one of the six small teak chairs that made up the waiting area, and glanced down at the reading materials stacked neatly on a narrow glass coffee table. Rather than the usual terribly-out-of-date magazine selection, there were books: *The Beatles Anthology, The Future of Architecture, Aesop's Fables, The Malacetic Atlas, Information Graphics,* and something called *Cooking for Your Future Self.*

If I were to imagine the Platonic ideal of a waiting area, this is pretty much exactly what I'd come up with—except for one thing. Hanging on the wall behind the receptionist was a huge framed photograph of a willow tree on the shore of a deep blue lake. The photograph was somewhat disconcerting at first glance, because it had been hung upside down.

"Somebody should be right with you," the receptionist said.

"Thanks." I nodded.

"Would you like water or coffee?"

"No, thank you, but . . ."

"Yes?"

"Is that photograph of the tree . . ."

"Supposed to be hung upside down?" The receptionist finished my question. "Yes. It's what the artist intended." He smiled.

"You must get that question a lot."

"Only every single day."

At that moment, Emily Connors rushed into the room and yanked me out of my chair.

"What the fuck, K?"

She pushed me out of the foyer back through the double doors and into the long hallway.

"You have to leave," she said.

"Did you kill Crow?"

"No, I haven't seen him yet, and you can't talk like that here."

Emily was wearing the exact same clothing she'd been wearing the last time I saw her, when she'd disappeared from the elevator in her friend's lakeshore mansion.

"How long has it been since I saw you?" I asked.

"An hour or two, why?"

"That's not true. It's been days," I said.

"Not all dimensions operate in the same temporal space, and crossing over can further distort time as well."

"How does that work?" I asked.

"How the fuck did you find this place?" she asked, ignoring my question.

"That's a long story."

Emily shook her head. "Okay. You're going to have to come with me."

"Where?"

She grabbed me, yanked me toward the elevator, and pressed the call button.

The elevator opened immediately and she pulled me inside.

"Hang on to this." She removed something from the back of her skirt and handed it to me. It was a small silver handgun. I didn't know anything about guns, but it looked like a model that James Bond would carry.

"A gun? What the fuck, Emily?"

"Please shut up." She leaned down, opened a hidden panel on the floor of the elevator, and pressed a button. Then she stood up, grabbed her gun, and slipped it behind her back into the waistband of her jeans like some kind of action movie heroine.

The elevator started moving down.

"Where are we going?" I asked.

"Jesus Christ, K. You really need to learn to shut up."

The elevator doors opened and we stepped out into an empty room, about fifty feet square. It was cool inside—well below room temperature. The walls were a glossy blackish-green. In the far-left-hand corner was a spiral staircase leading up.

The building started shaking, but it was strange. I understood that it had to be the building doing the shaking, but it felt like it was the entire world.

Emily and I leaned against the wall and waited for the tremors to pass.

"What's happening?" I asked.

"The Radiants are starting to fall apart," Emily said as she grabbed my hand and pulled me up the spiral staircase. She held the gun in front of her like the lead detective in some kind of network television thriller.

At the top of the stairs was a door.

Emily tried it carefully. It was open.

She put her finger to her lips and we stepped through into the pitch-darkness.

"What is this place?" I asked as Emily fumbled around for a light.

"These are my living quarters, K." Both of us jumped at the sound of Crow's voice.

And suddenly the room was illuminated.

Crow's living quarters were similar to the penthouse he'd shown me earlier—the same massive windows on one side of the room, almost identical floor-to-ceiling antique bookshelves on the other. And once again, the place was furnished with impressive pieces of art from baroque to midcentury.

Crow had entered from a nearby door along the same wall about twenty feet from us. He was flanked by two extremely large armed men. They looked like private military Blackwater types.

"Shit," Emily said.

Crow smiled at Emily. "You never stop impressing."

"You have to stop," she said. "The mechanism is failing."

"The mechanism, as you call it, is fine. It's simply going to be reset."

At that moment, there was another violent shaking episode. "Things are a little unstable, admittedly," Crow said, "but it's nothing to be alarmed about. Humankind isn't capable of permanently harming the universe."

"That's what they said about the environment, and now look at the polar bears," Emily said.

"You've always had a great sense of humor," Crow said, nodding to the security guards who took a couple of steps closer. "I don't expect you to understand all the intricacies of the work I've been doing here, Emily."

"Your wife and daughter are gone, Crow. They're not coming back."

Crow's face twisted up at the mention of his family.

"Please," Emily said. "They wouldn't want you to do this."

"You don't get to have an opinion," he spat.

"The Radiants are unstable; they're decaying rapidly. You have to stop."

"Hawk Worricker created his game under the auspices of stabilizing the Radiants, and by doing so, he effectively neutered the mechanism that exists beneath the world—the mysterious elemental force that Meechum's Radiants manipulate. Who is Hawk Worricker or Kellan Meechum to decide what's best for us? Who are they to play God?"

"You criticizing people with god complexes is fucking hilarious, Crow," Emily said.

"You'll see things differently when the game has been reset."

"Nothing's going to be reset, you idiot," Emily said. "We're all going to be wiped out of existence!"

As if on cue, the tremors started again and we were thrown against the wall.

"You're a fucking psychopath," Emily said as she pulled out her gun and pointed it at Crow.

Shaking again. It was getting stronger.

Emily steadied herself and aimed her weapon.

"I'm going to end what—"

But before Emily could finish her sentence, she was shot in the shoulder. The gun flew from her hand and clattered across the floor.

The sound of that gunshot reverberating through the room, combined with the violent shaking, felt like the end of all things.

"Fuck, Carl. You shot me!" Emily yelled, her hand bloody from touching the wound on her shoulder.

"You'll be fine," the shorter security guard said as he picked up Emily's gun. "I barely skimmed you. Just apply pressure."

The earthquake-style shaking had started to turn into something else—a deep vibration, a blurring of the world. The floor beneath my feet felt alive suddenly, sending a body-numbing shiver through my limbs into my stomach and chest.

"What's happening?" I asked.

"This stream is working to reset itself," Crow said. "It won't be long now."

"Bullshit," Emily said. "The stream is dying."

"I'm going to miss you both—and I promise you, I take absolutely no pleasure in this," Crow said, then nodded to his guards.

They slowly lifted their weapons.

"What happened to 'apply pressure,' Carl?"

Carl shrugged an apology as he and his partner took aim.

I closed my eyes and then . . .

Two loud shots rang out.

I covered my ears instinctively at the sound, and opened my eyes just in time to see the two guards crumble to the ground in a mess of blood and crooked limbs. They fell to reveal two women, each of them holding a huge handgun.

The twins.

"It's been a long time," Swan said as she stepped into the room from somewhere behind us.

All the color drained from Crow's face.

"No," he said as he took a step backward. "You can't be here."

"And yet here I am," Swan said, and nodded to the twins.

They stepped over the two dead guards and positioned themselves on either side of Crow.

Swan walked slowly across the room to join them. She didn't look at Emily or me as she passed between us. She was completely focused on Crow.

When she'd made it over to where he was standing, she looked him up and down as if he were an insect she'd just pulled out of a drain. Then she grabbed his face and looked into his eyes.

"I've been looking for you for a long time," she said.

Crow just stared, wide-eyed.

"You fucked up the Radiants, and now your world dies, you stupid little thing."

Clearly I was wrong about Swan. She hadn't been working for Crow.

"Once the mechanism is reset," Crow said, "this dimensional

stream will revert to its previous healthy state and we'll be able to start over. I've tracked everything down to the minute. It's—"

"Sshhh," Swan said as she shook her head, and I felt like I saw genuine sadness as she continued to stare into Crow's eyes. "It doesn't work like that. What happened to your daughter is irreversible."

"No. It's unforgivable, but not irreversible," he said. "What I'm doing is going to work."

"What kind of a father experiments on his own child?"

"No no no!" Crow screamed. "The mechanism is resetting now. We're going back to how things were."

Swan shook her head. "No. By manipulating things the way you have, you've destroyed the integrity of this dimensional stream. Every single soul connected to these events is going to disappear. Forever, just like your daughter. The Radiants are agitated. This world is dying."

"Lies!" Crow spat, and he turned and lunged at Swan, his face twisted, eyes full of rage. But Swan was blindingly fast, and before Crow was able to reach her, she'd pulled out a gun and shot him in the face.

The twins didn't even blink. They just stepped back in perfect unison as Crow's body folded to the ground at their feet with a muted thud.

Swan turned to face us.

"Hello, Swan," Emily said.

"Emily," Swan said. "It's been a while."

"You two know each other?" I asked.

Swan looked at me and then turned to Emily. "This must be hard for you."

"What are you talking about?" I said.

The room started shaking violently again.

"When is it going to stop?" I asked.

Swan turned to look at me, a pained expression on her face. "A universe doesn't die like a person." She looked down at Crow's body, lying twisted on the ground. "It's not light fading from a cage of blood and bone. It's billions of years of starfire and wonder."

I shifted my weight, and the shaking just about knocked me over. Emily grabbed my shoulder and stopped me from falling.

"I'd say you've got about an hour before the end," Swan said.

"The end of what?" I asked.

"Of everything," Swan said as she shook her head. "I tried to warn you."

"There has to be something we can do," I said.

Swan sighed. "The Radiants have fallen too far out of alignment."

"So there's nothing?"

"Maybe if you could win the game," Swan said, "but at this point it's corrupt, and no longer functioning properly."

"So, what's going to happen now?" I asked.

"When this dimension dies, every soul currently connected to the stream will be lost—all of their memories, lives, and families gone forever. And after that, each connected stream will fall into this one, then the others, like dominos. And then . . . the end of everything."

"Could you do it?" I asked Swan. "Could you win the game somehow? Realign the Radiants?"

Swan shook her head. "I'm sorry, but without Worricker's game in working order, I have no idea how to manipulate the Radiants to reset the mechanism. This world dies today. If you close your eyes, I can make it fast."

"What happens if we don't close our eyes?" I asked.

"This," she said.

And then the world went black.

43

YOU CAN'T HOT-WIRE A
FUCKING PRIUS

I woke up in darkness.

"Emily?" I called out as I stumbled to my feet. "Hello?"

"K?" Emily said.

I rushed over, following the sound of her voice, and smashed my knee into something solid. My eyes had adjusted a little bit and I could see what I'd banged into.

I knew where I was.

I hurried over to the front door, fumbled for the lights, and finally switched them on. We were standing in the familiar cool fluorescent glow of the Magician's arcade.

"Where the fuck are we?" Emily said.

"Arcade," I said.

"What arcade?"

"We're still in Seattle, close to my place." I looked out the windows. It was dark outside. For some reason, I'd always imagined the world would end in the daytime. "What time is it?" I asked.

"Nine," Emily said as she sat down on the floor and leaned back against the machine I'd banged my knee on. It was an old Atari game called Night Driver.

"Are you okay? How's your shoulder?" I sat down beside her.

"It's fine," she said as she moved a few inches away.

"You've been shot," I said.

"I know, thank you."

"By a gun."

Emily leaned back, shook her head, and exhaled.

"What's wrong?" I asked.

"Besides the world ending in an hour?"

"Yeah, besides that."

Emily stared straight ahead and bit her lip. I could tell that she was trying to stop herself from crying.

"What is it?" I asked.

She turned and pulled me closer, reaching her arms around my waist and hugging me hard. Tears started streaming down her cheeks.

I hugged her back. I could feel her body shaking as she struggled to hold back more tears. She was clearly in pain.

Then, Emily Connors pulled back, grabbed my face and kissed me. I could taste the salt from her tears as her lips met mine. As her lips and tongue moved across my mouth, I felt a surge of emotion move through my body.

Part of me never wanted it to end.

I'd fallen in love with Chloe, but I had no idea what had happened to her, and Emily Connors felt like part of a completely separate life.

Did Chloe even exist here?

I imagined how I'd feel if the tables were turned and Chloe was kissing somebody from her past, and I gently pulled away from Emily.

"I'm sorry. I'm in love with somebody else," I said.

And then I stood up and explained what had happened earlier, how I'd lost Chloe in a coffee shop filled with Harolds.

Emily looked as if she'd been struck.

I watched a wave of deep sadness move across her face as she absorbed what I'd just told her. I wanted to hug her again immediately.

But I didn't.

"Well, that's just fucking great, K," Emily said as she brushed the tears away from her cheeks.

"What's the matter?" I said.

"What's the matter?" Emily repeated, and shook her head. "What's the matter is you and I are fucking married, and I've spent the last four years looking for you."

"What are you talking about?"

Emily took a few seconds to compose herself before she began to speak.

"One day," she said, "about four years ago, you went out to try to save the world. I've spent the intervening years trying to pin down which dimensional stream you'd slipped into, and when, against astronomical odds, I somehow managed to find that stream—and against further astronomical odds track you down—it turns out you don't remember anything about the amazing life we built together."

"I don't understand," I said. "I haven't seen you since we were kids."

"But I've seen you," Emily said. "Up until four years ago, I saw you every single morning when I woke up and every night when I went to bed."

"That's impossible," I said—but I could tell by the way she spoke and the way she looked at me that everything she was saying was true.

"But this can't be real. I mean, I'd remember the two of us getting married."

"You would fucking think so, wouldn't you?" Emily laughed a little as she wiped the tears from her face.

I nodded, still trying to come to terms with what Emily had just revealed.

"I lose you to dimensional drift, and your girlfriend disappears from the world via a Starbucks bathroom. We're quite a pair."

The violent shaking and vibrating started up again. Emily and I held on to each other and waited for it to stop.

"You used that term that the last time I saw you. Dimensional drift. Is that why I can't remember?"

Emily nodded.

"What is it exactly?"

"Every time someone skips dimensional streams, there's a high probability that they'll experience some amount of drift. It's like deep-sea divers getting the bends when they surface."

"Decompression sickness?"

"Yeah, but for your brain. When you skip dimensions you're displacing all of the other instances of you, shifting everything over."

"Doesn't that mess everything up? All these different versions of somebody suddenly living in different dimensions?"

"It's actually mostly fine. Like I told you earlier, all of the instances share a kind of connection, and nothing is really permanently lost . . . it's like we're all drawn from the same source."

"But if we're able to move between dimensions, isn't it possible that I'm not your K? That your K might still be out there somewhere?"

"*You* are my K, and *you* definitely came here, to *this* dimension, four years ago. There was a displacement. If you don't remember us together, then . . ."

Emily blinked away a tear and wiped her cheek. I could see how hard this was for her.

"It's my fault," she said. "You left because I asked you to."

"What?"

"I discovered that Crow was manipulating the Radiants to try to bring back his wife and daughter, and that it was messing up not only the game but the entire multiverse. I tracked you down and convinced you that we needed to do something. We spent years together coming up with a plan, and then you changed your mind."

"What happened?"

"We fell in love. You told me you didn't want to leave me. You didn't want to risk forgetting."

"And then?"

"Four years ago, we discovered Crow's manipulations were causing more damage than we thought, and if we didn't act soon, the entire multiverse was in danger of collapsing. I talked you into slipping dimensional streams to try to stop him."

"That sounds completely insane."

"Does it?"

"Slipping into dimensional streams and forgetting a whole other life where you and I are married doesn't sound like the most likely explanation. My experiencing a severe break with reality feels far more likely."

"You and I used our connection to the Radiants to facilitate the slip."

"Our Gatewick sauce."

"Yes."

"You said you weren't sure how much Gatewick sauce I have."

"I'm still not sure, but I think it might be a lot."

I wanted to tell Emily what she was saying was crazy, but I'd been experiencing missing time and discrepancies in the fabric of reality. I wasn't sure what to think anymore.

"Okay," Emily said as she turned back to face me. "I'm going to ask you a weird question." She took a breath and steadied herself. "Do you remember the black well?"

"I—"

The dream came flooding back immediately. It was like being struck. I hadn't thought about it for decades.

In the dream, Emily, Annie, and I were walking in one of the farmer's fields out near their family's vacation home. We'd been laughing and running through the high grass for hours when Emily and I went back to the barn to get a drink from my backpack.

We'd reached the barn and were watching Annie running and jumping across the middle part of the field, chasing the neighbor's dog, when she just disappeared.

We'd been watching her run one second, and the next she vanished into thin air.

"Yes, I remember, but the black well was a dream," I said. "It was *my* dream."

"It wasn't a dream, K," Emily said. "It was real. It happened. We found those *Playboys* in the old house, you tripped and hurt your knee, we talked about a grasshopper army taking over the world and about Annie having nightmares after seeing part of *The Exorcist*. That was all real. I was there. Annie was there. It happened."

"It was a dream," I said.

I knew it was a dream; it had to be. But I'd never shared the contents of that dream with anyone. There was no possible way Emily could know those specific details.

Not unless she'd been there with me.

I'd forgotten all about that dream. But I remembered it clearly now.

I could feel the grass in the field against my legs as we walked, hear the beating of my heart in my ears, smell the evening rain forming in the air.

I remembered the two of us walking through the grass for a long time, looking for Annie, calling out her name. We ended up standing in front of a dark-ringed ancient stone well that we'd discovered the summer before. The stones had been blackened with some kind of burned ash or mold.

We called it the black well.

Emily and I yelled out Annie's name one last time as we slowly looked over the edge.

There at the bottom, in a pool of dark, shallow water, was Annie's tiny broken body.

She was dead.

I remembered screaming, falling into a pool of nothingness, the sky shaking and shattering in a brilliant flash and glow, and feeling every part of myself and the world around me break apart like a huge jigsaw puzzle.

Then I woke up in bed.

I ran straight into the room next door where Annie and Emily had been sleeping in the bunk beds.

When I opened the door, Emily was sitting up in the top bunk staring at me, her eyes wide with terror.

Annie was curled up in the bottom, sleeping soundly.

I went back to bed and fell asleep.

"Annie didn't remember a thing," Emily said. "When I told her the story, she thought I was making it up and asked me to stop. It really scared her."

"I imagine that would be scary," I said, "telling her that she'd fallen into a hole and died."

"For decades, I thought it was nothing but a terrifying dream. I didn't mention it to you back then, because I didn't believe for a second that you and I had actually shared the same dream."

"Why would you?" I said. "It's impossible."

"The following morning, Annie told my parents what I'd described and that I was scaring her. They pulled me into their bedroom and shut the door. This was the first time they asked me about false memories—dreams that felt so real part of me believed they'd happened in real life. I told them what had happened, and they nodded and listened. I don't know how to explain it, but something told me they believed that what I'd described happening to Annie in the black well may have actually happened—and not in a dream, but in real life."

"What makes you say that?" I asked.

"It was just something in the way they looked at me as I was describing the events of the dream. And . . ."

"What?"

"When I told them that *you* were there, in the dream, their faces changed. They were scared like I've never seen them. And there was something else."

"What?"

"A few days later, I overheard my parents speaking with a man in our kitchen. They told him about the memory I'd described, and he said that he believed I might have some kind of special ability, something they'd been looking for. My parents did their best to smile and nod politely, but I could tell they were worried, and that the fact that *this* man was saying *these* things might mean something extremely bad."

"What happened after that?"

"Nothing, really. Everything went back to normal. I didn't think about that conversation again until years later."

"What made you think about it again?"

"The man from that conversation showed up at my apartment."

"What did he say?"

"He told me he knew my parents from way back when, and that he wanted to make me an offer of employment. It was more money than I'd ever seen in my life. I told him I'd think about it. The next day I was working for him."

"Crow."

"Yeah," she said. "Fucking Crow."

"What happened?"

"At first, things were good. I believed that he really *was* working to make things better. I helped him track down discrepancies, patterns, and coincidences, and uncover some of the complex pathways he was looking for."

"But wait, so what happened with our parents and Gatewick? What eventually shut it down?"

"Our parents and a few others expressed their concerns, and Worricker himself shut down the project. It wasn't until after Hawk Worricker's death that Crow insisted on revisiting that avenue of research."

"And what happened when Crow started things up again?"

"Do you remember Natalie?"

"Kind of," I said. I'd met her once or twice, but I didn't really know her. "She was a bit older, around your age."

"Natalie was Crow's daughter. He was working with her to try to detect one of Meechum's Radiants, but when Natalie received the news that a friend of hers had died in a car accident, something happened. Crow believed his daughter's ensuing emotional distress resulted in her inadvertently causing an interdimensional slip, which led to her disappearance.

"None of us ever saw her again."

Now that Emily had mentioned it, I remembered Natalie going missing, but it had happened while my family was away in Europe for the summer, and by the time we came back, talk about Natalie's disappearance had faded.

"When Crow recruited me, I believed he was sincere about wanting to improve the world, that he was using Natalie's death to inspire his working toward genuine positive change, but any good that came of our work back then was simply a side effect of his actual goal, which was trying to bring his daughter back."

"Couldn't he just slip into a universe where an instance of her might still exist?"

"That was the first thing he tried—multiple times—but Natalie was never there."

"What happened?" I asked.

"We're not sure, but it looks like when certain people die or disappear, they do so across the board, so to speak. We don't know exactly how or why this happens with some people and not others. If an alien or previous terrestrial civilization created or managed the mechanism connected to these Radiants in the past, they didn't leave us any kind of instruction manual."

"So, Crow has been obsessively manipulating both the game and the Radiants in a fruitless effort to find a universe where his daughter isn't . . . dead, and that obsession is what put the multiverse at risk?"

"Yes."

"How does that work?"

"It used to be that when you messed with things in one dimensional stream, it didn't really affect the others. Sure, you'd get the occasional Berenstain Bears or Nelson Mandela controversy, but otherwise, memories and experiences would remain consistent along dimensional lines and stability was maintained. But, over the years, Crow's obsession with finding his daughter has resulted in him completely destabilizing the game and therefore the dimensional lines. It looks like now, if one goes, they all go. He's fucked up everything."

"How does it really . . . work?"

"What do you mean?"

"I mean, the science."

"What do you know about coherence and interference?"

"Assume nothing."

"Imagine the multiverse consists of waves. When you have coherence, there's no interference, and all the waves are functioning perfectly fine. But when there's something called constructive interference, waves can blend together to create a wave of greater amplitude than either one individually. Now imagine countless numbers of very powerful waves that used to exist in a coherent state suddenly coming together. The amplitude of that resultant wave would be impossible to measure."

"That's what's happening to the multiverse? It's becoming one giant, super-unstable, decoherent wave?"

"Yeah."

"The last time I saw you, you told me that my parents used my ability to slip me into another dimension in order to hide me from Crow."

"That's right."

"But that doesn't make any sense. Don't he and I both exist here in this universe?"

"Yes, but because of dimensional drift, the Crow in your primary stream no longer knew that you existed."

I shook my head. This was a lot to take in.

"So why do you think Alan Scarpio asked me to help him?"

"No idea, but the whole thing had to be part of Worricker's game."

"*Rabbits* sent Scarpio to meet me here in the arcade?" I said.

"I think so, yes."

We sat there in silence for a moment, then the world began shaking again—longer and harder this time.

"The tremors are lasting longer now," Emily said, squeezing my hand.

I nodded, still trying to come to terms with everything she'd just told me.

"So, in another dimension where we're married, you and I somehow figured out a way to send me here in order to stop Crow from killing the multiverse?"

"Yes. Well, we had a little help."

"Help?"

"From the woman who calls herself Swan."

"What's going on with her? Who is she?"

"You told me once that you believed she was what's known as a Warden."

"Wait, Swan's a *Warden*?"

"I'm still not really sure, actually. She's not a big talker. I just know that she's concerned with the integrity of the multiverse, and that she's capable of moving between dimensional streams."

"Did you ever think about, you know, slipping streams or whatever, to try to find a way to bring Annie back?"

Emily stared at me for a long time.

"You don't remember?" she asked.

"What do you mean?"

"The night Annie died."

"I remember everything."

"Are you sure?"

"Yeah, we listened to Tori Amos while you drove the truck up to the Petermans' house. You pulled out a journal or something, added some numbers together."

"One-oh-seven point three," she said.

"Exactly. You called it The Night Station."

"Years later, I discovered that Crow believed The Night Station was a kind of shortcut to a very powerful point of The Terminal. It turns out that one of the strongest of Meechum's Radiants is located right here in the Pacific Northwest."

"Yeah, Crow mentioned The Terminal."

Emily nodded, and the world started shaking again. If we hadn't been sitting on the floor, we would have been thrown to the ground.

"It's getting worse," I said.

"What else do you remember about that night in the truck?" Emily asked.

"Well, I remember you turning off the headlights at exactly six minutes past ten. We drove in the dark for a while with the radio tuned to that frequency. We were listening for something, and then suddenly there was a huge elk, and that's when you swerved to the left."

"That wasn't what happened."

"What do you mean?"

"*You* swerved to the left," she said. "Not me."

"What? No. I—" But she was right. Suddenly I remembered.

I was the one who had turned the wheel.

"And it was a tractor, not an elk," Emily said.

"That's right," I said, and in that moment something shifted in my memory. Maybe it was my proximity to Emily Connors after so many years, but it was like a fog had lifted and the entire scene was suddenly clear. I remembered now; the tractor was rust colored. "It didn't have its lights on," I said.

"The police told us later that if you hadn't swerved, none of us would have survived. You saved my life, but Annie died."

Tears streamed down Emily's cheeks.

I closed my eyes and brought myself back to that moment on the side of the road just after Emily and I were thrown from the truck. The truck had landed in the ditch, but somehow we'd ended up on the dirt shoulder next to the pavement.

When I woke up my head was killing me. I found out later that I'd suffered a massive concussion.

"I remember it had started to rain," I said. "There was a lot of smoke or steam, and you were crawling over to Annie in the truck. And then, I think you came back and dragged me over there."

"That's right," Emily said.

I could picture Emily's face, streaked with motor oil, tears, and dirt. She was screaming something. I couldn't quite make it out.

"You kept yelling at me."

"Yes."

"You kept yelling at me to help you save her. You said we have to save Annie, like before."

"But we didn't save her," Emily said.

"Then the man in the tractor came over, and then the police, and that's all I can remember."

While we sat there in silence, I could smell the hot metal on the asphalt and taste the copper tang of blood in the air. And I could see Annie's peaceful face as she leaned back in the truck, as if she'd just decided to rest her eyes for a minute.

"We couldn't save her," Emily said.

"Of course not," I said. "We weren't paramedics. We were kids."

"I know how it sounds," she said. "But what happened at the black well was real. We were able to save her then. We were able to somehow slip dimensional streams and save Annie. I know it seems crazy, but that's what happened. We saved her once, but we weren't able to do it again."

Emily wiped away a tear, and as if on cue the world began to shake again.

I stood up and put my hands against the Night Driver machine.

If our world had less than an hour to live, how were we supposed to go outside and walk around knowing what was about to happen? It all seemed so completely unreal.

I was staring at the screen of Night Driver, watching the car move along the road at night in the dark, when I had an idea.

I smiled.

"What?"

I grabbed Emily's hand and helped her up.

"What are you doing?"

"We need a car," I said as I led her through the arcade to the front door.

As soon as we stepped outside, I started to feel a low buzzing in my head and a woolly itching at the base of my skull.

I could tell that Emily was experiencing something similar.

Everything appeared slightly unreal. It was definitely night, but there was a dusty dark gray blur sticking to everything. The world was fading into a photocopy of itself.

The people walking around the streets and driving in cars didn't appear to notice that anything had changed, but the darkness was up there, hovering over everything.

I looked up at the host of faded swimming shapes that smudged and streaked the sky above us, and I started running, faster, pulling Emily along with me.

"Where are we going?"

"Lakewood," I said.

I could see recognition slowly move across Emily's face. She let go of my hand and stopped running.

"I'm not going back there, K."

"It's at least a half hour drive," I said. "I don't have time to argue."

"I'm not doing it."

"What if we can put everything back to how it was?"

"It doesn't matter. Everyone's still dead."

"You can't know that," I said. "Things could be different."

I had no idea how much of what Crow said was real, but I wasn't just going to sit there in the arcade and wait for the end of the world. I stepped out into the street, put my hands in the air, and almost got hit by a car.

"What the fuck are you doing?" Emily asked.

I started walking along beside the cars parked outside the arcade, checking to see if any of them were unlocked.

"We need a car," I said.

Emily shook her head and stepped out into the street.

I finally found a car that was unlocked and turned to Emily just as she flagged down a cab.

"You can't hot-wire a fucking Prius, K," Emily said. "Come on."

We made it to Emily's car in six minutes. There was almost no traffic. The cabbie smiled and thanked me for the generous tip. If the world was really ending, who gave a shit about an extra twenty bucks?

Emily put her car into gear and started to pull away from the curb when somebody knocked on the window.

It was Marianne Sanders, the detective with the scar across her face who'd taken our information at Fatman Neil's.

Emily rolled down the window.

"Where are you two off to in such a hurry?" she asked.

"Visiting a friend for dinner," Emily said.

Sanders smiled at Emily, then turned to me. "How do you know Easton Paruth?"

"Um . . . I don't. I mean, not really," I said.

"Then why do you suppose she was tracking you on her phone?"

"I have no idea. We went to see her, to ask her a couple of questions."

"Questions about what?"

"About the game I told you about."

"The same game that led you to speak with Neil Arroyo just before he was killed?"

"Yes."

"When was the last time you saw Ms. Paruth?"

"Um . . . a couple of days ago I think. Why?"

"She's been reported missing."

I shook my head. Fuck. I hoped she was okay. Easton was kind of terrifying, but she'd been (mostly) nice to me.

"I'm afraid I'm going to need you two to come with me," Sanders said, and moved to open Emily's door.

"Sorry," Emily said, "we're in a hurry," and floored it.

If the world was going to end, whatever Detective Sanders wanted to talk about really didn't matter. If we somehow survived, we could deal with her then.

I loaded Google Maps and found the quickest route to the freeway.

I listened to the sound of the tires on the wet asphalt as Emily guided the Volvo through mostly deserted city streets. I wondered if the lack of traffic was due to the violent shaking, or if maybe it was something else—something connected to the way the gray sky above us no longer felt like a sky, but rather like a permanent stain on the world.

Whatever was going to happen, it wouldn't be long now.

44

THE NIGHT STATION

WE MADE IT SAFELY out of the city and drove down I-5 in silence for twenty minutes. As we moved through the night, the chaos of the city gave way to the peaceful quiet of the suburbs, and I imagined the people who lived there feeling safe and warm behind their perfect lawns and creatively shaped mailboxes. They'd be getting ready for bed, reading stories to their kids while half-thinking about something else, signing forms for field trips, putting off sex to finish bingeing a show on HBO, and all the while, just outside their doors, the entire multiverse was most likely coming to an end.

I kept running back over everything that had happened—everything I'd learned about my parents, the Gatewick Institute, and Annie and Emily Connors. But if what Swan had said was true, did any of that stuff matter?

"We're almost there," Emily said.

I heard a slight tremor in her voice as we approached the road leading up to the Petermans' house. As we made the turn, I felt something pass through my body.

The darkness was coming.

"Can you feel it?" I asked.

Emily turned and looked at me. She could definitely feel it.

At that point, the world started shaking so violently that Emily could no longer keep her car between the lines. She somehow made the turn onto the old logging road and pulled over.

The shaking stopped a few seconds later.

"We should get going," I said.

"I'm sorry I was such a dick," Emily said. "It's not your fault you can't remember how amazing I am."

I nodded. "I'm pretty sure it's okay to be a dick when you lose the most incredible human being you've ever met," I said.

Emily smiled. "Even if you're not fortunate enough to remember how much you fucking love me, you're still the closest thing to family that I have left. We're family, K."

"You're goddamn right we're family," I said. "Now, let's do whatever the hell it is we're going to do."

"Are you sure?"

"Even if it means dying in an accident because we were stupid enough to drive in the dark with our headlights off," I said. "I'm no longer capable of giving half a fuck."

Emily laughed, and then she guided the car into the middle of the road and started driving up toward the Peterman house.

It was the exact same route we'd taken all those years ago.

"One-oh-seven point three," I said as I adjusted the frequency of the car's radio.

"You really think this is going to work?" she asked.

"Honestly?"

Emily nodded.

"Not really," I said.

"Fuck you." Emily forced a laugh. "Ready?"

I nodded.

Emily turned up the radio and the sound of static filled the car.

And I was brought right back to that night in the truck.

I'd relived it so many times, it was easy to get back there now, driving along the same road in the dark with Emily. The farther we moved up the road, the more I felt like I was actually somewhere else, somewhere back in time.

Then, Emily turned off the headlights and another wave of darkness poured into the truck and passed through my body. I could feel it slide into my skull, right behind my eyes. I shook my head and pressed my palms against my eye sockets. It wouldn't be long before the darkness coming from outside was everywhere and the entire world started shaking again.

Emily grabbed my hand and squeezed it tight. I could tell she was thinking about Annie. From the light of the touchscreen on the dash, I could see the tears streaming down her face. I squeezed back.

The last time we were here, speeding along this road with the headlights off, I was terrified. This time, even though I could feel that the end of everything was approaching, I wasn't scared. I was pretty sure Swan had been telling the truth, that our world was going to end, and if she was right about the timing, it was most likely going to happen very soon.

What did it matter if we died in an accident a minute or two early?

While Emily fought to keep the car on the road, I leaned forward and listened to the radio.

It was so quiet at first that I could barely hear it, but it was there. Music. It grew louder, eventually cutting through the static enough that I could make out the song. It was "Were You Blind That Day," the impossible song by Steely Dan.

Of course it was.

I turned up the volume on the radio, and I remember thinking, what are the odds of that song playing on the radio in that moment?

Suddenly Emily leaned forward. "Can you see it?"

I saw it.

There was something in the middle of the road up ahead. It was thick and dark, and appeared to be moving, but I couldn't make out any detail.

This time we didn't swerve, and Emily didn't turn on the lights.

We drove straight toward it.

As we sped forward, the shaking became unbearable and the darkness both inside and outside the car became something else— but maybe *someplace* else is more accurate. The reality of the space, or whatever it was that held the atmosphere in place, felt . . . thicker, almost slightly damp. It was as if we'd entered another world.

Then Emily screamed and a wild metallic buzzing, like a million wasps on a tin roof, filled the inside of the truck and burst into my head.

And then . . . we were definitely someplace else.

I was floating.

The familiar briny oily smell of wet fur and feathers filled my nose. It was peaceful, but I could still feel the powerful darkness all around me. It felt like we'd entered something like the eye of the storm. Whatever or wherever it was, the world wasn't shaking, and I could no longer feel the wheels of the car beneath me on the road.

As we slid forward into a thick blackness, the briny oily smell slowly turned into something else.

It was familiar, but it took me a moment to place it.

It was the scent of Dewberry perfume oil that I'd smelled back in the truck all those years ago.

And then I was suddenly adrift in the in-between place, but it was different this time—less chaotic.

Once again I felt the cool syrupy darkness, and the seemingly endless currents were rushing by just like before, but this time I felt more in control. If I focused my thoughts, I could see the colors and shapes of the currents, and if I closed my eyes, I could actually feel them and bring them closer.

This time I didn't reach down to try to find my mother's hand, or Chloe's.

This time I was holding Emily's hand, and I could feel her strength helping me focus. I could feel the strength of her desire and love for me.

I knew that it was time to make a choice.

I focused all of my attention on the currents, and immediately felt the familiar deep buzzing start moving through me, but this time, somewhere way out there in the darkness, I saw a distant smudge of light.

I knew what I had to do.

I squeezed Emily's hand, and once again reached down into the endless darkness.

I'd made my choice.

I cleared my mind and willed the distant light closer.

The smudge slowly became a flicker, then it morphed into a glowing swirl as it rushed toward me, slicing through the darkness, speeding, pulsing, humming, and burning, and then—

I was on my mother's knee in a strange house surrounded by our things, and—

Running through an open field jumping over the black well, and—

Broken and alone in the Harvard Exit Theatre waiting for The Passenger, and—

In somebody's kitchen laughing with my father as an old man, and—

In the truck with Annie and Emily Connors—

The left side of my body began to tingle as the light came closer, but just as it was about to reach me, I felt somebody grab my other hand and pull.

I turned my head to see who it was.

That's when the light hit me, and the world exploded in a blinding flash. I was stretched thin and twisted, all emptiness and cold.

And then the light was gone, and I was choking on the darkness.

I couldn't move or breathe. I felt like I was in a sensory deprivation tank filled with wet black cement.

And then I was back in the car with Emily.

Through the windshield, I could see the twisted shape of the gray shadow thing that had torn the Magician apart in that Super 8 film.

It was swaying back and forth, a melty twist of dark burning smoke.

I saw Emily close her eyes as she squeezed my hand tight.

I opened my mouth to scream, and suddenly I was a black hole, and I was pulling everything that existed into me.

There was a screaming from the burning heart of the world and everything exploded in a brilliant blaze of liquid fire and darkness.

And then there was nothing.

45

A THREE-HUNDRED-LANE FUCKMONSTER SPEEDWAY

I WOKE UP alone in a large bed.

Sunlight streamed into the room through two sets of leaded glass windows.

I was in a medium-size bedroom in what appeared to be some kind of cottage-style country house. I could see a thick grove of evergreens through the windows, which led me to believe I was probably still somewhere in the Pacific Northwest.

I could hear a song playing from a distant room.

It was "Third World Man" by Steely Dan.

I slipped out of the bed and followed the sound of the music.

It was coming from the kitchen. Somebody was in there, and it sounded like they were cooking. I moved down a long hallway, turned a corner, and saw Alan Scarpio standing in front of a stove making what appeared to be French toast.

"Good morning," he said. "I hope you're hungry."

Scarpio looked pretty much the same as the last time I'd seen him, although this time he was wearing dark jeans, a black long-sleeve cotton shirt, white Stan Smiths, and an apron with a saying on the front that read: MR. GOOD-LOOKIN' IS COOKIN'.

"Where's Emily?" I asked.

He shook his head. "You were alone when I found you."

I nodded and tried to remember what had happened in the car after we'd turned off the headlights.

Scarpio held up a spatula. "We got French toast, eggs, and some kind of vegan bacon."

"Where are we?" I asked.

"We're in Lakewood, in the summer house of somebody named . . ." Scarpio picked up a piece of mail from the kitchen counter. "Morris Peterman, apparently."

"How did I get here?"

"I went for a walk and found you just off the road in the middle of the driveway. I carried you up to the house."

"How did *you* get here?"

"I arrived a couple of hours before I found you. But I actually rented this place about six months ago, after I received this postcard in the mail."

Scarpio handed me a postcard. On the front was a familiar photograph. It was the willow tree that I'd last seen hanging upside down on the wall in the reception area in Crow's penthouse. On the back was a typed message with the address of this house and what I assumed was today's date.

"You received that postcard six months ago?"

Scarpio nodded and smiled. "Yep," he said.

I sat down on one of three high wooden stools positioned along the kitchen counter.

"How did you end up out there on the road, if you don't mind my asking?" Scarpio asked.

I gave him a quick summary of everything that had happened from the moment we'd discovered the map in *The Horns of Terzos* until I woke up there in that house.

"Wow," he said. "That's one hell of a series of events."

I nodded. "Yeah, it sure was. Where have you been?" I asked.

"What do you mean?"

"You were missing."

He nodded. "Over the next little while, you're probably going to notice a number of discrepancies between what you remember about the game and what others experienced while you were playing. I'd suggest saying as little as possible to anyone until you have a firm grasp of their understanding of events, but that's up to you."

"So you were never really missing?"

"Let's just say that I was working on something off-grid, something I needed to keep . . . to myself."

"Something you kept from your entire company?" I asked.

He nodded. "Yes."

"Were you playing Rabbits? Is Rabbits connected to the multiverse?"

"You sure you don't want to start with French toast?" He smiled. "You must be hungry."

"Do you mind if we talk a bit first?"

He smiled and nodded. "Sure."

"Is Rabbits real?"

"Of course," he said.

"What about the Meechum Radiants?"

"I'm pretty sure they exist, but I suppose it depends on who you ask."

"So, what are they?"

"Are you familiar with theoretical physicist Michio Kaku?"

"A little," I said.

"Kaku, using an analogy to discuss alien intelligence, referenced an anthill sitting next to a ten-lane superhighway. His question was: Would those ants be capable of understanding what a ten-lane superhighway was?"

I was familiar with Michio Kaku's analogy, but if that's the case, then the Meechum Radiants were more like a three-hundred-lane fuckmonster speedway.

"So what you're saying is that human beings are essentially incapable of understanding the Meechum Radiants?"

"Most of us, yes."

"Most . . . but not all?"

"Hawk Worricker understood, and he used that understanding to build something incredible."

"Rabbits."

Scarpio nodded and continued. "Way back in the 1940s, Alan Turing suggested that a machine shuffling ones and zeros could simulate any process of formal reasoning. Artificial intelligence grew in fits and starts, but as promising as AI was, it never came close to reaching its full potential."

"Okay, so what does that have to do with the game?"

"What if I told you that Hawk Worricker had developed an advanced cloud-based quantum computing system decades before the rest of the world?"

"You mean it's not some kind of multiverse repair mechanism?"

"Umm . . . are you messing with me?"

I shook my head.

"No, I don't think it's anything like that."

"So what is it?"

"What if everything that happened to you had been already been set in motion?" Scarpio continued.

"You're talking about determinism?"

"In a way, yes."

"How is Rabbits connected to the question of free will?"

"Let's take that book, *The Horns of Terzos,* as an example."

"What about it?"

"What if that particular clue had been planted decades ago?"

"A fake book was created by the game as a clue that wouldn't be uncovered until forty years later?"

"No. What if a *real* book was created by the game because you needed to find it decades later?"

"Shit," I said.

Scarpio nodded and smiled. "It's a mindfucker, isn't it?"

"You're saying it's all the Moriarty Factor? That this Rabbits AI did everything? There are no multiple universes?"

"I have no idea if we're living in a multiverse or not. I was never interested in quantum physics, I'm afraid."

"What about the discrepancies?"

"You're talking about the Mandela effect? The Berenstain Bears?"

"I'm talking about the Fremont Troll holding a Mini Cooper instead of a Volkswagen bug, a movie that used to exist but no longer does, a restaurant that closed permanently six years ago suddenly open again for business, a dead artist miraculously alive, writing and recording amazing new songs."

"Okay, so, based on what you've seen and experienced over the past few months, do you believe it's possible that, given absolutely unlimited financial resources and imagination, a group of people could have been hired to adjust the Fremont Troll sculpture and then put it back as it was? Or to reopen a restaurant? Or to manipulate your devices to avoid delivering search results related to one film? Or even create a new album from a dead artist?"

"I suppose so," I said.

"But there is another possibility." He paused for a moment, and appeared uncertain whether he should continue.

"What is it?"

"As you know, the game is extremely complicated. Uncovering sophisticated patterns, reality-questioning discrepancies, and unbelievable coincidences can be exhausting. Often this exhaustion— coupled with the mental and emotional gymnastics required to move forward during gameplay—results in some players experiencing certain . . ."

"What?"

"Breaks. With reality."

"You think I imagined the whole thing?"

"Not at all; I'm just describing a phenomenon. The scope and impact of the game is sometimes hard to imagine."

"Why did you come to visit me at the arcade that night?"

"I was led there, by the game."

"You were led there? What does that mean?"

"I was simply following the signs."

"Playing Rabbits?"

He just shrugged and then grabbed something off a nearby counter and handed it to me.

It was my phone.

On the screen was a video taken on the floor of what appeared to be a stock exchange somewhere in Asia.

"What's this?" I asked.

"This was running for half an hour this morning on the ticker at the Tokyo Stock Exchange."

It was The Circle.

Eleven Roman numerals and ten names (there was a blank space after VIII) moved along the ticker atop the huge displays that made up the index perched high above the trading floor.

Next to the Roman numeral XI was a one-letter name: K.

"Is this real?" I asked.

Scarpio nodded.

"Are you sure I was alone when you found me?"

He nodded. "Were you with somebody before that?"

"Yeah, a friend of mine named Emily Connors."

He appeared genuinely surprised.

"Emily Connors?"

I nodded. "You recognize the name?"

"I do," he said. "A friend of *mine* named Emily Connors occasionally uses my lake house in Seattle, in exchange for watering the plants."

"Does she have a sister named Annie?" I asked.

Scarpio shook his head. "Not anymore, but she did. Her sister died years ago."

"Do you have any idea where Emily Connors is now?"

He shook his head. "I haven't spoken with her for a few weeks. I've tried calling, but the number I have for her is out of service."

Emily's friend who owned the amazing lakeside mansion was Alan Scarpio. I suppose I shouldn't have been surprised.

"So, wait, if I won the eleventh iteration of the game . . ." I said.

"You're wondering if there's a prize?"

"Is there?"

"Oh yes. There most certainly is," he said.

"What is it?"

He shrugged. "Remember, we're talking about the most sophisticated artificial intelligence system ever imagined by humankind, capable of advanced recursive self-improvement, running on a limitless quantum system. Now imagine that system had access to every single piece of information ever uploaded, scanned, or spoken near a microphone connected to a modem."

"Okay . . ."

"The game knows your heart's desire. Chances are you already have it, or it's on the way."

"It is?"

He smiled. "And there's most likely money as well. I'd check your bank account if I were you."

"Do you know a man named Crow?"

"Not that I can recall, no."

"So you never went to visit him in The Tower at WorGames?"

I thought I saw a brief flash of recognition move across Scarpio's face when I mentioned Crow and The Tower, but before I could press him further, there was a loud knock at the door. I jumped.

"Come in!" Scarpio yelled.

The front door of the house swung open and Chloe rushed inside. She jumped into my arms, wrapped her legs around my waist, and kissed me.

Eventually, we stopped kissing, but it took a minute.

"How did you find me?" I asked.

"Got a tip from a billionaire who answered your phone." She turned to Scarpio. "Thanks."

He smiled. "No problem."

Chloe turned her attention back to me. "What the fuck happened?"

"What do you mean?"

"You disappeared."

"You're the one who disappeared," I said. "I looked everywhere."

"I was in there for like two minutes. When I came out you were gone."

I shook my head. "Either way, I'm damn happy you're alive."

"Me too, weirdo. Now, do you mind telling me what the fuck is going on?"

I handed Chloe my phone.

She stared at the phone for a few seconds. "Is that The Circle?"

"Sure is," I said.

As soon as she saw the winner of the eleventh iteration of the game, she turned to face me, her eyes huge.

I smiled.

"What the fuck have you been doing since I went pee?" Chloe asked.

I laughed. It was the first genuine heartfelt laugh I'd experienced in quite a while.

"The Magician is going to lose his mind," Chloe said as she took a photo of my phone with her own.

"He's alive?" I asked.

"He's fine," she said. "He said he was out of town for something personal related to his family. But it sounds fucking fishy, if you ask me."

"What about that Super 8 movie? We saw him torn apart."

"He says it definitely wasn't him, but he's demanding to see that thing ASAP."

I felt a wave of relief wash over me that quickly turned into something else. If the Magician was okay, was it somehow possible that Baron and Fatman Neil might still be alive?

I excused myself and stepped into the bathroom.

I ran water in the sink, sat down on the edge of the bathtub, and pulled out my phone. A quick search through social media revealed that Baron and Neil were still gone.

I checked my bank balance. Somebody had deposited what can only be described as a ludicrous amount of money into my savings account.

Just as I was about to put my phone back into my pocket, I received a message from a text-based mailing list of some kind. The message read as follows:

From WorGames, the studio that brought you Missile Strike: Silo and City of Falling Glass, comes a brand-new title that's going to redefine what it means to play a game.

Nothing is ever going to be the same.

Get ready to play.

The Door Is Open by Sidney Farrow is coming soon.

Preorder your copy today.

I sat there on the edge of the bathtub for a moment wondering how my number ended up on that WorGames mailing list, when there was a knock on the door.

"Who is it?"

"Who the fuck do you think? Let me in."

I opened the door and Chloe stepped into the room.

"What are you doing in here?" she asked.

"Just washing my hands," I said and handed her my phone.

"What's this?"

"Mailing list spam."

I watched Chloe's eyes as she read over the article.

"Shit," she said. "Is this real?"

"Looks like it," I said, sitting back down.

"Interesting choice for a title."

"Sure is," I said. "What do you think it means?"

"No idea," Chloe said as she sat down next to me.

We sat there in comfortable silence for a moment.

"So what the hell are we supposed to do now?" I asked.

"I guess we wait for the next iteration of Rabbits to begin."

"Then what?"

"What do you think?" Chloe asked as she grabbed my hand and pulled me up. "Win the game, save the world." She laughed, and the two of us went back into the kitchen to eat French toast.

ACKNOWLEDGMENTS

Many years ago I discovered something hidden, something barely visible in the cracks, a mysterious thing that nobody was talking about. Over the years I've done my best to compile the pieces, decipher the whispers, decode the messages, and come up with the best way to tell you the story, the story of the game.

This book is for those of us out there stumbling through the madness, doing our best to hang on to the magic of mystery, the rush of discovery, and a thrilling sense of wide-eyed wonder.

Although some names have been changed, and some real-life incidents adjusted to protect certain individuals, and even though you probably found it in the fiction section, Rabbits is real.

R U Playing?

With thanks to my smart, tenacious, well-dressed, and remarkably cool agent, Marc Gerald, for continuing to push me to write a book, and to my editor, Anne Groell, for taking a chance on me and acquiring *Rabbits* for Del Rey, guiding me through a journey of narrative discovery that would result in my typing more than a million words and then helping me choose the best 120K (or so) of those words and arrange them in the (more or less) proper order.

I must also deliver a heartfelt thank-you to those of you who have been kind enough to support my work in film and podcasting through the years. Without you continually watching, listening, and responding so positively to everything, I'm not sure Del Rey—an imprint responsible for a significant number of my most formative reading experiences via Piers Anthony, Stephen R. Donaldson, Terry Brooks, and many more—would have taken a chance on an unproven writer of prose (no matter how clever the cliffhanger at the end of my sample chapters).

And finally, thanks to my mom and dad for putting up with a kid whose nose was always buried in a book, to my wife, Isabel, for dealing with a husband whose face is far too often stuck in front of a computer, and to Ruby and Chelsea for lighting the way.